COLD BLOOD

ALSO BY JAMES FLEMING

The Temple of Optimism
Thomas Gage
White Blood

COLD BLOOD

James Fleming

For Isobel
from
James

JONATHAN CAPE
LONDON

Published by Jonathan Cape 2009

2 4 6 8 10 9 7 5 3 1

Copyright © James Fleming 2009

James Fleming has asserted his right under the Copyright, Designs
and Patents Act 1988 to be identified as the author of this work

First published in Great Britain in 2009 by
Jonathan Cape
Random House, 20 Vauxhall Bridge Road,
London SW1V 2SA

www.rbooks.co.uk

Addresses for companies within The Random House Group Limited can be found at:
www.randomhouse.co.uk/offices.htm

The Random House Group Limited Reg. No. 954009

A CIP catalogue record for this book
is available from the British Library

ISBN 9780224087216

The Random House Group Limited supports the Forest Stewardship
Council (FSC), the leading international forest certification organisation. All our titles that
are printed on Greenpeace-approved FSC certified paper carry the FSC logo. Our paper
procurement policy can be found at
www.rbooks.co.uk/environment

Mixed Sources
Product group from well-managed
forests and other controlled sources
www.fsc.org Cert no. TT-COC-2139
© 1996 Forest Stewardship Council
FSC

Typeset by Palimpsest Book Production Limited
Grangemouth, Stirlingshire
Printed and bound in Great Britain by
CPI Mackays, Chatham, Kent ME5 8TD

One

HAVING BEEN hailed as a genius at the age of twenty-three, I got too cocky. Everything had yielded to me. Fame had become my companion – lived in my pocket.

I was a naturalist. Old man Goetz was my mentor. Just the two of us – a team, like father and son. Museums competed for our services. Goetz & Doig: our names rolled off the tongue as if we'd been a shipping line. No one was better than us at discovering birds and insects that were new to science. In the name of progress we battled through jungles, waded torrents, scaled peaks, tramped through all the outer territories of civilisation.

The day everything changed for me we were in western Burma for the Field Museum. Our head porter had been murdered. We were obliged to remain in Chaungwa, a small trading town on the River Chindwin, while the matter was investigated.

I went to the post office to get a letter off to my mother, who was on an extended visit to her family in Russia. The humidity was oppressive to my northern blood. Listlessly I approached the clerk, wondering what rigmarole was in store as the passage of a letter from Chaungwa to Smolensk was considered.

It was here that Luck singled me out.

She was up there in the rafters, couldn't have been anywhere else. A stout lady with dimpled knees, spying on the throng. To get herself into the proper mood, she closed her eyes, sang her witching song and on opening them found it was I, Charlie Doig, she was staring at. Six foot two, strong across the shoulders and through the loins. Stubborn blue eyes, lumpy nose, awkward hands. Cropped hair. Travel-stained legs – scars, sores, etc. High curling instep and bouncing stride. Chest forty-two inches.

She couldn't have missed me. Goetz was out and about somewhere. There was only me and the brown fellows.

She took pity on me. She knew all about Goetz's temper, about malaria and the beige curse, that I'd had a hard time of it on the expedition. She weighed it on her scales – and smiled upon me: touched my shoulder with her wand. Then she instructed a certain jewel beetle to burrow out of the teakwood pillar on the far side of the post office, the pillar where it had been laid as an egg four years ago. Yes, four years growing and nibbling its way through the wood and into the world of man – into my world and my killing bottle.

It was the first of its sort ever to be captured by humankind. Noah had missed it and Abraham and all the merry crowd until the day that I sauntered into the Chaungwa GPO.

The glory was mine alone. Goetz never had a look-in. When the museum naming committee sat, that beetle went down in the annals of science as *Chrysochroa doigii* Brendell 1912.

Many times I studied the letter of award. Was I to be immortal? It could mean nothing less.

In return for a decent sum, this fantastically coloured beetle got to be the property of the Field Museum. They were looking for a show-stopper. Wiz, as they called him, fitting the bill, they dolled up my story and fed it to the newspapers. That Goetz and I had only been in Chaungwa because Hpung had been murdered there (throat cut) was the icing on the cake.

'A good killing sells,' wrote Amy Carson, the museum publicist. 'So mind you send us a photograph that makes you look as if you belong to the tale.'

The studio fixed me up with a patch of jungle and had me pose unshaven in my Empire shorts. The cameraman caught me crouching, my front knee sprung – the quarry was just ahead, I was holding my breath. At the last moment he made me grasp a stage rifle. In the proof I sent Amy, I appeared vigilant, murderous and decisive.

The Field mounted Wiz in a spectacular fashion, striding up a tilted piece of grey bark, looking back over its shoulder, its huge eyes liquid with nostalgia for the privacy I'd stripped from it forever. Over two thousand people showed up the day the exhibition opened.

Modesty would have served me well at that point. But I was young and bold with conceit. Had not the beetle been named after me?

Once I'd started on this line of thought, nothing could hold me back. I'd out-Darwin Darwin, go for the record – get fifty-eight *doigii* to my name and so beat the hero by one. I'd find a hidden-away island. All the firsts I needed would be there. I didn't know how this would happen, but having no concept of failure, I didn't worry. Somehow or other I'd get to fifty-eight species bearing the name of Charlie Doig. Medals would be struck for me. Mount Doig would make its appearance on maps. Or a glacier. Or a new island. Thank you, I'd say in my acceptance speech, thank you, *messieurs*, I always had these good feelings about myself. Success was inevitable.

But the world was not ready to submit to me. I should have taken the hint when it was offered, when Amy rejected the proof I'd sent her.

'I know what I said, but the fact is that it's a beetle, not a tiger,' she wrote and had me do something tamer, with a butterfly net.

She was right, and in another sense too. I should have been content to be a name on a museum label, should have allowed the idea of smallness to find a home with me. All my troubles have stemmed from that, my troubles, my joys, my loves.

Two

On the strength of Wiz, I was appointed in the summer of 1914 to document the passerines – birds that perch – of Russian Central Asia. Skins of every species that bred there were to be obtained. The expedition was mine, Goetz being over fifty by then and crabbier than ever.

Disaster struck immediately. Thereafter they followed each other like sheep.

First: the European war broke out, causing old Hartwig Fartwig Goetz to remember the Germanness of his soul. He deserted me: presented me with all his collecting equipment, stepped onto a train in Bokhara and went to a patriot's death.

Next: the Academy of Sciences stopped sending me money. The Tsar had none to spare because of the cost of the war.

Shortly after this, I broke my leg.

These sufferings were not sufficient. As soon as I was better I abandoned the passerines and set out across Russia to the Pink House, Popovka, province of Smolensk, the home of my mother's family, the Rykovs. For company I had a young Mongolian who'd attached himself to me as a bodyguard. His name was Kobi.

The train I was on contained only recruits and their lice. I caught typhus, or 'tif' as it's known with us. An inch of my life was all that remained by the time Kobi got me to the Pink House. An inch, as close as that: a few dozen breaths away from the mortician's trolley, which in my case would have been a shove out of a military wagon with a heavy boot.

But I pulled through, my will to live being stronger than the tif.

When I awakened in the Pink House, the hot summer sun was streaming through the open windows, I could smell the greenish scent of the Fantin-Latour that had been growing against the wall when I was a boy and was still growing there, and my cousin Elizaveta was writing a letter at a desk by the window. A bee came off the rose and loitered noisily half in and half out of the room.

She spoke to it: 'Kind and gentle bee, keep your distance, for here we have tif.'

I called out. She came to my bedside. Her dark, finely boned face bent over me. I said weakly, 'What have you done with your hair, then, Lizochka?'

Smiling at me, who was her patient, from the bottom of her black eyes: 'Four days a week I nurse our wounded soldiers in the hospital. None of us are allowed to keep our hair because of the lice. So we are alike, you and I, Charlinka.'

And I, who had until then treated women as a hobby, fell instantly in love. There was nothing of the dewy-eyed, walks-in-the-wood romance about it. The love I had for Elizaveta Rykov was gross. It concerned one thing only: complete possession of her, inside and out, until the day I died.

However, she was already affianced. The man was one of our most dashing young officers, a real idol. He had all a soldier's advantages: medals, fame, rank and, not least, the wardrobe of a colonel in the Garde à Cheval, which included trousers tight enough to make a maiden gasp.

Still, I went for her. Stuck my chin out and tightened my arse.

And I won her, led her from the altar as mine. She declared that her heart had belonged to me all along.

For seven days this woman was my bride – was Mrs Doig. Black hair, black eyes, brainy, angular, a small refined bosom – of greater beauty than is comfortable for most men. There can't have been a woman like her in the entire province of Smolensk, probably not in Russia itself. I'll bet you could have searched the ballrooms and apple orchards from Vladivostok to the Baltic and not found her equal. She had to be in the top twelve of Europe itself for beauty, intelligence and domesticity.

That I, who am imperfect, should have been found accept-able by such a woman filled me to bursting with pride. She was the sun, the moon and the milk of the stars, she was the purest treasure in existence. Sobbing with love, I'd dip my head between her sleek breasts and go back and forth kissing their nipples and murmuring of rubies, garnets and the rest of them until I ran out of words. Her eyes were jet, her skin like alabaster and her navel was folded like a cowrie.

Exclaiming, I would explore every inch of her as we lay on the bear cubs' skin in front of the bedroom fire.

One night towards the end we were on the bearskin, she naked except for the Rykov pearls. My great-uncle Igor had given them to her. They were famous throughout Russia, the largest weighing three ounces.

I was impatient and as stiff as a guardsman. She wanted to see how long I could hold out. Laughing, she lassoed my cock and garlanded it with the pearls so that it gleamed in the firelight like an elephant's tusk. This led her to thinking how tall our children would be. I said I'd have to measure her. Smiling – fireglow in her eyes, it was what she'd been hoping for – she reclaimed the cock-hot pearls (which had certainly seen nothing of the like when owned by homosexual Uncle Igor) and laid them out of harm's way. She reached back with her arms, right over her head. Using the top knuckle of my thumb as an inch measure, I started off at the ball of her heel. I went slowly, paying no attention to her squeals and giggles as I passed over dells and dimples, plains, forests and peaks. Up her neck I went and over her determined chin and nibbling lips. I balanced like a mountaineer on the ridge of her nose, made a detour to take in her upstretched arms and on reaching her fingertips and kissing them, one by one—

'How many?' she whispered, by then not interested in my answer.

I sat back on my heels. Now it was her turn to wait. She placed both hands round my cock and tried to draw me down.

'How many do you think?' I said.

'A thousand, I don't care.'

'Seventy-five inches to your fingertips. When you raise your arms like that, you're taller than I am.'

Squirming beneath me: 'What's important . . . do you want me to beg? Come down here, Charlinka.'

I looked at her long white body on the bearskin. I smoothed my palms over her flat stomach. She made way and I entered her with a rush, the deepest penetration in the entire history of love.

We were one person that night, when Dan Doig was conceived. She declared that the thud of my sperm hitting her egg travelled all the way up her spine. She'd felt it in her brain. More than just a tingle, she said: a definite crackle, like electricity.

To celebrate Dan's conception, she refastened the pearls round her neck. They grazed my chest as she smiled down at me, leaning on her elbow, tracing the grooves between my ribs with her forefinger.

'It was as though you fertilised me in two places simultaneously. Mighty Doig!'

All the happiness that had been lying around in the world unused was ours. It was drawn to us by the force of our love. I had only to put out my hand to feel it surrounding and protecting us like a soft warm billowy paradise.

Three

How THE gods must have detested our bliss. 'Break them,' they roared. 'Do it properly this time. Leave nothing to chance.'

The man they sent to do this was Prokhor Fedorovich Glebov. Pretending to be a Tsarist officer, he sought refuge in the Pink House just as our honeymoon and a week-long blizzard began. We were duped, all of us – my cousin Nicholas, his servants, my godfather Misha Baklushin, my wife. One night he murdered her ancient tutor in the room above ours. I was woken by the scream. He rode away into the forest, trailing his coat, inviting me to follow him. He was joined by a gang of deserters. Kobi tracked them through the snow. I shot and killed a man, believing him to be Glebov. It was not. Too late did I realise the depth of his deception. By the time I got back, he'd done his butchering.

He did it on behalf of Bolshevism, in the name of the common man. To compensate for the bad deal that this wretch has received from history.

It took Kobi and me two days to catch him. What I wanted to do was to cut off his eyelids so that he'd be unsleeping for the remainder of his life. Why not? Kobi wouldn't have given it a second thought. Not one person in humanity would have blamed me.

I did not. Instead, because I suddenly visualised his eyelids fluttering on the palm of my hand, I handed him over to some wounded White officers to let them torture him as they wished. When a couple of Zeppelins bombed their hospital wagons, he escaped. Even with a broken leg, the slippery bastard managed to crawl away and hide.

I have often pondered over that failure of mine to kill Glebov. I'm not a fastidious person. No one has ever called me nice. It's not in my born nature. I'm a vital, pushing, obstinate man. I have pride. I have ambition. I have a whole range of the minor qualities. But I am not and do not wish to be thought nice.

My uncle Igor had been a generous, unassuming, would-be pederast, the epitome of niceness. His fate – to be blown up in his carriage as he passed through the forest of Popovka. My cousin Nicholas had been almost unbearably nice. Elizaveta, Misha, Bobinski, Louis, all those slaughtered in the Pink House had been nice. Decent, honourable people, well suited to a civilised existence. And now? Dead. All these nice people were dead and gone, swept out of the way by swine like Glebov, by people indoctrinated to act without scruple or mercy.

So why did I risk staying in Russia? What did I want that I couldn't get in another country with a fraction of the danger?

Vengeance. Nothing could be clearer. I had one mortal enemy, this man Glebov. Never again would I let him escape. I would be his nemesis. I would hunt him as a dog hunts a rat, and when I'd caught him, I'd kill him with terrible finality. Then I'd get out of the country.

I'd find my way to America, where I had high standing at the Field Museum. If the war had made collecting impossible I'd take up accountancy. I'd force myself to learn their obscure language and their runes: buy a suit and become their ally. The sense of being a Rykov, even of being a Russian, would be moulted and a bright new Doig would step forth, a respectable fellow, an all-round good person.

Time would strip my memory down to the essentials. Mother – she'd be among the first to go: she'd been a stranger to me even before I broke free.

Papa – a glorious, seething, inventive Muscovite Scotsman, with curly black hair and flashing eyes and a skin so magnetic that my normally placid mother had been unable to resist touching it. He died of bubonic plague in Tashkent, at the age of thirty-nine. Boils, pus, vomit, crying out for help from his family while in the latticed room below, the turbans clacked away at backgammon and shut their ears to his lonely terror.

I was fourteen when this happened. I was caught flat-footed.

It had never occurred to me that people whom one loved could die. At first I was tearful. Then I grew angry. Then it was revealed how completely hopeless Papa had been with money, and I vowed that no one would ever take advantage of me. I would be the opposite of my father: I would devour the world.

His debts were huge. I estimated that had he been caught in the revolving doors of Moscow's Hotel Metropole, where he often took me for lunch, and had all his IOUs, liens, mortgages, pledges, arrangements and fantastic paper schemes for our enrichment been stuffed in around him, only his curls and his laughing brown eyes would have been visible. He was a sober man, the most sober of the many Scotsmen in Moscow. His downfall lay in having a brain like a mushroom cellar and a belief that the world was nice.

So let him abide in my memory forever, central and sturdy on account of his unfulfilled dreams and of the love that we had for each other.

And above him let Elizaveta shine on the highest pinnacle visible to man. Every woman after her would be a lesser experience. Beside her in my imagination – podgy hand tugging at her long blue skirt – must be my impression of how Dan Doig would have turned out at the age of three. Belly, bluster, baby biceps . . .

At this point I take my leave. Some scenes are too painful, especially those that spring solely from the imagination.

In the hateful month of March, 1917, when all this happened, I was twenty-eight years old. By then I'd had a beetle named after me, catalogued the passerines of Central Asia, survived typhus, had my only family members slain by the Bolsheviks – and been compelled to shoot my wife. If that isn't learning the hard way, I don't know what is.

Four

ALL THIS experience, this weight of life, drained me. My Darwinian preoccupations seemed silly. Love, money, position, reward – they were nothing. In that one murderous hour at the Pink House, Glebov had chopped off all the ligaments by which I was bound to society. I was left with one purpose in my life: to kill him. It didn't worry me that he could be anywhere in this huge country of ours. When the Revolution came, there'd be only one place for a top Bolshevik like him – the capital. So I went to St Petersburg and waited for the storm to break.

Kobi enjoyed mocking me by saying things such as, 'There are 155 million people in Russia and you want to find one of them?' But I knew Glebov was alive and I knew he'd show up. He was one of those people you want to see turning green before pronouncing them dead.

We went to the old Rykov Palace off the north end of Nevsky. Joseph, Uncle Igor's house steward, was still hanging on in the hope of better times. A number of pauperous families calling themselves Socialist Revolutionaries had taken the mansion over and stuffed him into a tiny back room. He was forty-three years old, a single man of slight build, with long black ringlets, a thin black face, soft eyes and a certain gracefulness of speech and character.

His narrow face went lopsided with pleasure when he saw me. Waving the SRs away, not even glancing at Kobi, he came right up to me. 'Ah, Doig!' he exclaimed, wrapping my name in a great gush of liquory breath. 'Back again! Out of the blue! Like an aviator!'

I need to explain something. When my father was wooing Irina Rykov, it was not grasped by the servants that he was just a classy Scottish adventurer. They believed 'Doig' to be his title. The word sounded so outlandish that they couldn't believe it to be his name. So they'd always called him Doig, thinking it to be the Scottish version of 'Your Excellency' or 'Your Worship'. I'd inherited it.

He put his arm through mine and held me tightly. 'The family – I never believed I'd see any of you again. The disgracefulness of these times' – he thought better of his arm – made as if to withdraw it – ended up by leaving it there. He waved at the leering scum. 'Go away, proletariat. Go and learn how to use a toilet.'

To me: 'They distrust it and shit on the floor. So long as the weather's cold, one can tolerate such behaviour. But when May comes, there'll be a stink all over the house. Lilac blossom and thawing shit, there's a Russian spring for you . . . Off you go! *Provalivai* – scram!'

We walked arm in arm into the next huge room. There was no purpose to it. Joseph just wanted to walk somewhere with his arm through mine, to have the contact.

Something lurking in his eyes, he said, 'The SR muck say there are soon to be no servants and no masters. We are all to be the same, even you and I, Doig.'

'One of us needs to be the leader. You?'

He sighed. 'It would be best if the Germans finished off our armies and put the Kaiser on the throne. They wouldn't stand for any of this nonsense. Doig, if we were to be equal . . .'

'Joseph?'

'My first wish would be to become your servant again. You will take me with you when you leave?'

'Of course I will,' I said, and he began to weep, out of gratitude that the family had returned and come to his rescue. He steered the talk round to Elizaveta, wanting to know why she wasn't with me. Pretty soon there was no alternative but to go to his room and drown our sorrows. We polished off the Plymouth gin that he'd salvaged and moved on to vodka. We could have had the remains of Uncle Igor's claret but I said it was important to transfer between drinks of the same colour.

Joseph lit a tiny mouse of a fire. After a bit he grew reckless and put on all the coal he had. It became warm. He slipped his braces and took off his shirt. The armpits of his woollen vest were a strong yellow – gamboge. He said, 'But you have to tell me this at least: did she suffer?'

'Worse than Christ.'

'You cannot leave me to imagine it. We must share, as we share in the agony of Our Lord.'

'She was seized by a bunch of deserters and raped in chorus on the floor of the stable. A Bolshevik called Glebov was behind it. He wanted to ingratiate himself with Lenin by carrying out an act of class warfare. Also there was this, that his own woman had been hanged as a Bolshevik saboteur. After they'd raped her, they razored a strip of flesh off each leg, from thigh to ankle. That was to mock the officer class, because the trousers of the Garde à Cheval are white with a blood-red stripe. She was in agony when I found her. The hospital – miles away – no drugs – it was a nightmare. She begged me to – and I did. I shot her. Now you know.'

Joseph collapsed into the ghastly chrome chair my uncle had bought from an American catalogue. His mouth buckled. He bawled – howled, the tears cascading through the hollows of his gaunt cheeks.

To begin with we weren't really tight, just high on misfortune. Then things got too much for us. We wept, we drank, we slept and night became day again. Still we continued drinking.

For some period of the second day, I got loose. Kobi came in pursuit. He captured me dancing down the centre of Nevsky. I was insane with grief and liquor. Elizaveta was in my arms. I had her ass tight in my hand. I was kissing her, pinching her, engulfing her in my arms. Her black eyes were bright with love for me – for having spared her the agony of a slow death.

Then Kobi leaned out of a horse-drawn cab and, catching me on the lurch, scooped me inside.

When I sobered up, the desire to capture Glebov and bake him alive occupied my entire being. I thought of nothing else, day and night.

However, Kobi was out of harmony with me. He didn't drink – thought poorly of my bender. He hankered for the open road, a fast horse and a true rifle. What grabbed him was the idea of being a mercenary. It was rumoured that General K. I. Muraviev was recruiting in the capital for the civil war that he could see coming.

One day Kobi said to me, 'Muraviev'd give me five thousand to see me ride into his camp. You give me five thousand and I'll stay with you. Five thousand or that's it.'

I looked him over. Waiting was so alien to him.

I said, 'He's not going to want you without a horse.'

'You can get that for me as well.' He was hot about it. The drying spittle was a white rind on his lips.

I said, 'Listen, Genghis, why would I want to do either of these things for you? You remember what the Lux cinema was offered to me for? Brand new? Red plush seats, electric organ from Germany, the screen, American cash register, carpeting, spittoons, a list of fittings as long as your arm plus the usherettes and their uniforms. How much?'

'Don't make fun of me.'

'Four thousand cash. And you want me to give you five thousand plus a horse? Have a pull at your ears. It'll stretch your brains and make them go farther.'

'You can do more with a horse than a cinema,' he said.

'You mean eat it? But then it's gone. You're worse off than ever.'

'The girlies are probably terrorists,' he said, beginning to sulk. 'You can't escape in a cinema, you can't ride it away, you can't . . .' His bravado sputtered out.

And then events shut him up with absolute finality. For on the morning of Easter Monday, Joseph, who'd gone out early to queue for bread, came running down the corridor to the room he and I were sharing. Came flying, small quick bounds, like a man about to jump a barrier. I slipped out of my old Rykov campaign cot and threw open the door.

'What is it?'

'Posters, all over the city they say. One's even been pasted over the day's services at the cathedral.' He gulped, getting his breath back.

'For Kerensky, for the generals, for the Tsar – which?'

'Worse, the worst possible.'

'The Bolsheviks?'

'Doig, they've let him back in. LENIN ARRIVES TODAY. MEET HIM! That's what the posters say.'

Kobi had taken over the space beneath the stairs for sleeping quarters. Hearing our voices, he crawled out to join us. I said, 'You'll get your war now, that's for sure.'

With the trace of a sneer he said, 'Will the Bolsheviks put up posters for Glebov as well when he hits town?'

I said, 'Lenin means power. Power's the pogey bait for all these fanatics. Glebov'll turn up.'

Joseph put in: 'To think that Lenin dares arrive on Easter Monday! Has he no sense of shame? Does he suppose that God doesn't know what he's planning? Who does he think he is?'

'Your new Messiah,' Kobi said drily.

Five

THERE WAS no reason why I should go and see Lenin arrive. There'd be a great crowd of his supporters to whom I had no wish to expose myself. I was too tall, had too fine a carriage, looked too much like a Romanov. And there was always the chance they'd pick up on my accent.

My mother had spoken good aristocratic Russian, which has a soft smooth tone and is coloured by French words and phrases. But Papa, the Scotsman in Moscow, had ended up with an accent that everyone said sounded like the worst sort of Estonian. Of course I'd copied him and by the time I understood the importance of accents, it was too late to change. Just as dangerous were the odd Russian-Scottish manglings that I'd inherited from him. Try as I might, they had a habit of popping up. As a result of all this, Russians looked twice at me when I spoke. I wouldn't have wanted that at the Finland Station, not with Bolsheviks all around me.

But I wanted to have an idea of Lenin, to know how he looked in the flesh and how he behaved. I wanted to know what sort of numbers turned out for him. 'You go,' I said to Joseph, since Kobi had gone off to find Muraviev.

He demurred, saying all the bridges between the city and the Finland Station would be raised to keep people away from Lenin. He pleaded with me, said, Did I want to get him lynched? Why didn't he stay and prepare some onion piroshkas and a herring for my supper?

But I had another reason for wanting Joseph out of the palace for a while. I took him firmly by the elbow and steering him into the lane that ran into Nevsky Prospekt from behind the palace, bundled him into a horse cab.

Then I returned and went quickly to my uncle's library where I took possession of his funk money, which all Russian aristocrats kept handy in case of disaster. His hiding place was in the supplements to the eleventh edition of the *Encyclopaedia Britannica*, all of them dummies in the same tan binding. I was afraid the Socialist Revolutionaries might have got to them first. But in this Uncle Igor was a genius: for instead of trying to conceal them he'd put the fake volumes on an open shelf above his lectern, alongside his Russian reference books, in the belief that no robber would search in so obvious a place.

No one should ever treat money lightly, that goes without saying, but you know, when times are uncertain, you need a different view of its purpose. A good pair of boots can get you through all sorts of quagmires that money can't. Horses, carts and weapons are also primary, being the wherewithal for flight and defence. Anything fragile or heavy – leave it for an idiot. Children are useful – the best thieves in the business. Women can be bargained with.

Don't be rigid about money, that's what I'm saying. It doesn't have to be notes and coins. Igor knew that too.

What I had from my uncle's hoard: twenty-five thousand Tsarist roubles in the scarlet one thousand series and thirty-one gold strips carrying the stamp of the Imperial Bank of Russia. These were the size of a lady's dance card and had obviously been minted with an eye to portability. Worth about ten thousand roubles apiece in normal times. The colour of that reddish mustard from Angoulême, but shiny.

Straightway I took them to Shansky, Igor's old jeweller at 228 Nevsky. It was late. He was reluctant even to admit that he was there. But I knew he was because a light had been showing until he heard my footsteps.

I said my name. He shuffled to the door – pressed his ear against it.

I said, 'Shansky, now put your eye to the keyhole.'

Allowing him five seconds, I said, 'Tell me what you see.'

'Black, nothing but black,' he said hoarsely.

'That's a very special black. That's the muzzle of my Luger Kriegsmarine. Now let me in.'

I laid out the gold strips on his workbench, seven rows of four plus three underneath. The pressure lamp was wheezing on its hook. His anxious face peered at me over his half-moon spectacles. His wife, who'd always been stupid, still had her hand to her mouth. The Luger lay between us, beside the gold. Pointing at them.

Shansky said, 'I made thirty-two altogether for the Count. Where is the other one?'

'He's dead, you know.'

'Yes. Was it Joseph who stole it? Go to Paris when you leave. You'll get the best price there. The French love gold. But don't accept paper in return. Paper money's the curse of civilisation. Look at what Kerensky's done with it. The man who's meant to be governing the country. It's an insult.'

I was asking him what he would propose in its place, when suddenly his wife blurted out, 'But if not Kerensky, who?'

We paid her no attention, the answer was so obvious. Shansky didn't take his eyes off me for a moment.

I said, 'The wealthy are leaving.'

'Indeed, Excellency.'

'You'll have been buying their jewellery.'

He licked his lips cautiously, glanced at his wife. 'Yes, the widow Skobolov was here . . .'

'Did she have good taste?'

He gave me a wan smile. 'Ah, I begin to see . . . You wish to exchange your uncle's gold for something easier to carry? Something like jewels, maybe, Excellency?'

His wife butted in hysterically, 'But will times ever get better? That's the question you should be asking yourselves. When did we last have a full meal, with all the courses possible, in Russia? When will bread appear in the shops of its own free will? . . . And for that monster to come back on Easter Monday . . . It can never be the same. We're finished. I shall hang myself before they get me.'

'Quiet now, *matushka*. Nothing is ever as bad as it seems or as good. We both know that.' Going over, he kissed her head and ruffled her tired grey hair.

He said to me, 'Your gold for my jewellery, is that to be the bargain?'

'But only the best.'

He went to his safe and unlocked it. He took out a tray and laid it between us on the work table – beside the Luger and the gold. He checked that the key in the door was fully turned. Then he rolled back the napkin of dark blue velvet and gave the tray a little shove mixed with a little shake, which I construed as disdain. 'The Skobolov woman's.'

I said, 'These things must have belonged to her maid. Please, the best.'

So we looked at the Kuzminsky tray and the Morozov tray and we picked through an unsorted bag from Prince Gorevsky that Shansky had purchased only that morning. All I took from these was one emerald ring of Gorevsky's because of the magnificent vulgarity of its setting. Revolutions have winners as much as they have losers. Some day I might have to appease a Bolshevik warlord. It could be touch and go, a pistol to my head and the brute counting down to zero. Then I'd say, 'Wait a moment, comrade, I've got just the thing for your woman. She'll flash like gunpowder with this on her finger.'

Well, it took time but eventually my gold was translated into 180 brilliant cut diamonds, medium to small. Those are the sizes that are best for day-to-day use, for turning into the wherewithal for bribes, information, wages – the necessary costs of life. I didn't worry about finding buyers for them: there are always greedy people around.

For bigger purchases such as artillery or an aeroplane, I took three of the gaudiest Gorevsky necklaces, things designed for the huge pink flabby women in his family. Shansky offered me pearls, good ones, but I declined: too fragile for what might lie ahead.

Helping me wrap the diamonds in individual tissues and fiddle them into the woollen lining of my boots, he said, 'The moment I saw the posters this morning I said to myself the magic word – America. Have you read what Lenin's written, Excellency? This won't be the place for anyone who owns anything. My wife and I have often talked about this happening. She has reservations about America. The hard journey – our age – how to survive when we get there. She says, "Who will buy our jewellery? What do we know of American taste?" And then you entered and now we have an international currency bearing the stamp of the Imperial Bank. So we can get to America in comfort and when we arrive we can afford to take our time. I thank you, Excellency, I thank you from my heart.'

He carefully inserted the last of the necklaces deep into the wool. 'Why do you remain, Excellency, if I may ask? You are young. Your future is surely not here.'

'Glebov is his name. Prokhor Fedorovich Glebov.'

He sewed up the slits in the top of my boots and finished the thread with a roving knot so that I could get at the diamonds without messing up the whole arrangement. I watched his neat, lean fingers. He said, 'Glebov – no, I don't know that name.' Then ruminatively, 'The Tsar's gold is the purest in the world. Believe me, I know about such things. The same reddish colour as your uncle's, from the copper particles in the rock. When times are dangerous – well, Excellency, we understand each other about the value of paper money.'

Then he waxed the strip of leather to disguise his handiwork and to stop the stitching from icing over, humming to himself and smiling.

It was well after midnight that Joseph returned to the palace. I awoke – I'd been dozing in the chrome chair – to find his dark, sardonic face peering at me through the haze rising from the table lamp.

Without any preamble, he said, 'Vladimir Ilyich's sisters were brought to the station in a black car. On getting out, the fattest one missed her footing on the running board and fell over, as if unaccustomed to cars. They both wore black – waddling black dumplings, that's what they were. And his wife, the Krupskaya woman – one would not say that they are often intimate—'

'You want them to breed, for God's sake?'

'Permit me to reply like this, that he looked the sort of man who hangs his testicles up behind the door when he goes to bed. There is no danger of young Lenins. He has a big head. His mother must have had a bad time at his birth. He was smirking the whole time, not genuinely pleased and grateful as

I'd have been . . . As he was being carried along, someone noticed that his boots were new. Walking boots they were, Doig, not our *valenki*. This man called up to him, "Comrade Lenin, why did you not buy our Russian boots?" He laughed: "Krupskaya made me get these when the train halted in Stockholm. She said my old ones were a disgrace to the cause." Another man shouted to the first one, "Why do you say that? Proper boots they are, with iron heel and toe plates. Hurrah for Comrade Lenin's boots!" And a schoolmaster next to me said to all who could hear, "Comrades, how these boots will ring in history!"

'The sound of Lenin's words, many of which were long and completely unknown to me, was disgusting, like an enormous cud being chewed. But the fools, they all shouted, "Hurrah! Hurrah!" Then he climbed onto an armoured car and a searchlight shone its beam on him. The schoolmaster at my side called out loudly, "Look at him, like Jesus clad in the glowing armour of truth." I thought they weren't supposed to mention Jesus but of course I didn't say anything.

'To sum up, it was like a holiday to honour a great victory. Everyone was in high spirits. They'd have torn Kerensky to bits if they'd got hold of him. Several thousand people were there, men, women and children, even though it was late. I was shaking with relief when I got away.'

Six

I NEVER DOUBTED that Lenin's arrival would spell the end for Kerensky. Nothing is ever gained by quibbling with history. It contains a whole bunch of questions to which the only possible answer is the answer obtained. The smoke of victory already clung to him. It was that, not a halo, that Joseph had seen at the Finland Station.

Perversely, it cheered me to know Lenin was in the country. Somewhere Glebov was resting up, but now the cheese had got to the stinking stage, he was sure to pop out of his hole. Then I'd have him.

But there were others who believed in Kerensky and were betting on him. Here let me mention the name of Countess Cynthia Zipf, a child in Newark, New Jersey, a beauty in Paris, a bride in Berlin, and now the mistress of one of the most prominent members of Kerensky's cabinet. She had this man's ear, his money and the run of his houses in St Petersburg and Moscow and of his country estate at Kaluga. An outsider would have said she depended on him for everything. Such a person would have been wrong. She had investments of her own and above all she had her nerves, which she was fond of boasting were descended from the best Jewish nerves in America.

For a while, during that hot – that exceptional – summer of 1917, it looked as though her predictions would be proved right. Everything that Kerensky did was just what the country wanted from him. Though not from a military background, he struck all the right notes when he toured the battlefields of the European conflict. Some of his speeches to the troops were inspirational. He was everywhere at once, never short of an answer or a beautiful phrase. The newspaper photographs of him were invariably reassuring. The short dark hair, the shrewd eyes, the decisive forehead (neither too low nor too intellectual) appealed to men, while those lips of his, so fleshy and uxorious, conveyed to every woman the idea of a good family man.

Kerensky made it possible to feel encouraged. And when, in the brilliance of May, the purple trusses of lilac dangled over the sidewalks and their scent inflated the air to bursting point, when dreams began to stir of the creamy flesh of potatoes dug from our rich dark soil, and of baby onions and beetroots, there were many people besides La Zipfa who professed optimism. Everything was going so well for Russia. Could one invoke – at long last – after so many sacrifices – the longed-for word, victory? And if that were so and the Hun were bashed to pieces, might not his palaces and positions be restored to the Little Father, at present mooning around at Tsarskoe Selo, preening himself in his Jaeger underwear and cataloguing his collection of seaside postcards? If only, murmured these optimists, someone had taught him to think for himself, to articulate boldly – to make every word he spoke stand up and salute. He had such a nice voice . . .

The heat grew. Russia baked. Kerensky declared that along our country lanes the wild flowers had never looked so lovely in his entire life.

'Doesn't he express himself charmingly?' said Cynthia to me one day upon meeting by chance in Nevsky. 'But you know what he should really do, of course you do.'

She drew her forefinger across her throat and gurgled. 'Kaputnik. The only definitive solution.'

She swayed towards me. Such a fine, strapping body when viewed as a whole. With first-class technique, one could count absolutely on it just by the way she walked and by the confidence with which she moved her limbs, as if she were already in bed with her favourite man. She'd tried to jump my uncle, Count Igor, when she was down on her luck. She'd had herself driven over in a rented carriage to dine and play a few hands of piquet. She'd worn a strong scent – like a she-buffalo, said Joseph. Had offered my uncle several perspectives of her bosom but then had spoilt everything by tapping him reprovingly on the wrist when he made a poor play and calling him an asshole. Uncle Igor had sent her packing. Thud! went the heavy beam that secured the front door – with the Countess on the wrong side. Igor had turned to Joseph, put a mottled hand on his shoulder and murmured, 'Womanhood and its perils, my dear Joseph.'

In recounting this anecdote, Joseph had played the parts of himself and both principals, making free use of the floor space and not holding back on La Zipfa's idiosyncratic Russian.

'Of course you know what I mean,' she said to me, 'you're Russian yourself. One day he'll have Lenin killed, has to. Then – oh boy, shan't we have a party! Meanwhile you should be grabbing the common stock of the Archangel Timber Corporation. Trades at forty-five. Never been so low. Fill a barrow. Bye, Charlie.'

But all the successes that Kerensky initiated somehow failed to be completed. People began to believe him less. They had only to glance at the roadside flowers to see they were actually wilting in the heat. From that it was a short distance to noticing the pouches deepening beneath his eyes, that he was losing weight, that his clothes now hung poorly on him, as if he were a peasant. His voice grew hoarse. Was it cancer of the throat, perhaps? Then he took to bringing up Lenin's name gratuitously so that, it seemed, he could abuse him in a cheap, rather womanish way.

Gradually, by these imprecise but convincing signals, one began to understand that Kerensky no longer believed in himself. And the reason for this was sensed by all: Vladimir Ilyich Lenin.

Even though they'd grown up in the same small town, even though Kerensky's father had actually taught Lenin at school, even though Kerensky controlled the state, the army, the secret police and the executioners themselves, the fact remained that he was eleven years younger than Lenin and was afraid of him. I was sure of it.

By a flourish of his pen, he could have had Lenin killed. No one would have been shocked. In fact, the more imaginative his demise the more impressed Russians would have been. What was vital was to get it done.

Every day La Zipfa expected the discovery of Lenin's corpse

in some humiliating corner such as the outlet into the Neva of the main sewer. A fisherman would hook it. The leader of the Bolsheviks, drowned in shit! His cause would be totally discredited. Every day that she was disappointed, she grew gloomier.

I said, 'Cyn, it's not going to happen. Kerensky is too feeble. You should get out of the country. You don't have to live here, you know.'

'Me quit? After all the effort I've put into being someone who matters? Look you here, Charlie boy, I'm right about the old buzzard. And to show how confident I am, this morning I installed my servants permanently at the mortuaries here and in Moscow with orders to telephone me the *instant* Lenin's cadaver is presented. "Lift every sheet," I commanded them. "Vomit as much as you want." That's the language they understand. I'm telling you, one morning it'll happen. The phone will ring. Mine before anyone else's. I'll make a *killing*. Then shareholders will have the most fabulous Settlement Day that the Exchange has ever seen. After that I'll get out. Hey, did you buy Archangel when I said? They were down to twenty last night. Buy another barrowful. Follow them down. All the way. Yeah, that's right, corner the market. What's a few thousand roubles to a Rykov.'

The next time I met her, in the fog and mud of that fatal St Petersburg autumn, she came up with her best line ever.

'Charlie,' she said, 'I've made up my mind. You were right all along. That Kerensky doesn't have the balls for the job. I'm off. When the ship docks in the US of A, I'll be back to plain Cynthia Cohen again, older and wiser. But first I'm going to have myself a party and on the invitation cards will be printed this, like they print the headings in a book, all la-di-da – "*Every woman of blue blood should buy herself some stock when she gets her period, to celebrate it not being red.*" Maybe some of my friends will laugh enough to go out and buy. Maybe for a morning the Exchange'll soar. Then I'll be able to get out a rich woman. And you know what I'll regret most? Not having laid you. I'd have given you the time of your life. Too bad you're still in love with your wife. Couldn't you spare just one afternoon for me . . . ? I guess not. You're too honourable beneath all that warpaint. You know, Charlie, this could be the beginning of goodbye for our sort. It's not far off. I can feel it.'

We were both right: I about Kerensky being too weak, she about the beginning of the end. It gave neither of us satisfaction that when next we met, we could read in each other's faces exactly how right we'd both been.

By then, the only real question was when Lenin would strike. The city was alive with rumours. The day after I spoke to Cyn, I gave Joseph a hundred roubles and told him not to come back until he knew every detail of the coup.

On the morning of 25 October 1917, not having seen him for a week, I spotted him walking wearily up the steps at the front of the palace. I went to the door. He didn't come in, just leaned against the jamb.

He laid his forefinger across his palm: 'Tonight.'

His second finger: 'The Smolny Convent.'

And the third: 'Lenin, Trotsky – and Glebov. The three of them. By tomorrow Kerensky will be out.'

He was exhausted. I steered him down the corridor to our room. He collapsed into the American chrome chair. 'To do it a week ago was their original plan. Then someone remembered that Chaliapin would be singing *Don Carlos* tonight. So they postponed the coup. The first shots won't be fired until Kerensky is snug in his box and the man is singing.'

Seven

WE LEFT the palace at ten that night, going out the back way. I'd bought the trays and their smocks from a couple of *gribochki*, or mushroom sellers, as a disguise and wanted to have a stroll along Nevsky to see how best to carry the act off.

'Stoop, Doig,' said Joseph. 'Be common.'

That wasn't so easy from a height of six foot two with a tray round my neck. In any case no one gave us a second glance. And the reason that they didn't was they were watching open-mouthed as a file of Red Guards marched down the Prospekt – politely, disciplined, not on the pavement but in the gutter with the horse shit. You could even say they were marching humbly.

A group of young officers staggered out of the Makayev champagne bar clinging to their bottles of Krug Elite and their furred-up whores. Everything was funny to them. They bayed at the beggars blinded in the war, and tossing scarves round their long necks they bayed at the moon, which was gliding along behind the battlements of a dense bank of sea fog.

The Guards drew level with them. I heard the soldier in charge say loudly, 'Smarten up, smarten your step there! Swing those arms, pick up your knees, let's show the *boorjoi* swine who's who in Russia!'

'Make no mistake,' I said to Joseph, 'the age of cigars and palaces is over. This morning it was on its deathbed. Now it's a goner. Nothing's surer when Bolsheviks parade down Nevsky and no one can stop them.'

'What comes next?'

'The age of survival,' I replied, at which point Kerensky, in

27

an act of desperation, had the electricity turned off. For an instant the coils in the street lamps glowed orange, then there was darkness except for the charcoal beds of the chestnut sellers' braziers. Darkness and the smell of fog.

I was glad for that shroud of fog. When murder's in one's heart one looks different. One's nerves get taut. Slips are made. In fact one's entire behaviour is altered, and people notice this. They follow you with their eyes and quietly observe all the ways in which you've ceased to be normal. A man thinking of murder becomes a public spectacle.

We walked quickly, along Konyushennaya, right past the Church of the Resurrection and into Mikhailovski Gardens.

Everything was quiet. A couple of mallard lay tucked up on the lake, floating on the murky water like a pair of abandoned shoes.

I said to Joseph, 'This is a very tranquil affair. Are you sure?'

He replied in a low, intense voice – grabbing my arm, 'Doig, is it true that you've never been afraid?'

I could think of nothing I wanted to tell him.

We left the Gardens and went past the Circus to Engineers Bridge. The fog had overflowed the banks of the canal. I took out my Luger. All the Fontanka footbridges were haunted by cut-throats what with the canal being so handy. When the Tsars had the upper hand, Uncle Igor had told me, there used to be a policeman night and day in a box on the eastern side of this bridge. The name of the last one had been Tikhonov. He'd had a red beard.

But times had changed. They were fresh and sparkling with the dew of Utopia and the policemen, afraid of being knifed, went around in gangs. So no Tikhonov, no red beard pimpled with droplets of moisture, no friendly salutation. Instead, we were halfway across, with the uneven grid of the iron walkway clanking beneath our boots—

A trumpet – a single call, descending without a falter through two octaves, the player not squirting the notes out with force but releasing them reluctantly, as a mourner would the grains of soil he lets fall on a coffin lid.

Everywhere else the city was holding its breath. The trumpeter had no competition. Even the dogs were silent.

28

We too halted, for perhaps the same reason that old soldiers automatically halt when they hear a bugle call. The sound of that trumpet was magnificent, made larger and I shall also say poignant by the fog.

Down he went, the lugubrious fellow, down down down with his pure sweet steady notes. At the bottom he lingered, indulging himself in some delicate finger work on the pistons. The sound faded. Had he turned to look in another direction, at some Red soldiers approaching? To raise his tantalising eyebrows to a beautiful woman? Then suddenly, again at full volume, like a sailor running up a ladder, he took off and up the octaves he flew, note upon note, ever so quickly, until I was certain there was nothing further that could be obtained from the instrument – and then, after repeating three times an incredible crying howling note, which must have been heard all over the city, he ceased.

Fanfare to the past, that's what it was, a sort of burial. Nothing to do with what was to come – with the flame of optimism or the sacred lives of children yet unborn or going to the moon. Tonight was the end, and that man knew it.

I started down the steps, my pistol stabbing into the silent fog.

Never have I experienced such nothingness. Not a cough, not a footfall, not the rasp of a match struck. Not a tendril of tobacco smoke or the whiff of a tart's pussy or the smell of a dog long dead in the canal. Why no barking dogs? There were two million people living in the immediate vicinity. Had the two million people living in the area suddenly been struck dumb or pulled the blankets over their heads? What had happened to the city's four thousand Frenchmen who, fog or no fog, babbled like houseflies twenty-four hours a day?

That was how it was in St Petersburg on that October night. And the reason had to be this: the city was waiting. The stuccoed façades of the princely houses knew, the cobbles knew, the water, the bridges, the absent whores, the absent thieves, the cats, the dogs, the canaries, they all knew, and probably the rats as well, which at night were usually quite free with the city but now were showing not even an inch of tail. Everyone and everything knew that after tonight it would be different.

I said to Joseph, 'You should have had my pistol at the Finland Station and shot the cunt. You'd have got a monument – thousands of them. Every main square would have had its Joseph – Joseph what?'

'Culp. My mother fell in love with the short stiff moustache of the German watch repairer who lived next door to her parents.'

'Joseph Culp, then. Think what immortality you've missed.'

'I'm a coward, Excellency. They'd have ripped me to pieces. They were mad with love for him.'

'Besides, you don't know how a pistol works.'

'That is also true.'

'Keep walking, Joseph.'

'Yes, Excellency.'

'Don't call me that. We're mushroom sellers.'

For all my urging he remained a reluctant companion and I had to walk behind him. 'Left . . . left . . . left . . . Military precision makes a man courageous,' I whispered into his ear.

Suddenly the night was split by the scream of flayed rubber as a black Wolseley came lurching round the corner towards us on two wheels, the noise like that of a pig when it first sees the knife. Its headlights sliced the fog apart. Bullets from the three shadowy men on the running boards spattered the building behind us. Joseph flung himself down on the pavement – flat on his stomach. The driver whacked on the brakes, slewing the car round sideways. More rifles were pointed at us out of the window, behind them a jumble of beards and teeth. There could have been another ten men crammed inside it. The sharpshooters were off the boards while the car was still moving and came running at me, running and shouting, criss-crossing through the car's headlights, impossible to see clearly. I went down on one knee – it was in Joseph's back – and abased myself.

When you have to bow, bow low, even unto the ground. It really was my mother's best bit of advice.

I proffered my tray. 'Mushrooms! For the cause – for the proletariat – free! I beg you!'

The muzzle of a rifle barrel stirred the leathery chunks. The driver manoeuvred the car so that its headlights were full on us.

Being on one knee disguised my height. 'Take! Take! They belong to you!'

They started to stuff their pockets, all the time Joseph lying doggo beneath me.

One of them said to me, 'You're in luck tonight, comrade. The last men we stopped we shot.'

'All Russia is in luck,' I murmured.

They shook their rifles at the night and shouted, 'Onward the proletariat! Long live Lenin!' The engine was gunned – a small white face, scarcely bearded, was behind the wheel – and they hopped back onto the running board. The car went the wrong way round the statue of V. I. Smirnov, righted itself and took on an opposite list as the little cheeser flung it round the left-hander into Sergievskaya and headed west in the direction of the Stroganov Palace with a bubbling roar from its exhaust.

I took my knee off Joseph. He lay very still, all crimped and at a funny angle. I told him to quit shamming.

'Five years ago I thought I might make it to the end without ever being shot at,' he said.

'You thought that, in Russia?'

'Yes. Why would anyone want to shoot a man who'd soon be forty years of age, that was the way I reasoned.'

'Is the bullet your greatest fear?' I asked.

'Not the bullet, Doig, the bayonet. I shall try not to run away when we get close to the soldiers, but if I do, I beg your forgiveness.' He bowed his head. 'I am a coward. May you never meet a more cowardly person than your servant, Joseph Culp.'

Eight

THE NOISE of the Wolseley faded and silence again descended. I'd expected something different. Was Russia's torrent of grievances going to turn out to be a trickle? Shouldn't there be a chatter of machine guns – bombs – mobs on the rampage – the incessant drone of military lorries?

'What sort of a coup is this?' I cried to Joseph.

But a few minutes later I saw a glow in the sky ahead. From the direction of Smolny, just as Joseph had said. We stopped and got ourselves sorted out as mushroom sellers. Joseph again asked my forgiveness if he behaved like a coward. Again I forgave him. Then I led the way forward – slowly, crying my wares.

Low-slung black saloons were racing towards the old convent. Ever more frequently we were passed by dispatch riders on motorbikes and even by bicyclists. Of the latter one might know nothing in those darkened streets until at the last moment one heard the strained breathing of the messenger or the creak of a wheel.

Tentatively we approached the Bolshevik HQ.

What they'd done: got some student from the Electrical College to tap into the grid, then strung factory arc lights all along the bright blue pediment of that aristocratic façade so that Smolny was ablaze as far as the railings separating it from the square and its grove of trees.

It was as if a battleship paying the country a state visit was moored in front of us. I halted, Joseph's tray hitting me in the back.

The coughing motorbikes, the scarlet of the swaying banners, the runnings and bustlings, the engine fumes, the smell of fuel oil and of smoke from a bonfire, the shouts, the heftily saluting girls – the sheer virility and energy of the scene: one would have said that enough electrical force was coming out of Smolny to power the entire city.

'That's more like it. Glebov can't be far away. *Poshli* – let's go,' I said to Joseph, and I strode in front of him into the light, jiggling my tray of mushrooms. 'Here, boys! For the sake of the Revolution! For the betterment of man!'

As I expected, they hadn't eaten for God knows how long. Their Bolshevik stomachs were hanging from them like empty gourds. I was besieged, and Joseph also. He got his nerve back and was quickly parleying with the Bolshies in a fine prole-tarian whine.

But the outskirts of revolution weren't where I was aiming. I had my eye first on the barrier of machine guns placed outside the two white porters' lodges and then on the group of men chatting at the top of the steps. That was where I had to get to, up there with the nobs, if I was to get close to Glebov.

I pressed forward: 'Hey, what about the comrades on duty, are they to go hungry at this great moment? Are we to forget their aching bellies?'

'Never!' This from a terrific hulk of a fellow, bursting out of the seams of a uniform made for a much smaller man. 'They're as much humans as you or I. Go to them, Estonian man. Point me out as the fellow who sent you so that afterwards we can celebrate together.'

I got to the first line of guards. They were crouched over their machine guns. The ammunition belts hung down tidily and had been folded on the ground like piles of ironed towels.

My new friend shouted over to them. Not hearing for sure where the voice was coming from, the guards spanned the crowd with their guns. He caught their eye and jabbed a finger at me.

Feeling more confident with every step, I said to Joseph, 'Give me what you've got left and go home.'

With a laugh I chucked a handful of mushrooms between the gunners and walked through their line as they fell on them like pigs, spitting out the rough bits all over the place.

These fellows, they were pretty well all in. I suppose they'd been on the go for at least a couple of days. Enthusiasm is important, but food and sleep are vital. Five hundred well-armed men of Kobi's stamp would have swept them into the river in half an hour flat and declared it a picnic. The Bolshevik Revolution would have been over before it began. Then who'd have got his backside on the throne?

I was young, fit, bold – and I was there. It's not easy to get lucky, but when you do, the sky's the limit. If Lenin, why not me?

But that's one of those pleasant sofa thoughts that occur later. At the time I had nothing else in my mind except how to get past the guard post at the top of the steps and insinuate myself into the presence of Glebov.

Handing out more mushrooms, I said casually, 'Boys, what's the latest password?'

'*Radost* – joy. That's what it was an hour ago. However, they change it whenever something goes wrong. Joy! I'd rather have sleep. Pass, comrade.'

Up the steps I went.

It was exposed in the glare of those arc lights. I quietened my nerves and climbed with slow, humble steps, not raising my eyes.

There was a table at which anyone wanting to get into the building had to present himself. Two men were being questioned in front of me. I didn't catch what their business was. Seeing me approach, the guard officer waved them through instantly, as if clearing the decks for action. He crooked his finger at me and smiled ominously.

'*Vot, vot vot* . . . Well, well, well, who have we here . . . So tall! So princely! It's obvious you're not one of us. You look far too good – too *comfortable* with yourself. Put your tray on the table. Slowly. Here, you – search it and then search him.'

I said, 'Comrade, in the name of science I appeal to you. No weapon could ever be disguised as a mushroom.'

'You know about science? You're not who you're dressed up to be. You're educated. Start the search.'

I cursed myself. How could I have thought that the new Tsar would be any less suspicious than the old one? The Luger felt like a ton weight in my pocket.

I said briskly, 'No need for that, comrades, when you have duties to the whole of mankind. Matters of real importance,

I can see that. Look, I'll search myself in front of you. Down to the bare skin, if that's what you want. If I miss anything you've only to say. Shoot me whenever you want. But keep your hands off the mushrooms. That's proper food I'm giving away. Who wants the likes of that fellow's arse-wiping fingers all over his meal?'

It was the dirtiest and most squalid of the guards I'd picked on, which raised a laugh. I bounced the mushrooms up and down on the tray, saying, 'Bombs, little bouncing bombs, look at them playing!'

My interrogator said, 'OK, *kroshka* – little one – what's the password?'

'*Radost.*'

'That's the old one.'

'I wasn't to know that, comrade. I've been feeding the troops—'

He cut me short. 'A good password system is the key to victory. That's the way one catches traitors and latifundists.'

'May we be preserved from them, Excellency.'

His eyes roamed over me. 'You're from Estonia or one of those little relics, you're not a proper Russian. Here, show me your papers.'

'But he's offering us food,' murmured one of the guards.

'Yes, let the fellow go. Free food!'

'I'll eat his bombs,' said a third, snatching at my tray. 'I know a good risk when I see it.' His eyes glowed. His teeth, strong and white against the black pelt of his face, bit decisively into the crinkled dome of the mushroom. 'Bang!' he shouted comically. 'Bang, bang, bang!' – and took a handful.

'Very well, Estonian,' said the officer. 'But stay where I can see you.'

Nine

THERE WAS a knot of us at the top of the Smolny steps. Below was an anthill of activity. Adventure was in the air. People were taking deep breaths, as if to draw the future into their lungs and never let it go. Excitement! It was flashing like the neon sign of a lady's slipper that hung outside the Makayev champagne bar. Only my interrogator was out of it. Something was needed to sideline him – and here it was—

A brilliant beam of light came boring out of the night, picking out the trees in the square. Behind it, thunderously, was a motorbike and sidecar. The driver spun the outfit round with a sudden twist of the handlebars, spattering mud over some bicycle messengers who'd paused, toes pointed to push off, to see what was up. The man in the sidecar leapt out and stared up at Smolny. He lifted his goggles – stuck them on his head. He lit a cigarette, inhaled, removed it from his mouth with a dramatic swoop. Nodding at the guards, he stalked between the outer machine guns and mounted the steps.

Between his second and third fingers appeared a buff slip of paper. He held it like a dandy, as if it were something infinitely precious and exquisite.

Everyone watched this lean, confident fellow. He seemed to have walked straight out of a film. One had to look twice to get rid of the idea of a rapier in his hand.

Oblivious, my persecutor glanced at me and began to crank the handle of the field telephone. He licked his lips like a woman on heat – glanced at me again – was clearly about to tell someone he'd caught a Tsarist spy.

I pushed against him – not with the Luger side of my coat

– and said, 'Comrade, why are you so determined to turn a mushroom into a bomb? Look at the messenger there. He walked straight through.'

As I finished speaking there came from behind me this shrill, harsh voice: 'At last, news of the struggle – let me see that message, quickly now.'

It was Lenin. I knew him immediately, even though he appeared quite different from the police photographs. His shoulder brushed mine as he passed. Scanning the bit of paper (putting it close to his eyes): 'Then we've taken the Post Office? Good. Very good.' He read it again. 'Almost without a shot fired. Even their own people are giving up on them.' This last he said in an undertone, almost to himself.

He was wearing a dark suit of some thick material. The trousers were too long – trailed along the ground at his heels. His beard, which he'd shaved off during the months he'd been hiding from Kerensky, was patchy, as if he had ringworm. And his head, which the newspapers had always shown to be three-quarters hairless, was thatched with a wig that gave him the looks of a dark-haired gigolo of about eighteen. It was how he'd walked into the city from the suburbs, so that the guards on the bridges wouldn't recognise him.

Turning, he noticed me and my tray. Close up his eyes were grey green, hundreds of kilowatts in them. They perforated the skin of my face like a couple of nails. He entered my skull. Not speaking, just looking around inside as my tormentor denounced me as a Kerensky infiltrator.

Lenin stepped up to me. With Kobi's knife I could have reached out and popped his fat little belly. He took one of my mushrooms, snapped it in half and then into quarters and began to eat.

He swallowed – gulped, choked a little, and said to me and all those around me in that shrill, scraping voice: 'This is the first night that the people of Russia have ever been able to call their own. If this man is a spy, let him first be useful to us. Let him feed us for nothing. Then we'll shoot him. If he's not—'

He got no further. The soldiers fell on my mushrooms, almost knocking me over.

'I'm no spy,' I shouted at Lenin, throwing open half my coat to show him I had nothing there except strings of mushrooms. On the other side I had a loaded Luger. My boots were stuffed with diamonds. They'd have killed me for either. But Lenin was hot with luck that night and I reckoned that being so close to him I'd get a share in it.

His mouth twisted sarcastically. 'The tall man's no spy . . . That's what he says, so make out a pass for him . . . You, Baltic being, what's your name?'

'Sepp, Arno Sepp. Born and bred in Tallinn.' I knew it was a reasonably common name in Estonia but it was the mushrooms that triggered it off.

The man wrote it out, letter by letter. Lenin, Zinoviev and the rest of them looked on with indifference as I became Sepp of Tallinn.

'Welcome to the new Russia,' said Lenin. I bowed. An aide whispered in his ear. He went back into the building.

I stretched out my hand to my tormentor for the pass and said, 'Well then, where does this get me?'

'Nowhere,' he said, tearing it across and across, into tiny pieces. 'Arno Sepp of Tallinn, my shithole.'

'It's the truth,' I said, placing my hands flat on the table at which he sat and leaning over him. What was extraordinary was that in that short space of time I'd actually come to feel that I was Sepp. It felt a truly seaworthy lie. 'My mother's family name was Saar, and that also is a common name in Tallinn. What else should a man called Sepp do but marry a girl called Saar?'

He glared at me, his eyes festering with disbelief.

Suddenly there was a terrific racket below. A lorry had broken down and was preventing another of the usual black saloons from getting in. It was sorted out with a lot of shouting. Then the driver of the car, even though there were only fifty yards to go, put on maximum revs in order to draw attention to himself and to make people leap aside.

The car door flew open, kicked from inside. A soldier put up his rifle in alarm. 'Password! Now!'

It was a thin, youngish man who came sliding out, galoshes first. He stood up – tall, six foot four, let's say – planted a black fedora on his black hair and said in an American style of Russian,

38

'Christ, Ivan, I haven't a clue. At midday, when I went out, it was *chyerf* – worm in English, which I thought a good choice for a revolution. But midday' – he looked at his watch – 'that was a lifetime ago. Between then and now we've changed the world . . . Jee-sus . . . Can you believe it, Ivan, that we've changed every number in the equation? It's a goddam miracle, that's what it is.'

'Password, papers,' said the soldier stolidly.

The man flapped a reporter's notebook at him. 'That's all I've got for papers, the rest are in the hotel. Reed's my name, representing the finest socialist newspaper in the United States. That should be enough for you.'

He put the notebook back and with one hand braced against the car roof, leaned down and said to the person inside, 'Here we are then, comrade. Go easy on it, one step at a time and we'll get there.'

Crash! Rifle butts were being slammed against the flagstones behind me – for Lenin, back onstage, as calm and commanding as before. He paid me no attention this time. With him was Trotsky, unmistakable on account of his athletic hair and pointed beard. Behind his steel-rimmed spectacles, his eyes glowed. Victory was to the Bolsheviks and he knew it.

Their four hands were in their coat pockets. My Kriegsmarine was a semi-automatic. I'd have had time to shoot them both. That's another dream I often have.

They strolled in front of me, blocking my view of Reed. I heard him shout up, 'Comrade Ulianov-Lenin, wonderful news – the Telephone Exchange, the Telegraph, the Military Hotel . . .'

Lenin murmured to Trotsky, their heads converging, 'Our tame American. A useful man. He should be humoured.'

Trotsky, hands now clasped behind his back, swaying on the balls of his feet, said, 'He could be paired with your sister Maria. That would be an international dimension we could exploit.'

'I would tell her it was historically inevitable. She would obey me. Is he a homosexual? It would be easier for him if he were.'

'I'll have one of our female followers discover . . . Ah, here comes Prodt at last. Which of those two is our greater friend, would you say, Vladimir Ilyich, Comrade Prodt or the American?'

'Friend? I don't think we need speak in those terms,' and they moved to one side as Reed trotted up the steps towards them.

Halfway up he paused and looked back: 'Comrade, you doing all right back there?'

The man they were calling Prodt was limping, head bent so that only broken views of his face were visible, never the whole thing. But I didn't need to see it all. There were at least ten things about him that told me instantly who Prodt was.

Up the steps he laboured towards Lenin and Trotsky. He was making heavy weather of it. He'd put on weight while his leg was healing.

I'd hoped . . . I can't tell you what exactly. That I'd catch Glebov alone in an office or in the darkness of the night, something like that. As it was, he had only to raise his eyes and I was butchers' meat. I was up there with Lenin, Trotsky and Zinoviev, me and my tray of mushrooms. Just the four of us, the soldiers and my tormentor being a few yards away in the opposite direction.

I heard the hiss of Elizaveta's indrawn breath and a little catch in her voice as she whispered in my ear, 'I know that man. Now's not the place for heroics, Charlie. Scoot and make it fast.'

He was wearing a military cap with a scarlet band. His mouth was working. He was in pain from his leg, was having to use a stick. I *had* to study him. I was unable to do otherwise – for a few seconds I was hypnotised and stared at him in the most obvious way. Then Lenin and Trotsky moved forward to greet him. I heard the smooth, welcoming tones of their voices – and came to my senses.

'Right you are, Lizochka, scoot's the word,' and I melted away, sliding behind one of Smolny's bright blue pillars.

Lenin must have seen the movement from the corner of his eye. He called out to me, 'Sepp of Estonia, you've nothing further to give us. You've played your part. So go back to your city and tell them that tonight the proletariat has triumphed. Yes, Mr Arno, triumphed!' He raised his fist in salute. 'Tell them that, Mr Arno Sepp.'

Reed had his arms outspread to embrace Lenin. He was still a step or two below him. Glebov was tucked into Reed's shadow.

The American shouted, 'Kerensky's had enough! Fled! The revolution's certain!' He got to the top – skipped the last two steps in one.

He embraced Lenin and then Trotsky. Suddenly, as he stood back, the whole tableau shifted and regrouped so that I was no longer concealed. I was out there in the open. No more than thirty feet separated me from Glebov.

I looked down as if searching for a coin I'd just dropped – risked another glance. He had four steps to go, was leaning heavily on his stick, still had his head down. When he got to the top he'd take a breather, then he'd line up beside Lenin and Trotsky. The three of them would face out over Smolny Square to field the applause and unburden themselves of a few speeches. I'd be up there with them, only feet away – tall, young, distinctive –

'For Christ sake, Charlie, *scoot*!'

There'll be a musical direction for how I walked down those steps: neither too fast nor too slow. But no such direction can speak of what was going on between my shoulder blades.

I said to my wife without lip movement, 'Make my spine narrower. Armour-plate it or something. Don't just sit up there and pray for me, woman, help.' And she did. She must have.

I'd left my mushroom tray on the table at which my tormentor sat: had set it down to prove to him that it didn't hold a grenade. He flung it after me with a shout, 'Take it with you, trickster.' It clattered down the steps and struck my heel. Should I pick it up? I did, thinking, Glebov can't fail to look now. I said to Elizaveta, 'Preserve me from a common death. I want to die in a rocket, tearing through the heavens towards you, not from a bullet in the back fired by the man who led your rape.'

I took longer than I needed to get the strap snug round my neck. I was Sepp the mushroom seller, not a spy. I couldn't afford to show what a hurry I was in. Then I continued down the steps.

Here is a curiosity worth mentioning: that all the time this was happening, which was about two minutes, I had a really strong itch in the centre of my back, exactly where Glebov would have aimed, which is the sixth thoracic vertebra.

I also want to say this about expecting to be shot in the

back, that if it had been pre-announced, if Glebov had shouted down to me, 'I know who you are! Eight paces of life, that's all I'll give you. Walk, Doig. One, two . . .' – and thus I knew it was coming – death would not have been unpleasant. Smack! And down I'd have tumbled, seeing at the last not a human but whatever bit of the sky I'd have chosen for the moment of departure.

But no bullet came. What happened was that as the mushroom tray rattled down the steps behind me, a soldier threw a whiz-bang into the bonfire to celebrate the victory of the Soviets and everyone looked towards him, not me.

A roar of laughter went up and I went a little faster, saying to myself, Once I reach the soldiers milling around at the bottom, I'll be safe.

But no sooner had I thought this than I realised Glebov was toying with me. He was waiting until I thought I'd got away. Lenin and Trotsky were standing up there holding their sides for laughter as he winked at them and at last drew his pistol.

I thought, But maybe I deserve death? What I did to Elizaveta—

Sweat was pouring off me, even though it was an autumn night. With every pace bang went a drop off the end of my nose. Forget everything I've just said about death from behind being not unpleasant. I was hating the idea. I had my eyes tight closed for those last few steps.

Then suddenly, without being aware that my legs were taking me there, I was through – past the soldiers, past their bonfire, past the sentry boxes, past the lorries, the couriers and their motorbikes, and the dogs scavenging for scraps. I never ran. I had enough self-discipline left for this. But as the Smolny arc lights faded, I walked faster and faster until the trees in the square loomed darkly before me. I darted into them with the utmost gratitude, like a man reprieved on the scaffold. I was exhausted. My breath was coming in surges. I leaned against the nearest tree and kissed its dank bark with open lips.

Ten

THE TIME was a little after two in the morning when I got back to Nevsky. My brush with Lenin and Glebov had used up all my juices. I needed a drink.

I entered the basement of the Makayev, which stank of sweat and tobacco smoke. There I found something left in a bottle of Abrau, the cheap Kievan champagne. I gulped it down, not taking the bottle from my lips, my whole arm shaking uncontrollably. Only the owner was in the place, sitting at a round corner table. His arms were folded across his chest. A pistol lay on the dirty tablecloth. Tears were coming from his eyes and dribbling down his unshaven cheeks.

I offered to sit with him and commiserate. He waved me away and I left. In the small basement courtyard a man in a black overcoat was having a woman against the wall. Her skirt was up to her waist, her thighs gleaming like enamel. She waved to me over his shoulder, maybe to book me for the next round. Ignoring her, I went quickly up the steps.

Almost in front of me, three young Red Guards walked out into the street and with hand signals stopped a private automobile. No conversation was needed, no explanations, no orders. The driver, from his dress one would say an opera-goer, and his distraught, fur-bundled wife got out of the car instantly and the Guards drove off.

I leaned against the railings of the Armenian church, watching. It occurred to me that I should start to say my goodbyes: the conditions I'd been brought up in from childhood were on the brink of disappearing. First I would go to the Rykov mausoleum, which was in the cemetery beside the Botanical Gardens – in the northern part of the city. The living one can deal with as one goes along. But for the dead a special effort must be made, even if it's only to say cheerio. What counts is the respect shown by the action. It clears the slate of everything that's happened in the past and tidies up the relationship between the dead and the living, which is always tricky.

Most of the Rykovs were there except Elizaveta and my cousin Nicholas, whom I'd buried side by side, and Mama, whose English death, from flu, had gone virtually unrecorded. Papa was there, cleansed of the plague. A native of Dundee, he'd never have believed that he'd end up in a private mausoleum in Russia. In particular I would go and honour him.

Having reached this conclusion, it was easy to decide that I too would commandeer a car.

Within two minutes, I saw the very one coming down Nevsky from the Admiralty. Its headlights, the size of kettledrums, were ablaze. It was being driven in the middle of the street, in the space reserved for shovelled-up snow and horse cabs. No sane person had done such a thing before. When I'd danced down it I'd been drunk and crazy. Yet here was this immense automobile cruising down the centre of Nevsky as if it owned it. And on the morning of the First of Lenin!

A man walking past said to me in disgust, 'There's our new leaders for you. Just look at the swine. Already!'

I stepped off the pavement. I had the blood of Scotland and the Rykovs in my veins – hot, scarlet, elite blood, which also means discontented. I wanted better than a dingy Wolseley saloon, better than something that Lenin's sisters used. This was my car, the vehicle toddling down Nevsky behind its vast headlights. I ran out to cut it off, drawing my Luger.

The driver's white face bore down on me. I aimed at a head-light then shifted to the figurehead on the bonnet, a swooping woman. I'd do the Bolshies a favour. It was too opulent, it had no future in a Russia that belonged to the proletariat.

The woman flew off at my second shot. The car glided to a halt.

Lowering the window, the chauffeur – bakelite eyes, blue chin – said in a tone of utter resignation, 'Look here, Ivan, old pal, do me a favour, will you? Leave his nibs' bleeding car alone until this time tomorrow, when I'll be on a boat back to Blighty. Blimey, what a go! It's the last time I sign up to deliver a car to Russia.'

This Luger of mine is such a beautiful weapon. When you stick the snout of its long barrel against someone's head, he understands one hundred per cent that the bullet's for him: it simply can't go anywhere else. And you both know that with nine inches of rifling it'll have real velocity behind it.

'Who's inside?'

'My Lord Boltikov,' he said gloomily.

'He's dead.' I was thinking of Boltikov the sugar king, the man who'd gatecrashed the party that my father gave before Mother and I took the train to our English exile.

'Must be his son. Ever so rich.'

'Fat and pink?'

'You've said it. Tsuh!' He jerked his chin upward, to inform me that in his opinion the young Boltikov was a bum.

'So what are you doing in Nevsky? Haven't you heard there's a revolution?'

'Opera first. Then a slap-up dinner. Now he's insisting on saying his goodbyes, him and his woman . . .'

'Wife?'

'No, mate, no. This is a German lady. Looks after his children or something . . . Mister, let me get on. He's got the same sort of temper as his other rich friends. It's a wonder he's not shouting already. Please, do me a favour—' Suddenly his eyes swivelled to something behind my shoulder. 'Quick, mate, Bolshies coming. Jump in or get off, whoever you are.'

The Rolls had an outside brake. He dropped his hand and slacked it with a thud. The car jerked forward. One foot on the running board, I wrenched open the passenger door. The chauffeur accelerated: tipped me in head first. Lurching, I grabbed for a strap, missed it and fell.

I knew the car had a carpet: I'd glimpsed it as I opened the door. I expected to land on it. Instead I went smack into a body that was soft and shrieking. In fact I knocked her over, and as I sorted it out, I thought, What the hell was she doing kneeling on the floor of a Rolls-Royce, was she praying or what?

45

Eleven

THE BLINDS were drawn and latched. I could make out Boltikov's head. Two-thirds of the way down his face, a cigar blossomed. I felt the force of the smoke on my cheek. It had a distinguished, exotic aroma. His voice came rasping out of the semi-darkness.

'A visitor, Liselotte.'

'He fell on me . . . it hurts . . .'

She was squirming under my shoulder. It was hard to tell which limb was where. I felt around, found Boltikov's shoes, then the edge of the seat. I hoisted myself to my knees.

The collar of his opera cape was still up. He was wearing a boiled shirt – stiff collar, white tie. It was all I could be certain of in the gloom. He said, 'I was listening to what you said. There's an instrument in the glove compartment that picks up everything. I don't trust that English shuvver of mine. How did you know my father? Who are you?'

'Charlie Doig.'

'The son of Irina Rykov? You are the famous traveller?'

'Yes.'

'Liselotte, I've cooled down. This man will be enough entertainment for the moment.'

My eyes were now accustomed to the light. He was sitting in the centre of the back seat, his arms outstretched along the back. His cigar glowed mutely between his fingers. Below, like a white blanket on which a moulting black wolfhound has been lying, spread his hairy stomach. His thighs were naked to below his knees. Here one met the top band of his sock suspenders and the corrugations of his woollen underpants.

He began to rearrange his clothing. 'Excuse me, Doig, it's not every night that one says farewell to the city of one's birth – to one's country. One's emotions become excessive, especially after the opera. Liselotte has certain skills – *liebchen*, what are you doing? Stop scrabbling round down there. Come and sit beside me. We have company.'

I'd sent her flying against the far door. She said the door handle had bruised her ribs. She had a final snivel and crawled over the carpet to Boltikov.

'Your pardon, *barin* . . .'

I was in her way. I pulled down a jump seat from the division for myself.

Boltikov was thirty-five or so. He laughed across at me. 'Liselotte is the governess of my son. She teaches him German in the morning and French in the evening. This part of her job is a penance for the evil Germany has inflicted on us – to be exact, for paying Mr Lenin to come here and start his revolution. She volunteered for this evening, of course. What do you say to that, Doig?'

'To Liselotte?'

'Lenin.'

'Only an hour ago I was speaking to him.'

'You should have shot him. He'll finish our class. Tonight is for goodbyes. Tomorrow Liselotte and my secretary and I drive across the border to Finland. My wife and boy are already there. From Finland this idiot shuvver of mine goes home. If I find there's trouble in Finland, I simply drive over the border to dear old Sweden. No one will stop a man in a Rolls-Royce. Wherever I get to, I'll start again. I have good contacts.'

'The reason I didn't shoot him was that I didn't want to be killed myself.'

'Not a martyr?'

'Never.'

'You can't hide class,' he said reflectively. 'Something will give you away, however much you try to conceal it. You can start speaking like a really stupid peasant, you can make the palms of your hands as rough as bark, but you'll still get nailed. Intelligence will mark you out. Breeding too—'

I laughed. 'My mother pointed out your father on the train.

47

She told me there was no bigger snob in the world than your father.'

'But what do you expect? Out of shit he turned himself into gold. From nothing, Doig! From a handful of kopeks! And having made his fortune, he couldn't think of what to do with it. He expected to meet kings and queens every day. "What else is money for?" he'd say to me. Or to a cabinet minister whose family had been around as long as the Romanovs, "We who are at the top should confer daily as to how we're to stay there." Things like that. He was right – but pretentious. Liselotte darling, sit closer to me, I like your smell.'

'Have you been caught up in a revolution before, Doig? What about those South American countries you went to?'

By this time we'd motored to the east end of Nevsky, circled the statue of Alexander III and had started back up towards the Admiralty. It was the direction I wanted to go. I was content to be Boltikov's passenger. He was doing the right thing. A man on the point of going into exile should say a full set of good-byes and do so in company, to ensure he doesn't become maudlin. He should be tender with his self-esteem. If he thinks poorly of himself on departure, how will he ever prosper in a foreign country?

Waving his cigar around, Boltikov continued on his previous theme.

(Liselotte had opened the window to let the smoke out. We could hear the occasional outburst of shooting quite clearly.)

'It may be the way we walk, as simple as that. Class will always show and the vermin'll spot it. That's why I'm getting out. Helsinki tomorrow. Eighty miles an hour the entire way. That's what it says on the clock so that's what we'll do. Eighty miles – that's – what's that in Russian?'

'Fifty versts.'

'Sensational! I love speed. I'll pick up my family and go to Stockholm and from there take a boat across to Wick thanks to Mr Thomas Cook and his wartime bravado – God willing! Then we'll catch a train to London. I have business friends in London. Also money with a gentleman called Mr Baring. Do you know this man?'

He stopped. His face crinkled with the foretaste of adventure and corporeal pleasures. 'We heard all about your travel adventures from your old uncle. You know, you could have had the pick of our Russian women when the stories got around—'

'I did.'

'You mean . . . that was a horrible experience. But it's what we must expect from these people . . . Doig, why not escape with me? You're strong. You're ruthless. You want to win . . . I'd pay you well.'

I said I'd think about it. It'd mean writing off my life so far – my childhood, Elizaveta, my lovely father, my descendance from the man who'd sent Napoleon packing. Did I want that – to erase the past? To deny myself?

I whistled vexedly – only a bar.

'*Stoy!* Stop! It's bad luck in the house. This car's a house for me . . . By the way, no one liked my father. It was a great relief to Mamasha when he died in the street. Walking along like you or me . . . he was so fat . . . You can see how fat I am, Doig. It comes from having been fed from the start on the best products sugar could make. I was in Einem's every day. He named a chocolate after me. It was called a Bombe Boltikov. Seventy-two per cent cocoa and in a compartment in the centre the strongest apricot brandy that Bols make. A little candy peel on top for ladies to pick off. Shaped *tout à fait comme un suppositoire* – it was a huge success. I expect I've eaten several tons of my Bombe . . . Of course Einem was German and so had to sell when this war started. His shop was never the same with the new people . . . The thing about the Germans is first the Kaiser, and second, sending that bastard Lenin to us. It's Germany that's brought us to our knees. Liselotte, do shut that window. It's Russia and the end of October, not June in Paris.'

He produced a flat silver flask of cognac. Liselotte took a good swig, coursing it round her mouth and smacking her lips. She passed me the flask. But I declined, saying it was a night to be sober.

They finished the flask between themselves. He said, wiping his lips, 'I'm disappointed in you, Doig. That was Reserve Royal 1825, from the Tsar's Summer Palace in the Crimea.'

He turned on the reading light on his side. It made him no thinner or more handsome. And Liselotte looked a hard nut,

49

even though the light was coming from behind a scalloped shade of the most feminine hue.

He said, 'When you crashed in here waving your pistol, I thought I was certain to be shot. Then you told me your name and I thought, Here's a man worth saving. Strong, brisk, cruel, those were the adjectives I chose, going by your reputation. But someone who doesn't have the sense to drink the best cognac ever made – well, it speaks for itself. I'll take you to the cemetery and then you can walk.'

I said, 'Mama was right. Snobbery can be inherited, just the same as blue eyes. That's a poor reason, to turn against me because I wouldn't drink your brandy.'

'You think I made the decision because I'm a snob?'

I shrugged.

'I was only testing you, that's all. To see if you'd speak up for yourself. Tell you what, come with me as far as Stockholm. A week, a month, as long as you wish. We'll share Liselotte.'

The car stopped. We were at the cemetery – the Nobles' Entrance, as I'd told the shuvver.

He came round and opened the door for me. I stepped into the pool of light from the lantern hanging outside the night porter's lodge. From the city below came the slap of small-arms fire.

To speak to me Boltikov had to lean right over Liselotte. He sprawled on her, like a bear – I saw her wince. He called out of the door, 'You mean, you're getting out and leaving, just like that? Well, I'll tell you what you are – a simpleton. One way or another they'll get you. I've owned factories, I know how the Bolsheviks work. Your height, even the words you use – yes, a decent vocabulary will be an automatic sentence of death. Doig, you're a *sitting duck* – see, I know a little English, I can look after myself without you. What do you say to that? Eh, Charlie? What do you say to me not wanting you any more? What's your next move?'

He was determined to see the effect on me and getting hold of the passenger strap began to haul himself over Liselotte. 'Look out, woman,' he said. She tucked in her chin and flattened herself against the back of the seat. He got to the point where he was sitting sideways, feet out of the door.

'That's me, Alexander Alexandrovich Boltikov. If I want to do something, I do it the shortest possible way. I'm not one for preening and prancing and saying one thing and doing another. You all right, *liebchen*?'

He took a cigar from his case. Red spores grew beneath his lighter and burst briefly into flame. He puffed from the corner of his mouth and spat. 'Don't be obstinate, Charlie. Make a journey, come with the boy Boltikov. He knows his way around. Permits, passports, train tickets, he can get them – snap, just like that. Light espionage? Name your need.'

He beamed on me, this short fat fellow. The yellow lantern light was on his face at an angle. 'There must be something you want.'

I said, 'Yes. I want to know what job Lenin gives Glebov.'

'Why?'

'So I can find him and kill him.'

He sighed. 'You're a brave man. All right, I'll do it. For you. Because I like you . . .' He drew on his cigar and fixed me with a puffy blue optic. 'Tomorrow I want to get all of Russia with me in this car – the air, the soil, even the stinking breath of our people. Their oaths, their bedtime prayers, the flowers in their little gardens – God, how I love this horrible country of ours.'

I knew the score from my efforts to get Elizaveta to leave. Boltikov would be the same. There'd be tears as big as summer raindrops, howling, tantrums and such emotional self-mutilation that the situation could be rectified only by the 1825 cognac and the slippery lips of *liebchen*.

'You'll never leave,' I said.

He took out a huge English handkerchief and dabbed at his eyes.

I could see Liselotte watching us suspiciously, afraid that her employer was getting into some typically Russian entanglement that would prevent their departure.

He and I embraced. She made room for him and he climbed back in. The shuvver closed the door on him. The car rolled away on its fat tyres. After twenty yards it halted. The back door flew open. Hanging on to the strap with one hand, he called out, 'I'll get what you want and cable you. At the Rykov Palace? Think it'll get through?'

I waved him my thanks. The huge car vanished, exhaust pipe fluttering.

Turning, I found the entire episode had been witnessed by the night porter standing in the shadow of his own door. It shocked me that he should have remained silent throughout. He said, No, he wasn't a Bolshevik spy: he was more interested in the dead than the living.

Twelve

I FOLLOWED him into his lodge to sign the register.

'Pychkin – Razumsky – Rykov – here we are, *barin.*' He inked the pen and passed it to me. But the nib being new and still in its anti-rust dressing would leave only a watery trail. He handed me a newspaper on which I scribbled until the nib worked. It was farewell: it was important that everything was right.

All our family visits were recorded, nearly a century of them. From December 1821, a month after the Founder's death, to last December when my cousin Nicholas had signed in with his two spoilt brats.

I filled in the columns: 3.45 a.m., Friday October 26th, 1917. Number in party – 'one'. In the section for Comments, I wrote: 'The night of the Bolshevik uprising (Lenin). The evening started damp and foggy. Shortly after midnight the sky cleared. A bad sign.'

On reading this over my shoulder, the porter said, 'Our soldiers'll soon chase him out. I'd be joining them if it wasn't for my leg.' He took the key to the Rykov mausoleum off the hook and dusted it in a pannikin of graphite; clipped on a long metal tag so that I wouldn't forget to bring it back.

'It's something having your own burial chamber,' he said, leaning comfortably against the counter. 'The upstarts come and say, This is a fine outlook over the city for when I'm gone, how do I buy a plot? I say, The last one we sold was in 1881, so you don't. They don't like that. Upstarts don't like being buried in the suburbs.'

He remembered Uncle Igor's visits well. I said that I myself had been in charge of sending up what remained of him after the bomb blast.

'Many more Rykovs to come, are there, sir? Is yours a fecund family, if I may enter the enquiry? You see, sir, I like to keep track of our noble families. In fact, I'm thinking of writing a little book about my years here.'

I told him of Nicholas's death at the Pink House. The last I'd heard of his sons they'd gone to Paris with their mother. 'That's it,' I concluded.

'You're the end of them in Russia, sir?'

'The very end. Full stop.'

'No children anywhere, sir?'

'No. My son Daniel is also dead.'

'What date was—'

I turned on him. His sallow quizzy face swam up to me out of a mist. I grabbed at his coat and pulled him close.

'He was never born. He never got that far, the poor little bugger, on account of the teachings of Mr Lenin, who has just taken control of your life and the lives of millions like you.'

My strength was mighty. He hung from my hands like a strip of damp cloth. '"Dan Doig, dead in the womb of his mother, who was born Elizaveta Rykov and is also now dead." Write that in your book of toadying. You and your sort . . . I hold you in absolute contempt.'

His cheeks were bulging out, red and shining from the pressure of my grip. 'So now you know not to ask about the Rykovs. When I die we are extinct. Extinct – is that plain enough? Done for. Shit in the pit.' So saying, I dropped him.

He began to whimper about who'd pay for the tomb's upkeep and so on. I said he could grind up our bones for fertiliser. Then I grabbed the oil lamp, made as if to cuff him when he tried to speak and went out into the night.

Extinct! Not obsolete or out of fashion or temporarily extinguished like a candle but gone for eternity. The thick salty spunk that produces men of legend had got thinned out. It had been used too frivolously. The Rykovs were to blame, with their passion to be modern and European – lawn tennis, gardeners, all that consumed money. 'A little fun' – that had been the cry among my uncles and aunts when I was growing up. They'd forgotten that sperm and character deteriorate together. You had only to look at my cousin Nicholas: a noble death but a disaster in all other respects. If you want to have successful children, you must get it right at the beginning. What comes out depends on what goes in. Humans forget that when it comes to insemination; they think that the rules apply only to farm animals.

Or was it the fault of the Rykov ovaries? Too encrusted with the fatty consequences of the good life to get the full whack?

However, had Elizaveta lived and carried Daniel to the full term, to the standard length of twenty inches, which could have been a trial for her narrow hips –

I slipped the key into the great iron padlock of the mausoleum. The door grated on its hinges as I pushed it open.

The smell of my family: cold, musty, like a larder that's been empty for a long time. These people were dead in every conceivable sense. For there to be an afterlife, there had to be a God. And had God existed, there would have been some emanation of His presence: a blue pilot light burning above the door, for example. The odour would have been different. There would have been uplift of some nature.

The coffins were neatly racked according to the various branches of the family. Uncle Igor had an ivory label that said simply: '*Count Igor Rykov, born 18 May 1842 and died 6 March 1917.*' He'd lived for seventy-five years. It was long enough.

'Cheerio,' I said. 'Cheerio, all of you. Thank you for your gifts. Especially thank you, Papa. None of you thought such a day as this would arrive. You believed in monarchs, the Church and the values of a civilised world. Well, they're all gone. Cheerio again.'

I left the key at the foot of the door and scaled the palisade into the general cemetery. I found a piece of wasteland not yet cleared for graves. In the centre was a patch of wild lilac scrub. It was dry beneath them. I took out my pistol, wrapped my coat snugly round myself and lay down. It was good.

It's only Russians, with our melancholia, who actually gaze at the stars. Some nationalities are happy with a quick glance, others want nothing more than to classify them by size, brightness or their distance from the Earth. No one spends as much time in conversation with them as we do. This is because our stars are more brilliant than anyone else's. In consequence, a feeling of intimacy can be acquired. They become our friends. As a matter of fact the stars are a vital part of the Orthodox religion and even the clergy acknowledge this.

All our great novelists have found the night skies an irresistible subject. They call on their services whenever the hero is searching for inspiration or forgiveness. They rarely demand that anyone is slain by starlight or, come to that, by the light of the new moon – though both are possible and happen frequently in real life.

Hands behind my head, I looked into their eyes. I said to them, Is it possible for me to sink any lower without being dead? It's not my fault I was born into this dire epoch. I know that tonight history has been smashed. I know that nothing can ever be the same again. Tomorrow will dawn upon a way of doing things of which not one person in mankind has any experience. The question is, will the old behaviour be of any use to me at all? One must suppose not. However, very few people know anything about revolutions. Only very rarely does a man have a chance to practise. I shall try to act honourably, as my father would have. But there is also this: I wish to survive. Maybe only one of these is possible. Do you know which it is?

I picked up my pistol and aimed it at the Great Bear.

No, don't say, I expect I'll find out for myself. Just help me get to the shore. Don't be ungracious. You've favoured many more unpleasant men than myself. Real vipers. That tick Napoleon, for instance . . .

The stars eyed me comfortingly, bright with their wry humour, not a bit upset about my pistol being pointed at them. As one, they nodded to me, Get Glebov, then you'll find a real difference in your situation.

It was what I wanted to hear. I turned onto my side and worked a hollow for myself in the dead leaves – pulled my hat down over my ears.

Sleep should have come instantly. But it didn't, and the reason was this: had Glebov seen me at Smolny or had he not? That was the point at which we stuck, those stars and I.

Thirteen

THE NEXT event in the Bolshevik Revolution: the arrest of
Alexander Alexandrovich Boltikov. He failed even to get
to the border with Finland.

On entering Viborg on the Katarinegata – the cobbles slippery beneath a dusting of snow, the red flag hanging limply
from the neck of Torkel Knutson, heroic on his plinth, and the
town-hall clock on the dot of ten, exactly on schedule for a tip-
top lunch at Helsinki's Hotel Societetshus – he'd noticed the
unusual number of soldiers lounging around.

Liselotte was on one side of him. His secretary was in front,
with the English shuvver. Liselotte had been uncomfortable in
Russia. The Revolution had been the last straw. She couldn't
get out fast enough. The nearer they got to Finland, the more
she quivered. She'd brought some knitting but had several times
missed the pickup stitch her hand was so unsteady. A little before
Viborg she put her gloves on so that he shouldn't see the whiteness of her knuckles.

It was she who'd understood immediately why a van was
waiting up one side street and a cavalry patrol up another.
(Boltikov admitted that he'd been thinking about a plate of
oysters.)

'Get us out of here,' she screamed at the shuvver, opening
the window in the division and stabbing him in the back with
her finger.

But it was the secretary who answered. He smiled as he'd
never done before. His face lit up like the morning sun and his
eyes, previously so dead, danced like gnats on a warm spring
day. He'd shopped them.

The leaders of the Viborg Soviet approached wearing suits and overcoats. Behind marched a company of Bolshevik soldiers. The snow started to fall again, making everything quite silent, even the steps of the marching soldiers.

'Oh my Gawd,' said the shuvver, tipping his plastic-visored cap onto the back of his head.

The secretary got out, briskly and joyfully. The leader of the Soviet embraced him. They all did. He made an ironic bow to Boltikov and disappeared.

The door was opened on Liselotte's side. She clung on to Boltikov, screaming, her arm clamped round his neck. It made no difference. Two of the soldiers were ordered to drag her out. They climbed into the Rolls, treading mud and snow into the carpet on which she had so often knelt to pleasure him.

Defiantly, he lit a cigar.

With infinite gentleness, making emollient clucking noises, as if dealing with a recalcitrant child, they unpeeled Liselotte from him, each clutching finger in turn. No brutality, no ripping. They'd been told to get her out in good condition, and they did.

She was led away. Then he, Boltikov, got out of the car.

Jaw cocked, his eyes unholy in their defiance, Alexander Alexandrovich continued: 'The Soviet boss took the cigar from my mouth, had a puff, and handed it to an underling. I watched it circulate among these ignorant factory workers who'd only ever smoked *papirosi*. My Ortega Grande was too much for some of them at that hour. It got wetter and wetter. It can have given no pleasure to the last couple of men.'

Their luggage was in the rear compartment. They made him unlock it and lay his nice pigskin cases in the snow. They forced him to undo the straps himself. He had to kneel on the cobbles in the smart trousers he'd put on for his family lunch.

When they'd finished – his silk dressing gown, pomade, razor strop, stud hook, medicines, and God knows what frippery from Liselotte's cases spread out on the suitcase lids and loudly haggled over – the head of the Soviet put his hand on Boltikov's shoulder, turned him round to face St Petersburg and said, 'Walk, comrade. When you get to the city say to your friends, "Greetings from the Viborg Soviet! World Friendship to All!" Now go.'

'I'd only gone ten yards when he called me back. "That coat of yours is a good one, comrade. It'll give warmth to a night-worker." When I demurred, he threatened to have me branded on the forehead, M for *millioner*. Think of it, Charlie. Scarred for life, the flesh all livid and puckered. Later it occurred to me that Lenin might have been planning to have all us industrialists branded. If that had happened I'd have gone up to Pabst, whom everyone knows to be the meanest man in Russia, and said, "My dear fellow, you hid it from us so well!" But it would have been poor compensation for the pain. A corpse has more sense of humour than Pabst . . . The fizzle and then the smell. Horrible! Horrible!

'I didn't want to be seen any more in my smart clothes. I wandered round the station area and found a man who was as fat as I am. I offered him one hundred roubles for the clothes on his back. We did the swap in the waiting room – the first-class one. He was in such a hurry to get the money that he was stripped before I had my shirt off. He wanted my studs and links too, saying they were part of my clothing. I refused. His clothes smelt. Then I wound his scarf round my face as a disguise and stepped aboard a train back to town.'

There, his first thought had been to establish a new identity. He was on a Bolshevik list, a marked man.

He'd gone to his forger and within a day had become a new man. Then he'd set out to collect his funk money, which he'd sprinkled in small amounts among his business friends.

The idea had been that when he turned up and presented an IOU, they'd pay him. But the reality turned out to be far different. Many of these businessmen had already fled. And the others pretended they didn't recognise him when the only papers he could produce were under a name that was totally unknown to them.

'"My dear sir, it would be quite wrong to give this money to you. In an hour, Mr Boltikov himself may appear and sit in that very same chair. What would I say, that I gave his cash to a stranger, just because there was a similarity in appearance?"'

He'd scraped up a bit of liquidity. There were still some honest men left. But mostly his so-called friends were vermin. What was he to do?

'And the answer came to me in a flash: "Doig will think of a way forward. Doig's the man for a tricky business." So here I am, Charlie, a beggar at the palace door.'

Inspecting Alexander Alexandrovich Boltikov and noting the worldly tenor of his eyes, and their usedness, and the tightness round his mouth, a man could easily say to himself, even a man who knew nothing about his Rolls-Royce, there goes a capitalist shit if ever I saw one. But I liked what I'd seen of him. As my father once said (I believe attempting a reference to himself), genius only does clever things: it's enthusiasm that makes the world spin.

Helping him out of his Viborg coat, I said, 'OK, so long as you can tell me about Glebov.'

'It wasn't easy. But for Charlie Doig . . . your friend is now People's Commissar for the Political Re-education of Prisoners. He was Lenin's second appointment.'

'Trotsky first?'

'Yes. Glebov has left the city already to work with the army at the front. When the war's over, he's to start work on the Tsar and all those fat children of his. That's what my spies are saying.'

Fourteen

MURAVIEV WOULDN'T employ Kobi in his army because he didn't own a horse. 'Get one and I'll give you a squadron but until you do . . . well, frankly, my dear fellow, you've spent so much of your life on a horse that you scarcely know how to walk. Next!' That's what Joseph, sparkling with glee, told me Muraviev had said to our Mongolian killer.

Kobi prowled round the palace sullen and rebellious, picking quarrels with the SR lodgers and itching to have a fight with somebody. He'd fixed up a system of weights and pulleys to keep his sabre arm in tone. I listened outside the door. The swish of his sabre thrashing the air was like a palm tree in a gale.

From somewhere he'd picked up an old cavalry greatcoat with narrow lapels, shoulders made for a blacksmith and a skirt that brushed the floor. (I may remark that within a week of Lenin's coup every conceivable style of Tsarist costume was for sale on the streets.) Beneath it he had an officer's dark blue dress trousers with a sash of faded scarlet covering the patch where some of the brocade had been ripped off. I caught him parading in front of a mirror.

Intending to humour him, I said, 'You could be the Prince of Siberia.'

He strutted, flaunted, glided his palms down his hard thighs, flashed his oriental eyes at himself in the mirror. He looked at me sideways, which with those eyes he was able to do without moving his head.

'Prince? I believe so too. "Prince, here are your female prisoners." Such words would fill me with pride – my parents also, whoever they were. Every Mongolian envies a ruler who takes female prisoners. The men they don't bother with.'

He saluted himself, standing rigidly. Or maybe he was practising taking the salute from his troops.

'You're too young to lead a revolution,' I said. 'What you need first is a spell shovelling coal.'

He circled me, drawing the sabre a little way out of its scabbard and then thrusting it back in so that it gave off an admonitory hiss.

'You'll blunt it,' I said.

'Keep that coal piddle to yourself,' he growled. 'Me, a Mongolian horseman? What's more . . . I've been thinking . . . who's to say I'm not of noble birth? Those missionaries who brought me up didn't know. You don't either. You're the one who should do the shovelling.'

I waited until he settled, which he did as soon as I mentioned the Trans-Sib railway and his manifest destiny as Prince of Siberia. Then I told him I was going to buy a train – the whole lot: locomotive, tender, carriages. The marshalling yard behind the Nicholas Station was choked with them. A bold man wouldn't even have to take his wallet with him, that's what people were saying. This done, we'd cruise the tracks until we picked up Glebov's trail.

'But General Muraviev—' he began in protest.

'– has now left to gather an army in the Urals. That's where we'll be going, east towards Siberia. We'll armour-plate the train and mount machine guns on the forward platform. We'll have a hell of a time, shoot every Bolshevik we see.'

I painted a picture of our huge grey locomotive shuddering through the snow-storms as he crouched behind a *machinka* and shot to ribbons the hordes of Red cavalry. Of course it appealed to him. Suddenly he saw that as a means of warfare, being on an armoured train was greatly superior to being a horseman with a sabre.

His eyes lit up. 'Every single Bolshevik – dead!' He counted the categories on his fingers. Men, women and children – that went without saying. Then, 'cripples, the insane and the pregnant, even if they come out waving a white flag. Gun them down. Ta-rat-a-tat-tat. Throw the bodies in the river.'

Joseph coming in heard the last few sentences. When Kobi had left, he said, 'In a world of equality such as Vladimir Ilyich talks of, will butlers still be expected to risk their lives on behalf of their masters? In Your Excellency's train, for instance . . .' He'd been ruminating about the dangers he'd faced on the night of Lenin's coup, when we went to Smolny.

'Yes. You stole a bar of my uncle's gold, that's why.'

'Excellency! He presented it to me! It was my reward for having saved him from disgrace.'

'What are you talking about?'

'He made friends with a young man from the racecourse –'

'The usual?' The only fame my uncle achieved was through his assassination – blown up in his coach. Otherwise his life had been spent in seclusion, listening to the murmurs of his chronic hypochondria as he whiled away the hours turning the wondrous folio-sized pages of Redouté's *Roses* and glancing from his library window in the hope that some passing street Adonis would catch his eye and leading him upstairs by the wrist, would teach him everything.

'The boy tried to blackmail him.'

'A jockey?'

'Yes, Excellency. Your uncle fell in love with the colours he rode in. He wanted to make each of his footmen wear silk shirts in those same colours and carry whips jutting out of their boots. I had to deal with the boy. When he cooled down, your uncle saw his error. That was when he gave me the gold.'

I couldn't be angry with Joseph. He hadn't tried to deceive me, had come straight out with the truth.

I said, 'Then you're a rich man, Joseph. Why are you still here?'

'I gave it to my mother. She owed money for my father's burial, despite that he ran away and left her.'

'It must have been a funeral on a royal scale.'

'There were debts also. You know about debts, Doig . . .'

His eyes glinted. He shook his dissolute locks at me challengingly. Everyone knew about my father's borrowings. Kobi had probably told him I was soft. Joseph wanted to see if I'd compel him to pay it back somehow. It was what a proper Russian *boyar* would do.

I let it pass – smiled instead, for I wanted something tricky of him.

Fifteen

C ONTRARY TO popular opinion, it wasn't a buyer's market at all in the marshalling yard. In fact, it was hard to find a rig in any sort of condition. The best price Joseph could obtain was two thousand Tsarist roubles for a modest locomotive, its coal and its driver, an enthusiastic young Tsarist called Valenty.

A good riding horse was priced at around six thousand – or three locomotives. You'd have thought the economics were out of kilter until you considered the expense of coal. Whereas a ton of hay would have got a riding horse from Moscow to Warsaw and halfway back, a ton of coal only took you sixty miles.

Later that afternoon I added the Pullman carriages that had carried the Grand Duke Dmitry into exile and a tender with a connecting passage beneath the coal between the driver's cab and the front coach. When men get killed in the cab you don't want to have to halt to replace them.

Those Pullmans were quality. It was a truly dismal St Petersburg day – fog, a light drizzle, the acridity of coal smoke, apathy as heavy as lead. But the carriages were gorgeous in their yellow-and-chocolate livery and equally splendid inside, with the Romanov coat of arms everywhere and photographs of their palaces in the sunny Crimea screwed to the walls – in a charming family sequence there was one of the Tsar on a yacht that showed clearly the tattoos on his upper arms.

The business completed, I told Joseph we were quits over the gold bar he'd stolen and sent him home. I had a useful conversation with Valenty, then left the yard by the main signalling box and walked along the rails into the cavern of the Nicholas Station. The public having given up on the possibility of using the railways, it was quite empty – no passengers, no officials, no porters, no pigeons.

A deserted railway station can eat into a man's soul more deeply than rust. But the idea of travel – of movement, of the unknown – was good after the months of hanging around in St Petersburg. I was like any Russian. While earthing up our potatoes, we may suddenly be struck by the notion of going five hundred miles to call on an aunt or a childhood friend. We down tools and surrender instantly, walking however far it is to the station with a smile in our eyes and an absolutely clear picture of the engine, scarved in smoke, that's going to carry us there.

Light-headed, idly debating how I'd find Glebov and kill him, I walked through the echoing iron-spanned hall and out into Znamenskaya to catch the no. 5 tram.

'Every end doth not appear in the hour of its beginning.' My godfather Misha Baklushin – who, let me remind you, was himself murdered by Glebov – latterly read only two authors. After a certain age (which he put at fifty) one comes to realise, he said, that most writers' texts are virtually identical. Read one and you've read twenty. His exceptions were Sir Arthur Conan Doyle and Herodotus, whom I've here quoted in the version that Misha had me read. The words may not be correct but the meaning is.

I'm referring in this context to my tram journey up Nevsky.

Sixteen

THE IDEA of freedom from the system of Tsarist government was infectious. To be living in St Petersburg during those confused weeks after Lenin's coup was like being among children let out of school early.

So when the light fingers first took a pinch of my trousers, the inside leg no less – but let me go back a moment, to the tram stop.

At long last a no. 5 rounded the statue of Alexander III. There was a crowd of us waiting, and more came running out of the shadows as the tram glided to a halt in its creaking galleon style. Its rubber jaws peeled back with a yawn and I elbowed my way inside with all the others. There was no reason why I should have paid attention to any of them.

The cigarette smoke, the gabble, the steam rising from the unwashed bodies and the liveliness written across those faces were glorious. It was the Russia I loved. I surveyed it happily from my six foot two as we all swayed, lurched and jolted to the same tempo. Like a firework party, screeching and throwing off squibby blue sparks, the tram bore us north-west up Nevsky.

But not for long. As we rattled over the intersection with Liteyni Prospekt, the usual happened and the pole connecting us to the overhead wires flipped out of its socket. People went on with their chatter or mocked the conductor, whose job it was to climb the outside steps onto the roof and fiddle the pole back in with a rubber-handled trident kept up there for the purpose.

He passed the strap of his scarred leather change-pouch over his head and locked it in his cubbyhole – bending awkwardly since its key was on a ring at his waist. He buttoned his jerkin, said something with a laugh to a babushka, and went out.

The roof groaned beneath his footsteps. We all stared upwards, not convinced that we wouldn't suddenly see the studded sole of his boot and perhaps his ankle appear through the metal.

Two sailors wearing *Aurora* bonnets were telling everyone around them, whether they wanted to listen or not, about the shell that the cruiser had fired as the starting signal for the Revolution.

I looked down at the *shapkas* and shawled heads, at the flat naval bonnets, at the beards and the sunken eyes and the blanched northern faces. I smelt the odours lifting off them – onions, tobacco, horses, oil, humanity. So where was a woman's perfume to be found in our new Utopia? Nothing was the same nor ever would be without the possibility that on entering a room one might catch the drift – of which one? Elizaveta had worn Soir de Paris and none other. Had Glebov smelt it on her when he—

Ting-ting! It was the conductor who'd come in from the roof, removed his gloves and thumbed the bell. He opened his locker and slung the change-pouch over his shoulder. He pushed his way through to the woman he'd been called away from, the babushka wearing pink mittens. They resumed their conversation.

A child was squirming his paw through the press of bodies to anchor himself to his mother. I felt it snag my left trouser leg.

The tram stopped: more people piled on. I held my ground. We were squashed up against each other like herrings in a barrel. I was unable to move. I was standing with my arms folded across my chest, like Octavian at the Battle of Actium when he saw Cleopatra's flagship turn tail and bolt.

Extinct! I'd show that gravedigging swot what Rykov spunk could do. When I'd sired a large and boisterous family from the docile Swede who was waiting for me in Chicago, I'd bring them all back and parade them in front of the fellow. I'd ask him how the research for his book was going, play with him for a bit. Then I'd push the children forward and say, 'There, there's extinct for you, Mac.'

It was at this very moment, when the organs of reproduction were on my mind, that those fingers again visited my trousers. The first time the pressure had been so fleeting that it could have been the child. He was right under my nose, a well-dressed lad wearing a little-man soldier's cap, a fancy thing from a nursery. But this, this was lingering and deliberate. No six-year-old was that interested in what my trousers were made of.

It wasn't an itch.

Nor was it an insect, all of which have learned to be delicate walkers.

It was fingers.

Fingers at my trousers: an inch closer to my manhood.

My immediate instinct was to look for Cynthia Zipf. She'd said she desired me. The approach would have been in her style.

I looked carefully down at the people within range. But none bore the remotest resemblance to Cyn. And I'd have heard her voice a mile away: she'd never have been able to hold back on her extraordinary brand of Russian.

It had to be one of four: anyone else would have had to make too long an arm. The candidates were the child and his mother, an elderly man with a rheumy nose, and a woman turned away from me, her expression unascertainable.

I ruled out the old fellow. What could he have hoped for from me?

The tram stopped again, at the Public Library. The boy was dragged out by his mother. The old man was now facing me at close range. His eyes were pouched and cloudy. They touched briefly on mine, acknowledged that we were at closer quarters than either of us would have wished, and passed on.

Which left the remaining woman, who had her back to me.

Can anyone think poorly of me if I say I was flattered?

I could see nothing but thick black tendrils drifting out from beneath a blue woollen headscarf. Her coat was made of a decent material and its colour was in good taste – deeper than tan, the brown of early autumn. Her shoulders were slim. I got the idea that with shoulders like that she'd have a narrow, bony face, cosseted eyebrows and an expression that was supercilious.

I saw her shoulder twitch and the next I knew — but there was a problem: my trousers were made of thick winter wool. However, this only increased the work rate of my imagination. I thought of a pastry cook with fat pink arms caressing the dough. I thought, God, what a woman can do with dallying fingers. I eased my loins forward, invitationly . . .

Then the fingers were gone — not abruptly, but drifting away, sliding down the barrel. She made a slight adjustment to her shoulders — to the outer point of her humerus. She gave a little toss to her blue headscarf and inched backwards. I felt the mound of her right buttock against my leg. Had my arms not been trapped across my chest by the pressure of the other passengers, I could have got a grip on her.

I tried to peer round the blue scarf. I tried to find her reflection in the window, but it was completely fugged up. Was she a whore? Or had she been dispatched by Shansky the jeweller to capture the fortune I was carrying in my boots?

The tram slackened speed. There was a general stirring down the car. It was the stop for Kolomenskaya, the poor area to the west of Nevsky.

She got off without a backward glance. Her shopping bag was in her left hand, which tallied with her movements in the bus. She hefted it into her right hand. It was clearly heavy. So she'd got up early, had been lucky in the shops, had gone to her work and was now returning home. She'd better watch out, especially if it was meat she was carrying. Kolomenskaya was a tough area where everyone was always hungry. I tucked myself in about twenty yards behind her.

She had a quick decisive step. Her plain wide skirt swung with her stride, grazing the top of her black polished ankle boots. Her feet turned slightly outwards as she walked. She had a good carriage: I could have balanced a wine glass on top of that blue scarf.

She never looked back. I expect she learned to distinguish my footsteps. After a while the two of us were the only people on that street.

Then it struck me. These were hard times. So she was the family's breadwinner, it made absolute sense. I was going to take my pleasure and then be obliged to deal with the husband

70

or her brothers. Maybe she'd cry out in such a way that the listener behind the screen could accurately gauge the tariff of ecstasy. Maybe it was her mother who did the bargaining. Maybe it was yet more sinister – a roomful of cripples or sufferers from some ghastly disease of the poor who'd strip me of every single possession and turf me out naked, perhaps dead and naked.

My next thought: bet she's as plain as a drainpipe living out here. So far I'd seen only her nose, from both sides, as she turned the corners. She was wearing glasses.

Again I watched the go of her. Sensible and balanced, as any decent woman should be . . . hang on, Charlie! She was no slut. A librarian, that's what she was with those glasses. There were plenty of possible reasons why she'd got on at the Nicholas Station and not at the Public Library, where presumably she worked. She'd had enough of books for the day. She wanted some fun. A woman was entitled to think like that.

At no. 12 she stopped. She put the bag between her ankles, took a key from her coat pocket and inserted it into the lock. Her fingers still on the key, she turned and looked straight at me.

The street light was directly above her head. Everything about her was clear.

A little over thirty. A triangular, small-featured face. Clean complexion, in the sense of sleeping well and being free of doubt. General skin colour: milk and vanilla. There was nothing buxom about her, nothing remotely whorish that I could discern. No jewellery, no make-up, no pretensions towards elegance.

Her spectacles had wire frames. She regarded me over the top of them – they'd slipped a little down her nose. For the first time I saw her eyes. They were lovely and large, atropine green, not deadly at all.

So this was she, the librarian who rode the trams and took risks with men.

Chance, it has a sweetness and purity all of its own.

Seventeen

Our boots were muffled on the stone stair treads. She led the way, two steps in front. I watched the sway of her skirt. Underneath she was wearing woollen stockings. The seams at the heel of her ankle boots were as polished as the rest of them. A meticulous miss, my librarian.

An argument between two men was taking place in the rooms on our left. Above and on the right someone was practising a violin to a woman's piano accompaniment. 'Cock your wrist more, *malenkiy*. Remember what your teacher said.'

Upwards we went, to the fourth floor. Neither of us spoke.

She had two rooms: a bedroom and a tiny scullery. The latter was painted light green. The bedroom, however, had a warm, good-quality wallpaper – pink bushy objects like huge roses on a cream background. The bed was a small double with a clean white counterpane. Along one wall was a curtain of a floral pattern similar to the wallpaper. Behind it were a squat and a water tap, also her toiletries on a scrubbed wooden shelf under a mirror. In a recess beside the door was a rail for her clothes. At the foot of her bed stood a chest of drawers. On it was a framed photograph of a girl aged about six. Huge eyes, like moons.

She went into the scullery and set her bag down.

'A good cabbage. A turnip – they're much tastier now that the frosts have started. Bread.' She aligned them on a narrow fold-down table. 'Lastly,' – the blood on the brown-paper wrapping was still damp. She slapped the parcel down beside the turnip – 'horse. My ration card for a fortnight.'

'You were lucky.'

'I know the man.'

'Even so . . .'

'Do you want to share it with me?'

'Of course.'

'It was killed four days ago. The man told me before I bought it.'

'Four days is fresh in these times.'

Without spectacles, her face was elfin, small-boned and even fragile. But it was shrewd. When people took books from her section she'd make sure they registered them with her, and when they returned them, she'd check that the maps hadn't been cut out. She'd be diligent, I knew it. Russians are always ripping maps out of books. They manufacture travelogue dreams from them.

She said, 'I'm famished. Let's eat first. We both know how things stand between us. You wouldn't have followed me otherwise.'

There was nothing coquettish about the way she said this, nor in the way she unwrapped the meat and began to trim it.

I said, 'How do I help?'

She went into the bedroom and took a metal token from a painted wooden box on the chest of drawers. 'Hand this to the porter and he'll give you a bucket of coals. It has to last me a week. We have to be careful about when we light the fire, when we eat and when we get into bed. I've learned how to do all three things in comfort. If I use more than eight coals a night, there's one night I have to do without. Make sure he doesn't put too much slack in the bucket.'

We ate on upright wooden chairs on either side of the fire. Hanging over the fireguard was her nightdress – pink with blue piping.

She said, 'I'm no beauty, you can see that for yourself.'

'Some women don't need to be.'

'I was sixteen before I discovered that.'

'How?'

'For exactly one year I'd been working in a corset shop. It was my first job – in fact I'm still there. When Madame Zilberstein's out, I run it.

'This day Madame was behind the counter. A man came in

with his wife. The woman began to discuss her needs with Madame – maybe it was a special corset for an important dinner, something like that. I was in a corner, checking a new delivery of stock against the order ledger. The man waited for a good moment. Then suddenly there he was in front of my table. He leaned over and pretended to help me count out a package of whalebones. He said nothing but his eyes – I knew what he meant even though I was a virgin. It was an instinct I had, plus the fact that I tingled down there. I wasn't offended. Not maidenly, not at all,' – she flipped her hands sideways, a number of times, rapidly. I steadied her plate for her. 'I realised it was what I'd been waiting for. So I returned that look of his. Then Madame asked me to bring over a particular style of corset, one with a dipped waist. But we both knew, he and I.

'He was waiting for me when I finished work. Down the street a little so that Madame wouldn't notice. He gripped my arm and said, "I have to fuck you." His voice was absolutely urgent. I said nothing, continued walking. But actually I was longing to hold his cock, with both hands, because I knew that's how it'd be with him.'

She broke off: took my plate and put them both on the chest of drawers. The fire was drawing well. Sitting down and crossing her legs, she said, 'What was curious was the strength of that instinct within me. I only ever talk about it with men. They understand. The women I know would think me cheap.

'Walking at my side, the man (who was not unattractive, let me tell you) said, "Your eyes are too soft for disagreement. I know a hotel, five minutes away, that's all." A few yards later, he said, "What'll it cost me – is a good meal enough?"'

'What did you say?'

'None of your business. What's your name?'

'Charlie.'

'Well, Charlie, in fifteen minutes this room'll be as cold as a tomb. Believe me. Come to bed.'

The kettle was mewing on its trivet. She filled a bowl from it and went behind the curtain to undress.

I raised my voice: 'Yes, but the meal – did you take him up on it? Did you demand the best menu or did he just give you money and leave?'

'You're going too fast. What happened was that I loved what he did to me so much that I fainted. My mind just couldn't deal with all that pleasure. Remember, it was my first time. I had absolutely no idea what was possible.'

'You actually fainted?'

'Yes. After only a few strokes.'

'How long were you out for?'

'I don't know. I came round when he bit me in the neck. Of course he was extremely proud of himself. If you really want to know, he gave me dinner and a good present as well. Afterwards he wanted to see if he could make me faint a second time.'

'Did you?'

'No, but he said that he very nearly did. As it happened, though, we never met again. It's the nature of these relationships.'

'Did you think you were in love?'

'Not for a moment. I've never known what it's like to be in love and I expect I never will. I think it's an excuse people make to delude themselves that they're happy . . . Are you getting undressed too? I don't hear anything. If you're one of those men who just want to talk, you can get out.'

I took off my boots and stood them where I could see them from the bed. I checked the door was locked. It was extraordinary, the whole incident, everything being handed to me on a plate like this. I reckoned I could quickly pick up the smell of a dangerous woman. But here there was nothing – except for the sudden aroma of vinegar as she prepared herself.

She said, 'I'm assuming you don't have any contraceptives. Anyway, they're clumsy and expensive . . . How far have you got?' A white arm appeared and threw me a white towel. 'That's for your feet. At a minimum.'

It was warm in the room, warm and cosy among the flickering candles. Even with that small amount of coal, the fire was throwing off good heat. Outside, the street was quiet. Directly above us, someone else was also preparing for bed.

She called out, 'I want you completely naked. Don't think you're just going to undo your buttons and fuck me against the wall as if I were a station whore. I know what I like. I like the weight of a man on top of me. His skin, his hair, his strength – his bruteness. It's the differences I want. That's what gives me pleasure.'

'Any rules?'

'No Frenchmen. Once was enough. A pervert of the worst type.'

'What about doing it alone?'

'I've told you, I'm after the differences. With a man I feel warm and confident for days after. When I look at the Neva I know I could swim it easily. If there was a mountain in the city I'd be able to run up it like a fly going up a window. With a man I feel good. Alone – nothing.'

Her fingertips appeared in the gap above the curtain rail. What was she up to now?

'Are you sure you're not just a talker? I didn't think so when you came out of the station. Virile, that's how you looked, a proper man. If I was wrong, you should have said so before I gave you that bit of meat. I can't afford to waste anything.'

A stopper came out of a bottle and again the tang of vinegar flooded the room. Was she trying to pickle it?

Suddenly it infuriated me that this horny little thing should be calling all the shots, hectoring and lecturing me. I peeled off my coat in a rush and ripped that footling curtain aside – sent it zinging down the rail.

'At last! Quickly, grab me. I'm getting cold. I don't know how they ever get babies in Siberia.'

Her underarms were black as Tartary and her underbrush – tarantulas could have lived in it and never been glimpsed, or goatherds playing pan pipes as they wandered around. I thought, Christ, what must it be like in spring when everything's warming up and it's growing like fury? As she turned to dive into bed I grabbed her rump. She held still. With my other hand I unbuttoned myself. My cock bounced out – stood up, looked around.

'I know what's going on back there,' she said, and whipping round she led me by my tether to a low footstool which she mounted to make easier between us what nature had made awkward by the difference in our heights. With one arm tight around my neck she slid her neat belly down mine till she had me nudging her groove.

76

Watching her eyes change colour, I prised apart the folding gates and entered my full length. We shuffled around. I kicked away the footstool so that her thick calves were against the side of the bed.

'Shamans,' she said, 'that's how they do it. They hire out for people in Siberia who want to make babies.'

'With mushrooms from the forest, special ones that get a man going in really low temperatures . . . You know, you'll come off worse if we fall like this, with you underneath.'

'It's quickest.'

'Slow is best,' I retorted.

We uncoupled – hurled ourselves into the icy bed where I made love to her thoroughly and she to me, all the while amid the reassuring scent of brown vinegar. When we'd finished we lay back, well pleased with each other. I said, 'But you can't have my heart.'

Eighteen

HER NAME was Xenia. As it got light she lit a tallow candle. It smoked and smelt of mutton fat. She looked lovely lying there, her small pale face sunk deep into the pillow and the light trembling on her cheekbones.

Her first words were, 'What did you mean, about your heart?'

So I told her. Confessions, every man has a store of them.

She heard me out. Occasionally she gasped or cried out in revulsion but generally she kept silent. She had good sense – a shopgirl with a steady eye on the columns that record the debits and credits in a life. That's what a man needs for confession. Someone who wants to set up a debate or a competition soon causes the flow of guilt to dry up. It's a good quiet woman who does the trick.

I spoke of my adventurous father from Scotland, of the impossible wealth of the Rykovs, of my peregrinations as a naturalist, of my discovery of the beetle that carries my name – of how Nicholas and Misha were butchered by Glebov and his rabble.

Abruptly she averted her face. I'd painted the scene too strongly. It was the sheer meaninglessness of the violence that upset her.

And thus we reached Elizaveta.

I went at it slowly and in a roundabout way. I made Lizochka less attractive. I had us only engaged, not married. I smoothed and flattened the story. But try as I might I was unable to avoid the crisis. In fact, my own voice cracked as that whole snow-filled scene came back to me – the stable floor, the frosty sun snooping at the skylight, the woman, my wife, lying naked beneath the horse blanket.

Xenia saw it coming. To begin with she refused to listen. 'It's every woman's nightmare. Why would anyone want to cause pain to a woman when we suffer so much anyway? Only men are capable of cruelty like that.'

I said in a low voice, 'Those eyes of hers – may God have pity on me and never show them to me again.'

Maybe she'd never understood until then how utterly simple men are. She raised herself onto an elbow. Her huge wise eyes gazed upon me. She traced a path down my nose and round the edge of my mouth. 'Go on,' she said.

'Then I committed an abomination, which was perhaps greater than Glebov's. It wasn't a crime or a sin. The God of mercy must surely have looked down at me with approval. But what I did was an abomination. To shoot one's own wife can't be anything else. In fact, you could say that of all the disasters that have hit me in Russia, falling in love was the greatest. But she begged me. Do you hear that? It was her wish. Yes, begged . . . She saw the pistol. Her eyes brightened – the look she gave me was extraordinary. I could never describe it. We said our farewells. She closed her eyes – waiting. I went back a little so as not to powder-mark her skin or cause her fright at the last – in case she suddenly opened her eyes to see how much longer I'd be. She had a mole at the tail of her right eyebrow. I took it as my mark.'

I wasn't after Xenia's approval: I might never see her again. Nevertheless I was like any other man, wishing to be thought of favourably by the woman he's in bed with. I glanced sideways at her. Her expression told me nothing. She just stared at the ceiling.

At length she turned her head towards me and said angrily, 'That was in March? How could you even think of another woman so soon?'

'Soon? Is ten months soon?'

'Yes. It's not decent. The love you speak of must have been a sham.'

'You're the first woman I've lain with since her death.'

It wasn't good enough for her. 'What do you give your women in return?'

'At my best I'm capable of any sacrifice.'

79

'Give me an instance.'

'I shot Elizaveta.'

'Is that a sacrifice?'

'I took the life from the only woman in the world I shall ever love. What else could you call that?'

Her green eyes interrogated me, just staring into mine in an unnerving way. I said, 'Ask me again how I feel about women once Glebov is dead.'

'That's me, in case you're wondering,' she said abruptly, pointing to the photograph.

I wasn't. But I was relieved to change the subject. I said, 'Do you ever wear jewellery?'

'No. It doesn't suit my personality.'

'Which is? Give me some adjectives to think about during the day.'

'Number one – tired. It's a long day for someone on her own. Queuing for food, then work from eight until six with no real break. Then finding—'

'A man?'

'And have him eat most of the food? That won't happen again, Charlie! What comes after Charlie . . . ? Oh, I see, that accounts for the foreign accent . . . After tired – I don't know. I've never given myself much thought.'

'I want to pay for the meat. Stay in bed a bit longer. You've got plenty of time. I'll come with you and get you out of any trouble with Zilberstein.'

'I don't want to be late. I learn from her. One day I'll set up my own shop.'

'So who's it going to be, me or Zilberstein?'

'Zilberstein.'

Then she said, 'But you could have taken her to Smolensk, to hospital. The night was fine and the ice hard. You said so. You could have gone like the wind.'

'The horses were knackered. We'd ridden them into the ground.'

'Yet you found fresh ones when you wanted to.'

'I've admitted it was a dilemma.'

'I'd choose a stronger word, whether or not to shoot my wife.'

'She begged me to do it. The rape – all of them, mind you;

the strips of skin razored off her legs. She was at the stage beyond agony. No hospital could have saved her. They had no drugs left, nothing. Do you think I haven't gone over the scene a hundred times a day?'

'Are you sure? Charlie Doig, are you absolutely sure? Would you make that declaration on oath to your Maker?'

'What would He know?' I said sarcastically.

'God knows everything. It's His forgiveness that sustains us.'

I couldn't tell how sincere she was being. She might have been just mouthing the stuff she learned from her parents. On the other hand it was possible she went to church, knelt, prayed, had visions, believed in everything that was going. I decided this wasn't the moment to start finding out. Those green eyes – I'd never met them like that before. Cross her and they'd grip you while she was twisting your balls off.

I said impulsively, 'Come on my train. We'll need a mascot.'

But she was clinging to the death of Elizaveta, which clearly fascinated her.

'What did you do with her?'

'Misha, Nicholas, Louis and Elizaveta, we buried them side by side in the stable dungheap. It was the only place soft enough to get a spade in. We were working by candlelight. Steam was rising from the pit. It was their souls leaving. It broke me utterly. It was there that I settled up with her.'

'Then you shot those men . . .'

'Yes. It was good. Shooting Glebov'll be better.' I gripped her to me. 'Live your life properly. Have an effect on something. Come on the train with me. You were meant for better than corsets.'

'You've got the wrong woman for a mascot, Charlie.'

The clock on the chest of drawers chimed seven. She jumped briskly out of bed and disappeared behind the curtain. 'Brrr! What would I give for a heater, like you see in magazines!'

'You'll never get Lenin to give you one. Equality is all that interests him. Every man as happy as his neighbour, that's his motto. So where's he going to get 155 million heaters?'

She was washing low down, in the warm places, I could tell by the gasps. I said, 'My train'll have hot water throughout the day.'

The wet sounds ceased. 'What?'

'With me you'll have hot water all the time. Here's my plan—'

'Oh, that again. Listen, the shop opens at eight. The first hour of the day is the most important, when last night's broken corsets are brought in. Often they have to be repaired by lunch. I don't have time for your plan.'

'I'll pay for everything. You don't need to even think about money.'

'If you get killed, what then? I'll have given up my job. I'll be stranded in some provincial town, all mud and duckboards. I'm not interested. Kiss your elbow to the idea.'

She came out glowing, the springy black bush doing handstands. She stepped into her woollen knickers and pulled on a woollen vest. She was speaking before her head came out. 'As for finding this man Glebov, it's not possible. How many people did you say there were in Russia – 155 million? That's one five five zero zero zero zero zero zero – six zeros of humans and you're going to stumble across him? The death of your woman has fevered your brain.' She was bent at the mirror, teasing out her hair. 'Mascot! Only a prick'd say a thing like that.'

She was going to wear a little dark felt hat today. She settled it carefully – in an instant was the shopgirl on the tram.

'Lenin'll always need corset shops. Think of that Krupskaya woman of his, what's going to hold her in place? Anyway, that's all I know about.'

She picked up a tin off the chest of drawers and rattled it at me. 'Here we have whalebones from one-sixteenth of an inch to three inches wide. Krupskaya will take the largest, we can be sure. In the next compartment, binding tape. Twenty-four yards a piece, six pieces to the gross. Some manufacturers give you short yardage. You have to watch out . . .' (She wagged the cardboard tape holder at me.) 'Here's stay silk for the stitching . . . This is my life, Charlie. Don't get me involved in your adventures . . . If you want to shit, you should do it now. I'm leaving.'

On the street she stood against me and fingered my greatcoat – suddenly looked up. There was great knowledge in those eyes. I couldn't hold it against her if she believed in God. She said, 'A little less of the high and mighty and I might have taken you seriously. Goodbye.'

I watched her go: a small solid woman in a brown coat and a tit of a hat – a corset seller. No one seeing her would have guessed her secret – her vice, her genius.

Nineteen

T HE FRIVOLITY and pranks didn't last long in St Petersburg. Soon from every street vent there rose the hateful stench of Bolshevism. It was the worst sort of craze – a philosophical one, which meant it had to be imposed by force. You couldn't walk anywhere without seeing a gang of ruffians bearing rifles and red cockades. An ordinary educated man could be accosted and ordered to justify the French novel under his arm or his porpoise-leather bootlaces, in fact the tiniest middle-class thing in his appearance. One morning I saw a man in a *polushubok* or winter coat, which had a really ancient fineness to it, forced to his knees and made to kiss the boots of one of these men. That coat of his could have come from the Middle Ages, perhaps from some Mongol khanate. The leather was on the outside, scarred and weathered like an old hunting dog. The stitching was still tight. At the neck, the cuffs and the skirt, where the wool was showing, it wasn't bedraggled as if the man had slept in the coat but was trimmed and combed in the modish way that one sees in portraits of Peter the Great's courtiers. It was a fantastic coat, still supple, and its owner had been wearing it in the manner it had always been worn, with an upright carriage and a swagger.

The friends of the man whose boots he'd had to kiss thought it very funny. He was forced to kiss them all, and to do so in a prescribed way, making obeisance to each man with outstretched palms. After this he was hauled up and had one arm of that stylish coat cut off at the shoulder. Then he was sent, weeping silently, on his way. He'd been humiliated in public and the coat, that *boorjoi* totem, had been ruined. The common man was in the ascendant.

Boltikov, who was now my permanent guest in the palace, saw what was happening and began to calculate how long it would take for all the stolen treasures to navigate the traditional economic processes and be re-offered for sale – in a different place, with a different owner, maybe in a different shape.

'We should be there, Charlie,' he said, waving a cigarette around as he reclined in the chrome chair with his feet up and an atlas spread across his thighs. 'Constantinople, that's where the stuff'll pop up. Europe's blocked by the war so Berlin and Paris are out. Leipzig doesn't have the money it used to. Where else is there? No one'll want to send valuable goods across the Atlantic with German submarines waiting for them. They'll find their way south. Moscow – Kiev – Odessa, and across the water to the Turk. Whatever the common man can't eat, drink or fuck he'll sell. Just think of all those furs and pictures and jewels going down to Byzantium.'

He leaned forward – 'Become a trader with me, Charlie. It's a chance in a thousand. Think of your Scottish father. Think of your mercantile inheritance. Forget revenge.'

'How'll the effendis take to you being among them? They'll want the business to themselves.'

'Not with you beside me. They'd soon see things our way if they had to deal with you. Imagine it: the docks at Galatea – a foggy dawn – a fast sloop from Odessa about to berth – the effendis won't argue if it's a man like you striding down the gangplank. They respect character.'

I supposed that Boltikov was missing his wife and boy: it'd be inhuman to believe otherwise. With them were all his most valuable possessions. His factories – gone. Liselotte, servants, the Ortega cigars – gone. Even as we spoke, the common man was trying out his bath, his cellar, his wardrobe, his capitalist shoes and Madame's jewelled garters, sniffing his pomade, testing his gold cufflinks between his teeth – wallowing in luxury. Boltikov had been reduced to a shred, to a few rouleaux of ten-rouble gold coins that he'd kept buried in his garden. Yet here he was, in all his fat cheerfulness, already up to his ears in schemes.

I didn't know whether I liked him 100 per cent. But it was impossible not to feel something positive.

'Glebov first,' I said, smiling because he'd suddenly reminded me of my boisterous father.

He crinkled his big face and clapped his hands. 'So be it. A tour of Russia! Put an extra wagon on the train. I'll fill it somehow, and once you've dealt with Glebov . . . you know, Charlie, if we managed to collar the Tsar's gold reserves, even you'd go cool on Glebov. Terrific purity, my friends tell me, and a wonderful red colour from the copper in it. Picture it, gold flaming like a girl's hair . . . and, Charlie, just consider for a moment all that purity. If you got a hundred women in the same room, you'd never—'

'Glebov first,' I said again, laughing.

'Very well. The show's yours. But afterwards . . .' He opened his eyes wide and raised his eyebrows as far as they'd go. 'There's good money to be made somewhere.'

Then he waddled off to see if his father's jeweller was still in the city. Something valuable had once been left in his safe . . . His homely thighs brushed against each other as he walked. He had leather facings on the inside of his trousers as if he were a cavalryman. His head moved incessantly to alert him to the dangers from which he could never hope to escape by running.

In the corridor he halted. His footsteps came padding back. He stuck his head inside the door. 'First proposition: there is only one God. Right? Second proposition: there is only one big chance in life. Right? Which do you believe in more, Charlie?'

Thinking of Xenia, I told him that some people would believe that his two propositions were in fact one, that God was the only big chance.

He wasn't prepared to debate that, saying he preferred to think about the Tsar's reddish gold. I said we'd be moving out in thirty-six hours – at dusk the following day. If he wasn't at the palace then, we'd go without him.

Twenty

GOING BACK to the question of extinction, there were Rykov relics that I very much wanted to take on my train. One day the tide would turn for me and I wished to have mementos of these good-bad times for my children.

For instance: silver banqueting sconces, a stuffed bear with eyes of red glass, two French kettledrums from Napoleon's war, banners captured during the Caucasian campaign against Shamil, Uncle Igor's chrome chair and a life-size wooden jockey in the Rykov racing colours (black with pink sleeves) holding out a tray in which visitors to the palace could leave their cards. They weren't valuable, but to each a story was attached.

However, the SR lodgers, whose revolutionary bile was increasing daily, were incensed by the sight of Joseph trundling the jockey out of the palace. It was demeaning to the nobility of man, averred the twats. Having confiscated the figure, they posted an armed guard outside the storeroom, which they also sealed.

I was not to be defeated. Did they expect me to slice myself down the middle and throw away the Rykov half, to abandon my Russianness?

My last afternoon in St Petersburg arrived. It was getting dark. Boltikov – God knows where he'd got to. Joseph, Valenty and I were loading the cart to take to the station. I'd put Kobi on guard duty. He'd taken up position behind the plinth holding up the bust of the Emperor Tiberius. From it he could cover the whole of the front of the palace.

'Take care of the old Roman. I'll be back one day. Me or my kids.' The SR leader to whom I'd spoken looked down from the palace steps, at the three of us beside the cart.

I went on, 'Bet you never thought you'd be standing where you are.'

He had a famished, black-stubbled face – said: 'All layers of society should be shaken up once every century. In that way no one bears a grudge for too long. None of this would have happened if more aristocrats had been killed.'

'Thanks, pal,' I said, thinking of Elizaveta.

Relenting, he said, 'Take the Emperor with you. It's nice work. It'll only get smashed if it stays here.'

Extraordinarily, he then helped Kobi carry the bust of Tiberius down to the cart. The only suitable place for it was behind and above the driver's bench, so that he became our figurehead, gleaming palely in the dusk.

Kobi climbed aboard. Valenty took up the reins. Joseph, who'd gone to the gates, lifted the centre pin and glanced out, up and down Nevsky. He raised his hand. All clear – then he darted over to the flagpole.

I stood and faced the palace. I saluted it. In the corner of my eye I saw the Rykov flag set out up the pole. In a second – yes, there it was, the searchlight we'd rigged up with a stolen battery. Joseph trained it upon the slinking wolf of the Rykovs. The animal writhed and snapped in the breeze – bared its fangs at the common man. Having saluted the palace again, I saluted the wolf.

I looked across at my little Joseph. He too was at the salute, crying unashamedly.

It was far too precious to leave behind. 'Take it down,' I said, 'and make sure you keep it somewhere dry.'

'Lupus has had his day,' said the SR man, not having heard what I said.

'Don't you believe it,' I said.

He sighed, the sort of noise one expects from a half-hearted anarchist. 'You and I, for instance, our levels of society could have enjoyed a true meeting of minds had circumstances turned out otherwise. It's the Bolsheviks – and Lenin, they're the problem. They're so unbending.'

To hell with Lenin! Maybe we'd go and the palace gates'd close behind us and a new breed of historians would write kaput to all nobles. But they'd be wrong.

I climbed on to the cart. 'Good luck,' I shouted up to the palace, to all the Rykov spirits that still inhabited it. 'You'll need it with these bastards on the throne. Let's go.'

The horses took the strain, leaning into their collars. The big wooden wheels rumbled over the cobbles. A kettle fell off. 'Kobi,' I said, 'nip down and—'

With a howl of its klaxon the armoured car bowled in from Nevsky and made Joseph jump for his life. It rounded my uncle's collection of marble catamites – boyfriends of Tiberius – and halted face to face with our terrified horses, its single roof head-light shining over us.

I said to Valenty, 'Lenin's fuckers. Leave them to me.'

Kobi shouted, 'I'll shoot the first head that appears,' which was a waste of words since we couldn't see a thing on account of the blinding roof light.

But it was Boltikov. His muscular voice came booming through the semi-darkness.

'One gold rouble it's cost me, this escort party. They'll see us to the station and then see our train out of the yard and onto the main line. Not bad, eh!'

'Who's they?'

'Bolsheviks, Mensheviks, what do we care? They've got the armour, that's what counts. I said to them, Boys, come to Odessa with us, there'll be rich pickings down there in the sun. They said, Enough excitement here, comrade. Joseph, put a rug over the Emperor. We don't want the wrong sort of excitement going down Nevsky.'

Kobi: 'He's dead. Leave him behind's what I say.'

But I wasn't going to have that. Tiberius was another memento. Joseph agreed with me. Uncle Igor had told him that Tiberius had been a lucky mascot for the Founder and should never be sold or abandoned.

'Every adventure needs an emperor,' he declared loudly.

A hollow voice from inside the armoured car said, 'Shoot them both. Down with all emperor swine.'

Boltikov smiled over to me and rubbed his thumb and fore-finger together like an imitation Jew. 'We needn't listen to him. Money speaks loudest,' he said in thick English. 'It's the sort of thing they're taught to repeat by people like Glebov.'

Then to Joseph, who had opened up an abusive exchange with the voice behind the metal slit that was demanding his death, 'Stop all that. Just cover the statue.'

We rolled out into Nevsky led by Boltikov in the armoured car, its klaxon blasting at the curious group gathered at the palace gates.

Joseph was sitting sideways, his legs dangling over the edge of the cart. I leaned over to him. 'Actually, better a woman as a mascot than a dead emperor. More useful.'

'Best of all would be a live emperor, our little father,' sighed Valenty.

'No chance of that,' I said. 'Lenin's got him and Lenin'll keep him. One day we'll be told he's died of a fever.'

Joseph said, 'Every army should have its woman to act as mascot, cook, whore, sweeper, seamstress and disciplinarian. That's what a man needs to make him fight at his best.'

'See one around?' said Kobi sarcastically.

'You want a woman, Mongolian prick?' Joseph said. He always spoke with his face closed, giving nothing away, perhaps from working with my uncle. Whenever he said something un-expected, it came as a double surprise.

'Don't be stupid,' said Kobi.

'Well, she's here,' said Joseph.

It was Boltikov's headlight that picked her up. She was walking out into Nevsky to intercept us. Quite calmly, a canvas suitcase in each hand. Boltikov shouted to me, 'Something to do with you?'

Her face was as pale as a moth's. She stared up at me, a triangle of white topped by the same dark felt hat she'd been wearing when I left her. It clung to her springy hair by a miracle.

We'd come only a couple of hundred yards from the palace. Had she been waiting for me? How had she known? Was it chance? Was it love? Was it an ambush?

'You got her just like that?' Kobi said suspiciously.

Boltikov was jutting out of his armoured turret like a sub-marine commander. He looked Xenia over. He was like Kobi, rough and disbelieving. 'Did she fall from the sky? Charlie, have nothing to do with her. She's dangerous.'

But she was resolute. She shoved her suitcases aboard – giving them a final push with her shoulder – and clambered up beside Valenty. It was the point at which she should have been refused if that was what I wanted. But I said nothing and Valenty – he neither helped her nor shoved her off. So she got to be there with us, one of the party, which she did neatly, in a quietly determined way, no squawking.

She folded her skirt beneath her and sat down in one continuous movement. She crossed her hands in her lap, tipped her chin and said firmly, 'I have an invitation.'

Boltikov, turning right round in his turret, said, 'What's all this about?'

She said to him, 'I'm no Bolshevik. A week ago this man was in my bed,' – with a glance in my direction. 'That was when he invited me to join his train. But he said as a "mascot", which I didn't like, so I turned him down. Since then, I've changed my mind.'

'Why?' he demanded. 'Why at the precise moment we're leaving?'

She removed her hat and tossed her head.

No man can resist a woman doing that. A bell rings. If not in his heart, then somewhere.

'There's no food here any more. I don't want to leave but I don't want to starve. Which would you choose? If you think the same as I do, you have my full answer to all your questions.'

She was a goer all right was my girl.

Boltikov looked across at me with narrowed eyes. People were beginning to gather.

I waved at him to get on with it. He suddenly grinned. 'Hope she's as obedient as Liselotte.' He shouted down to his driver who noisily engaged gear. The engine coughed and a cloud of choking oily black smoke enveloped us. The horses snorted and blubbered their lips. We were on the move again. We had a mascot.

Twenty-one

WITHOUT ANY warning, not even a preliminary flicker, the electricity was cut off. The night fell over us like a giant tarpaulin. One moment I'd been able to distinguish the clothes and expressions of the passers-by and the next unutterable blackness held sway along the whole length of Nevsky, gripped between the buildings on either side and pressed down on us by the weight of the sky. The stars were black, the moon was black, God and His saints and His angels and all the stuff volleying around in the cosmosphere were black as well, that's what it felt like. I thought, Do Lenin and his people not understand how power stations work or has coal become a rarity? Is the day about to arrive when we give our friends a lump of coal as a birthday present? Then another thought came to me, that deep in some subterranean vault, Lenin had his own private generator humming flat out while he sat at Smolny bathed in light and heat, his huge skull glowing, thinking of a name for his next red setter as he signed death warrants.

That such a man could have stomped down from his attic in cuckoo-clock land to take control! As well to be ruled by a croupier, who never pretends to be anything other than a cheat.

God damn all thinkers.

God damn V. I. Lenin and infect him with a hideous death. V for Vladimir, vile and vermin and VD and for the small red grave-worm and for the greatest of them all – vengeance.

But one had to be alive to enjoy it—

Run, prince!

Run, miller!

Run, every beautiful woman in Russia! Bury your jewels, muzzle your jangling breasts, dirty your milkmaid cheeks, let your buttocks fall and travel only by night. Trust no one. If cornered, trade Jerusalem for protection. Men don't lose their appetites just because times are troublesome.

Run, every man of principle, everyone who likes to wear a clean collar, can count to ten or knows more than five hundred words. Run like blazes, for the frontier, for a train, for a ship. Don't be embarrassed to fire first. Don't look back. Don't bother praying. The gods of the past have had it and the new gods are monsters. Accept this. Continuing to put your faith in the morals that were your grandfather's will bring you nothing except a share in a mass grave.

Run, run, run, children, you above all. Run till your pudgy legs come off.

I rose on the cart and jabbed my fist into the darkness.

Xenia looked up at swaying me and said, 'What are you doing?'

I was crazed. My visit to the Rykov mausoleum – my thoughts upon extinction – and now quitting the palace, which goddammit belonged to me and no Red bastard, had caused my brain to sprout with every sort of resentment. Neither father nor mother was left to me. Brothers and sisters – none. Friends – the tempo of my life had been too rapid.

I said to myself, Doig, this Lenin and his brutish philosophy has not only destroyed your youth: it has made an orphan out of you.

Orphan! What loneliness there was in that word.

My fingers, splayed like a shuttlecock, were on Xenia's head to steady myself. I was squashing her hat, which was damp with the evening mist. I thought, Therefore my vengeance will not only be on Glebov but also on the entire Bolshevik system for having exposed me to this awful state.

'If that is possible,' I said out loud, taking a grip of her hair as we lurched over the Liteyni Prospekt tramway. But was it? One thing at a time. Everyone knew that.

'If what is possible?' she asked.

And suddenly the street lighting returned and I was standing

93

there, all of them looking up at me and my rage already ebbing. Joseph said, 'Lo, the universe again,' and I said to myself, Once I get Glebov I'll go to Chicago and everything will be for me as it is for others.

Twenty-two

INITIALLY WE haunted the metropolitan lines round Moscow and St Petersburg. Valenty had used his connections to frank us into the railway system. The signalmen kept the points open for us to enter the line and the depots let us take on coal and water for free.

We became in effect a ghost train, and in those chaotic conditions were bothered by nobody. We drifted around, listening and waiting. 'Special' trains interested me mightily since they were only put on for the Soviet bosses. Thinking to find Glebov this way, I made a point of shadowing them. Sometimes we got too close. One apple-crisp morning I saw Trotsky, laughing, sweep back his hidalgo's cloak and urinate off the platform of the guard's van of his private train. I could have sworn that his mane of hair had been sprinkled with hoar frost. It seemed white, like a saint's. That can't have been right but what was indubitably the case was that he had a fine arc for a man with so much on his mind. This may be true of all revolutionaries who are physically very active. Ambition, which I know from Mongolian medicine to be a really hot emotion, must burn away the plaque in the body's watercourses and allow the liquids to gush. That urine of Trotsky's, which may have been his first go of the day, soared over the guard rail of the van all yellow and glittering like the sort of champagne one only reads about. What was he chatting about so gaily over his shoulder? A dream he'd had? The day's plans?

'Call out to him, invite him in for a meal,' Boltikov said sourly, grabbing back his binoculars.

Everything was elastic during these months. All information, both the true and the false, was available to everyone. But none of it related to Glebov. He just wasn't where we were.

New Year passed and the worst of the winter. Peace was made with Germany. April arrived and our armies began to come home from the front – by now Bolsheviks to a man, even the officers. More and more troops became available for the struggle against the Whites. Lenin was getting a grip on things: the holiday season was over. That was my judgement, and to support it, our chums up and down the railway started to say that there was no coal to be had, even though I could see mountains of it glistening in the wet sun. Oh, but it wasn't *steam* coal, it'd be terrible in a locomotive like ours. I didn't argue. One day Joseph returned from the railway canteen and reported that he'd been asked to pay a rouble for a posy of six matches tied by a scarlet thread. A month before he'd have got them for nothing, a whole carton. I didn't argue with him either. I could tell the way things were going.

Boltikov, sensing my despair, sidled up and whispered, 'So why don't we forget about Glebov and slip down the line to Odessa? A boat to Constantinople, a spot of the old commerce with the orientals – restore our fortunes?'

My anger returned. Why should I have to fight everyone? Who was paying, who was the piper?

I eyed him. For the first time I noticed the touch of crocodile skin about his face, the twist of his mouth and the way he worked his eyes, which were constantly probing me, as if certain that in some corner of my brain I'd hidden the alchemist's secret.

He said, 'You're obsessed about going east. If you're so keen on it, why not keep going until you get to China? Gather an army of Chinks. Get yourself some Manchu pussy.'

I was poised to go for him. But Xenia saw the heat in my eyes and laid a soothing hand on my sleeve. Then very softly, those green eyes dancing, she produced the clincher: the Americans were landing in Siberia. Someone had received a letter from his brother in New York who was in the habit of drinking with a man who worked for the government . . .

'Americanski!' That one word transformed everything, like a magic potion. If we went east we'd meet up with them, couldn't fail to.

'What?' I shouted.

Very sweetly she said, 'I speak a better Russian than you. I come along after you've been wading around in your lordly manner and smooth things out.' (Saying which she rubbed my arm again.) 'The lives of these men are poor. They can't see how they're going to get better. But they want to believe in fairy tales and they like a woman with a pretty manner. So they tell me what they won't tell you. Anyway, the Americanski are on the way. They'll reach Siberia this summer. What else can I help you with, Charlinka?'

Boltikov had no answer to that. Only a madman would turn his nose up at the Americans. Who had the latest machine guns, the surest ammo, the best tinned food, tents that really were waterproof? Who had the tip-top wireless kits? Who'd invented money? The guys who were up to that would surely know exactly where Glebov was.

Then on Mayday itself my girl heard something else: that the Tsar and his family were being taken to Ekaterinburg, which was about as far east as they could go in Red territory. She withheld the news until night, when we were turning in. I'd knocked two compartments into one and had a carpenter build us a honeymoon bed.

I was kicking off my trousers when she mentioned the word Ekaterinburg.

Combing out the thicket of her hair – tugging at it – peeking at me in the mirror with a fetching smile: 'Of course I'm sure – I wouldn't be telling it you if I wasn't.'

'You know what this means?'

'We follow them?'

'Yes. You know what that means?'

'Bye-bye Moscow, bye-bye St Petersburg, bye-bye civilisation. Hello mud, cold, boredom, Siberia – I need compensation for that, Charlie.'

She turned to me, slid out of her dressing gown, stood akimbo with a different sort of smile – fetching plus. Strong, meaty, white-fleshed body, full breasts growing from a wide base. How could I ever have imagined her checking the maps in library books?

She said, 'I need full compensation. Glasses off or glasses on?'

'Didn't you say you liked to watch?'

'I'm not that blind.'

'Take them off then.'

She bent over me, naked, reached down with her lips. She could do tricks with them, with the muscles round her mouth, like a giraffe plucking leaves from a tree. Having worked her way up me, she said mischievously, 'But what's this written on your chest? I'll certainly need glasses to read it. Stand up, you lazy fellow!'

I did so, with some pride. 'What are you talking about?'

She scrawled a forefinger across me from east to west, nipping at tufts of hair for emphasis. Her belly against mine was like a water skin warmed by the sun. '"The rules of behaviour in Siberia," that's what it says here. "Number one, go a bit more gently or you'll bring the partition down." That happens, we'll end up in the corridor, both of us, Charlie boy.'

'Number two?' Her buttocks were hot and soft and massive, proper Russian buttocks.

'No number two.' Her tongue was like a conger eel in my ear and her legs were quivering. She was ready to topple. One hand had my cock tight against her stomach so that I shouldn't get away. I said, 'OK, then we'll lie the other way round.'

But by then she didn't care, I would say from having considered the details of the compensation in some detail.

I eased her down – she wasn't heavy, about 135 pounds. But it was awkward: I had to go with her on account of her having hold of me.

Pinning her I said, 'One of these days I'll get you to faint. I'm not going to be beaten by some city shyster.'

Her eyes opened wide, green as the sea. 'You've nothing to be jealous of. I faint from the sheer pleasure of having you. Every single time. If you looked into my eyes more often, you'd see. Yes? Hey, Charlie, yes?'

Somewhat later, she said, 'If I go topsides, the partition'll be safe.'

The two of us moving smoothly, I said in her ear, 'It was built in America, for God's sake, a Pullman. It's not going to collapse. Let's not be over-dainty.'

'But to fall into the corridor would not be stylish,' she said.

'I know what would be,' I said, and the next day I stuck Tiberius on the front of the locomotive and thus we quit the home front to head east, in the direction of Ekaterinburg and Siberia. The Emperor shone with divine right and was sniped at by the Reds from every bridge until we cleared the danger zone.

Twenty-three

J OSEPH CAME tripping down the corridor – the town of Tulpan was in sight. I was for running straight through it in order to put more distance between us and the Reds. Joseph said that another train was using our line, that it had halted at the station.

'What of it?' I said irritably. 'Go round. You'll only have to set a few points.'

He slid into the chair beside me. 'Indeed, Doig, but what Valenty says is that the locomotive is armour-plated.'

'Why didn't you say so before?' I was already on my feet.

'Apologies, Excellency.' He pressed his palms together and bowed, his brown eyes glancing humorously up at me.

I said, 'Joseph Culp, you're a dark dog. Go fetch the lady to me.'

My peacheroo sauntered up, arched her back, stuck out her breasts – saluted. She was in good fettle, despite that we'd had our first real argument the night before – God.

A quiet unpretentious God's fine by me. Like Buddha. When I was in Burma, I'd noticed the locals had a good relationship with him, no fawning or unhealthy behaviour. But to go at it blindly as Xenia did and kowtow to Him as if every minute of your life He was standing above you with His hand on the guillotine lever and if you didn't have the right answer Crash! and the 140-pound knife'd slice your head off, well, that was patently nonsense.

(She'd sat quite still, hands folded over her fanny, as I let rip.)

Moreover, if God was capable of making such evil bastards as Glebov, didn't He have to have some evil in Himself? How did He know what to put in him otherwise?

She smiled – I would say pityingly. She mentioned a few things that were central to her beliefs. Hogwash, I said. She smiled again, knelt to say her prayers. Afterwards she asked if I wished to make love to her.

Of course, I said, and we fairly went at it, continuing our argument by other means.

Now she said with a grin, 'You've converted, that's why you've got me here.'

'My spirituality has always been visible to those who know where to look. Listen, Miss X,' (which I said in English, the letter being an aggressive sound in Russian) 'there's an armoured train at the station ahead. I want it. You and I, we're going to discover how mighty it'd be as an enemy. I'll take Valenty and quiz the driver. You see what you can get from the passengers.'

We stopped to plug a bullet hole in the boiler so that we wouldn't arrive looking like a cripple. Valenty brought us up casually behind this train with its nice grey locomotive. No whistling at it or getting furious, all very friendly.

The money was bolting. I knew what was going on as soon as I saw the passengers wandering around. Which they were doing languidly but at the same time looking over their shoulders. Not convinced that the Bolsheviks would actually slit their throats but feeling a good long train journey was a sensible precaution until the storm blew over.

The question was whether they'd got bodyguards in there with them.

Valenty and I strolled down the platform. All these refugee aristocrats studied me in their covert way, checking me off against the Romanovs they knew.

We got to the loco. It was a devil of a thing with a four-wheel bogie and six driving wheels. The armour-plating was backed by two inches of concrete. I wanted it immediately. I lusted after it, yearned to be howling down the open track behind its grey steel baffle plates. No one could put a bullet through the boiler or shoot the driver. In a machine like that we'd pierce the walls of Jericho at the first go.

Valenty walked over to the cab and engaged its driver in trade talk.

I leaned against a post and watched the passengers saunter round smoking their Northern Lights cigarettes.

It wasn't clear to me why they'd halted in Tulpan, which was the sort of plains town that's reproduced a hundred thousand times in Russia. One railway station, two churches, four hundred wooden houses of one storey, twenty of two storeys, and mud streets. The main sounds in these places are the wind in the telegraph lines and lonely men shouting at their wives.

Valenty came over with the driver. He was fat but carried his weight better than Boltikov. One felt that the fat was necessary to him. His name was Yuri Shmuleyvich. 'He believes as we do,' said Valenty. 'He'll do anything to defeat the Bolsheviks.'

We got talking. It turned out that one of the passengers had had a heart attack while dancing and had died, that was why they'd stopped in Tulpan. The undertaker was there. Someone was dealing with the paperwork.

Shmuleyvich said to me, 'If you fart in this country there's a paper to be signed.'

'Dancing?' I said. 'He snuffed it while dancing?'

From the corner of my eye I saw Xenia working her way up the platform. I'd had her prink herself up with some rouge and a little rose water. She hadn't wanted to but I persuaded her by saying she'd meet a better class of traveller if she looked the part. That did it: she was a snob, no point in pretending otherwise.

'Yes, dancing,' Shmuleyvich replied.

'So you're carrying musicians, not soldiers, then?'

'These are the bravest men on the train,' he said humorously, nodding towards the carriage door that was just opening.

A man, black as the back of a fireplace, six foot six in Uncle Sam pants, dithered on the step. His great white eyes appealed to me: 'Mister, can you tell me why I ever agreed to come on this goddam trip?' Behind his shoulder was another much smaller Negro.

Shmuleyvich, winking, said to me, 'Jazz, *barin*, Americanski jazz. You understand now?' He raised his arms and wiggled his backside. 'That's how he died dancing.'

The giant called out, 'Hi, Shmuley,' and in his long glossy black shoes and short white socks came gingerly down the steps, put his arm round Shmuleyvich's shoulder and held him tight. 'Holy shit, what an asshole of a place you've got here. Couldn't we have just pitched that guy over the side, you know, opened the door and said, Out you go, feller?'

Shmuleyvich, laughing, not trying to get out of the black man's grip, said to me, 'You deal with his foreign talk, *barin*.'

Which I did, and it turned out that the man had died doing a jazzed-up polka and that he'd been seventy-six years of age.

But this was not the first thing on the black man's mind. He was so glad to find someone other than his friend who spoke English that he nearly cried. Then, 'Now what's really bugging me is this – man, it's so good not to have these savages babbling at me – here it is, like I read in the papers back home. What's your name? Charlie? OK, Charlie, there's this King of Russia and he's a really bad piece of work, putting people in prison and shooting them and really treading on them, yeah, pounding them into the ground and stopping them from voting. Then this other guy, another Russki, the baldish feller, comes along and says, Fellers, this old King of yours is a piece of shit and no mistake. I'm gonna give you equality, and land, and education, all for free. You don't get to pay one red cent. Yup, free! No more stomping, no more bad times for any of yous.

'I says to myself, Isn't that to be commended? Look at it how you will, those are great ideas. But what happens? My President and your President and lots of other presidents, they get together and say, The bald number's a real bad feller, we'll have to send our armies against him, he's a threat to the entire world . . . I mean, Charlie, can you explain that for me?'

The corpse was lowered from the train. The undertaker appeared holding his hat: the doctor put his on. The first whistle went. The passengers drifted closer to the doors.

The smaller of the jazzmen said, 'Who'd want to have a war over a town like this? I mean, fancy being killed for—'

'You keep out of it, fat face. I got to Charlie first. Didn't I, Shmuley?'

The second whistle went. Shmuleyvich patted the black man on the cheek and walked off to his cab. Xenia glanced at me. She'd trawled through the passengers and was now only a few yards away. A neat white hand was beckoning to her from the train door. She shook her head at him – hatless, oh, that rich swag of hair, worth a fortune at the wig-makers.

The big man said to his pal, 'C'mon, let's hop back on. I don't trust these Ivans. They'd dip us in shit any day.'

The black men waved at me and made a run for the train. The giant scrambled up the steps. White socks, three four inches of bare flesh, bruised to purple by our Russian winds, then the Uncle Sam stripes leading the eye to the long fat crack. The third whistle went and the train began to move as the last of their stripy buttocks, like the flank of a vast tropical fish, toiled through the door.

The giant stuck his head out of the window. 'I mean, Charlie, what does it all add up to? Is the rest of the country as bad as this? Like my friend said, what the hell are they fighting over?'

His smile and his white teeth grew smaller. Black smoke began to billow down the side of the carriage towards him. Ruefully I spread my arms.

Twenty-four

W E SPENT the night at Tulpan getting our hands on a couple of coal tenders. Coal was always a worry. Even a full tender took us only five hundred miles. If I came across a heap of the stuff, I had to have somewhere to put it.

Also Xenia had to be taken into town to post letters. I said to her, 'How perverse, during a revolution.' But the station-master had assured her the posts were still moving and she'd seen for herself a couple of trains heading towards Moscow. So she was determined to do it: farewells to her sister and mother whom she might never see again, that's what she said.

Then we set out in pursuit.

You know how it is with time, its metre varies: now plodding, now squirting out the seconds like it's going to lead you right to the end of the world just as soon as it can. In central Russia it scarcely budges, the country is so featureless.

However, in the middle of the afternoon the brakes came on, quite gently. Thinking the armoured loco was in sight, I pocketed my Luger and went up to the cab.

In front of us, about half a mile away down the dead straight track, was a tiny wayside stop. A length of grassy platform, a small shed for waiting passengers, a loading bank – and one would have said nothing else because emptiness was what the mind expected.

Not so, very much not so.

On the platform stood a gentleman in a long fur-edged coat, even though it was early summer. God had given him a round red face and long blond moustaches. He was leaning on a knotty cane in the manner of Voltaire.

To his left were a couple of peasants. Each had a station flatbed on which were lined up a succession of dark blue and dark red leather suitcases, one colour per barrow. They were ranked by size, the largest being nearest the edge of the plat-form.

Additionally – astonishingly – in the centre of our track, standing four square on a sleeper was a pin of a woman with foxtails round her neck and on her head a swooping green straw hat. She was waving us down with short, hysterical, flapping motions of one hand. At her bosom, in among the furs, was a dog, only its white head visible.

Valenty said, 'Could be an ambush?'

Kobi got ready to shoot.

Valenty: 'Run her down, Excellency? This isn't a refugee train.'

But I'd spotted a mansion house set back among trees and I remembered Uncle Igor saying that he never spent the night at anyone's house unless they had a hundred tons of coal in the backyard. I said to myself, Igor, old duck, come to my aid this day and give these people a hundred tons. No, double it. We'll shift it somehow.

To Valenty I said, 'No, but give her a fright.'

I'd no idea precisely where she was standing since I couldn't see round the front of the engine. We could easily have gone a foot too far with a bad result for the lady. But Valenty had taken his side bearings perfectly and when I climbed down I found her anchored to the sleeper, eyes tight shut, the palm of one outstretched arm warding us off, wraiths of steam rising round her as if she were being burned at the stake.

I lifted the brim of the green hat. She had a pinched, narrow face beneath greying hair. She was murmuring a prayer of some sort. Her lips – I couldn't tell if she had a deformity somewhere round her mouth or not. They made a strange shape as she muttered away.

'You can look now,' I said.

Her eyes opened like a blast of phosphorus – small, greeny-blue chips, nothing soft about them. The dog, a poodle, inspected me.

She said, 'You've got to help us.'

I said, 'Why?'

'We have money.'

'Coal's what I want,' and saying this I took her by the elbow and helped her across the rails to her husband. He bent down and pulled her up by the hand. Russian platforms are low to the ground, but it wasn't dignified.

She straightened, reasserted herself. 'Oskar, it's you who must explain matters to the young man.'

He had medals on his chest – good ones, St Andrew and St Alexander Nevsky. They swung and clanked as he bowed to me. 'Count Oskar Benckendorff at your service, sir, Gustavus Order 1st Class in the Swedish nobility, family resident at this place for two hundred years. My wife – the Countess Delicia, née de Conde. She has always been the braver of us. She was for staying, telling me she'd poke their eyes out. But my instinct for the correct balances in society have prevailed. We are leaving our home. Two hundred years we have worked these lands, two hundred honest years. The present can be so spiteful to older people. But there it is. We must say thank you to the past for what has been good and not become morbid about the bad – not stay growling in our beds. We have decided to travel to Vladivostok. There we shall winter and see how the wind blows. It may be a seven-day wonder, you can never tell in Russia.'

'And I'm to help you?'

'Any assistance, however small . . . I heard what you said to my wife. Please take our coal. Obviously we cannot carry it.'

I felt sorry for the old boy. He'd seen trouble coming three years before, when Russia had marched on Germany and got pasted at Tannenberg. He'd made it his policy never to have less than three hundred tons of best-quality coal on hand. With that he'd thought he could sit out anything in comfort – could die in peace and quiet and warmth. But it had been the wrong danger he'd foreseen.

It took us the remainder of the day to move that coal. By the end we were filthy. The last ton we used to fire up the mansion boiler and wash ourselves.

What on earth had Oskar and Delicia done in that vast elephant-footed cast-iron tub? Did they have swimming contests? We stripped and piled in two at a time; lathering, laughing, singing while waves of black water slopped over the Countess's lemon-and-grey-tiled floor and disappeared via a trap and gulley into a gurgling cavern that was very soon rimmed with a scum of coal dust. We were like boys. Three hundred tons! The glee that Joseph's first fart provoked as it echoed eerily off the iron hull was infectious.

While we were at the coal, the Benckendorffs had supervised the loading of their luggage onto the train, then clambered in and sat down with their books. As I'd shovelled, I'd been able to see them reading. They clearly had no idea about survival. Having ploughed through their Dumas they probably reckoned they'd picked up all the tips that were necessary for handling risk and danger. Russia had lots of educated people in that position.

I watched them in the train as I towelled myself dry, thinking how well the Countess had done to trap Oskar, who was clearly a decent gent. When I said that her lips were deformed, I meant that she had a square mouth. One could see how this had come about when one saw the exceptional length of her incisors, which were like planks. The mouth had to be like that, pushing her lips out in a bunch, or she'd never have got to speak. The first time Oskar kissed her must have been out of curiosity. Of course she'd swallowed him whole thereafter.

Joseph's voice called to me up the staircase (which was a very fine double one, bare wood, the risers being made of a much darker wood than the banisters). He'd set out on a tour of the house to evaluate the status of the Benckendorffs vis-à-vis his old employers, the Rykovs. When I found him he was in the conservatory.

In stoking the boiler for the bath, we'd also put heat into the pipes of this long high room of glass and iron. The dank, decadent aroma of warm air mingled with rotting humus was straight from the tropics. There was a memory in all this for me.

Resting my hand on the back of a warped bamboo chair and having in my ear the plink-plink of the tap that fed a little rill of strange cuspidate rock plants, I murmured to Joseph, 'The whore on the boat, the boat on the lake . . . that night in Burma – all night I was at her, a great backlog of lust to be worked off. You can have no idea of my frenzy . . . That was just before I discovered my beetle and became famous. And now this smell

– the smell of Burma – the musk of that woman! Oh, Joseph, those were better times! This world we've reached disgusts me.'

'Yes, Excellency.'

'At that time I alone held the key to my future.'

But my jungle experiences were too difficult for a native of St Petersburg. Either that or they were so far removed from the present as to be completely without meaning to him. 'Indeed, but Excellency, look up there! To join the Emperor!'

He was pointing up at a pedestal of which I could see only the base on account of a cascade of bright green ferns, ledge upon ledge of them. Moving to a different angle, I saw it was a bust of Louis XVI (it said so on the plinth). Looking farther down that gallery of weird spiked plants and bulbous stems and lianas writhing like tortured snakes up into the metal cross ties of the roof, I discovered the Count owned an entire avenue of French monarchs.

Joseph said, 'We could get four more heads on the front of the loco.'

I said, 'Do what you want,' and sitting down at a small round bamboo table, I put my fists to my head.

The Benckendorffs had lived easefully on their estate for two hundred years amid the public duties of the provinces and the customary sins of the wealthy. Now they were leaving – were sitting in a Pullman carriage with a white poodle named Kiki and were boiling to be gone.

Already they'd forgotten their comfortable bed, the names of their gardeners and how the conservatory smelt. They'd probably forgotten what they had for breakfast. What was important to them was the future. The calculation having been made, they'd discarded this entire section of the past – had done it mutually, looking into each other's eyes, like a suicide pact.

Should I be dealing with Elizaveta in the same way? Should I say, 'That's it, my darling,' dust off my palms and abandon her? Was her memory becoming a drag? A nuisance – even a danger to us as we searched Russia for Glebov?

The thought was so loathsome that I cried out and knuckled my temples.

I went out into the clean summer's day. Standing on the terrace I drew in chestfuls of our Russian air. If I forsook Elizaveta,

I forsook Russia. It was not what I wanted, I knew that now. My cousin Nicholas and my godfather Misha Baklushin had both been right. I'd tried to persuade them to leave before it was too late. They'd wracked themselves, wept torrents – and refused. Because the world could never contain a second Russia, and they knew it. I'd cursed Elizaveta for baulking at exile, oh how I'd shouted at her on that last night. Yet she too had been right. And all my countrymen and women who'd tarry too long would be right also. Exile was for shirkers. I would follow my heart, would avenge my bride with Glebov's blood or be killed doing so.

It was my answer.

Boldly down the carriage drive I now went, the train in front of me. Oskar's reddish, tobacco-soaked moustaches and the rat-like incisors of Delicia were pressed against the window, urging me to hurry. Kiki jumped off the Countess's lap onto the table and began to yap at me. Her breath made an oval of smoke on the pane. The cockatoo tuft on her head quivered from her efforts. Oskar's blond-haired hand angrily scooped the creature onto the floor and he tried a smile on me.

Going straight into the Pullman, I said to her, 'Lady, that dog is your death sentence. Without it a Bolshevik might let you go. With it you're sunk. My advice is to throw it out or give it to Valenty for the firebox. You wouldn't hear even a squeak.'

I left her scowling. The way her mouth was shaped she couldn't clamp her lips. She tied them up into a sort of knot and shook them at me.

Joseph had taken me at my word and with Boltikov had pressed Oskar's men into their service. One was pushing the heads of four French kings in a barrow and behind him another two were making heavy weather of a consignment of pictures in large gilt frames. I waited until they were aboard, until the pistons were hissing and the wheels tugging. Then I went and lay down. Xenia was gone, cooking us a meal. I slumped across the bed feeling unhappy again. Maybe finding Glebov was an impossible task, like everyone said.

I was in some halfway house between sleep and waking when I heard footsteps, not Xenia's, coming down the corridor. The Countess's knuckles rattled on the door like Spandau fire. Her voice had the metallic screech of a shipyard in full employment.

'I wish to protest. It is my right. Even in these illegal times, every person has the right to protest . . . I know you're in there.'

A pause – and the handle began to whip back and forth. She was using both hands on it.

'Under our noses did they do it! Even as we watched they stole our property. It is an outrage. I shall inform the Governor of the province. I shall demand full compensation in the courts. Or you can take us to Vladivostok for nothing. I don't mind. Do you hear me, you inside?'

My unhappiness redoubled. If she couldn't forget the busts and pictures, which she'd abandoned in any case, how was I ever to forget Elizaveta? Everything seemed hopeless, and not just hopeless but intrinsically bad, like a piece of meat that is rotten through to the centre of the bone.

I leapt off the bed. 'Woman' – I was at the door attacking it. The bronze turnlock came away in my fingers as I hurled it open. 'Woman,' I roared, gripping the throat latch of her coat and twitching her up till she was on tiptoes and her jaw horizontal. I bent my face towards hers. Her eyes had become tiny, folded around with loose skin. From somewhere in there she fluttered the lids at me. I said, 'Don't play games with me, French baggage, you'd left those things forever, chucked them away. What are you talking about?'

She closed her eyes, showing me her lilac eyeshadow. Her lips began to slither around. She hung there in my grip. I thought, I'm becoming a true beast, that's what this life without hope is doing to me.

She whispered, 'I *adore* masterful men,' and as the train rocked, she pressed her loins against mine and showed me the tip of her tongue, which had a grain like the back of a Burmese river slug, whose pink and fleshy young I have often eaten. I said, 'Keep it for the Reds,' pushed her away and went to feel sorry for myself with Xenia.

Twenty-five

THOSE ARISTOS were such idiots. Thinking to hide from the Revolution and make merry with American jazz, they'd sauntered down a spur into the forest without remembering to switch the points back behind them. They might as well have painted a trail of arrows in the Romanov colours. I sent Kobi to reconnoitre.

He slipped away into the fir trees like a ghost, looking up just once, to see where the sun was. When he returned, he tricked us, creeping up beside the train and suddenly showing his Mongolian face to the Countess from a distance of three or four inches, flattened against the window. She tried to shriek but Oskar's big red hand was over her mouth in a flash. They were learning.

The line stopped at a quarry that had been used for ballasting the rails. There was a turntable. They'd managed to get their train turned round, but that was all. Kobi had heard the throb of loud music. He'd seen the two black men through the window, one at the trumpet, the other playing a double bass. There'd been a third man at the drums. He couldn't understand why they'd stayed in the coaches and not had a regular dance outside, a festivity, as they did in Mongolia.

The quarry was less than a mile away. I said we'd go in at dawn.

Boltikov was unusually quiet. He was busy estimating the bales of stoles and capes that would shortly be his, the fur-lined coats, the muffs, cloaks, mantles, pelures, busbies, bootees and other furry items that would be snug on a woman and warm with her smell. He was thinking about how to get them down to the warehouse in Constantinople that in his mind was already his.

I took him aside and quoted our proverb: '"One can decide whether a horse is good or whether a horse is bad only after one has ridden it."' Maybe there'd be no booty. Maybe there'd be a different problem, one that was altogether more complicated.

'Suppose,' I said, 'that some of these people turn out to be old friends. Maybe your best school friend ever is among them ... An old flame, think of that ... Or a woman you once treated badly and whom you remember with shame. That would be the worst of all. She looks imploringly at you ... Or maybe she's too proud to be a supplicant so that you have to take the full weight of shame upon yourself. What are you going to do then? Shall we abandon old chums to the wolves?'

'I'm still young. A man with money can always find new friends.' He'd lost weight, was tauter and meaner than I'd ever seen him.

'Still, I'd try a disguise, Alexander Alexandrovich. You know how friends can be when they're in a tight corner.'

The Countess took up my theme: 'Oskar – darling – suppose it is not Alexander Alexandrovich but we ourselves who find that we know people on that train. Suppose, my dear, suppose that that scheming bitch, Sophia Elektrovina—' her hand went to her mouth but couldn't quite stifle the gasp – 'we'd have to hide. I couldn't trust myself to keep quiet. I might cry out – she'd recognise my voice, come looking, and then what would we do ... ? I mean, people who've been our neighbours for centuries, what if they're on that train? We can't just leave them to their fate – can we?'

Slowly she looked round at all of us in turn. 'How thrilling that would be!'

She melted coyly into Oskar's side. He put his arm around her. One could tell from the formality of his expression that duty was at work. It would be impossible ever to know what he was thinking. I believe he was made of a baulk of red-haired wood in which there were a number of small slits his parents had cut to contain information notes on certain aspects of existence: economics, the orders of the Swedish nobility, pleasure and food. The Countess Delicia would be the doer in that union.

I mistrusted leaving the main line. An enemy could come along behind and shut me in. But I wanted that locomotive: I badly wanted its armour-plating backed by concrete and the power of all those wheels.

At dawn we slipped at crawling speed onto the spur line and halted in the forest. We were five effectives: Kobi, Joseph, Boltikov, Valenty and myself.

Joseph was nervous, asked if he could remain behind and help Xenia with breakfast. His eyes had the glitter of fish scales in the half-light. I reminded him that it hadn't gone so badly for him the night of Lenin's coup, when we went among the soldiers at Smolny. But he wasn't persuaded. He told me again that nature hadn't made him brave. He was wearing a black woollen hat. His hair was down to his shoulders. His cheeks were green and hollow. Ah, Joseph, my Joseph . . .

I had no intention of taking Oskar, despite his medals. I could hear him snoring as we moved out, our boots noiseless on the litter of spruce needles.

A wisp of steam was showing from the chimney of the armoured loco. Valenty nudged me. I knew what he meant: it'd have taken three hours to get away if the firebox had been cold. We'd agreed he'd be a useful fellow, that other driver – Yuri Shmuleyvich. He was a Tsarist. His interests were the same as ours. We'd take him as stoker, whether he wanted to come or not.

I doubted they were up to posting sentries – and was right. We just walked straight up to the train and stepped aboard.

We had to fight our way through to the dining car so thick was the miasma of debauchery. Joseph threw open the doors at each end. When the haze cleared, I found the double bass propped in a corner wearing a scarlet dressing gown. Beside it was the set of drums. Joseph drew back the curtain to the pantry and there, sitting in the white enamel sink, his greyish legs and bony kneecaps hooked over the edge, was the unclothed corpse of an elderly man. His head was propped at an angle – wedged between the taps. On it was the cap and insignia of a senior colonel in a Hussar regiment.

'Must have been the heart,' said Joseph, tapping his own.

'Climbed up and undressed and said, OK, I'll die now?'

'No,' he said in agreement. 'Maybe shot?'

We looked all around that man and were still wondering about him when Boltikov entered. The cause of death didn't interest him for a moment. But the cap of a Hussar colonel did and finding it fitted, he kept it on. Shmuleyvich was definitely on our side, he reported. Valenty had gone back to bring up our own train. Kobi had discovered a light machine gun plus ammunition. And he'd yet to find anyone awake on the train.

'Dead men and women. We could go up to any of them and shoot them as they lie there. Easy meat. For the Reds as well as us.'

I sent him to tell Shmuleyvich to give the coaches a good to-and-froing.

That got them on the move. They began to creep into the dining car, broken and bitched, in their last night's outfits. Pretty soon the room was filled with the stink of their exhausted pleasures.

Kobi had been going through the train checking everyone was up. He came back to the dining car and nodded. He emptied his rifle and reloaded it. Every Russian knows what that oily rattle stands for, also the snap of the bolt as it locks, also the instant of silence as a man curls his finger round the trigger.

'Who are you?' shouted a bold voice.

'Charlie Doig.'

'What do you want from us?'

'You're going to run a race round the coaches. First two past the post get lucky.'

'And the others?'

'Won't get my full attention. Now get moving. Quickly there, *zhivo, zhivo.*'

I got out and was scraping the finishing line with my heel when Valenty appeared with our old train. Xenia waved to me through the dining-car window, then came swankily down the steps. She was wearing a blouse I hadn't seen before. Her arms were bare to just below the shoulder. She sashayed over and kissed me in the ear – in front of all those people. It was terrific, like a water bomb going off. I was anyway awash with adrenaline. Every fibre was singing like the telegraph wires: heat was coming off me in clouds. She'd have had only to glance at me in a certain way or shift her breasts and I'd have been at her.

She looped an arm round my neck – drew my head down to her level – whispered: 'Now I know what they mean when they say that all victorious leaders have a strong physical odour.'

Chortling, she retired a couple of paces.

I had the giant black man play the call for Assembly on his trumpet. Boltikov in his red colonel's cap lined them up, all this nightclub riff-raff. Forty-two souls in all. Kobi had our new machine gun trained on them.

'All of you!' – I spread my arms wide – 'You are alive! Be grateful for that. The clouds are high and the light is good. A reasonable day is in prospect. Be grateful for that also. I'm leaving you your warm beds, your food, your drink, your snow. I am leaving you your money and your dignity. Everything that you value most will remain in your possession. All I'm taking are your weapons, which in any case you have no idea how to use, and your locomotive. In return I give you ours. You'll travel slowly in it until you can find someone to put a weld on the bullet hole in the boiler. That's all that's bad about this day as far as you're concerned – all that I know about. The rest will be of your own making.'

Well, that's all right then! You could see the relief on their faces.

Just behind me Xenia hissed, 'Watch out, Charlie!'

Simultaneously there was a shrill call from the direction of the Pullmans, 'You can't go without us, wait!'

It was the Benckendorffs, the Countess Delicia leading. Behind stumbled Oskar, furnace-faced in his heavy coat, a large suitcase in each hand and a small one under each arm.

Everyone watched in silent amazement as the Countess, cool, commanding and elegant in a frothy white blouse buttoned at the sleeves, grey skirt to the ankles, deep black belt and that saucered green hat, came tinkling through the mess of quarry rubble. The sun had come out in force. It was going to be a belter of a day.

Boltikov said to me, 'Does she think she's at the racecourse?

Trouble's coming. Let's get the competition wrapped up and be on our way.'

Xenia was at my elbow again. 'If you allowed them their footwear, it'd be a better test. Look at those broken bricks they've got to run over. Glass as well, I expect. And some of them are old people. Don't be an ogre, Charlie.'

But it wasn't softies I was after. I wanted people who'd figure out the jagged bricks and the shards of glass and the bits of the old iron stone-crusher that were lying around. I wanted clever dicks, two of them. Besides, if I allowed them their boots, the losers'd come running after us and catch us if we had to stop to switch the points onto the main line. Then we'd have to club them down, as sailors do when the lifeboats are full. There'd be shooting, it'd turn ugly. I didn't want a battle. There could be Reds somewhere in the forest who'd get curious.

Some of the people had heard Xenia, had watched my lips and read refusal in them. Now I saw hatred in their faces. The old, the fat, the ill: those who'd had tuberculosis or had once broken a leg, the ones with diarrhoea. How were they supposed to compete?

Two women looked at each other and then at me. I saw in succession hope, fear, despair. 'Us too?'

'Yes . . . no . . . wait! Anyone volunteering to go on the slow train can drop out of the race. No point in busting your balls in this heat.'

The black jazz players sauntered over in their Uncle Sam pants, daintily picking their way through the bricks. 'I reckon Tom and me'll do just that. We got the tunes. Everyone loves tunes. Them Reds ain't no exceptions. As for running . . . no one I know does that.'

They wandered back to their carriage. Others joined them. Only six were left in the end. They gathered in a bunch in front of me. I explained the rule, which was to finish first – and felt the brim of a hat graze my ear. I leaned away. It didn't stop her. She spoke like a cat stalking a mouse, quietly, each syllable falling in its precise place.

'Darling, that couple on the left are the Davidovs. They bought a house from us in Moscow five years ago. There is money still owed to my husband. How I would adore it if they failed to win.' She craned her neck forward and sneered at them, baring her camel's teeth from gum to gum. 'It's him. He deserves to be shot. All swindlers should be shot. Without a trial – you know.'

Disgusting but honest was Delicia Benckendorff. I dropped my handkerchief to start the race.

Twenty-six

THE DAVIDOVA woman was a roomy sort, big-boned and yellow-haired, not obviously nimble. Except maybe in the water: I could see her as a powerful swimmer, full of natural buoyancy. It was obvious that she'd given the business some thought and had decided she was going to ride on the fast train and to hell with the others. Her husband was a thin, pallid fellow, with a trimmed black beard. By himself he'd have been nothing. But she was loyal as well as determined and was clearly going to carry him if necessary.

Holding her nightgown up, not caring what anyone saw, she struck out into the trees, a completely different direction from the others: a slow start to be sure, and they'd be going the long way round, but once on the soft bed of needles, they flew. Like a scene from a classical legend, they sprinted through the firs, heads tossed back, her pink limbs pumping amid a flurry of white garments.

The other four, all men, scrabbled over the rubble, jostling and cursing.

I knew immediately who the clever dicks were.

It was the Davidova woman who appeared first round the end of the train, her breasts swinging like church bells. A murmur of disbelief rose from the spectators. They'd been betting on the result. The weight of money had been on one of the men.

She'd cut her leg badly. Her feet didn't look too good. But she kept going – not looking back at the competition, just glancing across at me, to judge where the finish was. I admired her. And I admired her even more when the Countess rose from her ambush and began to call Mrs D. out for being a crook, all in her shrillest shipyard voice. Mrs D. veered to her right, to pass close to her. She drew back her arm – let fly – pam! – fetched the Countess one in the gob with a back-hander.

I said to Boltikov, 'Round up the Davidovs and get them on the train. No time for their baggage. Just do it.'

Then the Countess was in front of me, bleeding from the mouth. 'Did you see that? An unprovoked assault. She should be shot as well as that man of hers.'

Out of the corner of my eye I saw Boltikov shepherding the Davidovs towards the Pullmans.

'If you won't do it, Oskar will. I've told him to find the pistol. He thinks it's in his small suitcase.'

Kobi still had that bunch of dissipated failures covered with the machine gun. The morning sun was blaring down on us in the clearing, bouncing back off the raw rock of the quarry walls. The air was absolutely still. The only smell in it was of coal smoke. Not clouds of the stuff, black or white, but a haze of light grey vapour coming from the chimney of my new train, the colour you get when the fire's hot, when the loco's primed and ready.

Kobi was getting ready to gather up the machine gun and make a run for it. He looked over his shoulder to see how near starting Valenty was.

There was a shout from Oskar. He'd found his pistol. His clumsy hands were fumbling with the ammunition. It was time to go.

I seized Delicia Countess Benckendorff in my arms. I hugged her to me – all bone, her vertebrae crunching like railway clinker. In a flash she had her arms round my neck. I kissed her hideous mouth, firmly, with full lips and a little dart of my tongue to show penitence.

Then I scraped her off. I held her at arm's length. 'Darling – I'm sorry. It's goodbye.' And I ran for the train, which was already moving, Valenty hanging out of the cab and judging my speed nicely.

Somewhat out of breath I went to the dining car to meet the Davidovs. At last I was as well equipped as anyone on the railways. An armour-plated locomotive, fuel, men, money – I had them. Weaponry could be better. I would have liked to be pulling a flatbed with a three-inch howitzer. No matter, at least I could make an impression on events now.

Success puts a gloss on everything. I smiled wolfishly at Xenia, who was laying out the glasses for the samovar. The Davidov man was leaning against the wall, fingering his beard, sizing us all up with lidded eyes.

I said, 'What are you any good at?'

Whatever he replied, it didn't add up to what I'd expected. I thought, Shit, have I made a mistake getting these two? and barged into the cooking galley. This was of a decent size, the Pullman being appointed for royalty, but Mrs Davidova filled it nobly – had Xenia stuck in the corner, a mite by comparison. I said straight out what was on my mind: 'Are you as useless as your husband?'

Her blue eyes gave me the sort of tungsten look that said, I know you're the boss but I'll get you later.

'Well?' I said, flushed to have got a new loco so easily and standing my ground – in fact squaring up to her with my hands on my hips.

'Your wife said you needed a full-time cook. My friend here agreed,' – she indicated Joseph – 'so that deals with that. I am she. Also I am useful in another respect. For eleven years I was in charge of the children's ward in the Protestant Hospital – at the end of Ligovskaya. So I can be your doctor as well as your cook. Is that sufficient, sir?'

Xenia put her hand to her mouth but I could tell from her eyes she was sniggering at me, confident that I'd found my match.

I said sternly to Mrs D. that I'd judge her by her work and told Joseph to show them to a compartment.

The moment they were gone, Boltikov said, 'I've remembered about him. He was involved in that new block of apartments on the west side of the Tavricheski Gardens. Something went wrong with the money. He had to retire to the country to avoid a scandal. Two years ago?'

'We'll make him head waiter.'

'But she's OK. And a survivor.'

Survival, here was the word again. Never used by my parents or their friends but now to be heard freely among all sections of their class. Two 'v's in it, which was interesting. Vile, violent, V. I. Lenin – and now survival, which in Russian is *vyzhivanie*, to reinforce the position.

Add Venus to the list – I trapped Xenia's eye. I wanted her very badly.

Suddenly – out of nowhere – like a thunderclap – the roar of an aircraft overhead, inches away; and its Spandaus bursting p-p-p-p-p-p-p-p into our chatter and self-congratulation and the racket drowning everything except the shattering of glass and the splintering of wood and Xenia's scream as she dived under the table. As if by magic two lines of bullet holes appeared in the roof of the dining car. A foot apart, dead straight, immediately above my head. Had rain fallen vertically, a drop could have come through one of those holes and hit me in the centre of my eye.

Xenia had me by the ankle, was climbing up my trouser leg. Her lovely face appeared above the table, wide-eyed and frightened. 'Where can we hide? Are we doomed?'

She fell to her knees and started to pray, hunched right over so that her hair brushed the floor.

The door crashed open. It was Kobi, drenched in a sheen of excitement. He'd come for the machine gun. He was going to set it up on top of the coal tender. 'It came in so low, the angle would have been perfect. I could have shot it head-on, in the propeller, right in the guts.'

I understood now why the bullets hadn't struck me: the angle had been too shallow. He should have come in at a steeper pitch and been prepared to be tough on his aircraft when pulling out.

Kobi went on: 'It's gone to shoot up our old train. We were being used for practice.'

I didn't understand that. Having an armoured loco, weren't we the more important target?

Xenia, having dispatched all her fears to God, looked at me as if I had three heads. 'Oh, but they're easier, that's why. The pilot'll have seen them lounging around. It's what I'd do.'

It made sense and it didn't make sense. But I didn't follow through and started to wonder where the plane had taken off and what its range was. Were the Bolsheviks that close behind us?

Twenty-seven

Valenty had the damper wide open. We were going at a good clip. Leaning on his shovel, the sweat starting from his forehead in blisters, Shmuleyvich said, 'Don't worry about the coal, Excellency. The faster it takes us away from that pig, the better. Look at him. Look back there, will you.'

It was a black Fokker triplane that was hammering our old train. (You can recognise them at any distance by the tail, which is shaped like the ace of clubs.) Taking its time, looping and swooping like one of the huge black velvety butterflies that we'd found throughout our Burmese expedition. (Another lifetime, the era of Goetz.) Hell, that was tough on the Benckendorffs, the jazz band and the rest of them. Sun, music, a snort of cocaine – visions and the beauty of being. Then out of nothing she'd come, Dame Death, to wake everyone up before killing them. Bloody black death, Fokker death.

Oskar would be dead. He'd never have made it to the forest in time, not over the rubble in his winter coat. The pilot'd have picked him out, gone specifically for him as he fled stumbling. That broad dutiful back, no Bolshevik could have resisted it.

The jazzmen would have been next, the Uncle Sam pants also irresistible to a Red gunner who'd heard he'd soon be fighting the Yanks. Black bastards, he'd have said to himself, thumb knuckles white on the firing buttons.

They'd been wrong, those two. Tunes were for winning women not wars.

We watched as that Fokker spun round the corpse of the

train. Shmuleyvich said, 'We're getting the clean end of the stick.'

'So far,' I said – and immediately the Fokker pilot lobbed a couple of small bye-bye bombs on our old loco from the cockpit and headed down the line for us, dodging to keep in our smoke so that Kobi, who'd set up the machine gun on top of the coal tender, couldn't get a fix on him.

I said to Valenty, 'How far to the points?'

He peered through the porthole. We were on a slight bend. He couldn't see. He leaned out, one foot in mid-air, hanging onto a bracket. His voice, very small, reached us above the wind. 'Hundred yards.' Then: 'They're against us. They're set for the main line.'

He started to pull himself back into the cab. I heard the unhurried high-pitched beat of an aero engine. I heard the Spandaus open up. And I saw Valenty flung out of the cab, spun right round by the force of the bullet so that he was facing us, his young face wide with astonishment. Then his grip slackened and he fell, without one single noise.

Shmuleyvich's massive hand pulled down the brake lever. The wheels screamed. Kobi came sprawling down from the coal pile.

The Fokker was turning in front of us. It arched up, flipped over in an Immelmann and headed for us, a little higher than before and straight out of the sun. Just a round black barrel getting bigger, that was all I could make out.

Kobi was scrabbling to get back up. The train was shuddering to a halt. That pilot had seen the points were against us. He only to go round and round until we were forced to stop. Then he could finish us off at his leisure.

The points were forty yards away. Beyond them the main line glittered in the sun.

Shmuleyvich looked at me. I knew what the look meant: I keep the loco going, you get the points, boy. No Excellency this or Excellency the other.

The Fokker made a couple of passes down the train without shooting, to mock us. He had the new guns that were synchronised to fire through the propeller arc. I could see their slits quite clearly, jet black behind the grey blur of the propeller.

The pilot was alone in the cockpit, just his leather helmet visible. No canopy. Goggles. Must have got a mouthful of smuts flying into our smoke.

We were almost stopped. Now the Fokker was coming at us in earnest, with short bursts, the bullets singing off the rails like bees.

To Shmuleyvich – 'How many levers for the points?'

'Two. One to release the rail, the other to move it. Could be stiff. Go out the wrong side of the train. You'll gain yards on him.'

I looked up. The Fokker was putting in a new row of hemstitching down the coaches. My girl'd be under the table again. Joseph too, probably.

'Fuck off, Bolshevik prick.' I'd have it painted down the carriage roofs, scarlet on black, Elizaveta's favourite combination. *Krasni khui*. Red dick, the cockerel. Then I leapt.

The pilot had seen that one coming. I should have had the Davidov man go first. Given him the choice, get shot by a Red or get shot by me.

I ran to the front of the loco, as best I could across the sleepers. Their spacing was awkward: one slip and he'd have had me for carrion. The bullets crackled off the rails and the armour-plating. They passed so close I could smell them. The shadow of the Fokker seemed to be sitting on top of me. That's what it felt like. There flashed through my mind two of the illustrations in my first Bible. They'd given me nightmares. *The Herald of Death* and *God Strikes a Sinner*. I thought, And I've still got to cross the open ground, switch the points and get back to the loco.

At last the shadow moved and went racing down the track in front of me. I knew the next bit. Another Immelmann roll and he'd be back. I'd be caught at the points. That'd be it. Six foot two, no real covering fire and clear light. Some part of me would get hit, couldn't be otherwise.

Kobi opened fire, but only for a short burst. 'Come on, man, what are you doing, for Christ's sake?' I shouted.

Then I gathered myself up, tucked my head in and went

sprinting out from the front of the train. Death was chasing me. What would it feel like afterwards . . . ? Why hadn't they put the points closer to my bit of the line . . . ? How actually did the lever shift the moving rail, was there a cable – then my boot caught it and I went flying, got smacked face down into the clinker by my momentum. For a second I was stretched out like a man already dead. But I wasn't where the Fokker thought I'd be and his bullets went wide.

Next: Kobi had got his machine gun balanced and opened up. I was on my knees, scrambling – scrabbling – to put some fresh speed on. P-p-p-p-p-p – it was a great noise that, the clump of Kobi's gunfire. It was the best I ever heard. I was thankful, not almost beyond words but actually so. My tongue was frozen – God was holding it. Yes! It had to be God. At that instant I believed in God, in the Apostles, the Miracles and every one of the ten Johns.

Cautiously I looked around. What was even better than the rattle of Kobi's machine gun was the fact that the Fokker didn't care for it. Or maybe he was running low on fuel or was out of ammo. Whatever the reason, he rolled away, the red star bold on his fuselage. I glimpsed white teeth in a filthy face. The sun flashed on his goggles – he was gone.

I was shaking all over. Had the points offered any resist-ance, I'd have sat down and cried. As it was, the lever came sweetly over and Shmuleyvich, grinning broadly, passed the train onto the main line. I walked towards the cab – tottered, my calves like jelly.

I climbed the ladder. Kobi was still up there on the coal stack, his face streaked with black. He said, 'Glebov, I know it was.'

I said that a man who'd broken his leg like Glebov would never be able to handle an aeroplane. He just wouldn't have the strength in his leg muscles. I didn't have this as absolute knowledge. But it seemed obvious. Moreover, Glebov was a commissar, not an airman. He wouldn't have time for that sort of caper. He might have had the pilot dispatched to patrol the railroads. It made perfect sense. I'd have done the same. But it hadn't been him in the Fokker.

Kobi said again, 'It was Glebov. I was closer to him than you were.'

'You were? That's balls. I was up there at the same level as God. At His front door. Hammering on it for mercy. Give over, Genghis.'

But he stuck to his opinion and I wasn't going to argue. He'd been wanting a change ever since we'd got holed up in St Petersburg. Let Muraviev take him off my hands, that's what I thought.

Twenty-eight

WE QUICKLY buried Valenty and Shmuleyvich took his place as driver. I told him to burn coal. I didn't believe for a moment that Glebov had been in the Fokker. But I didn't like the idea of being within range of the Bolsheviks' planes. So we went like hell for a week before easing off to pick up the news.

It was in this way that we began to hear more about the Tsar's imprisonment at Ekaterinburg, which was some way to the north and east of us. It was said that Commissar Glebov had charge of him, which fitted in well with what Boltikov had first heard. There could be little doubt about the Tsar's eventual lot unless Muraviev and the Whites could get to him in time. And whether that was possible – but here it became complicated. The Americans, British, French, Italians and Japanese had all sent forces to Siberia. Each wanted something different. As a result there were so many generals who might conceivably end up with the decisive role that I got giddy even thinking about them. There were too many arrows heading in too many directions – too much space for events to occur in. Something was needed to bring matters to a head and thus make Glebov accessible to me.

The death of the Tsar would obviously be one factor.

The other was brought into range not by kindly Fate but by the far from benign figure of Alexander Alexandrovich Boltikov.

I'd taken over Valenty's berth and there rigged up a drawing board on which I'd pinned a large map of Russia. On it I was shading the direction and extent of the Bolshevik advances as per the news that I judged reliable. I wanted to discover where that Fokker had been operating from.

'Charlie,' said Boltikov, coming in and looking unusually contrite, 'I'm feeling guilty about my wife and boy.'

'Do you want to feel guilty?'

'No! I sleep so badly.'

I asked him what she looked like. 'A beautiful *blondinka*, like a willow tree in spring. Her figure is sensational and her mind excellent. Therefore she is interested only in strong men. When I said we were leaving Russia, she said she'd go to Finland as an advance party and prepare things for my arrival. What did she do? She grabbed everything. Millions in cash. Plus my father's pictures. All the furniture, carpets, jewellery *und so weiter*. Said she'd wait for me to catch up. Ha! She'll have gone off with another man, I'm sure of it. That's her style. What I'm asking is this: do I have a duty to be loyal to her in the circumstances?'

'None.'

'May I forgot her?'

'Completely.'

'What about the kid? Six roubles to four says it's mine.'

'Then invest a proportion of your available love in him. And when you meet up with him as a young man, hand over the same proportion of your new fortune to him and say, "This is yours. Let's drink to our prosperity." Next problem.'

He smiled slowly. Conspiracy was in his eyes. Leaning forward so I could smell the salted fish on his breath he said, 'Well, Charlie, that was all chat. What I really came about is the information that's just come to hand.' He took the pencil from between my fingers and began sketching – thick, decisive slashes. 'Here's Kazan and the Volga flowing down to Samara. Right? And here's Ufa, which is on the River Kama, which connects to the Volga not far below Kazan. That's the geography that concerns us. Think of nothing else but that triangle. Plus what Joseph's just told me.'

'My Joseph?'

'Yes. Your Joseph and my spy. He's made of earhole. Turn the map round so we can both see it. The thing is this . . . would it surprise you to know that in one of these three cities there's a vault full of gold? Maybe it's on flatbeds between two of these cities, maybe in a string of barges. But the gold exists. "Next problem," you say – I can read you like a book. It's this: how to make the gold ours. Yours and mine, Charlie Doig.'

I studied him. The existence of the gold didn't surprise me. He had a monstrous nose for money. 'No. The first problem is its value. From that we know how much effort to make. Whether it's worth the risks.'

'That's the second problem. The first one is to get this dreary business of revenge out of your head . . . But let me tell you the story. When the German war started, our monarch did a wise thing and sent half the country's gold stock to Samara in case things went badly with the Hun. From Samara it was shifted to Kazan to join up with a small quantity of gold that was already there. That's how it got to these parts. Then the things happened that we know happened, like the Whites capturing Kazan. Now the Reds wants to grab it and the Whites want to keep it and our brave friends in the Czech legion think they're owed it for all the fighting they've done.'

'What's it worth?'

'United States dollars?'

'Yes.'

'Three hundred and thirty million.'

I said, 'That has to be hypothetical. Some will have gone missing. It always does.'

'Wrong word. Celestial, that's what it is.'

'Weighing? Even a million dollars' worth sounds heavy.'

'At $17.80 per troy ounce it comes in at 690 tons. Four-hundred-ounce bricks. That's thirty-three pounds each. The Russian double eagle on every single one. Purity – 98 per cent as assayed. As fine as Britain's. Each brick stamped and dated.'

'Year?'

'Nineteen fourteen.'

'And the reddish colour to it, is it a stigma?'

'No. The British have taken shiploads of it in payment for arms . . . Why so negative, Charlie? Do you have a bad relationship with money?'

'I was a naturalist. I've never had any money.' I couldn't think why I should tell him about the diamonds in my boots.

Going on: 'I'll tell you what makes me especially negative. Getting 690 tons of gold out of Russia without being hacked to pieces.'

'We don't have to take the lot. Ten million dollars would start me off. In five years it'd be twenty. Five-year doubling, that's my rule of thumb. What about you?'

His financier's eyes were trained on me saying, What sort of a problem is this that you have, and hurry up, and just think of a figure that'll give you everlasting happiness. Anyway say something, that's what his impatient stare said to me.

He continued, 'You've shot Glebov or strangled him or pushed him through the ice. Now what? Going to retire and live out your life in poverty, are you? Of course not. Now's the time to think about your future. Test the horizon. Think of all the women you want to make love to, the wines you want to drink. Racehorses, bung a few of those in while you're about it. A decent house or two. Yacht? Of course, with a crew of a dozen and your own flag at the masthead. Don't stint yourself, man!'

Anyone who can't admit to wanting money has a blocked nature. But I foresaw trouble with that quantity of gold.

However, he was in no mood to listen. 'Glebov'll be after the gold as well. He's only got to pop down from Ekaterinburg. Two for the price of one, that's what we could be talking about here. Looking at it from your point of view, of course, Charlie.'

The door opened. It was Xenia, come to look for me. I kissed the side of her neck, plunging at it. She smelt great, of laundered cotton.

'What were you talking about hidden away like this?' she said.

'Oh, the price of coal,' Boltikov said. But the words didn't ring true, and my girl stared long and hard at him as he went out into the corridor.

Twenty-nine

WE WERE approaching the Urals, which are the frontier between Europe and Asia, between Russia proper and a lower degree of civilisation. Beside us, bumping up against the railway from time to time, was the dusty old track used by exiles since God knows when – the Road of Sorrows.

Romantically for a change, her nose pressed to the window, Xenia exclaimed, 'Look! I can see their footprints of blood. Their tears were so salty they made holes in the ice! You can even see the scuff marks of their chains in the dust. In the ditches are their bones. But their dreams – I don't know where you'd look for those. Exile, forever and ever: it's a horrible idea. How their women must have suffered.'

'Often they went with their men.'

'As I'm going with you? Is that it? To Siberia? To a free sort of exile?'

I buried her questions in silence. Exile – the fatal question, the one that had killed Elizaveta, Nicholas, Misha, all of whom I loved. I had difficulty speaking about it. The truth was too deep, even if I could recognise it when I got there. And Xenia was a stickler for the truth.

She was perfect for me, my corsetière. I'd had enough of beauty. What I wanted was a solid, faithful woman: quiet, neither imposing nor annoying. You can find women who are not attractive in a popular sense yet who radiate an inner beauty and a potential for loving a man until the world comes to an end. That was the sort of woman I wanted. I deserved her. I had a lot to give in return.

Xenia was all of those things. I was growing fonder of her

every day. Yet there was a piece of grit in our relationship that I couldn't put my finger on. It never reached the surface. But I was aware of it. Something behind those huge green-grey eyes, something undisclosed. I didn't think it was to do with our disagreement about God. But there again it could have been. That subject is so vast and delicate that I could easily have dropped a clanger without knowing it.

The matter of exile wasn't the only reason I got dispirited travelling next to the Road of Sorrows. Lenin had walked it and probably Glebov too, the creature who haunted me. Its existence bore too closely upon the Revolution. It stood as the symbol for our war, for the reason we were tearing each other apart, Russian versus Russian. Moreover, every time we rounded a bend and found it appearing before us, the sight of it would provoke those ardent Tsarists among us – Mrs Davidova, Joseph and Shmuleyvich – into the most pessimistic discussion imaginable concerning the fate that awaited the Tsar and his family and what the repercussions would be for all the ordinary, God-fearing people of Russia.

It got me down. Where was the end to it all? Life after Glebov – what would it look like? Where would I fit in? How should I prepare myself?

In this way I started to think more closely about the Tsar's gold. And I was still thinking about it when we steamed into Strabinsk, the headquarters of General K. I. Muraviev and the 6th Siberian Army. The date: the evening of 26 July 1918.

Strabinsk was very much a frontier town. Colonel Zak, though wounded and obliged to lead his Czech legionnaires from a hired droshky, had captured Ekaterinburg the day before. A rumour was now spreading that he'd found evidence that the Tsar had been murdered. Drunken White soldiers were roaming the streets on the lookout for women, a fight, tobacco – mischief. Their officers were shooting anyone they didn't like the look of. Gunfire echoed through the dusk, and women's screams.

Boltikov and I kept to ourselves as we made our reconnaissance. In the end we found a man sober enough to guide us to the house of Muraviev's aide-de-camp, whose name was Blahos. By then it was late. Blahos, who was not over thirty and had a weak mouth and waves of auburn pomaded hair, was down to a vest and cavalry breeches, scarlet braces hanging below his waist. He had a female companion. I told him who I was and requested an appointment with Muraviev the following morning.

'Busy, busy – can't you see?' He must have been from our borderlands, maybe from Galicia with a name like that.

We were to return in the morning. He already knew about me – said I was a troublemaker. He'd obviously heard about the Fokker's attack on the train.

We looked vaguely for somewhere for Xenia to start a corset shop, that being a constant desire with her, had a beer in Strabinsk's big hotel, the Moderne, and returned to the station.

I kept guards posted throughout the night. Soon after dawn, Boltikov came and woke me. The night had been so hot he'd had difficulty sleeping. He said, 'Muraviev won't want us here. The reason he'll give is that you're too dangerous to have around. Because the Reds are obviously after you and that'd make trouble for him, that's what he'll say. But the real reason is the gold. He'll be in on it. Same as Glebov. Doesn't want the competition.'

I muttered, 'Christ, are we going to have to stand in a queue?' Then I nuzzled up to Xenia, both of us naked in the heat, and went back to sleep.

Thirty

B LAHOS WAS waiting for us outside the Moderne, a creamy, three-storeyed building that took up the whole of one side of the main square. The sun by then was brilliant, almost white in colour. The shadows in the folds of the Tsarist flag above the hotel were so harsh that it appeared to be made entirely of black cloth. The morning breeze had died. By mid-afternoon it'd be stifling. It was a typical Siberian summer's day.

He saluted, to put us at a loss, and bowed insolently to Xenia. He said to me, 'I am instructed to tell you that the General does not wish you to remain in Strabinsk. He has given your train priority and immediate clearance to Uralsk, which is as far as his jurisdiction reaches. You are to leave by midnight.'

'Why's that?' said I.

'The man you're seeking is operating in the area to the west of Uralsk. So the reason you have come here is no longer valid. Another reason is the murder of the Tsar. We only await word from the Supreme Commander for our foremost regiments to march forward and afflict the Bolsheviks with such a wall of flame, bomb and bayonet that they will be wiped from the earth. In the circumstances, your presence will be a distraction. Those are the reasons, Doig.'

'Sure there's nothing else?' Boltikov asked.

'Nothing.' He bowed, showed us his pink scalp beneath his crinkly hair. 'Come to my office, please. Your exit papers need to be dated and stamped. They must also carry your signa-ture as well as mine to be in accordance with the General's regulations.'

We fell in behind him, trudging across the hot square with the hotel behind us.

A troop of round-shouldered cavalrymen appeared, kicking their nags along. Many of them had strips of linen tied over their mouths against the dust, which was hanging in the air like a tattered brown curtain. The horses moved wearily, not picking their hoofs up properly, behaving like slippered old men. Their heads drooped: they were not even interested in the jangle of their own harness. Everyone was listless, everyone was expecting the worst.

'These foremost regiments of yours are quite something,' I said to Blahos.

Only the small, shoeless boys who were running behind the horses to scoop up the dung had any energy. They were going to dry it and sell it in cakes for fuel.

A few minutes later and another troop went past – then a third. There were about twenty men in each, some with rifles and some without. None were carrying lances. One could never have said what regiment they were part of.

When the dust collapsed in the intervals between them, one could see on the wooden sidewalks men curled up asleep, or begging or praying or smoking or arguing or just watching all the things that will happen in a revolution when everyone is helpless except the sponsors, in whose interests this helplessness is. Homeless mothers were giving the tit, at the same time flapping at the flies that swarmed over the milk dribbling from the infants' mouths—

I want to say more about these flies, which were making everyone's life a misery. They were small, about the size of a spring raindrop and extraordinarily quick. I think they were *Sarcophaga carnaria,* or flesh flies. It was impossible to say for certain without a microscope. To attempt to kill them was pointless. I only ever saw White officers trying to do that and took it as proof of their stupidity. The sole solution was to ignore them. But this was difficult for men, and here's the reason. Whenever a man pissed they gathered round his cock, even settling on it – for the usual reason, that the ammoniacal smell reminded them of rotting flesh, from which they draw their protein. No blame can attach to them for this: it's what nature taught them to do. But let me say that the tickling sensation of their feet is extraordinarily disagreeable. I've often thought of the diseases they carry and even woken in the night convinced that what I was feeling was an egg being hatched in one of my passages. Once this has entered your mind at two in the morning nothing can come between you and the ravages of syphilis. Boltikov also suffered the same discomfort.

My girl, however, was untroubled by them.

Blahos turned and said to me, 'I'm sure that Jones, the American cipher expert, will confirm that People's Commissar Glebov is not in the province. Nothing gets past him. You'll find him in the Moderne.'

We walked on. Blahos said in an aggrieved tone, 'He has a room to himself. So does the other one. They always have clean clothes.'

'Where's he keep his wireless stuff?' said Boltikov.

'At the station. It's in a wagon, heavily guarded at all times . . . Down there, that's my office.'

Nothing could have been more dismal than the centre of Strabinsk on that day, when people were still digesting the news of the Tsar's murder.

Over there: a mongrel licking the face of a child sleeping on a mat – guiltily, glancing up every few seconds.

Beside it: a man sitting on a stool and begging – holding out a tin. One temple had a terrific dent in it, like a dew pond, and his eyes were completely skewed. His tongue was hanging out in a great pink strip – or what would have been pink had it not been covered with flies. I don't know how he took food. Maybe it was only liquids. But managed he must have, for he was a fleshy fellow.

Xenia wanted to give him money but we wouldn't let her, saying that the man was faking it, how else could he be so fat.

Still on dogs: on the sidewalk leading to Blahos's office the ugliest mastiff in Siberia was humping a gasping pop-eyed King Charles spaniel which had a blue ribbon round its neck. We had to step round them. The mastiff had an identically guilty expression to the mongrel licking the child's face. It was going at the spaniel with the desperation of a dog experienced in the ways of man and fearful of being booted off before he could spill his seed. Its tongue was hanging out of the side of its mouth, which gave it an additional expression, one of conceit. Its hot yellow eyes darted left and right as it worked its loins.

As we drew level, the dog spent itself, arching its head upwards and giving off an eerie howl. 'Wolf in it,' Blahos said.

From nowhere a woman came running. She had on a white cotton dress and black leather shoes. Behind her, grinning, was a bellhop in the maroon-and-gold livery of the Moderne. She stood at the entrance to the street, shrieking for her dog, which was obviously the King Charles. She reminded me so much of Delicia Benckendorff that I heard this woman shout for Kiki to begin with. In reality it must have been Fifi or Weewee or something. The spaniel, of course unable to move, raised its soft brown eyes to her in an apology.

Boltikov said, 'Even the dogs are copying Lenin. Look at how the brutish mastiff has nailed the pretty and helpless aristocrat.'

Blahos said to me casually, 'By the way, see that house there with the small window under the eaves? Want new papers or anything in that line and that's where you'll get them. A Jew, of course. You'll pay a Jew's prices. But he's busy. He works late hours.'

Nodding to his guard at the door, he stood aside for us to enter his office. On the walls were large-scale maps of the province and a couple of identification charts of German aeroplanes. A heavy, sweating woman was seated at an upright typewriter, threading a new spool of black and red ribbon. She'd hung its grey oilcloth cover over the back of her chair like a cloak. A corporal was on the telephone. Cradling the receiver, he whispered to Blahos that it was Colonel Zak speaking from Ekaterinburg. 'Only a situation report, sir . . . Tell me the number of that regiment again, Colonel?'

I said to Blahos, 'You've repaired the telegraph lines a damn sight quicker than anything else seems to happen round here.'

He studied a thermometer which had Celsius in one panel and Réaumur in the other. 'It's too hot to make a success of thinking . . . It's not us who've repaired them, you can be certain of that. It's the Czechs. The General hates having them so close.

He says their energy makes us look like South Sea Islanders . . .
Shablin, bring me the exit papers for Doig.'

The woman finished with the spool and rose from her chair.
She was solid all the way down. She went into a side room.

Boltikov said to Blahos, 'All right, we'll clear off. Now tell
us the real reason.'

His face was a study in blandness. There were quicksands all
round. At no time since Lenin stood in front of me at Smolny
had I been confident that I had truth by its arse hairs. He said,
'That's simple, we need every inch of railway track for our troop
trains. We've no time for frivolities.'

'Glebov a frivolity?' I exploded. 'That murderer?'

Blahos shrugged. 'This afternoon we'll be interrogating the
Reds captured when we took Ekaterinburg. I invite you to be
present. We'll soon discover if they know of anyone named
Glebov.'

'Or Prodt, that's another name he uses,' I said. 'But that grade
of prisoner you're talking about lives in total ignorance of what's
happening at the top.'

'As you wish.'

'He may even have a third name. What I know for certain is
that he was at Ekaterinburg with the Tsar.'

'You know everything better than we do . . . Sir, your papers.'

Mrs Shablin raised her skirt to sit down. A gamy flatulence
spread through the room. We went out into the heat.

Xenia said in a tired voice, 'Nothing is ever as it seems.'

'Being mostly less,' I said curtly.

We couldn't find the street she'd dreamed of for her corset
shop and when we got back to the station I learned from Mrs
Davidova that Kobi had succumbed to the reputation of
Muraviev as an exciting cavalry officer and had decamped.

Thirty-one

I TORE UP the permits we'd been given for Uralsk, tore them across and across. 'Best thing for them,' grunted Boltikov, sitting opposite. We'd got our hands on some more beer at the Moderne. It was helly hot in that compartment of mine.

'It's the only way to deal with these *chinovniks* – flat-arses,' he said. 'It's the clerk class that's brought Russia down. Papers, papers, papers, they stifle a man's desire to do better for himself. Every other clerk should be impaled in public as a lesson to the rest.'

Joseph entered and picked up all the scraps of paper. He read aloud, '"Rail Permit Good for Uralsk,"' observed that it would be worth money to someone were it pieced together and went out backwards, not disturbing the order of the torn papers, which he'd placed on the flat of a book.

Boltikov went on, 'Open another beer for me . . . That gold, is 690 tons still too much for you to think about?'

A fortnight ago I'd have given him the usual reply: Glebov first. But these doubts I had about ever finding him were growing stronger daily and I said, 'We should think about that, you and I.'

And a voice in the doorway said, 'Well, 690 tons ain't too much for me.'

It had to be the American, Jones. I gave him a brief look and said to Boltikov, 'How's your English?'

'A few business phrases – "My very last offer." "Twenty per cent minimum." "When dividend last paid?"'

'That about deals with everything important,' the fellow said in English. His voice was so deep and measured that it could only belong to a really solid citizen. Then he said to Boltikov in Russian, 'But I can handle your language. Anything except chess problems.' He said it humorously but slowly, with a strong accent, as if in pain.

He wasn't as tall as I was, but he was well framed, had an open face and brown eyes and hair. He was wearing an army necktie, which made him unusual in Strabinsk.

'Leapforth Jones at your service. Captain attached to Military Intelligence, Section 8. That's the Bureau of Cryptography. The Black Chamber, as we call it back home.'

He looked me over carefully. 'I guess you're Charlie Doig. Our friend Blahos has been talking about you.'

He recognised the provenance of our beer, which had on its label the picture of a man in a dark green fedora smirking through a triangular moustache, the sort of expression that showed he was pleased to have made the sale. Jones yelled out of the door, 'Hey, Ivan, bring me one of those.' Then he pulled up a chair and said to me, 'Anyone who gets fired on by the Reds is a friend of mine. That's what's important to us, to know who's on our side and who isn't. Darned tricky in a place like this. All the coming and going – in these guys' heads, I mean. How to make out what they're actually thinking, where the truth lies—'

Joseph arrived with a bottle. We eyed Jones as he drank from it, trying to divine how much of the sucker was in him. He belched and smiled on us, dazzlingly, teeth like cliffs of chalk. Then, tipping his chair back as a man walked down the corridor, 'Hey, Stiffy, I've made us some friends at last.

'Meet my wireless operator, Timothy H. Brown, known by all as Stiffy. My small genius, I call him. Heck no, that came out wrong. My wireless operator who though small is a genius. That's better. Came from your side of the Atlantic once, Charlie.'

Brown wasn't a dwarf but he didn't have to duck for doorways, put it like that. Wide, light blue eyes, and lank, gingery hair that he'd grouped into a few thicker strands raked carefully across his skull.

'Tell our friends about yourself and get it out of the way,' commanded Jones.

Stiffy gave the three of us a vague salute, trying to fit everyone into its scope. Looking at me, 'The "H" in my name stands for Hardman, sir. So I've been Stiffy from my first day at school, Stiffy on the steamer to the Americas and Stiffy in New York. Now I'm Stiffy in Siberia – sir!' He came to attention and saluted us again.

Jones said, 'I meant it when I called him a genius at his wireless. He can read thirty words a minute. If we were sailing across the ocean and saw a pod of whales, Stiffy'd only have to put on his headphones and twiddle a few knobs to tell us what the ninth whale was digesting. Yeah, he's good – the best I know.'

Stiffy said to me: 'Sir, it's not difficult. We all speak Morse.'

'Then I put on my thinking cap, that's where I come in,' said Jones. 'We do pretty well between us. Well enough to have the President of the United States of America send for us. Himself.'

'So who controls you,' I said. 'Uncle Sam or the big White cheese, Kolchak?'

'You bet that's Uncle Sam. The 27th US Infantry'll be landing at Vladi any day now and he controls them as well. Plus he controls Mr Gray, who's our Consul in Omsk, plus another guy down in Samara. Plus a few thousand more here and there in Russia, not wishing to be exact about these confidential matters. To hell with that Kolchak guy.'

Joseph brought Stiffy a beer without being asked. I didn't want to run out of the stuff so I told him to take it back and bring us a samovar. It was my best one, the one I'd brought from the palace, a resplendent, boastful construction from the period of high empire with mahogany handles and a great silver belly on either side that Joseph still polished once a week. In my uncle's time it had always been preceded into the room by a footman to prevent a child knocking against it and being scalded.

'Call me Leapforth, boys,' said Jones, watching Joseph make a space for the samovar. 'Christ, that's some urn, a real beauty. Only trouble, Ivan – it doesn't leave much room on the table in case we want to lay out any papers. Just bring us the tea in glasses.'

'Not the same thing at all,' said Boltikov sourly, not having taken to Jones from the start.

'Yeah, I know you Russkis are tied to the old ways, but the tea'll taste the same.'

There wasn't a great deal of room in the compartment, the bed being for me and Xenia and not a fold-up. Boltikov and I sat at the table with our backs to the window, the two Americans opposite.

Jones went on tipping his chair back. It was a good one from the palace. I told him to stop messing it around. Joseph brought the tea and a plate of knish, fried dumplings filled with potato that Mrs D. had knocked up. When he'd left, Jones leaned back and locked the door.

He took out his pistol, jokingly blew some imaginary smoke from the muzzle and said, 'This country's fuller of rats than a bin of wet corn.' He laid it on the table in front of him.

Then, 'All the principals being in one place, let's get things clear between us. First, what my good fellow citizens are paying us to do, second, how we do that, and third, how you and us are going to make a cooperation. Yessir, that's how I see it, a multinational effort on behalf of international tranquillity. If you're game, that is, gentlemen. No pressure. Just holler if you want to go your own way . . . Mr Boltikov, you say if my use of the lingo isn't clear.'

He took a sugar cube from the top pocket of his tunic and dropped it into his tea. 'Now the Tsar's dead, my only remaining commission is to report on the depth of the Bolshevik movement and the balance of strength between the Reds and the Whites. Will Russia become another Balkans? Are there outstanding national leaders either Communist or Tsarist whom our country should be seeking to influence? What are the policies of the Soviet leaders? These are some of the questions to which my government needs an answer.'

He sipped at his tea, grimaced and slipped in another cube of sugar. 'I'd rather be paid by Uncle Sam than Uncle Muraviev. Not much sugar at the Moderne . . . You'll want to know how we can accomplish this. The same way that we know about mostly everything that's happening out here: by keeping our files up to date and our ears open. At the moment our information comes from the reports that the Red commander in this region files twice a day with HQ. Regimental identification,

144

troop movements, some planning details – you can piece it together quite quickly once you've got the hang of their minds. Mind you, Charlie, they're hot stuff with their ciphers. They used to change them every other day but the trouble with that was that some commanders didn't receive the new one by the due date or were just too plain busy with stuff like fighting. So now they change once a week, that seems to be their routine. At the moment they're using a Variant Beaufort, which is about as low as you can get—'

'Thought you said they were hot stuff,' I said.

'Yeah, beats me why they've gone down to a Beaufort. Fifty years ago it was being sold to schoolboys as a bit of fun. Maybe they're having trouble getting decent cipher clerks.'

'Explain it,' I said.

'In ten words,' said Boltikov, bored, picking the seeds from the raspberry jam at the bottom of his tea glass.

'The whole thing? Transposition, substitution, the ways a cipher alphabet's constructed? Why, you could write a book just about the use of nulls – that's letters you put in to confuse the enemy. They don't have a meaning – or do they? You don't want to know about cryptography, Charlie. The war can't last that long.'

Stiffy said, 'Repetition is straightforward, sir – with respect.'

'OK, Stiff, you're right. I'll give them repetition seeing how it's the basis of everything. Now, boys, the only cipher that stands a chance of winning is the one that avoids it. OK? Start using the same symbol for one particular letter and you're sunk. If the frequency tables don't undo you, there's any number of mathematical formulae that will. Short is good. Short wins wars. But the type of information that has to be sent by cipher is rarely short. That's why ciphers are so complicated. That's why I have a job . . . Codes and code words? Forget 'em. They're for kiddies.'

Boltikov was lolling in his chair, snapping at flies with one hand and flicking their bodies into his glass. He caught my eye. He was waiting for the cooperation bit.

The heat was hanging on to the bitter end of the day. Without the trees, there was no baffle against it. It rolled in from the plains, filling the hollows in the fields and the river valleys, the streets, the courtyards, the houses, rooms, beds and at last the brains of everyone present in Strabinsk in those first days of August. It was why Muraviev drank champagne at ten in the morning, why the mastiff was humping the spaniel and why Leapforth Jones was fingering his pistol.

Thirty-two

HIS VOICE was deep, solemn, serene, all the effects for which men get trusted and called Uncle. His steadfast brown eyes rested patiently on mine. His tunic had come off and his tie. His khaki shirt had razor-sharp creases. He was wearing a wedding band. In every single respect the Captain was a skilled and wholesome employee of the US Army.

He said, 'You don't seem very curious about us. No questions? Like how did you guys get from the States to Strabinsk?'

Boltikov said in his heavy English, 'We wait for pay day,' which made Jones smile.

'So tell us,' I said.

'When we left the US there were six in our unit. Four have copped it, three from tif and one from falling into Vladi harbour between two vessels. So I have to press-gang men as I go along to put up the aerial. Hundred and twenty foot to be swayed up and guyed. Not a job for Stiffy and me alone. End of story.'

'You want a labour force.'

'Yep, that's it,' he said, looking me straight in the eye.

Obviously the two were in it together, the wireless king and the cryptographer. They'd got hold of something juicy. Had to be the gold. Everyone was hot for it. Why should they be any different? They couldn't bring it off by themselves: they needed us. To be precise, they needed my armoured locomotive and my driver and my workforce – *nota bene*, my reliable workforce, not dying of tif or getting squashed to death.

I said, 'Leapforth, let's not play games. Where's the gold? Now, as we speak?'

147

That big white smile again. 'I like a man who pitches fast. The answer is, Kazan. The Czechs and the Whites recaptured the city last week. They plan to ship the gold east in barges. Kolchak wants to have it where he can see it.'

'And what you have in mind? – let me see if I can guess . . . It'd be frowned on in the States?'

'Right on, Charlie.'

'But in Russia, where the rule of law has gone down the pan—'

'Down deep, man, real deep.'

'Anything goes?'

'That's it,' he said. 'Morality – forget it. You can't find a trace of it in Strabinsk. You should see what I get offered in my hotel room – every night.'

Wanting to put him right on that I said, 'Hold it there. I'm not here just for myself. If that makes me a man in a thousand, well, that's the way it is. I'm here for one thing only. Revenge. Revenge, full stop. The man I'm after is People's Commissar Prokhor Federovich Glebov. When I've nailed him, maybe I'll have time for your gold.'

'Man in a thousand, eh? That's a pretty high figure . . . OK, I wasn't making enough allowance for the sincerity of your motives. So revenge is your game . . . yeah, well, looking round Strabinsk when the news got out about the Tsar, I'd have said every single person here is hot for revenge . . . You'll have a good reason for going after Glebov, probably something he did to your family. That seems to be the pattern . . . So you're not interested in this gold story, have I got that straight?'

'Glebov first.'

'I see . . . Maybe I can help you, Charlie? How would that be for a deal, if I helped you with Glebov and you helped me into Kazan?'

'We could discuss that,' I said warily.

The next thing he said: 'You know, it's a different class of winner that surfaces in a revolution. Sure, the guys with the usual unpleasant qualities'll pop up, the vultures and the criminals, but to make it to the last cut . . . to have a chance at the big house . . . yeah, you've got to have one hell of a good story in a proper revolution, one where the whole system of living is up for grabs. Like you're the first man to discover how to make bricks or the first woman with tits. You get me?'

Thinking he was shooting a line for himself, I asked him what his story was. But he shook his head. 'Not me. Stealing gold ain't much of a story these days. I was thinking about some of those Reds we could be up against, the guys who've made it to the top. Trotsky and this Glebov of yours. They'll be as full of tricks as a pack of monkeys. Now, this is what I was thinking . . .'

The essence of his plan was to vanish from the US Army, he and Stiffy. Not to desert, but to get themselves artificially killed and thus disappear from the army's books. That was what really made him nervous: having the US authorities on his trail. So once they were dead they'd buy new documents from the counterfeiter opposite Blahos's office and when they made off with the gold, why, they'd just be regular desperadoes who'd got lucky.

'The papers, the witnesses to our execution, I can arrange them all. Then burial in a mass grave. I've got a photographer for that part, here in Strabinsk, name of Smichov. That's all that's needed. My wife's not going to send her lawyer to Siberia to sift through a heap of bones just so she can have a good weep. The kids neither. Pa was a soldier, so he got himself killed, that's how they'll reason. Stiffy here's only got a sister for a family—'

'Two.'

'OK, two. What's the second one called, Stiff? Back in Bristol, so how was I to know that? Older or younger? OK, she's the oldest of you three so what she's going to say is, That little Timmy was never going to come to any good, not snotting like he did. It's his just deserts. Forget about him . . . Listen to me, Charlie, Stiffy and I can check out of Strabinsk any time we want. Out of here, out of the army, out of our lives. No one'll be any the wiser. Anything goes. You said it yourself.'

Boltikov, seeming asleep, opened for me one brusque, bright, intense blue eye.

Stiffy was twiddling a hank of his anaemic ginger hair round his index finger, girly fashion.

Jones, looking directly at a vertical line drawn halfway between me and Boltikov: 'And you're no different, you two. You could vanish like us.'

I said, 'Why'd I want to do that? I'm not the one in the US Army.'

'OK, maybe you don't need to for the same reasons I need to. But you'll be the very first man to exist if you don't want – let's put it like this: to renew yourself. You name me a man who's not running away from something.'

'Didn't I just tell you, I'm a man in a thousand?'

We regarded each other in silence. Had I bought the Cinema Lux, this would have been the bit in the movie where my Russian audience would have stopped spitting out their sunflower husks – when the four gunfighters played a card game, loser to be hanged in the morning. Through their fantastic system of eavesdropping, Jones and Stiffy had uncovered information that was available to neither the President of the United States nor the King of England nor the Pope, the Infanta nor anyone in the entire and teeming billions of the world save Colonel Zak and a handful of top Bolsheviks.

I looked round the table, moving my eyeballs only. Behind each of the others' masks, I could make out the shape of a giant truth that was glowing red hot: that never again, though we were each to be immortal, would we possess the knowledge that could place 690 tons of gold in our possession.

Women – if you miss one, there are more on the way. Wealth isn't like that. It's not stacked up back to the horizon. It has to be earned.

Mouth at an angle, Jones said, 'You ain't no man in a thousand, Charlie Doig. That's bullshit. You're a scavenger just the same as Mister Ordinary.'

'Tell me what you know about Glebov. Blahos says he's nowhere near here.'

Jones picked up his pistol, aimed it casually through the window at bossy Mrs D. who was on platform patrol on that side of the train. 'Good-looking dame, the big one . . . your friend Glebov, People's Commissar for the Political Re-education of Prisoners, was in charge of the arrangements for the Tsar and his family. The late Tsar, God have mercy on him . . . You heard

Glebov was doing anything different, you were being fed bird-seed. He's one of the Big Three. Lenin, Trotsky, Glebov, that's the line-up. Glebov ran the show at Ekat. He had them shot. Except maybe his daughter Anastasia, the chubby one. I'm hearing a rumour that she survived and your fellow's trying to organise a ransom for her.'

I sat silently, trying to work out if that told me anything more about Blahos than he was a liar.

Jones snowed me with those teeth of his. 'That's first-class information I've just given you. See, Charlie, there's not much around here that I don't know. Do a deal with me and there'll be more.'

It enriches the spirit of mankind to be desired, especially after a period of down. Pressure builds again in the heart cavity and in the lungs. We are invigorated by a new form of oxygen, that of popularity. Our organs swell, our blood fizzles, our kidneys grind like fury and smash the toxins to pieces.

I smiled like a prince on Jones. Nevertheless I said, 'Glebov first.'

'Here's what I say to that,' he said, and sent a bullet between Boltikov's head and mine, shattering the window.

A scarf of blue smoke curled past the jagged ends of the glass. He said, 'Without our information you'd still be at base camp.'

'Without us you'll be digging latrines to hold red piss for the rest of your life.'

Stiffy said, 'The room was getting too warm anyway.'

I said to Jones, who was still in his chair, still holding his pistol, 'A bullet's a poor argument. Maybe it's a big thing in America, but in this country loosing off like that is a way of saying good morning.'

He said, 'Glebov's chasing the gold as well. I know it for a fact. Come with us and you'll get to meet him face to face. Is that a better argument?'

I said, 'But I give all the orders, understood?' and saw him nod. I said, 'And we split the proceeds four equal ways, understood?' and saw him nod. We shook on it. Then the door started to rattle and the handle to turn.

It was Xenia, in a state of high alarm after the shot. I scooped her up and kissed her until she squealed and the others went out grinning into the corridor.

I told her what had been said about Princess Anastasia. Her hand went to her throat. 'The poor love! I shall pray for her,' – which is what she did while I idly watched Mrs D., who'd been joined on patrol by Shmuleyvich.

Thirty-three

B UT HOW, practically, were the deaths of Jones and Brown
to be faked?

'Why fake them?' said Xenia, who saw the Americans as
competition. 'Why not do it for real?'

However, that wasn't the way to get at Glebov so I declined
her proposal. As it happened, it was Jones himself who solved
the problem of his own death.

Strabinsk gaol was on the far side of the city. From its
hanging shed a cart track led to the burial pits about half a
mile outside the city. At the moment the gaol was full, all the
Bolsheviks captured at Ekat having been sent down for
Muraviev to interrogate.

'Why didn't they shoot them there?' said Boltikov one afternoon. He'd come to tell me of Joseph's latest report, that a
huge new pit was being dug at the burial grounds. I called
Jones in. It could only mean one thing: that the gaol comman-
dant was going to exact his own revenge for the murder of the
Tsar.

'That's old Lev Stupichkin. He was born in the days when
the heroes of Russia danced mazurkas with their spurs on,' said
Leapforth. 'If he's going to exterminate a crowd of Bolshies,
that's our chance. Stiffy and I'll slip in there with the corpses.
Get it done in a flash.'

I thought, Christ, cartloads of bodies going to the dump and
he and Stiffy are going to volunteer to get in there among them?
To be tipped out higgledy-piggledy, legs and arms all over the
place? Uninhibited death and he wants to mimic it?

I looked up at him, washed, crisp, tanned, wearing his easy

American smile. 'How's that going to be, lying in a burial pit with a lot of Red stiffs?'

'You squeamish? Only needs to be done once. It'll be worth it. Smichov'll take some photographs as proof of our death. "Two of our gallant boys being chucked on the heap by the barbarians," that's what Consul Gray'll say to himself when he gets them. He'll have his clerk read out the covering note. "Captain Jones and Wirelessman Brown, that's who they are, sir," the fellow'll say. "Murdered by the Bolsheviks. That's them being buried." "Enter them as died on active service. Next!" says Gray. That way we'll vanish from the records. Nothing easier.'

But Stiffy was having none of it. 'I don't want to lie in other men's blood. My clothes'll stink. All right, sir, I know we'll burn them but I'll still have the smell in my mind. It'll stay with me till I die. I'll never be able to smell flowers ever again, not properly, know what I mean. Not roses, nothing like that.'

'Cut it out, Stiffy. Your share of the gold is worth eighty-two million US dollars. That's worth one hell of a pong.'

Stiffy snapped to attention, saluted. 'Beg pardon, sir, but I cannot do it. You know I was brought up as a Boy Scout. Courteous, kind, obedient, smiling, trusty, loyal, helpful, brotherly, thrifty: pure in body and mind, that's what our patrol banner read. Furthermore, sir, I must tell you that those dead men will have infectious diseases. I already have eczema behind my knees.'

'Stiff, I don't care about the Boy Scouts. I don't care about behind your knees. For eighty million bucks you'll jump in and get your tootsies dirty, you bet you will. Don't be so goddam sensitive. They're not going to bite you or breathe all over you, they're goddam corpses. What's got into you? For money like that?'

Two men work side by side for a time and there's always a price to be paid if one of them won't budge. Stiffy's price was that the baths at the station that had been lately closed down should be fired up again. He'd scrub the filth off, that's what he'd do, and then he'd have himself scourged with birch twigs. His strange blue eyes lit up. His buttocks would be of a spectacular whiteness, I knew it. Except for a strip of pink pockmarks up his crack where the fleas had been jostling for the extra warmth. Probably a little rasped where he'd been itching them. A hefty babushka'd lay into his meagre Christlike flesh with a besom and he'd go dancing and leaping and yelling, bollocks flapping . . .

He wasn't finished. 'I'll take that bottle of Vladimir that Mr Doig's got hidden in the water cistern.' He looked at me challengingly, but I thought, Good luck, and said nothing.

That satisfied him and we started to plan the folder of death that I would cause to arrive on the desk of Consul Gray.

'Leave some blanks,' growled Jones. 'This isn't just any old war, this is a war fought between savages in the centre of Russia. Who'd expect the reports to be apple pie?'

That said, he went off to find Smichov, the man who was to take the photographs, and to get the ground spied out. Xenia and I took a horse cab to look for her corset shop again. When I had my way she'd be settling down thousands of miles from Strabinsk but I wasn't telling her about that now. I was happy to be with her. So long as she wasn't in one of her Jesus moods, she had a neat, hard mind.

'If every woman could afford a corset, every woman would own one.' That was her philosophy. What woman wouldn't want to present the best figure possible to the world?

'Look at Krupskaya – where did she spend the first pay cheque Lenin got? Down at the corset shop, you can be sure of it. What have we got here in Strabinsk? Corsetable women – about twelve thousand. Put your mind to work on that, Charlie. Madame Zilberstein had only three hundred. That's what she grew fat on, three hundred women. She grew enormous. When she sat down she was like a rowing boat upright in the chair. So why do you think I'm mad? I can tell you do from your mouth.'

The cab jolted us over the dusty potholes. Strong black hair bulging out from under her lilac dust scarf, the huge green eyes, the bubbling lips, the downy jawline. Strabinsk was a vile place and her idea rotten. But I was enjoying her independence, her strength – her very presence. I adored it, didn't want to stop the words coming out of her. And thinking this to myself, plus being inundated by the absolute force of my delight in her, which left me gasping for breath, made me say something that I'd not intended.

Walking her away from the cab, hand in hand, I said, '*Moya dusha*, when this is over, I'm going to get you to Odessa. The British Consul . . . I still have papers proving who I am – the old documents from the expeditions with Goetz. There shouldn't be a problem. Then—'

'Then? Tell me, Charlinka.'

'Then I'll marry you.'

That's how it came out, crudely, not a bit like I'd meant. I gabbled on: 'I was thinking . . . if there's trouble . . . it's this, my plan. The Whites aren't going to win the war. The Bolsheviks have the discipline and what they think of as the just cause – the flame of righteousness and all that. And here's the point – should anything happen to me, then you, as Mrs Doig, would be able to get passage on a British ship. Just walk up the gangplank and wave goodbye to Russia. Tough, but at least you'd be safe.'

I raised her hand and kissed her knuckles. 'Does it make a man feeble if he loves his woman?'

She looked carefully into every corner of my face. She raked me with that look, cleaned me off down to the bone. She said, 'I never thought that I'd receive an offer of marriage from any man. Are you sure that's what you meant?'

'Yes.'

'Not something connected with Elizaveta, is it?'

Those eyes, I could hide nothing from them. And the truth of the matter was that she was right. Marrying her was my atonement for having killed Elizaveta. The whole thing was for my benefit. The instant the words had started to come out, I'd understood what I was trying to do. I'd taken one life, now I'd be saving one life.

And she'd picked up on it in a flash – had got me confused, made me falter. Beginning to sweat, I said, 'Your whole position would be improved. Dramatically.'

She was still looking straight into me. I knew what she was thinking: 'That's not a great line in a proposal of marriage.'

I said, 'I'm not a saint and never will be. But I love you. I'll give you protection. In times like these, that's what a woman needs most.'

'Love?' That's what she said, that one word, with a flick of an eyebrow.

Then she put her arm through mine and walked me over to where the cab was waiting. Quite gaily, she said, 'You're an attractive man, Charlinka. But would you be an attractive husband? I have to think about that.'

Thirty-four

WE SLUNK along the rails through the hot evening dust. On our right – to the south – lay the teeming mass of the city, brooding revenge not only on the murderers of the Tsar but on all associated troublemakers – semi-fanatics, sympathisers, waverers, even those who just believed that some adjustment to the system would be beneficial.

Stiffy, Jones and myself, just the three of us. Plus Smichov, whom Jones had arranged to meet where the railway track crossed the lane going up to the burial pits.

A little way past this point was the siding for the brickworks. Its owner had fled. Shmuleyvich was going to lay up there while we were busy.

Smichov was waiting beside the track with his brown leather suitcase and tripod. We got down from the train. Jones introduced him. I passed round a bottle of juniper brandy. We made some jokes. Shmuleyvich departed.

Bang on 7.30 p.m., just as we'd been told, the staccato rattle of machine-gun fire shattered the evening.

'Listen to that! Better than Strauss, better than the best music ever written!' Smichov stood to attention. 'God bless the Tsar and his family! God bless the Romanovs forever and ever!'

We waited. Presently there came a few pistol pops – the wounded were being finished off.

A little later the tumbrils creaked into view, three of them, horse-drawn. No black plumes here, no boots backwards in the stirrups, no muffled drums. Blood was dripping between the planks into the dust, that was the tone of this burial parade. The bodies were moving of their own accord as the carts rolled along – in particular the heads of those on the topmost layer, which were wagging and nodding.

A short distance behind was a small black carriage drawn by a white horse. A soldier sat on the bench beside the driver.

'Stupichkin, the prison governor,' said Jones. 'Probably has to sign a report to say he's seen them go into the pit.'

Stupichkin's guard waved us forward and we stepped into line behind the carts.

Stiffy was sweating like a brook, his cheeks the colour of wallpaper paste. Jones was upright and silent, chewing on something. Smichov was the talkative one among us. By counting the corpses he could see, which was in effect the top layer, and multiplying by the vertical number of layers, he was trying to establish how many Reds had been executed.

Conversationally he remarked, 'Look how many horizontal strokes there are in bodies when a pile of them's lying flat. Two arms and two legs for each to start with. Then the lines that originate from their boots – if they've been left with them. Even their hair makes lines. A photographer notices these details – hey, HEY, watch out, that bastard's still alive!'

It was a man in the second cart who'd chosen this moment to be resurrected. A clenched and bloody fist was rammed into the air. A second or two later – groans, very deep, from the bottom of the scale, as of a cow calving. Tousled hair appeared over the side as he strove to raise himself: bandaged forehead, eyes as blue as gentians, nose, mouth, beard – they appeared in turn, his face streaming blood except for those eyes, which were of so startling a blue that they might have been screwed in by a jeweller.

He hauled himself up. The blood, somebody's blood, was down his neck and down the front of a once white shirt. Backwards and forwards he swayed, bubbles of blood forming at his mouth as he attempted to speak.

The carts bumped to a halt. The fellow was jolted off balance. He slumped forward over the side of the cart, his body folded at the waist and hanging down – his arms in their white martyr's shirt, his long dirty brown hair, the loose end of the bandage round his head, all of them pointing at the dust.

Smichov had his tripod up in a tick, I never knew it could

be done so fast. He came out from under his black cloth and started shouting, 'Yes! Yes! Kiss the cart, whore! Your last kiss before you get to the Devil's arse.' Running over to the man, he seized him by his hair and started to crash his face into the side of the cart – one, two: one, two, rhythmically. 'Watch his teeth fly out, boys! You over there,' – to one of the carters – 'get ready for a catch.'

He paused in his rhythm to speak to the wretch. 'Have I broken your nose, Mr Lenin? Pray pardon, for I am but a clumsy boorjoi.' The bloodied face, in which only the eye surrounds were white, which Smichov was holding up by the hair to speak to, suddenly convulsed. A spout of blood flew from his mouth, spattering Smichov's linen trousers. He jumped back: 'You filthy Red traitor . . . you dirty little sod, you . . . Look what you've done to me.'

The man somehow raised his head. I could see right into his mouth, could see the struggle his tongue was having to get the words out, all its knots and contortions:

'Long live the people of Russia! All power to the Soviets!'

And then, even more extraordinarily, this so-called corpse shook his head and, by pressing his hands flat against the top rail of the cart, started to push himself erect.

Kneeling on the bodies beneath him, he faced me. I had the impression that it was me alone he was speaking to. '*Svoboda! Ravenstvo! Bratsvo!* Believe nothing else! I shall not die!'

'Oh yes, you will,' cried a soldier, clambering up the mound of slippery corpses.

'My strength is greater than the sun, my words are a library, the force that is within me will never perish . . .'

Now the soldier was balancing above him, feeling for a foothold. The setting sun was directly behind the soldier. He was in its very centre and thus was turned from a shoddy conscript into a statue of black marble in which no feature of his face was discernible. He stood poised, magnified by the sun. His rifle was at an angle above his head, the butt readied to club the man beneath him. The military cap, the vindictive nose, the thick spraddled legs wound round with puttees, they were above me – then down they came and there commenced the barbaric pounding at the man's skull and the sounds arising from this, which included not even one small prayer or sigh of regret but consisted solely of thuds ranging from hard to soft and interspersed among them the unceasing and stupid oaths of the soldier.

I looked away. Each blow was terrible. The man must have died immediately. But still the blows rained down. I heard someone retch behind me. Turning I saw Stiffy sitting on the ground with his hands over his ears. Jones – I can't remember.

But beside me Smichov was egging the soldier on, driving his fist into the palm of his hand. At the end he said to me, 'Do you know what the Reds did to that man's family, in front of his very eyes? If you did, you wouldn't blame him. No one could.'

The soldier climbed down grinning. The carters returned to their tumbrils. We started off again to the burial pits.

Behind followed Stupichkin in his black box, like a priest.

The flies arrived in their millions. Their noise was unbelievable. A roar, that was how it reached me.

We came to a stinking rivulet coated with a yellow mousse of foam from the brickworks. The carter cracked some grisly joke as we hopped up beside him to save getting our feet wet, but I couldn't understand his accent. Laughing, he pointed with his whip at the sleek, waterlogged shapes of dead rats drifting beneath the foam as the passage of our wheels stirred it up.

At the top of the bank was one of Strabinsk's slums. Pye-dogs came slinking out from underneath the huts. They were after the human blood, to get their fill of protein. No one made any attempt to keep them away. When the horses began to trot, so did the dogs, their loose, ringwormed dugs jiggling in time to the slapping hoofs. It would have been comical if it hadn't been so disgusting.

The more educated a person is the less he understands about survival. He thinks that because the learning of it is arduous, the fact of it must therefore be sophisticated. There is nothing sophisticated about survival. The next breath, that little puff, that colourless, weightless, invisible essence, that's what counts. What comes after it? Not known by any soul – and in fact unknowable. But at least one is alive: at least one can hope that the next instalment will bring an improvement. The pye-dogs knew that. The aristos and musicians in the shot-up train – they did not.

What about Stupichkin, how much did he know about survival? Beyond caring, if he was the age that Jones said. I looked over at his carriage. Some of the yellow foam was still on the spokes of its wheels. A panel in the side was open. He was staring at me, his face a glimmer of white in the back.

The soldier sitting beside the driver beckoned to me, making it clear that I and no one else was intended. I walked over.

Stupichkin's sallow face peered at me from beneath secret eyelids. He laid his hand on the sill: nothing but bone to his wrist, then a ruffle and a sleeve of pink-striped seersucker. He said in a soft, careful voice, 'I know who you are. Misha Baklushin was your godfather. You buried him.'

'I wish that it weren't true, Excellency, but it is.'

'His mother, Lydia, the pianist – I was married to her once. Your father – Pushkin, as we called him. I knew him too. Come to my quarters when this business is over. I have some information for you.'

Thirty-five

THE COLUMN moved on, closer to the burial pit. Walking beside Stiffy, I said, 'Chin up.' But he was done for. His scalp had caught the sun earlier in the day. He had a white handkerchief over his head knotted at its four corners. He shambled along, stooping and dreadful.

I said, 'Don't be so anxious. You'll soon be someone else.'

The pye-dogs continued to lap at the blood dripping from the carts. Not bothering with the frame for its toes, Smichov whipped up his tripod and took a photo of them. 'I'll sell it to Muraviev's paper with the caption, "Dogs and Bolsheviks sup from the same bowl." They'll enjoy that in town.'

'You'll be eating those dogs soon,' I said. 'Wouldn't surprise me at all.'

'Not a chance. Killing the Little Father was a terrible error. People will really turn against the Reds now. I give them a fortnight, a month at the most. Our armies'll roll them back like carpets – into the sea, into Poland, Germany, I don't mind where. We'll send their heads bowling down the streets, lots of chopped-off heads with those filthy ink-stained beards their sort grow to show they're not women. But they are. They're red cunts, that's what they are, useless to everybody. Now let me get these photographs done so I can go and have my dinner.'

In no other country of the world is human life valued so cheaply. The proof was in front of me in those pits. And it was in the odour that rose from them, of decomposing flesh. Once experienced, the smell of rotting humans is impossible to forget simply because of the associations that accompany it.

I thought, one slip and I could be down there with them.

It wouldn't have to be my slip. Someone a bit drunk, someone who took me for a Romanov prince, someone who wanted to try out a new pistol or someone who just hated me on sight: for any of those reasons I could be down there in the swelter.

Or stuffed into a hole in the forest, at any rate tossed out of life.

Elizaveta – I took a deep breath. It was what I'd done to her. What Glebov had started and I'd finished. I'd shot her through the temple, aiming for that mole, from three paces. It hadn't been Glebov who'd squeezed the trigger. It was I. But it was he who'd loaded the pistol and pointed it.

That was how it stood between us, between the three of us you could say – four, if you counted Death itself.

Yes, you had to count Death as a person. He was always there, behind the screen or not, whichever he chose. Watch in hand, tapping out the seconds left. Striking through names on the register – address, occupation, collar size, the lot: mopping his brow and thinking about humping his girlfriend, Time. The two of them, deadly conspirators. Barren, thank God, like Lenin. There were some people in the world of whom a single example was quite sufficient.

Harden up, Charlie, I said. Nothing is wretched unless you think it is.

I looked down at the pit before me. It was no wonder the priests were so powerful in Russia. Not much religion was needed to believe that what lay down there was a mass of sins, writhing and spitting like snakes, trying to crawl out and get among the population. I offered thanks that Xenia wasn't with me. No woman should have to face such a scene. The bodies, the dogs, Smichov the twizzle-moustached photographer getting copy for the newspaper – for the benefit of posterity, detailing what men were capable of.

It was awful what was happening. I swore that from now on I'd treat Xenia with unfailing compassion. In fact all women, until I died. Their burden of responsibility was too great. It wasn't their fault that from their wombs came forth tyrants and the like, real monsters screaming for power from the word go. But of course it was they who got the blame, the fathers waltzing away scot-free. And accepted it, went staggering beneath its weight for the rest of their lives.

So on behalf of womanhood I'd take Xenia to Odessa and make her Mrs Doig. The children we'd have would be beautiful. I'd do my share of raising them. They'd call me Papa, slide their trusting hands into mine as we walked, get me to tell them stories—

'Watch your heels,' shouted a carter. He unfastened the traces and knocked out the backboard pins. The cart tipped up. The bodies slithered out of their own accord.

Stiffy stood on the brink of the pit, peering down expressionlessly. Jones was with Smichov, setting up the camera and getting it clear about the shots he wanted. Smichov had lit a yellow *makhorka* and was taking huge puffs from it, drawing his cheeks right in as if he were an underwater swimmer. He queried something with Jones, making a new camera angle with his hands.

Jones nodded, patted him on the back and went over to Stiffy: 'Eighty million dollars. One jump. Not bad.'

'Yes, sir.'

'Put your forage cap on.'

'Why, sir? It came off when I was fighting the Reds, didn't it?'

'You're right. Hold there, I'm going to sponge more blood over our faces.'

'Yes, sir. I'll just have to take a chance with disease, is that it, sir?'

'We'll go to the baths immediately. I said to the guy, have them hot by eight.'

'Yes, sir.'

'Stiffy, believe you me, you'll never be poor again.'

'I would like that, sir. Bristol docks are no place to be poor. If you saw my home, you'd say, "Stiffy, why the heck didn't you get out sooner?" Is the geezer over there ready? Then I'm jumping. Mr Doig, sir, fetch me that box from over there, would you? I'll do it off that. It'll look more like the real job.'

He balanced on it, Jones holding onto his tunic. Smichov hid himself under his black cloth. The carters stood back looking bemused. There was a click as Smichov inserted the plate. He raised his hand. Jones gave Stiffy a shove.

He was inspired – I'd never have believed it of him. He'd thought how a corpse would appear as thrown by two men and he did it, hurling himself sideways like a bolster. When he landed his body collapsed into the careless position of the dead lying all round him. His blue eyes stared right up at me, not blinking, his jaw slack and his mouth open.

Smichov was moving around beneath the black cloth as he inserted a second plate. His head came whipping out. He shouted to Stiffy, 'Don't move, Yankee corpse,' and squeezed the bulb with the same hand that held his cigarette.

Jones was stilted in his method of falling, even though he took a run at it. But it'd be good enough to convince Consul Gray. If anyone began to say, That guy wasn't thrown, he jumped – if an expert got around to studying the photographs closely, they'd be busted, that was all there was to it. But it was good for a pair of amateurs, good enough.

They lay together, overlapping, criss-crossed, bloody. The flies were going in and out of Stiffy's mouth.

Smichov asked if that was it. Just then I saw that the creases in Jones's tunic were too sharp. Men who'd been fighting the Reds for a day and a night without food or water shouldn't be looking as if they'd just marched off the parade ground. I jumped down and lugged one of the corpses over so that it was sprawled across Jones and obscured the evidence. I climbed out. Smichov took a last plate.

'Thank God for US Army boots,' said Leapforth as he oozed his way to the edge, where I was waiting to give him a hand up.

'We'll deal with all these rags back on the train,' he said. 'We'll have Shmuley burn them in his furnace. Civvies! I've got myself a nice blue cotton shirt awaiting me, and summer slacks, special lightweight for Siberia, and a natty blazer from Scott's in Main Street. Two-tone shoes, long fawn socks, all that I need to be John S. Piler, haberdasher from Columbus, Ohio. You guys want to test me on my life history? Parents, parents' parents, schooling, dates, football, all that sort of stuff? You're welcome. Come right in, folks, and spread yourselves around, door's wide open. Any time you think you're getting to my true line of work, I'll wink and say, Munitions, old fella, leave it at that. John S. Piler, thirty-five, nice wife, two kids, great to see ya.'

'Leapforth – by losing that name, you lose some distinction,' I said.

'Hell no! I only got that stuck on me because my ma and pa were friendly with a preacher fella and thought to oblige him. Leapforth! I'll be glad to see the back of him. Stiffy here – what name did you choose, Stiff?'

'Dave Cram. One of the crew on the boat to New York was called Cram. I was in love with him. He never knew about it. I've always wanted to be a Dave.'

'Nothing in the middle?' I asked.

'Dave Cram'll do me fine, sir.'

'OK, Dave . . . goddam these pesky flies,' Jones said. 'Stiffy, cut the regimental buttons off before Shmuley burns our tunics and throw them in a lake somewhere. Can't be too careful.'

'Yes, sir, and then I'm going to take Mr Doig's Vladimir and get drunk. Even for eighty million dollars I wouldn't do that again. If I don't scrub every inch of my skin it'll get infected and turn grey.'

'First thing in the morning we'll go to the passport place that Jew runs. He'll fix us with new papers in a day.'

'Blahos'll have a stake in that business, I shouldn't wonder,' I said.

Jones said, 'Every game you can think of is going on in Strabinsk. What worries me is whether he'll have the blank sheets for American passports. It has to be a special weave, as I recall. Special watermarks too. I don't want to have to become a citizen of Panama or some goddam anyoldwhere like that.'

I said, 'At the very least he'll have Brazilian paper. That's where all the crooks head for.'

Which I said encouragingly, grinning, for they deserved a pat on the back for having jumped into that pit. But what was actually on my mind was the extreme difficulty they'd have running all that gold out of Russia and then converting it into fluffy clouds of happiness.

Thirty-six

THREE HUNDRED and forty-five tons of gold would fall to Jones and Stiffy. No burden at all for a boat once it was aboard. It was on and off that'd be the problem areas. And getting value for it.

They'd entered Russia at Vladivostok and come up the Trans-Sib. It was what they knew: it was how they'd want to get out. But Admiral Knight and the US Navy were anchored in Vladivostok harbour. They wouldn't fancy running that gauntlet. So they'd be looking to do something nifty at Chita and transfer on to the Chinese Eastern Railway. Who was top man down there? The animal Semenov was in it somewhere. He'd want a good chunk. So bye-bye 10 per cent. Then south through Manchuria via Harbin and its fleapits and its counter-feit countesses whose glacé silk petticoats would make a soft frou-frouing that an outdoor man could easily mistake for the murmur of bulrushes. Oh perils most horrible for Stiffy! But they'd get through somehow and reach Port Arthur.

There they'd meet a delay occasioned by a savvy customs officer who'd take to wondering about the contents of so many identical packing cases that required two coolies a case. So off would go another 5 per cent, a customs officer having only half the clout of Semenov. But in the end they'd decide it was worth the price, a deal would be struck, and they'd get to dockside.

Through the China Sea their vessel would glide, a swish schooner powered by the new Gardner diesel that had indi-vidual cylinder heads. No flag would be flown. Though Dave Cram had sworn to keep his pinkies off the Marconi wireless set, he'd still stroll along and, um, just cock an ear to the maritime radio traffic – listening through one headphone only and so not calling down the wrath of John S. Piler, who was now much exercised by the difficulty of finding a private buyer, cash only, for what remained of the dead Tsar's gold.

Obviously they'd play mah-jong, which they'd learned while delayed by that customs officer. By day they'd drink green tea, infused with an oriental tincture to loosen their anxious American bowels. By night the best clarets in the world would be theirs, which in the hands of their previous owner, the last Prince Kuprin ever to exist, had travelled from Bordeaux to St Petersburg to Moscow to Harbin where the Prince and his Princess had died from stab wounds inflicted on them by a maniac in the bar of the Hotel Popov.

They would start to grow a little chubby.

The voyage would continue with apparent serenity. The fish would fly: the sea would sparkle: the rigging would moan and the Chinese crew remain obedient. To pass the time, Dave would compose a number of decrypt exercises for John S. The latter would solve them all solely by observing closely the shapes taken by Dave's mouth, which he'd watch as diligently as if he were a deaf man attending choir practice. He'd never ask for a reprise, never write anything down. With his yachting cap pulled well down against the dazzling marine light, he'd just stare and stare at Dave until he found the answer.

Try as he may, Dave'd be unable to think of enough keywords without letter repetition. Piler would twig everything and criticise him for lack of originality.

Unflagged, incommunicado, the good ship *Anonymous* would plough its furrow across the Pacific Ocean. In its hold there'd now be only about two hundred and eighty tons of the reddish gold.

So where'd be the buyer with a hoard of cash? Would they find him in Valparaiso or have to run the Horn to Rio? But would the Chinese crew stand for all that rough and tumble with the waves? Another thing, the Gardner had been spluttering a bit of late. How the devil did one clean that new type of cylinder head? It'd never do to be without power off Cape Horn . . .

And what was to be done if they failed to find a buyer? Would they have to hole up on a remote island, eyeing their unsaleable gold as they eked out the last of the Smith-Haut-Lafite and listened to the patter of coconuts?

I couldn't see happiness anywhere. I could see nothing but worry and the potential for misadventure.

I said to Leapforth, 'Fat lot of fun that gold'll bring you. You might as well stay ordinary folk.'

'Man,' he said, 'you're welcome to your opinion. Meanwhile, I'm for the baths with Stiffy, to wash everything away and start my life as John S.'

I left them to it and walked over to Stupichkin's black carriage. The door swung open. Bending my head, I mounted the two steps and sat down beside this crumbling old man.

Thirty-seven

'I HAD THE prisoners brought out of their cells and gathered below me. I said, "Do you want to be shot in the evening or in the morning?" I could have had them shot at any time I wanted. I thought they should be given the choice since the only reason they were being shot – well, there was actually no reason, not as a Frenchman would understand the word. Because they'd been captured, that's as close as you could get.'

In the centre of his desk, on a square of black velvet, was a skull. He picked it up, hopped it around on his fingertips. 'My second wife, not the mother of poor Misha Baklushin. This woman, to whom I would gladly have given all my chances of going to Heaven, died in a carriage accident. I had the greatest difficulty making her head my own. Religion, undertakers, tradition, you can imagine the barriers.'

I murmured about letters and pressed flowers in a book and even photographs being not quite the same.

'Yes,' he said. 'With a skull you know where you are. You can speak to it without feeling you're going gaga. Your people, they have similar feelings so they don't look queerly at you . . . It's good to have your company, Doig. Your father was quite a scamp, you know, always getting into one trouble or another. Your mother . . . But that's all in the past. Everything worthwhile is in the past. How were we to know that what we were doing was wrong? We'd been doing it for centuries. No one ever thought before that it was wrong to have servants or money. Yet now that little tradesman fellow is calling us names that were only ever used for the devil. Thank God I'm not young.'

He gave the skull another twirl. Puffed at the eye sockets, dusting them. 'We never had children, no little Stupichkins. The doctors said her shelf was lying the wrong way. I'm glad. To have one's children die before one must be an unspeakable pain. And today they might well die first, you know. There's so much mischief around. Whenever peasants take over, you get bad government . . . Misha Baklushin, my stepson, he was the closest I got to having a child. Lydia, his mother – we remained friendly. When I became a widower and got sent here, she would write to me almost every month.'

'Was that how you heard about Misha?'

'Yes. It was the most frightful letter I ever received. Misha, your cousin Nicholas – and of course your wife.'

'Elizaveta.'

'Yes, Elizaveta née Rykov, the same as your mother's family. You did a brave thing. I could never have done that to either of my wives. I loved them too much.'

We were drinking vodka. His drawing room was on the first floor. Below the window the soldiers were changing guard. The windows were open, the curtains undrawn except for a light muslin drape to keep the insects out. There was enough of a wind to make them bulge, a hot wind coming up from the deserts in the south.

He said, 'Everyone knows why you're here. Blahos tried to get rid of you because he and Muraviev hope that when the gold pops out from Kazan, it'll pop down their throats. They don't want a man like you around.'

I smiled and raised my glass to him.

He said, 'I can see why. When I first saw you, I said to myself, If he's only half the man his father was, I'll help him. Come to the window with me.'

The floodlights were on. The compound was octagonal in shape. At each angle was a blockhouse covering the smooth glacis where they reckoned to kill any attackers who got through the coils of barbed wire.

'The greatest danger is from within,' Stupichkin said. 'One of these days the prisoners will attempt a breakout – and my guards will not resist. It'll happen as I say. The Reds are certain to win. We have nothing to set against the notion of equality.

172

When they do so, they'll murder me as painfully as they can . . .
Those machine guns of mine down there, they have a water-
cooling jacket that surrounds the barrel. In winter there is often
no water, but there is always snow. The design of the jacket is
so bad that it is impossible, or at least very hard, to stuff them
with snow. If a soldier is in a hurry he can't afford to boil up
the snow. Otherwise they fire when wanted and will kill
Bolsheviks if fired accurately. Therefore I am giving you two of
them, here and now. Do you have a little . . . ?'

He stroked the palm of one hand with the fingertips of the
other, smiling delicately as he did so. 'Something in the Tsarist
currency will keep my men happy . . . scarlet would be the best
colour . . . yes, two thousand is a perfect sum. Now what else
do you need, Doig?'

'I have two objectives. The first, to kill Glebov—'

'That's what my information concerns. Second?'

'To seize the gold in Kazan and get out of the country.'

'For which purpose you will of course need to get into Kazan.
If the Whites are holding it, you need no disguise. But if Trotsky,'
– his wizened monkey's face twisted passionately – 'who is the
most unprincipled monster in the universe, has taken it, you'll
need something. We can help you with Red Army clothing, from
the men we executed . . . Also, ammunition for the machine
guns, *bien entendu*. I will give you six boxes with a thousand
rounds in each. What else does a modern caballero need?'

I asked for an armoured car, at which he laughed. 'If I had
one, I'd set off in it right now for America. But I'll tell you
where you can find one – in Blahos's yard. Go past his office
keeping it on your left, down the lane that opens up in front
of you and at the end you'll find his compound. He may keep
a soldier sleeping in the car . . . What else, what else to defeat
the Bolshevik? Of course you know why I'm doing this. Because
I'm as good as dead, because of your father, because – because
I wish to make a clear and unmistakable contribution to the
civilisation that has born and nurtured me. My country has
served me well – it has kept me going for seventy-seven years!
Now I shall return something to it . . . Horses! You must have
your own cavalry! What can I have been thinking of!'

He drained his glass, throwing his head back. He drew a

handkerchief from the lace at his wrist and wiped his lips. He smiled up at me. 'Smash them to pulp, Doig!'

We started to move downstairs, when suddenly—

'Wait! I haven't told you about Glebov. The most important thing of all.'

I now learned everything that Stupichkin had extracted from his prisoners.

On the subject of Anastasia, the unaccounted-for princess, nothing was certain except that men had been withdrawn from each Bolshevik regiment to search houses round Ekat as well as every train that left the city. Some of the men sent to Stupichkin as prisoners had taken part in the train searches, pulling at women's hair to see if it was a wig and making them stand up and be measured in their stockinged feet.

'Where is the Princess? I don't know. But Glebov doesn't have her. I interrogated his driver. On 24 July, the day before Colonel Zak and his Czechs entered Ekaterinburg and a week after the Tsar and his family disappeared, Prokhor Federovich Glebov got into a Wolseley six-cylinder motor car with new tyres and was driven south-west towards Kazan. He was alone except for his bodyguard. At Sarapul the driver handed him over to another one. This man then tried to return to Ekat but was nabbed by Zak's men at a roadblock and sent down to me. Glebov's talk in the car concerned what was to be done if Kazan fell to the Czech forces. This has now happened. So we must suppose that he's near Kazan, probably having joined Trotsky whom all reports agree is massing his armies for a counter-attack.'

'Do you have proof that Glebov's after the gold?'

'That's a silly question. Nothing can be proved during a revolution. There is one thing more, Doig. I have known you were on the way for a fortnight. Three separate men have told me of this. Blahos also knew it, independently of my information. Strabinsk is a nest of spies. Do you suppose that Glebov has heard nothing about you?'

Something in his parchment face caught my eye, some flicker of ambiguity. I said suggestively, 'I wonder what he'll hear when I leave your house.'

He sighed deeply and laid his hand on my sleeve. 'The horror that we have of a violent death doesn't stem from the fact of death itself but from our unpreparedness. When I die I wish to do so with dignity. For that I may need assistance from my enemy. There, you have your answer. During the long span of my life I have concluded that truth exists nowhere except in certain mathematical data. If I make two pronouncements with opposing meanings, it doesn't mean that one of them is a lie. Whichever happens is the truth. Truth exists only in the past.'

He calmed me, this small old man who didn't even come up to my shoulder – 'You wish to see an avenue stretching out before you and to know that this road only is the one paved with sincerity, honesty and decency. I'm sorry. It's impossible to live without lies. Every human comes to realise this. Maybe you are starting to discover it too when you make love to your young lady. There may be times when you tell her something that is not up to the highest standards of Christian truth. If that is indeed the case then be tolerant, I beg you, and when you remember old Stupichkin, think of him as a radish – a red skin maybe, but round the heart and in all the vital areas, white as the snow. Now come. Let me give you these weapons I spoke about.'

A duty soldier was at the door to his rooms. Stupichkin told him to go and fetch his sergeant.

Thirty-eight

THE MACHINE guns were to go forward of the cab on either side of the locomotive. It wasn't ideal. Without swivelling turrets an armoured train has limited offensive potential but I didn't have time to get into that branch of engineering.

Moreover, two machine guns took up the services of two men. They could only be Boltikov and Kobi.

I said to Stupichkin, 'Muraviev's got one of my men. Seen a Mongolian around the city? He'll be unhappy by now, 'll be chewing his whiskers.'

He asked his sergeant. Yes, such a man had been seen. No one had been able to understand why a member of the great warrior nation had got mixed up with a layabout like Muraviev.

The sergeant had got an off-duty detachment to wrestle the machine guns onto a large station trolley. Some sacks of Red uniforms were thrown on top of the ammunition boxes. A piebald was led round to be hitched up, not a handsome horse but with solid quarters and good bone.

It shuffled forward into the floodlights with alert, suspicious movements of its head, which I saw were caused by the fact that it had a wall eye. Its name was Buran, meaning gale or tornado. It regarded us each in turn, expressively, probably out of hunger. As he was being backed up to the trolley, I heard a seashore slapping noise and, looking beneath him, I saw that we had a stallion.

'Christ, how did he get past the pincers?' I asked the sergeant, who was standing between me and Stupichkin.

Stupichkin smiled – they both smiled. The cavalry requisitioning department refused to accept piebalds because they stood out so much. The enemy invariably concentrated their fire on them. No cavalryman would accept a piebald for a mount. Therefore all the farmers naturally wanted to breed piebalds and keep the requisitioning men away. Tornado was in demand.

'Now you understand the fullness of my generosity,' said Stupichkin.

'Whoa, Tornado, whoa,' I addressed him as he began to play up, I suppose having masculine pride about pulling a station trolley through town. 'It's dark, no one'll see you.'

Looking into his wall eye, I saw that it was exactly the same vivid blue as those of the man who'd been bludgeoned to death on the cart. The other eye was wonderfully quick and virile, almost human. I said to that horse, 'Hairy hoofs or not, I must ride you through Kazan or die,' and because of Stupichkin's vodka and perhaps also through being light-headed in reaction to the gruesome episode at the pit, I saw myself in a wall-eye-blue pyjama suit riding bareback on Tornado with Glebov's severed head at my saddle-bow, his livid blood flowing like sauce onto my curling vizier's slippers—

Stupichkin had taken a pinch of my coat and was leading me out of the floodlights. He checked none of his guards were within earshot. 'Kazan, sometime in the first week of September, that's when Trotsky'll attack. The Czechs'll fight like rats. The second day'll be chaos. That's when you should go in.'

This time I didn't even begin to wonder how he knew that. I thanked him and said goodnight. However, he was reluctant to let me go. Did I want a hand or two of Boston? One for the road? I wouldn't try any rough stuff with Blahos, would I? He'd be a vindictive adversary . . .

In the end he gave up – grabbed and hugged me as if I were his son, I suppose also saying farewell to what could never be repeated, the Russia into which he'd been born. Tears were pouring down his cheeks.

He stood back. He said harshly, 'Well, goodbye then, Doig. We'll never meet again.'

I bowed to him – and led Tornado and the trolley of weapons away with the old feeling of machine guns trained on my spine. At the gatehouse the soldiers lamped back to the gaol for clearance to let me go. It came immediately – a stutter of flashes – and they conducted me through a maze of barbed wire and left me on the cart track that went up to the burial pits and thus to the railway.

We set out for the train, Tornado and I, the horse at my elbow, snuffling and rattling his bit.

The moon was riding above the city, our Russian moon. It was impossible to suppose that this was the same moon that shone over any other country, for Russia is a world complete in itself and has no need to share a moon with another nation any more than it needs to share its vast rivers, lakes and mountains, its language, its God, its savagery. How could there be any moon left over for anyone else after it had peered into our forests, silvered our endlessly winding rivers and climbed the peaks of the Tien Shan? It must have been possible, for every school textbook told us it was, but in my heart as in the heart of every Russian, the moon was ours, and so were the stars. It was in Russian pockets that God slipped them for the duration of the day, deep down there, tingling in the furs. And here they were once more on display, spread out above me, a wreckage of sparks scattered over the immenseness of our Russian skies – and I thought again how strange it was that in the pit of a civil war that could have been waged by no other nation on the earth, I should find two Americans bumping along with only the haziest notion of the dark forces around them.

Could it really be as simple as Jones said? That the President had given them a wagon of expensive wireless equipment and said, 'Go find out what's happening at a little place called Kazan. Can't be more than one of them on longitude 50. Off you go now, boys, and no slacking while you're out of my sight.'

Was that how power worked? And then the sweet odour of gold had risen to Leapforth's nostrils and he'd jumped into a pit of corpses and lo and behold was now John S. Piler whom no one would ever finger for having once been Captain Jones of the Black Chamber.

I said to Tornado, 'Somebody came to me with a tale like that I'd say to him, "Do I look like a flat-earther?"'

Thirty-nine

M Y TRAIN wasn't where I'd left it: Shmuleyvich had obviously taken Stiffy to the baths on the far side of town. Having no intention of leaving my new weapons unguarded and no wish to have Blahos wander by and find all these sacks of Red Army uniforms, I sat on the loading ramp of the brickworks and waited for his return.

The moonlight bounced off Tornado's good eye, giving him a rakish look. Tam o' Shanter, my old father would have named him – probably with a few complimentary verses in his stalwart Scottish declaiming voice. It was a curiosity finding in the gaol of this frontier town a man who'd known him well enough to call him a scamp. Which man had given me two machine guns complete with ammo and the rectangular black japanned tin boxes that held all the different-sized spanners and keys with which to disassemble them – and a horse.

Stroking Tornado's nose, I said to him, 'Don't want to be uncivil, old fellow, but even if I had ten thousand of you, it'd make no difference. You're old hat. There are subs under the sea, tanks on land, Camels and Fokkers in the air and a flotilla of motor torpedo boats on the Volga. Christ, there's mechanisation everywhere. Consider the tank. Thereby, a soldier's connection with the horse has been almost completely severed . . .'

I babbled on to him about the tanks the Bolsheviks had captured from the Germans. They had red stars on them now and a name painted on the hull – 'Sword of the Proletariat', 'Revenge', that sort of thing.

'Revenge is a good one. *Mest*'. Maybe I should get it painted on my loco. What do you say? And how come those bastards Jones and Stiffy were entitled to get a ride to the baths in my train, eh? Couldn't they walk? Thought they already had the gold in the bag, did they? Stiffy all excited with my bottle of 60 per cent Vladimir and a sachet of Roget et Gallet's Elixir of Carnations. To celebrate becoming Dave. I overheard him telling my woman about it. You'd never believe what men get up to, old fellow. Nor the lies they put about. That Jones and his damned smile – no woman could marry someone who smiled all the time like that. If you were a woman instead of a horse, could you lie beneath a man whose teeth were phosphorescent in the night like a shark's? I'm telling you, Tornado . . . Yet he's claimed a wife back in the States, in Grand Rapids . . .'

I fell to wondering what the horse smelt of so strongly. It was stale, it was musty – yet it was something more, like the smell of a new roll of felt.

He shook.

A piebald horse shaking in the moonlight, the beams bouncing back off the areas of white hair together with a spray of dust and mites . . .

So scampering Stiffy and toothy Jones had been chauffered to the baths at my expense and were steaming their impurities away without paying a blind bit of attention to the standard notice, signed by the Governor and therefore meant to be obeyed, oh my God yes, obedience compulsory except maybe in a revolution, 'Strictly No Farting'. They'd have volleyed away as they gulped down my Vladimir and would return all clean and precious whereas I—

I was rank, no other word for it. Was Xenia the same, was that why she didn't complain—

Like Cyclops, Shmuley came rushing out of the darkness, the single light on the front of the loco growing from the size of a ping-pong ball to a saucer to a bright white plate as he halted a few yards away, steam wreathing him as he leaned from the cab.

'That you, boss?'

'It isn't Karl fucking Marx so go and find me a horse wagon for Tornado here. How long did it take you to get round the loop and back to the station? OK, go round again. There's sure to be wagons at the station. Get two – I'm going to try for an armoured car. If the stationmaster objects, shoot him. Hitch up to the Yanks' wireless wagon while you're about it.'

'Boss, the spiv has bolted.'

'What does Mrs D. say to that?'

'Only really special men from now on, that's what she told me.'

'Then that's fine. Send Stiffy to me.'

He appeared soused with Vladimir 60 per cent and Elixir of Carnations. He'd got a babushka to trim his eyebrows.

I said, 'Stiffy, I don't give a shit that you're now Dave Cram. You've an hour to get cleaned off. Then your wireless'll be here and you're going to listen at that set day and night until you get word from me personally you can stand down. Yep?'

Hearing me speak, Xenia popped her head out of the carriage. I asked if she'd like to sit in the silky night air with me and Tornado for a while, but saying it in a rough voice from being tetchy.

'Why?' she said, because that's how her mind worked. I said to keep watch over two *machinkas* plus ammo plus Red Army uniforms while Shmuley went for wagons.

She agreed provisionally – so long as I guaranteed there were no Reds operating outside the city at night. 'If they crept up and cut your head off, where would I be then? This is exactly the sort of situation I fear most. I told you so, back in St Petersburg.'

I said, 'I keep a spare neck up my sleeve, now come on out of there and join me.'

She said, 'Is that a horse?'

I said, 'Yes. It's called Tornado and it's got a complete set of balls. Now come on down before I get impatient.'

Does one allow things to happen or does one force them? It's always the question. An optimist does the former. Musket balls beat against his cuirass like raindrops and he smiles: 'They're doing me no harm, see, I've got my armour on.' Idle men are also tolerant people. They say to themselves, If I lie in bed for long enough I'll die there, nothing worse can happen.

But I was aflame. The Reds'd be attacking Kazan in the first week in September. Glebov would be there. I wasn't like a woman who sniffs everything before tasting it, not just the milk. I was buzzing, cocked, hot to go.

Xenia was prickly, let go of my hand as soon as she was on the platform. I quickly discovered why: Stiffy had spilled the beans to her about the antics at the burial pits. She realised that she'd got into more than she'd bargained for – which was to have me look after her and set her up in business as a corsetière. She said she hadn't understood the Bolsheviks' true intentions. The black Fokker had really scared her and now this . . . It was disgusting what the two Americans had done. At least they'd been to the baths afterwards. Whereas I—

'I was never party to the change of identity,' I said, hearing the underlying change in her tone. 'What's it got to do with you anyway?'

'You've been drinking,' she said.

'I've had a scoop . . . What are you bawling about, you had enough men to protect you.'

'How can you go drinking and then tell Mr Brown off for doing the same thing?' she said petulantly. It seemed the moon was dodging round the sky. One moment I could see her expression clearly, the next her face was in shadow – or what was worse, half her face, so that I was continually glancing from one side to the other to see where reality lay.

I said, 'What's biting you, lady?'

She didn't answer that and didn't have to. She was afraid, that's what it was. The Thomas Cook railway tour of Russia that she'd signed up for had turned into something else. She was a shopkeeper. She was out of her depth. It'd be hell getting her to Odessa. She'd be a drag the entire way – and I'd proposed marriage to her.

I said with a kindly manner, 'It was that attack by the Fokker, it's just beginning to get to you, isn't it?'

'I can't get it out of my mind. We might all have been killed.'

'Then there would have been no cause for worry.'

'Do you want to make a scene out of this? Are you deliberately trying to misunderstand me? You . . . you . . . all I'm here for is so that you can reap me whenever you feel like it. Silly Charlie Doig, you're so puffed up with yourself, so arrogant . . .'

There was more, a great deal more about my character. She got hysterical – and jealous of Elizaveta. So *that* was the heart of the trouble, not the Americans jumping into the burial pit.

Everything came flooding out. It was crude of me to blame Elizaveta's death on Glebov when the decision had been mine and mine alone. Glebov was obviously a pawn of Lenin's, no worse than any other hired man. It had been I who was the bastard. I hadn't done all that I could have done to save Elizaveta. I'd been brutal – selfish – lacking any sense of decency, even of morality. She'd seen this side of me time and time again: she'd had enough – she wished to return to St Petersburg and Madame Zilberstein's shop.

'My girl, my darling girl . . .' Penitent yet manly, I took her in my arms and chuckled her until Shmuleyvich came clattering back with the extra wagons and Stiffy's wireless rig.

She was assuaged, but only somewhat. Most worrying from an operational point of view were occasional remarks about where my money was coming from. I thought, Did I let slip something about the diamonds in my boots when drunk? Had she unpicked the stitches and got in there with her little corset-maker's fingers? I didn't think so. I bent to scratch my leg and found the stitches were intact. Nevertheless there was a sweetness in her voice that didn't match up to her words – and I made a note to be extra careful. The moment Shmuley brought the train to a halt, I shoved her into a Pullman with my hand up her backside and said she could twiddle her thumbs for a bit.

Joseph sticking his head out, I told him he was in charge until I got back. I was going to take Boltikov into town to get hold of Kobi. I needed a full establishment. I wanted to get set up for action.

Forty

Kobi was no trouble. Not being a drinker, he had nothing in common with Muraviev's mercenaries. We found him on patrol – six men altogether.

I said to them, 'Which of you wants to get rich with me in Kazan?'

How rich, they wanted to know; what artillery would they have in support; which regiments would they be up against . . .

I made a mistake here: I spoke Trotsky's name, not knowing that in Muraviev's news-sheet that very day there'd been a quote from the bastard promising five hundred roubles and the enjoyment of a countess to whichever soldier raised the Red Flag above the kremlin of Kazan.

The patrol didn't like the idea of fighting against men going for that sort of reward. They flinched, I saw it in their eyes. I asked them if they'd seen Blahos around. They shook their heads. They couldn't have cared less about Blahos. They were thinking about five hundred in cash and making a countess squeal and which side was going to win.

I was sorry I couldn't recruit them. Numbers make everyone more confident. I did a quick check. Kobi, Boltikov, Shmuleyvich and myself made four full-time operatives. Joseph and Stiffy would be wasted on the firing step but useful elsewhere. Jones was a doubtful asset. Xenia – nix. Mrs D. – I'd score her half. She had guts. Anyway, not enough of us.

We got to Blahos's yard, which was exactly as Stupichkin had described. A dog wanted to give the game away until Kobi had a quick word with it. Now everything depended on Shmuleyvich being able to get the armoured car going. I was relying on him:

he was the fellow with engine grease down to the third layer of his epidermis. He viewed it thoughtfully.

'Well . . .' he said, stroking his chin.

I said, 'You'll be pushing it or else.'

Nettled, he opened the bonnet. I was keen to have this machine. It had two swivelling turrets set on the diagonal to make the car slimmer and a rear access door to them. Maxim machine guns. There was a headlight on the roof. Boltikov thought the glass in the front slots was bulletproof. We walked round it several times. Narrow wheels, so probably for road use only.

Shmuley called softly to me. He'd solved the problem of how ignition could be achieved in an Austin-Putilov 50 h.p. engine which had no key. It had fuel, he said, it had reverse gear: he could get it turned round and out in a minute, no more. He reckoned it'd shift along at about thirty, faster than anything else in Strabinsk.

The big man looked at us, smiling. He spread his arms wide. It was hard to say whether the shadows on him were shadows or puddles of oil. '*Pochemu nyet?* Why not, boss?'

He grinned, his teeth strong like the gates to a fortress. 'God be with Russia!' he exclaimed – and the armoured car burst into life, volleys of oily black smoke blasting from its exhaust and its metal sides rattling like a charity collecting box.

Boltikov and I jumped onto the running board one side, leaving the other one for Kobi and it was exactly as Shmuley had said. No one could have possibly caught us as we went rumbling through Strabinsk.

At the brickworks siding, nothing had changed except that Joseph had put the ramp down. Shmuley roared up it. He cut the engine. I opened the rear access door to see how we were placed for ammunition.

He was crouched there, very young, very white in the face, very afraid. It was Vaska, Blahos's nightwatchman.

I said, 'How old are you?' He was sixteen.

'How tall are you?' He didn't know.

So I had him come out of the turret and when he unfolded himself, showing that he was a good tall fellow and ruined only by starvation, I signed him up. 'Vaska,' I said, 'you're mine. Go and get the biggest meal of your life from Mrs D.'

Ten minutes later we were out of Strabinsk and going west – direction Kazan.

Forty-one

THE FIRST trick Glebov played on me – but before that I
have to say something more about Xenia, who by this time
had been my lover for nine months.

Her nature was open – also firm. I never knew her say anything
that didn't have a purpose. I don't remember her ever venturing
onto speculative territory, not even in relation to her religious
beliefs. God was there in the same way that gravity was: nothing
further had to be said. All that interested her about Lenin and
his policies was the effect they'd have on the price and avail-
ability of the basic foods and on the future of shops like
Zilberstein's. The grand theories passed her by.

What I'm coming round to is that she was dull. She
commanded no passionate arguments, had only niggling prej-
udices, wore no jewellery and had no feeling for bright clothes'
colours – by this stage a blouse of birthmark purple was her
sunniest garment. And here's another thing: she insisted on
hanging her clothes up every night. Before she said her prayers,
let's not forget to mention that too. Tidiness is good and our
compartment was modest. Nevertheless there are excellent
habits which pall on a man, such as constant telling of the truth,
obsessive hygiene and hanging one's clothes up.

For a woman with such astonishing eyes, a fine figure and a
good commercial mind, she didn't make the most of herself.
Not in conventional ways, I mean. That was because of her
vice. Sex was her secret, the means by which she kept on good
terms with the world.

One evening after we'd left Strabinsk, I came late into our
compartment. She was sitting on the edge of our bed, fully

187

dressed, holding in the candlelight a piece of foolscap covered with pencil jottings – figures for her planned shop.

I said something suggestive. I must have, I can't hold quiet before a desirable woman.

She looked up. 'You feel that way too? I was hoping so. I've got nothing on under my skirt.'

I said, 'Show me then,' hurriedly sitting down to unlace my boots.

She carefully laid her paper down out of harm's way. She stood upright on the bed. Crossing her arms, she pulled her skirt up to her forehead – then lowered it, peeping at me over its hem.

God! Her thick white thighs towering above me, her Hottentot's bush, her smooth belly, the dark noisettes of her nipples, those spanking green eyes – and yet she was so straight, so pedantic, so prudent in her character.

The fact is that within her sexual soul all these limiting factors had been wiped out. There was nothing there except balmy welcoming air which gave her flesh a sort of buoyancy. You could see it in her face too when you knew what to look for – the fullness of her lips in particular, and the way they strove to make contact. This was her secret, and it was impenetrable to everyone, both men and women, who lacked the magic key. It was why she didn't wear jewellery or fancy clothes: she didn't want to clutter up what was important to her and make it unrecognisable to those who might be attracted to her sexually.

I expect she'd had women in her bed as well. With that buoyancy went generosity and an absolute appreciation of the importance of dedicating some inviolable part of one's life to pleasure. In her case one part was consecrated to God, one part to screwing and the remainder to the struggle to remain alive. That was how she explained it to me.

So the 'vice' was a form of genius. She knew she was rare among women.

'I can recognise lovers from some way off and they me. There are signs – in the way of walking, how the body is carried, that's the first one. I never pay attention to the clothes, only to the person's eyes. It's mutual. We pair off immediately. There, in the street. One of us will know a hotel in the neighbourhood that caters for our type. Sometimes we don't exchange more than a few sentences. I never ask a man's name. I've never been disappointed.'

'Never?'

'Never. The best and only the best – oh, Charlinka, how lucky I've been. Not one man has wanted more of me than I've been willing to give.'

I can remember the conversation almost word for word. By then we were lying across the bed, both of us naked. My cock was splayed out across my thigh like a dogfish on the slab. She started to trifle with it.

Shmuleyvich had his foot down. The engine tugged, the greasy pistons acted and countered, the carriage swayed, rickety-tick rickety-tick. I looked down at her. Those exquisite lips came squirling up for mine.

'Only the best,' she murmured.

'Not for much longer. Top lovers will be executed by Lenin in the name of equality. We'd better hurry.'

'Will every man have to be equal to every other man? Is that what he means?'

'In all respects.'

'All?'

'I'll have an operation,' I said.

'Don't say that. I want you as you are.'

With perfect timing the train entered a tunnel. The rush of the wind changed tone and became hollow, boom-boom-boom, reverberating in my eardrums. We passed beneath an inspection shaft. For a second the noise emptied up it. Then with a sudden crack it was trapped again. Boom-boom-boom – and I entered the winner's enclosure.

Her breath just beginning to scurry, she grabbed at my buttocks, said, 'But equality is stupid.'

'What a thing to say now—'

'I like to have something else to think about in the middle stages. I've taught myself to hold the pleasure back for as long as possible, to heighten it.'

'And when it arrives?'

'It's as if I'm in a canoe and suddenly I burst through a wall of jungle into the treasure cave. Whoosh – oh, Charlie, what you do to me—'

I was still on the long strokes. We were bucketing along, lurching and swaying but when we came to the place where the goods lines from the Kushka quarries joined, a real labyrinth of points, we had to hang onto each other to stop being thrown out of bed. Binding me with hoops of iron, she whispered:

'—entire shelves of treasure stretching as far as the eye can see, glittering and fabulous, lit by cunning little lamps and the light shuddering with the excitement of it all – and then I think of Solomon's cock, which I see as sharp and tawny, not like a Russian cock at all, not thick and juicy, and that keeps me under control – oh my God, Shmuleyvich, get that whistle ready—' then she said nothing more, being busy with her orgasm.

We reached calmer waters. Her eyes cleared. The threads of longing dimmed from blood red to the colour of the air between us – air that had been somewhat jostled. I kissed in turn her little pink fruits and blessed them for their presence. Resting on my elbow, I traced the coastline of Africa round her tingling face, Libya being her forehead and the land of the Boer her doughty chin. Her great green eyes were the emerald mines of Xanadu.

She said, 'Trim the candle, Charlie.' Then, in a low, replete voice, 'We're travelling west now. It's towards trouble. I can feel it. Must you really have that gold?'

'What do you make of Mr Jones?'

She smiled. I kissed her eyelids, wondering how I could ever have thought ill of her. She said, 'I think he's someone other than he seems to be. Putting a bullet through the window is the sort of thing a young aristocrat does in one of our novels.'

'He wants to steal 690 tons of gold and remove it from the country.'

'That's a lot,' she said.

'Yes.'

'Are you going to help him?'

'A little. I'm after enough gold to get you and me to Odessa with some left over for when we reach London. Stupichkin gave me good advice. He said I should limit my ambition to what I can move and watch at the same time. A wagon, a barge, a suitcase, a canister. Makes sense.'

'So which are you looking out for?'

Talking to her was like having a corset fitted. A tuck here, an inch let out there, get it all lying perfectly. I said, 'Best would be a barge. I know the rumour that the Volga's got a fleet of Red torpedo boats on it but I'm ignoring that. According to rumour, the ground is clogged with their troops, the air is stiff with their planes and the sea black with their cruisers – believe all that and we might as well open our veins.'

'Keep death out of it, Charlie.'

'Disappointment is worse.'

'I know. England might disappoint me. Have you thought of that?'

'Keep England out of it. Odessa first, my peacheroo.'

There was a quick, sharp knock at the door. I wrapped a towel round my waist and opened it a slit. It was Leapforth. He said, 'I think you should hear what Stiffy's just picked up on the wireless.'

I said, 'You tell me. Six words or less.'

'One'll do.'

'Which one?'

'"Anastasia". It's the keyword they've just used. Four identical letters in it. It breaks every rule in the book.'

'Then they wanted it to be intercepted. What does the message say?'

'Haven't broken it all yet. Something about the barges lying in Kazan. Give me another hour.'

'Tell Stiffy he can listen, but if he sends out one single message he's on the next train to Siberia.'

'Why'd he do a thing like that, Charlie?' he said in an insolent way.

I closed the door on him. Xenia, lying there with the sheet up to her chin, said, 'When a Russian does a thing like that, there's a trick within the trick,' which even a child could have told me.

191

Forty-two

*T*ISHE EDESH, *dalshe budesh* as our saying goes: he who walks softly, goes far. I reckoned it must have been Glebov who'd sent that message. His spies would have picked up my trace in Strabinsk. It wasn't a difficult guess that I'd team up with the Americans.

'What's his game, then?' I was in Boltikov's compartment, just the two of us.

'He's after the gold. Everyone's after it. Change the system and all you get is new forms of treachery. Nothing alters at the heart of things.'

'But why bring Anastasia into it?'

'The man's waving to you.'

'Peekaboo?'

'Yes. He wants to lure you to Kazan so he can kill you. He'll be eager to get you out of the way – to finish that episode completely.'

'Before I get him.'

'It's what I'd do if I were Glebov.'

I said, 'I wonder if he has a conscience. Does he ever wake up in the difficult hours of the night and think to himself, I shouldn't have done that to her?' Then I went down the train to have a word with Shmuleyvich. There were only two ways to get to the centre of Kazan – and I wasn't going to have us walking.

He'd just put into a siding for the night and was blanking off the fire. I looked round to see what extra protection he might need. We'd fixed up our two machine guns forward of the cab, on either side of the boiler. Kobi and Vaska, the new boy, were going to be firing them. So Shmuley'd be covered from in front. And the wings of our armour-plating should protect him from the side. But I wanted to be certain. I didn't have a spare Shmuley.

He said, 'Where are we going, boss? Kazan for the gold?'

'You too?'

'Small train, big ears,' and he laughed, a terrific rumble that made his stomach quiver. 'You'll need to hurry. The locomen in Strabinsk said Muraviev is after it as well. And the Czechs, to pay their way to Vladivostok. Also – your enemy.'

This surprised me. 'Glebov?'

'That's what they were saying. Everyone knows everyone else's business.'

'Especially mine?'

'Yes. Gold easy to get at, is it, boss?'

'On barges lying on the Volga. That's what the Americans tell me. They listen to the Whites' wireless messages.'

'If it was me, boss, I'd wait till they've put it onto a train and then move the train. Get someone else to do the lifting. That'll be sore work.'

'I hear you. But first we have to get into Kazan. How do we do that, Shmuley?'

'Not in a hurry. There's only one way in from this side, on the Sarapul line. That's a one-track railway. We want to have it to ourselves. Follow me? We don't want to be meeting stuff head-on.'

'Sure. Once the fighting starts in earnest, there'll be refugees coming out in their thousands. We'll park up in a siding while their trains go through.'

He put his python's arm around my shoulders. 'I'll get you in, no need to worry about that. But will you get us out? At the end of this I want to be rich and I want to be alive. The wife died on me. I need a mate and it works better if the man has money. Get me? So the big question for me is this: How are you going to get us out with the gold if we get caught between thirty thousand Reds fighting thirty thousand Whites? You a magician, *barin* Doig?'

I said I'd figure that out.

But actually he was asking the wrong question. What he

should have asked was how I was going to get Glebov alone for long enough to kill him – and *then* get out. Get them all out. Right down to Vaska the sixteen-year-old with his fluffy cheeks.

Jones was at me first thing next morning, he and Stiffy together. 'What could he have been thinking of using Anastasia as a keyword? I got it in seven minutes precisely. See here, Charlie, keywords aren't usually chosen at complete random. They're almost always things that are on a guy's mind. "Armistice" or "Bolshevik" would be good examples for right now.'

I said, 'He was turning a knife in my hip joint. You don't know Glebov like I do.'

Stiffy opening his mouth to speak, I said, 'You didn't respond, did you? For one thing you're meant to be dead and for the other the Reds'll have a range-finder somewhere.'

'No one likes to have us around,' he said plaintively.

'Of course not. Wherever you set up your kit, shells will surely follow. Shells or planes, comes to the same thing. So keep your dabby fingers off the sending key. I don't want another black Fokker – Hey, you smile like that again, Leapforth Jones, and you can run out and switch a set of points over while I shoot at you. It was no fun. Nor for the guys he killed.'

'They've got spies everywhere,' said Jones.

'Why make it easier for them?'

I glowered at Stiffy, who was back to twining a lock of hair round his finger. I knew he'd find it hard to resist that sending key. 'If your fingers get an itch for something, stick them in your fly.' I bared my teeth like a dog and growled at him.

Jones said, 'There's something else. "Anastasia" was yesterday. Today we have "Elizaveta". I thought that'd interest you. Note the repetition again. And the "z" – only beginners use a rarity like that. Up to now their keywords have been real snorters. I've had to lever them open letter by letter. Here's an example: the last one they used before "Anastasia", I found it meant a drawing of a staircase that has an ambiguous perspective—'

'"Schröder",' put in Stiffy. 'The umlaut was doing duty as a null, but it wasn't really a null, so the Captain was thrown completely. Very clever.'

'You see what I mean?' said Jones. 'We're going along with

these keywords that have a real sarcastic twist to them, and now they give me a couple of sitters. What's the story, Charlie? What's with this Elizaveta? Anastasia was just a tease, you were right there. But this other dame—'

'Let it go, Jones.'

'I would, but I have to know whether it's going to affect my operation. That's fair, isn't it? All I get from Joseph are hints. Whenever I press him about the exact reason you're gunning for Glebov, he dreams up some urgent duty. Urgent, in Russia! So's my asshole. Whatever it is between you and Glebov, I reckon it's pretty gruesome. Got to be about money or a woman. Isn't nothing else in the whole wide world that could fly so far. Am I getting warm here, Charlie? Do I feel a little heat rising...? OK, you're taking the Fifth, that's up to you. But you know, vendettas, sideshows, they mess up everything.'

I said again for him to let it go. Boltikov entered the room.

'This Elizaveta – beautiful name. Really gets my balls twitching. Was that the lady in the contest, la belle Russki dame?'

The smile had gone. His look was as hard as flint, those languid brown eyes of his having shrunk to the size of centavos. 'If it's that personal, like a duel between the two of you – and I'm not forgetting you're half-Russki yourself and that you guys are a riddle to the rest of us – then I don't want to get caught in the mesh. Out-of-plan things'll happen. That's no way to win a fight.'

He eyed me like a bull eyes a small dog. No trace of pretty boy Jones now.

'I'm thinking, Charlie, that maybe something happened to this Elizaveta that where I come from would land a man in gaol for a century. Now is that getting warm or am I baking fucking hot?'

Smoothly, as if opening a packet of cocktail sticks, I un-buttoned my holster and took out my Luger. He was right across the table from me. I pointed it at the cartilaginous knob at the base of his breastbone – four feet away.

Stiffy stopped twiddling his hair. The handful of kopeks that Boltikov was jiggling in his pocket lay still.

The blood had left my face as all the poundage of my love came thundering up from my heart. Hard on its heels was anger that this smiler, whose idea of love would be having the fat girl from next door over the sofa arm once a week, should take it on himself to defame my woman.

I said to him, 'Elizaveta Rykov was my wife for exactly seven days. On the eighth day I was lured out of the house by a trick. By the time I discovered my mistake she had been raped by Glebov and a gang of soldiers. Why? Because she was the daughter of a nobleman, no other reason. Then they tortured her. Don't think of the worst, think past it. I shot her to put her out of her agony. At present I have only one purpose in my life: to find Glebov and kill him. If you mention her name again, I shall kill you also. With this pistol, the same one that I used on her. You have my word for it, the word of Charlie Doig.'

But he still held me with his eyes, probing. 'So you shot her, huh. I guess she'd have been lying down . . . Pretty dramatic, snow on the ground and so forth. Yeah, snow, blood all over it, the smoke from the shot . . . that's hellish.' His face softened a little. 'Hellish,' he said again.

Then briskly, turning over a new leaf, 'Charlie, I don't want to mess with you now or at any time. I'll tell you straight out what's bugging me. You're after Glebov and we're after the gold. How do we get those two things reconciled? I only want to deal fairly with you.'

It was the second time he'd used the word. But the fact was that from rich to poor, from dunce to genius, no one in Russia had the smallest interest in fairness, hadn't even any knowledge of the word. Power, that was the brew in the black bottle. Trample the common man. To hell with fairness. Surely Jones knew enough about the country for that.

There was a fiction in him, maybe two or three or four.

Looking directly at him, I said, 'Someone here is after something I don't know about. And that's too bad for him, cos I'm only making plans for myself and my payroll. Shmuleyvich! In here!'

When he came I told him to take a no. 22 screwdriver and dismantle the armature of Stiffy's sending key and bring it back to me. That or break up some of his nice soldering.

'No!' Stiffy grabbed Shmuleyvich by the arm and held him fast.

'It's my life! It's given me friends all over the world – a family. Without it I'd be a null. The wireless, it's who I am.'

Boltikov growled at Stiffy, 'In what way are you necessary to us? Why don't I just shoot you and take your share of the gold?'

With an upward, preening, corkscrew movement of his neck, Stiffy said, 'I'll tell you why. Because you want to know the exact date Trotsky'll attack Kazan, that's why.'

Boltikov said, 'I'm waiting.'

Stiffy looked at him with total disdain. '3247813127829311T. The "T" is a null to complete the series of digraphs. I'm not just a secretary taking down shorthand, you know, some stupid little polly.' He made Boltikov a tiny bow, a lovely piece of rudeness.

Jones said, 'It's the usual checkerboard cipher with the transposition coming from the keyword. Like a Vigenère with reversed alphabets. An altogether better class of cipher than a Beaufort.'

'That's shit,' bristled Boltikov.

'You think so? You think I'm bluffing?'

'How do you know it's from Trotsky?'

'Came from Stavka. His HQ. Can't be anyone else.'

'How do you know it's for attacking Kazan?'

'Short is always orders. Decipher what Stiffy just told you and you'll find an abbreviation that stands for "Treat this as confirmation of the tactics already discussed". The rest is date and time and target coordinates.'

'Who's he speaking to?'

'Kreps. He's leading another army up from the south . . . Gee, you're a quick man on the draw, Mr Boltikov.'

I sort of shouted at Stiffy, quite a release of breath, 'So what the hell day is it in September? I'm not interested in your schoolboy number games.'

Stiffy asked Jones if he could tell me the date. Jones nodded.

It was to be 5 September. On that day the Reds were going to pile in with every man they could lay their hands on. Trotsky and his armies were closing in from the west, were attacking the Romanov Bridge even as we spoke. Kreps and the 6th Army'd be the other arm of the pincers.

I said to Jones, 'Was this another Elizaveta message?'

'No.'

'So this date isn't part of their game? They're not leading us up the garden path?'

He shook his head. 'It's for real. Stavka wouldn't play games with Kreps. It'll be on the night of the 5th because the Whites don't care for night fighting. The Anastasia and Elizaveta messages are probably being sent by Propaganda Bureau. They put out all the dummies – create false armies, sow suspicion, get the other guys jumpy . . . Mr Boltikov, mind if I ask you something? Where does the paranoia come from in your countrymen?'

'In the nation's milk, from titties.'

But it wasn't paranoia that was tapping out my wife's name. What I was hearing was a whore rattling the curtain rings of her booth and the name of the whore was Glebov. The golden rule: a man is never more easily hunted than when he believes he's hunting another. A cold tremor rippled from my heart into my arms and legs and down to their very tips.

Forty-three

CHIRILINO WAS the place I chose to lie up until the time
came. We cruised quietly into the station one evening with
men at both machine guns to show we meant business. We
needn't have bothered. The only person who hadn't got out was
the stationmaster.

His name was Blumkin: short, stout with a chipped front
tooth and a gold watch chain as thick as a skipping rope hanging
between his waistcoat pockets.

His story was a sad one the first time we heard it. Every
evening he'd take out his stepladder and light the twin rows of
oil lamps that stretched the length of the platform. Every hour
of every day he expected to hear again the thunder of the Trans-
Siberian expresses and see his lamps set a-swaying by their
billowing bow wave. He loved the expresses, he loved the little
stopping trains, he loved the ladies in woollen scarves who
popped out from town to sell glasses of tea and offer napkin-
covered baskets of warm piroshkas to passengers who were
delayed. Bells, whistles, coded messages on the railway telegraph, locomotives on the potter (columns of sooty smoke like
mushrooms in the grey sky), changing the date on his ticket
machine, triple-stamping dockets for the shipment of heavy
goods, all such matters were his life blood to exactly the same
extent that the wireless was Stiffy's.

He wasn't downcast by the fact that we were his first train
for over a week. He was one of those people who are on top
form throughout the day. He and Jones were like twins, smiling
away at each other from the moment dawn broke.

One particular reason he was so cheerful was that he too had worked out what the fall of Kazan would mean in terms of refugees. The ticket office and both waiting rooms were crammed with everything from blankets to jars of kerosene, not forgetting the Kapral cigarettes that he was going to sell at five kopeks each to these desperate people instead of the usual five kopeks for twenty. When he'd sold three-quarters of his stock, he was going to jump aboard the next train and make a run for America.

So his story became less sad and I foresaw that his chipped tooth was in line to become golden.

I got Blumkin to give us one of his sidings so I could observe the refugee trains passing. It's not every day one hits off a revolution plumb in its spinning eye. Wasn't I going to sire kids sometime? Wouldn't they say to me, 'Hey, Pa, what did all those escaping princes look like? Were they crying their Russian eyes out, dressed in the family furs, had emeralds up their asses?'

Blumkin said, 'Why be interested by them? They'll soon be poor or dead.'

'Damned right they will if they buy anything from you,' I said. Then I got Kobi to persuade him to fill my coal tenders.

Hearing the roar of the stuff coming down the chute, Jones stuck his nose into my affairs. 'What's all that for?' he asked. 'It'll take us miles past Kazan. Isn't the idea that we board the gold train and use their coal? Why buy more than you need?'

Here I became certain that he was either a dope or a fraud. First, I wasn't paying for the coal. Second, if all that gold, 690 tons of it, left Kazan on a train, everyone in the province'd be after it. There'd be spies hidden in culverts, snipers, bombardiers, army commanders, tarts, lawyers, dentists, jewellers, makers of weighing scales, assaying agents – Christ, there'd be no limit to the number of spoons in the stew if 690 tons of gold got loose. To stay anywhere near such a train would be fatal. Yet Jones hadn't thought of that?

I tapped my nose. 'All part of the plan, Leapforth.'

Then I had Shmuley take the train down into our siding, which ran alongside a lake with ducklings (a second brood) strung out like commas behind mamasha, who'd be tomorrow's dinner if I knew Kobi. Chivvying the ducklings along, lowering its neck and hissing at them, was a swan, compensating for its bad temper by the snow-white elegance of its plumage and its stateliness.

It was like a real Russian summer paradise down there. Stupichkin should have been with me, should have lain down and died there so he didn't need to look upon any more awfulness. At any moment Chekhov could have strolled out from the shimmering birch trees in his crumpled linen jacket and scuffed brown shoes and said something witty to us. The hand coming from his trouser pocket to take out his notebook would have been hot and moist. Shoving his cap onto the back of his head, he'd have shown his brown hair to be lax with sweat. He'd have leaned against a birch and lit up. Mrs D. would have come to the door of the galley. Skillet in hand, warm fat dripping onto her apron, she'd have stood there gazing upon him, eyes soft with admiration. In her mind she'd have been murmuring to him, 'Come and have a little breakfast with me, dovey.' With a smile he'd have pushed himself upright and shrugged his jacket straight. (That would have been the moment for his witty remark, not earlier.)

The birds sang softly, the wasps shone with health, the crickets chirruped and the bees were happier than they had been for years now there were no peasants left to steal their honey. In the evening the mosquitoes would be bad but it wasn't evening yet and next to the lake was a meadow full of grass and bursting white clover for Tornado.

The ramp of his wagon came down. Out he trotted, the horny old bruiser, with his head up and his big bold eye on full alert. He halted to sound his trumpet. Greetings, girls! went out to the mares of Chirilino and when he had no reply he lowered his head in resignation and strode off in step with Kobi, whose shoulder he rubbed affectionately with his muzzle. Better than hauling the Strabinsk death cart, that's what my charger was thinking.

Kobi loosed him in the meadow, slapping his dusty rump.

I was at the bottom of a telegraph pole chatting to Stiffy, who was up there with his headphones listening to the traffic between Strabinsk and Kazan. We watched Tornado roll, we watched him drench a couple of molehills with a volley of glittering sun-blest piss. Then Stiffy said to me in a most ordinary voice, 'Horses are easy to understand. But none of you get me.'

'Beg pardon, Stiffy.' I squinted up at him. He was leaning

back in his climbing harness, dark against the blue sky and all odd angles like a pterodactyl.

He held up a hand for hush. A message was coming through. Out of the corner of his mouth he said, 'The Whites are so thick. If it's important, they have a special group, a letter–numeral mix that they put at the beginning of a cable. It means, "Clear the line immediately . . ." Bloody stupid. Tells everyone to listen . . . Hang on, let's just see what this is about . . . Feeding prisoners, nothing interesting to us . . . May I go on, sir?'

I nodded.

'I'm not a complete coward, sir. I just don't want to be trapped in a woman's vagina, that's what I'm most afraid of. It's not as if I haven't given it a try . . . Got a moment, have we, sir?'

There followed the history of Stiffy's sexual experience with women, which he spoke partly to me and partly to the sky and partly towards the birch trees, where Chekhov's image persisted for me.

The day was a cracker. Listening to Stiffy's voice from up the telegraph pole made me wonder what God's voice would be like. Shouting? Smoochy? Cajoling? Probably a wheedling bullying mixture—

'Masturbation's the best. Wanking's trumps, that is. That's why I enjoy listening to folk on the wires. I get all the excitement and have none of the cost. And why I'm telling you this is because I know there's a battle coming soon but, sir, well, sir, the truth is that I'll be at my best out of the line of fire. I'll be worth more to you at my wireless than with a rifle in my hand, and that's God's own truth, sir.'

When I said nothing, he called down anxiously, 'Have you been listening, sir?'

I said, 'You mean you want to be in a bunker? Both you and Joseph?'

'Merely being alive is enough danger for me, sir. You can't avoid women.'

He unclipped his taps and came down the pole. Kneeling on the ground, he packed them into a canvas satchel with his headphones. 'I'd shit myself. You'd think less of me . . . The thing is, if you're in a uniform, everyone thinks you're brave. Well, I'm not.'

'But you still want your share of the gold?'

'I'd die rather than be poor again. Being poor in America is the same as committing a criminal offence. So if it's all right with you, sir, I'll earn it by my work on the wireless. I'll even sleep up a telegraph pole if you want me to. No one's better at his job than Stiffy.'

I regarded him in silence. Behind me Mrs D. was shouting at Vaska. They'd got out the bags of Red Army uniforms and were sorting them.

'I'm a confusion, that's what I am,' Stiffy said. 'When I came into the world, some wires were placed in the wrong plugs. I'd like to be like you, sir. You're like Noah's blooming pigeon. You always know exactly which direction to go in.'

I didn't see him as being important in the soldiering line but I didn't want him to think he could get away with anything. I waited to see what else would come out.

He gave me a quick glance, said, 'Early this morning I took down another Elizaveta message. I think it was Glebov himself at the key. A really heavy fist, without any fluency, as if he was reading the Morse off a chart. That was at the start. Then one of the usual senders took over.'

'What did he say?'

'Ah, sir, everything has a price. Working with Captain Jones has taught me that.'

I said, 'That's going to be a bad deal for one of us. Blackmail always is.'

'Only making the suggestion, sir. No real force behind the shot. Only, when we get to Kazan would you remember that it was Stiffy who told you that Glebov had grown a moustache?'

'Hell, Stiffy, that was not expected.'

I had him describe to me the exact circumstances of the message. It turned out to be Glebov and Kreps exchanging cracks about Glebov's job re-educating the Tsar and his family – having his moustache trimmed regularly as a courtesy to royalty.

'So he's got to have one, sir, before he can talk like that.'

'Has he? Stiffy, when you lie down with dogs, you get up with fleas and don't you forget that. I'll know about Glebov's moustache when I get him in my sights and not before. The chances are that he's sitting there in the Propaganda Bureau having a good laugh at me. Doig-baiting. I'd say he no more has a moustache than a billiard ball has one.'

He continued to watch me.

I said, 'More to come, is there?'

He said, 'It was painful he was that slow in his transmission. I wanted to start sending myself, to help him, but you'd ordered me never to do that. I played with the dial as I listened. The set was going well. The valves weren't burning too brightly, weren't howling at me as they can do in some conditions. Then he finished. "Goodbye" – a single stroke. I said to myself, That's that for the moment. The next thing I knew he'd started up again in cleartext. No cipher, no code. Plain Morse for the whole world to hear.'

'What did he say?'

'"Are you reading me, Americanski?" That was what he sent.'

Forty-four

I<small>N VIEW</small> of this conversation it was vital that no knowledge of our position should reach Glebov. So I didn't reply to his taunts, set a guard round our encampment and pulled in Blumkin. The Reds had people everywhere. There wasn't a single Red who was a White on the side but there were lots of Whites who faced both ways, people like Stupichkin. On which side of the line was our plump profiteer? I sent Kobi over. He rode Tornado and returned with Blumkin stumbling along in front as he thrashed idly at him with the reins. I shut him up in Tornado's wagon. He complained like anything, putting his mouth to a gap in the planks and yelling in a curious high tenor voice, just like Lenin's. But we fed and watered him well enough so he could have had a great deal more to shout about.

By now everyone knew we were going into action in three days. Of course they were expecting me to come up with orders and plans. Jones's brown eyes rested on me more snidely than usual. I got the impression he wanted to see what I was up to before committing himself.

Still, he lent me his map of Kazan. He had a set of six-inchers for each of the large towns of central Russia. They came in a polished brown leather pouch that carried the stamp of the Admiralty War Staff, Intelligence Division, London. He was mighty proud of it, not having thought what the Bolsheviks might do to him if they took him prisoner and found the pouch.

This was how I figured it out:

The line from Chirilino entered Kazan at a slant from the north. Trotsky and Kreps would launch their attack from the west, keeping the river on their right flank. There'd be chaos. Therein lay our best chance. We had Bolshevik uniforms. Our armoured car now had a Red Star on its bonnet. Stiffy would use the wireless to lure Glebov to a tryst – and there the deed would be done.

However, I needed somewhere to leave Xenia. It'd be a dangerous time. And I didn't want to risk Glebov getting hold of her.

I spread the map out. I was immediately attracted by the Zilantov Monastery, which stood on its own hill and had water on two sides. It'd be defensible. It had good access to the Volga through the old Admiralty Quarter. It commanded the neighbouring ground – and would obviously give refuge to a woman. Some old monk would glare at her through the grille – suspiciously, in case a leftist was concealed beneath her headscarf. But she'd have the right words. She always had the right words where God was concerned.

Jones smarmed up to me wanting to hear what the plan was – salients, re-entrants, passwords and the like. 'It'll have to be mighty fine if the six of us are going to get the better of four Red Armies. Is it to be abracadabra and all's well, is that the idea, Charlie?'

I longed to knock his white teeth flying.

To keep him quiet I put him to work painting the slogan boards we were going to hang on the side of the train if we were likely to run into Reds. 'Slay All Bankers', 'Plunder the Plunderers', that sort of stuff. On the coaches themselves I had the Pullman colours painted out and on the goods wagons neutral but heartening messages painted, like sheaves of corn and horses pulling dray wagons and wise men presiding over councils of the people. I wanted it to resemble Trotsky's train – but not too closely, in case it was Whites we met first.

It was Joseph who took charge of all this. With a Red Army cap on his head, sitting in my uncle's chrome chair beneath a gnarled apple tree, he did the entire layout, somehow managing to render less potent the nightmare yellow that we'd found a heap of in Blumkin's stores. 'Zobb's Incredible Circus. Firm Sale. No Return' – that's what the paint-pot labels said.

His dark locks strayed from beneath the cap and brushed his shoulders. His pencil flitted across the paper with the certainty of a rapier. The tip of his tongue darted in and out as he worked.

I said to him, 'That's what revolution can do to a man, Joseph.'

'Excellency?' He was sketching out the lettering for the last board: 'Anarchy: Does the Shoe Fit?'

'Releases the spirits of the downtrodden, brings forth genius. You and Stiffy. Maybe neither of you would have discovered your talents without a revolution. We've come a long way since I walked in off Nevsky and told you Elizaveta had been murdered.'

He laid down his pencil, took off his Red Army cap and stretched like a free man.

'Tomorrow we could be dead, Joseph. Be shot in the stomach like Alexander Pushkin and linger – hang on for days calling out for God to make an end of us – screaming, smelling our own gangrene – our souls rotting.'

'It'd be God's will.' Joseph raised the pencil to his eye to estimate proportions. 'He cannot be defied.'

'You afraid?' As a man he was so slight, so precariously based, that it was easy to think of him as dead.

He laid down his pencil. 'Excellency, when I was twelve and a footman at Count Noselov's, I was afraid I'd never earn enough money to get me as far as the point of death. Years and years I'd have to survive and I didn't see how I could possibly do it. When I was your uncle's butler I was afraid something awful would happen to me, like dropping a piece of his china, and I'd slip back to being a footman. When the revolutionists barged into the palace I was so afraid of having a bayonet stuck in me that I walked around with my breath drawn in to make my stomach disappear. I now understand that God made me to be some sort of artist and not a servant at all. This too makes me afraid. Even the Bolsheviks need servants. But who needs an artist? So now I ask myself, how shall I, Joseph Culp, ever get to the end? What I think, Excellency, is that fear is part of all our lives. So tomorrow will be no different from any other day.'

'You're braver than you make out. Remember our walk to Smolny, to see Lenin?'

'Doig, the Reds have *organiziert* as no Russian force has ever had before. This devil called Trotsky, this Jew, has every tenth man in a regiment shot if an attack isn't pressed home. In a charge they run towards the enemy shouting "Karl Marx! Karl Marx!" because they've been told his name'll protect them from the bullets.' He spat. 'Like savages.'

'That the bullets'll bounce back off them, is that what you're saying? Where did you learn this?'

'I speak to lower people than you. Such people believe what Trotsky tells them because of the rewards he promises. The beautiful women get sent to the transport wagons at the rear but the rest are available on the spot. The soldier-peasants infect them and give them babies they don't want. They destroy the lives of women who are completely innocent of any malevolence. They do it just so they can empty their balls and boast afterwards. *Svoloch* – scum. They deserve to be boiled alive.' He spat again. 'Doig, I don't want gold.'

'What's it to be then?'

'I want my old mother to come back and see how her sorrow turned out. That German watch-repairer who was my father ran away. That was her first sorrow. But I was her greatest sorrow because after I left she had nothing. *Barin*, what I would like most in the world would be for her to sit up alive and see the drawing that I'd do of her.'

He rose and taking up my uncle's chrome chair, moved down to the next carriage to be painted. It was Tornado's. I saw Blumkin eyeing us from his spyhole.

'Elizaveta,' I said, 'let's do one for her. In scarlet.' It'd been her best colour, always. The walls of her room, her dancing shoes, innumerable scarves, even the frames of her glasses.

Joseph shouted to Vaska to count the remaining tins of paint. We still had an over-supply of the yellow and only a few pots of scarlet. He said, 'What we'll have is a sky filled with thunder. And in the blackest part of the thunder we'll paint in red – Excellency, would it be in order to put "For Elizaveta"?'

As the painting started, Blumkin began to shout abuse at us. We would see first his blabbering mouth and then one eye (which looked brown against the wood even though it was in fact blue) as he gauged the effect of his words.

'The paint's got harmful chemicals in it,' he said eventually, more soberly, squeezing his lips and his chipped tooth up against the chink between the planks. 'That's how I got it cheap. Pyotr Stefanovich Malkevich – do you remember his case? He had a factory down in Rostov. The police got suspicious after some of his workers died. They found he was putting something illegal into his paint to make it go further. When they began to look into his affairs, they discovered that he was keeping three wives, each one living in a different part of his mansion. Then it turned out that one of the Mrs Malkevichs was also married to a man called Zobb who owned the biggest circus in the province, had ten dancing bears, four hairy women, all from Albania, a gorilla that could talk in Chinese—'

'Shut your trap, old man,' said Joseph.

'It turned out they were in it together, Zobb and Malkevich, and shared the woman. Mrs Zobb-Malkevich's name was Grishka. I saw a photograph of her. It surprised me that two men should desire her. It was how I got his paint, after he was sent to prison . . .'

Vaska walking past, I told him to get a piece of wood and nail it over Blumkin's hole. 'Nail it to his tongue if he argues,' I added.

Joseph remarked, 'A storyteller, like every stationmaster I've ever known.'

Mrs D. came marching through the grass in bare feet. She'd got hold of a pretty green summer frock that ended just below the knee. She had a healthy skin. Everything in her strong round face shone with the pleasure of life.

'When do you want to try the uniforms?' she asked.

I'd told her to sort them by size and rank and sew up any bullet holes. If Stupichkin had executed a general who stood six foot two in his socks and had a forty-two-inch chest then that was the uniform for me. Any medals in the pockets, I'd have those as well. I didn't want to look sloppy: didn't want to wear trousers that trailed behind me on the ground, like Lenin's.

'Got something for me then?' I asked.

She really had a lovely bloom to her cheeks that day. Her lips were pink and full. It was clear that mean thoughts and deeds refused to come near her. How could she have fallen for that spiv of a husband?

Smiling, she saluted me: 'Destiny calls, Colonel Doig.'

Forty-five

TWO RED Vereys over a green one. Shmuleyvich, whose watch it was, lumbered down the train to waken me. Midnight exactly. He hadn't seen the flares themselves but he'd seen their reflection off the clouds. Like the aurora borealis, especially the green flare, which had left a flat stain in the sky for a good two minutes.

'It spooked me,' said the big man, 'until I realised it must have been hanging from a parachute. I wouldn't have done that. Every minute it was up there was a minute for the Whites to have target practice.'

I said for him to get some sleep and call everyone at dawn.

'Thank God you didn't ask him about the coal situation or he'd be here still,' said my drowsy love, moving away from me.

'No coal, no hole – putting one's pole in the coal-hole – any hole's a goal – a man could go on for a long time on those lines,' I murmured into her ear, pulling her back so that I was right in there behind her power-station buttocks, my cock nestled up against her smutch and growing hard. But it was no good, for soon she was gruntling away as she dreamed of corsets and whalebones and of swanking through her shop with a tape measure round her neck.

I tried a few things to get her interested but they came to nothing. That was a pity for I was keen to have her, that midnight of 5 September 1918. Here's why, nothing to do with carnality.

The fact is, when a man's keyed up for some great ordeal, he's restless. He doesn't want to read a book or discuss a famous picture. Appreciation of form and beauty must wait for settled times. What he wants to do is to hop onto a woman and get busy inside her. It's the combination of solace and power that he's after, the one in case he gets killed, the other to put him in the mood for victory. Only a woman can give him this. Only her incomparable organ, the one that's of the greatest importance to the world, far more than any other, including eyes and ears and even the digestive processes, can bring peace to a man's soul.

Say what you want but that's how it is, that's man for you.

God save all women! God bless and protect them and make them perfect and have them ready for when we return.

So I said to myself, despite my frustration. Then some other eve-of-battle considerations started to spin through my mind and before I knew it, I was having a hard time getting to sleep.

What part would the Czechs play? All sorts of stories were on the go about their armoured trains. Reinforced concrete behind the armour-plating – field guns being fired off flatbeds – machine-gun turrets that swivelled through a complete circle – five hundred men per train, each of them desperate – what the hell would I do if they set upon me? How was I to convey to them in their troublesome language that I wasn't after all the gold, just one bargeful?

Then again, what if Glebov didn't bite? How would it be if in fact he were the bloodhound and I the fugitive?

One thought led to another . . .

The next I knew was that the air was filled with the crash of cymbals and trumpets, with gongs, with factory hooters and earthquakes. I sat up sharply. Crackety-crack, crackety-crack, crackety-crack – it was the first of the Kazan refugee trains rocketing through with Vladivostok in their sights. Our siding was fifty yards away from the main line and concealed in a slight declivity. Nevertheless our windows quivered, the putty fell out of them and the cap on the pipe leading up from our stove bobbled like the lid of a kettle. The noise faded, with a last whistle as it raced through Chirilino.

That train was the first and it was the fastest, the rig of someone who'd had the foresight to purchase the coal and a driver before the rush. Not just any old coal but the best that was around in Kazan, leaving for the rest of the flighty the slack at the bottom of the heap, which was as hard to shovel as dust and burned poorly.

'They'll get slower and slower, you wait and see,' I said to Xenia, throwing back the covers and slapping her pink haunch. 'The last'll be scarcely able to move.'

I was proved right. The rest of the refugee trains wheezed past us, moving so gently that one could examine the patterns of rust on the wheels as they passed. Stray dogs from the town ran alongside the carriages, snapping at the ankles of the refugees sitting sideways on the coach buffers, making them draw up their legs and cling to each other.

Here a question should be asked: Did any of us wave to these unfortunates or call out a cheerful greeting? How much of the good Samaritan was in us?

The answer is, Yes, Vaska, our young naïf did. When the first of the slow trains arrived he walked beside it saying things like 'How are you?', 'Where do you come from?', 'The day's still young', and other rural commonplaces, his wide peasant's face full of smiles and goodness.

But that was the last time he did it. Mrs D. smacked him down fiercely, saying it would only encourage refugees to abandon their hopeless form of transport and take their chances with us.

'You ask the Colonel if he wants a bunch of useless hungry layabouts under his command. Go on. He's only five yards away.'

Bewildered, Vaska did just that. Of course I said No. And I looked at Mrs D. in a different light from then on.

All day long the trains came past us, Boltikov scanning them avidly for signs of wealth. He wanted to believe that tubs of icons, tiaras, pearls, rubies, emeralds – every species of jewel, not to mention cloaks of Arctic fox and rolls of medieval Bokharas – were still being shifted out of the country. He'd already filled a wagon with stuff to sell from his dreamed-of warehouse in Constantinople.

'Kazan is rich. Think of the Tartar cattle merchants and the like. Don't tell me they still put their trust in bank vaults.'

I replied, 'Alexander Alexandrovich, a for apple you'll be lucky to get to Odessa let alone Byzantium and b for baksheesh the goods that you seek will, for the most part, be leaving Russia not with their owners but through underground channels unknown to either of us but of a certainty in existence since conditions were primitive.'

He was not persuaded. 'But Russia is so huge! Twelve days from Moscow to the Pacific on the fastest train! Think how much wealth there is around. Some of it must be in these trains. Let us at least stop and search them. It can do no harm. You never know – some of these Siberian gems, Charlie, you've never seen anything like them – just one prime diamond would buy us a palace on the Bosphorus – OK, every other train, then – OK, so we have to put the Kazan job back a day, what of it . . .'

I said he should go and open Blumkin's store to work off his appetite for profit. But selling candles and the like didn't appeal to him. He went to watch Kobi giving Vaska sabre drill.

We remained where we were, observing the movements on the railway. By the evening the refugee trains had ceased: the line to Kazan was clear.

Forty-six

WE SHOWED no running lights. A fuzzy patch of sparks above the chimney was all that gave us away as we slid through the belly of the night. Even the kerosene lamp that played on the water gauges had been hooded.

Pressure was right down. The dampers were virtually closed. We were just trundling along because Stiffy was at his wireless and bracketed to his wagon was its aerial, all 120 feet of it. For the moment we were travelling through open farmland with no bridges over the line to foul it. When we got nearer Kazan, we'd be close enough to Glebov to pick up his signals without it. In the meantime I wanted to know about every single piece of wireless traffic, Red and White. We had to have the aerial up and we had to travel slowly.

Dawn was my deadline: six thirty. By then Glebov had to be dealt with and the gold had to be ours. I didn't want us to be wandering round Kazan in daylight in Bolshevik uniforms.

In front the sky had a bruised tinge. Like the Verey lights that had signalled the Bolshevik onslaught, it was reflected onto the clouds over the city, turning them into huge violet pillows.

There could be no doubt: Kazan was burning.

No, said Shmuleyvich, it was some queer relic of the day's sun – to do with the coming of the equinox. He'd seen it before, in Siberia. But whatever its cause, it was a bad colour. 'Pitch black would have suited us better for the gold.' Glancing at me, 'Though perhaps not for the other thing.' He made a stabbing motion with his hand. 'For that you must be able to see clearly. No good guessing where the bastard is.'

There were just the two of us in the cab. Our rifles were propped in the corner, below the coal. The iron wings meant we were safe from anything except a grenade or a direct hit from a shell – or from gas. I hadn't heard of anyone using it in Russia but only the worst was to be expected from Trotsky.

For a moment Shmuley's face was profiled against the sky. Remarking to myself upon the strong nose of a man who enjoys women, I asked him the same question as I'd put to Joseph, How did he feel about being dead by this time tomorrow.

He grunted. 'If I could be certain it was going to happen, I'd want to lie in bed with my woman and smoke and drink simultaneously right up to the moment of death. That's what I most like doing. I'm a basic man, born from Adam's seed.' He chuckled. 'My feet know where the ground is. There's nothing airy-fairy about Yuri Shmuleyvich.'

The night was smooth on my face. It was a companionable feeling being alone with this large, vigorous man. It was as if the two of us had sworn a pact to take on all of Trotsky's armies by ourselves.

He continued: 'Any fool can have a woman at the same time as he's smoking. If he's taking a long time about it, she'll probably want a cigarette as well. The problem is with the drinking. Let's face it, we like to use our hands to get a grip on things, wouldn't be men if we didn't. And she likes us to get a grip, let's not forget that a woman likes being gripped. Annushka—'

'Annushka?'

'Annushka Madam Davidova,' he said with a chuckle.

At that moment the bell we'd rigged up to the carriages rang, barely audible above the noise of the engine.

I said, 'Too bad. Will Annushka wait until next time?'

'She'd better, boss. She'd better wait forever.'

I went back through the coal tender and was met by Vaska. He led me down the train to the dining car. We had blackout stuff at all the windows – cloth from Blumkin's stores. Jones was at the table with decrypt papers strewn all round him. His smile was ragged at the edges. He probably thought he should be in his bed.

'They've opened a new code.'

'But you broke it and here I am, Leapforth. No need to be dramatic.'

'Yeah, I broke it . . . in the end. They've moved on from the Caesar alphabets and all that Vigenère stuff. What they're at now – a polyalphabetical substitution. Greek and Russian only so far. Makes sense for the Russkis to use Greek. I guessed that one right away. Then they used a repeating keyword, which was kind of them.'

'They're through with Elizaveta?'

'It's only Propaganda who've been using it, I told you that. This was to Trotsky from the commander of the Northern Army. The Reds have captured the railway in two places. Our railway.'

'Doesn't surprise me. I haven't seen any foot traffic the whole night. Capture the railway and you capture the road, that's what it looks like on the map.'

The road ran alongside the railway, dead straight, no bridges, not twenty yards away. Even in that light we'd have seen movement. Handcarts, wagons, dogs, horses, donkeys – encampments round a fire with prayers and weepings and songs of death, animals and humans alike suspicious of the promises flying around. We'd have had to be blind not to see ten thousand refugees hoofing it east.

I said, 'The Reds'll have done it to put pressure on the city. There'll be all these mothers and children and old people crying out for food and water. Getting in the Whites' way. Getting desperate.'

He said, 'So it doesn't worry you that the line they've captured is the very one we're on? That we're shafted?'

I looked him over, chin resting in my palm. I said, 'Why do you suppose we have all these Red uniforms? What's your game, Jones? You're not behaving like a man who expects to be moving out soon with 690 tons of gold. You're acting too sluggish. No modest man ever made a fortune. Keeping something back, are we, *plut*?' – that being slang for a confidence man.

'The false whiskers are in my pocket, Charlie boy,' he said,

217

moving quickly out of his anxious mode and pouring that smile of his over me like syrup.

I shouted for Vaska and sent him back to Shmuley with orders to stop the train. We needed to prepare for meeting the Reds. I'd take the aerial down at the same time. 'And then go through the coaches telling everyone to get changed into their Red kit. Run, boy! *Zhivo!*'

Jones made to leave but I stopped him. 'It's time you and I got things cleared up. Tell me straight what you're doing. Arrange the words so that I believe you. Otherwise I leave you behind.'

I took out my Luger and laid it on the table.

That got his attention. He opened his palms, spread them wide as if to show he was unarmed – or at least innocent.

'Sure I'm not after the gold. That sort of thing's for kiddies' storybooks. Stiffy thinks we are, but he's still got a lot of kiddie in him. All that playing around with wireless sets . . . Well, I guess I'm sorry for the deception, for undermining my commanding officer' – he laughed pleasantly to prove we shared a joke – 'but what I've been sent to do is highly confidential, you get me, Doig? Top, top, top secret. I can tell you now because tomorrow I'll be out of your life. What's going on is this: my country and Lenin's lot want to have unofficial talks about the relationship between them – you know, what's to happen to property owned by American corporations, what's to happen to Serbia, Johnny Turk, the war with Germany – all that sort of heavyweight stuff. OK? Am I getting myself believed? However, there is a problem here for both sides: they can't be seen sitting down at the same table. For our President it'd be ruin and for Lenin likewise since the only reason he got where he is was by telling Russians that all capitalists were evil. It'd look like one big cheat if he suddenly showed himself as our buddy. So I'm the go-between. Me and Trotsky first. If that goes well, me and Lenin. Then maybe me and Lenin and the President. Now you see why I had to vanish from US Army records. These fellows at the top, they hate to have loose ends lying around that some busybody'll trip over.'

'So why are you telling me if it's top secret?'

He chuckled. 'By tomorrow night you ain't going to be around no more. You and your crowd – believe me, you'll be food for the crows by this time tomorrow and it won't do you a blind bit of good looking to me for protection. I'll be gone. Underground. Me and Trotsky. Big time.'

Forty-seven

THE GENERATOR bulb glowed green in the semi-darkness of the wireless van. A chink of light came from the back where Stiffy had his box of tricks. I slipped into the canvas-backed chair beside him. The valves were burning gently, just right.

'What's on?' I mouthed. The time was 2 a.m., as near as makes no difference.

He glanced at me, the headphones making him look top-heavy. He was on Receive, his fingers taking the dial through the wavelengths a hair's breadth at a time. Every fibre in him was concentrating on the diddidahs – on eavesdropping, on that other life of his.

His eyes held mine as he scribbled on a shorthand pad.

He pushed one headphone forward at an angle and said, 'Muraviev.'

'Doing what?'

'His signaller. Asking Kazan for a fresh report on the Bolshevik regiments, identification thereof. Routine stuff.' He looked at his pad.

He could have married this wireless of his. I said, 'Stiffy?'

'Yes, sir.'

'Do you have a problem sending a message in cleartext?'

'You mean, not encrypted at all?' He removed the headphones entirely and stared at me.

'Not at all.'

'Letter by letter? Standard Morse?'

'Yes.'

'Well, sir, as long as it's short . . . they'll have a direction-finder somewhere.'

'It is short. Trust me. I know what long is.'

'What call-up signal shall I use?'

'Same as for the Elizaveta messages. Same wavelength, same everything. Whatever that sender used, you use.'

'Let's have it then, sir.' He held his pencil ready.

'NEMESIS TO GLEBOV STOP . . .'

I paused, not having the next few words quite right in my mind. The nail of his index finger tapped nervously at his pad as he waited for me. He jumped up, tugged his trousers straight, dug around in his arse, sat down again – spat into his palms and rubbed them together. If he'd had five sets of fingers, they wouldn't have been enough to do all he wanted.

I snatched the pad from him. It took me a couple of goes before I got it right.

His hand glided to the set, clicked the switch to the right for Send. Finger above the black button – hovering, itching to be social . . .

He turned to me, his eyes very serious. 'Sir, are we being wise?'

'Do you think he doesn't already know I'm here? Don't think your wireless is the only set of lugs in town.'

'But on his doorstep? When he could have a plane over us in ten minutes?'

'Stiffy, I have some advice for you. When in Russia, be a Russian. That means not being a fucking Anglo-Saxon and democratic and quibbling. When I say, Give Glebov a fright, you do it. Yes or no?'

'Yes, sir.'

'Very well. Your usual speed. NEMESIS TO GLEBOV STOP WATCH OUT BEHIND YOU STOP THE BIGGEST SHADOW IS DEATH – then the letter for goodbye. Or however you end a message. Go on, do it now.'

Every Red signaller'd pick it up, shake his woolly head and rush off to find out what it meant. Tension would be created. Look over there, the shadow in that doorway, it's Doig. Bang-bang, down he doesn't fall. Only Glebov would understand how profoundly I meant what I'd said. For all I knew there could be a hundred thousand people in Kazan tonight. But only two of us mattered. And then there'd be one.

Forty-eight

SCUNNERED, THAT'S what my old man would have said of them. Yelling 'Karl Marx! Karl Marx!' as they charged had turned out to be a worthless certificate of immortality. Sixteen inches of Czech steel, honed every morning to a frosty blue, had punctured that one. Other reasons for the poor Red morale: ammunition, victuals, morphine – nowhere to be had except by conquest. Boots – likewise. Their foot wrappings stank like a slaughterhouse in August. Nothing had happened as foreseen except for the flies, which had grown to the size of blackberries on the rich diet of flesh.

Victory, where was it, then? Where was the loot, where the tender white princesses who were now to be the property of all?

And that five-hundred-rouble payout that had been promised each man when Kazan was taken, what good was that going to be if a fellow could no longer enjoy it – if he'd been executed by Trotsky, got tif or had had his balls lopped off by a White sabre?

'Capture the place first, *duraki*, idiots,' said the lieutenants and junior captains wearily. 'Can't you understand even primitive reasoning?' But they too were pretty well scunnered. What was the point in having officers whose orders could be refused if disagreeable to those being ordered? Why not run away if one's destiny was to be taken to the back and shot for failure?

But fear is powerful and it was fear of Trotsky that had given the Reds the courage to secure the railway line by which we were entering Kazan. Having pushed out the Whites, who'd always loathed fighting in the dark, they'd driven a couple of lorries onto the foot crossing, set a few sentries and then climbed into the lorries and gone fast asleep, piled on top of each other like a mob of piglets because they'd been fighting non-stop for two nights and a day.

That's how we found them, that's how I know.

Boltikov said, 'Let's smash through the lorries, Charlie. Get Shmuleyvich to put up some smoke and then wap them in the guts, send them sky-high.'

I said, 'Why'd we want to do that carrying Bolshevik slogans on our train and wearing Red Army uniforms? What'd happen if they've torn up a rail and we hit the gap at speed?' My idea was to shimmy through the cordon into the no-man's-land between the armies and do the business discreetly.

'We'll keep the fireworks till we're leaving,' I said.

He said, 'You sure the Whites are going to try and run the gold out tonight?'

'That's what Stiffy says the intercepts say.'

'So that's the strategy at the top, but as their great plan is unfolding, some of it just squirts out on our side, that it, Charlie? What's with the women while this is going on?'

'Xenia'll be in the monastery. Annushka has volunteered to go swimming.'

'Annushka?' he said.

'Shmuley has got familiar with our good doctor. It's Annushka and Yuri now. One moment there was nothing between them and the next . . . That's how things happen, whether there's a war on or not. Anyway, the two largest people on the train turn out to be the strongest swimmers, how's that?'

'Sounds like true love.'

'They'll be too busy for love.'

Boltikov, daintily scratching his nostril with his pinky then clearing his throat: 'Now – hmm – ha ha – know something, Charlie? That we're within a rifle shot of the greatest fortune in the world? I'm not suggesting we give up on Glebov. But the thing is – one small barge – do we really have to be so frugal? Listen, if we were to cut the Yanks out of the loop, then it'd be you and I alone as principals. That'd be 330 million dollars more for us. Huh, Charlie? I mean, we're men, aren't we, Charlie? To anyone with his full quota of spunk it's got to be tempting.

The whole caboodle. The entirety of one hundred per cent, that's what I'm referring to.'

'How'd we get it out of Russia? Then how are we to find a buyer for such a quantity? Think I haven't thought about it?'

'You just leave all that to me. You get the stuff and I'll deal with the rest.'

'Get through this rail block first, shall we?' I said.

'One thing at a time,' he said, mimicking me.

Shmuley tooted twice. It was my signal. Slowly, in an appeasing way, he brought the train to a halt about fifty yards in front of the barrier of red lamps strung across the rails.

I said to Boltikov, 'You can pray they haven't torn any of the track up. On your knees. Proper praying.'

Then I opened the carriage door and dropped onto the clinker – stayed there crouching, waiting for the challenge.

The sky and the clouds still had the same queer violet tinge, which was even reflected onto the rails at my feet. Because the shot was late in coming, I had time to notice that. Plus the smoke drifting across the sky from the burning warehouses.

The sentry must have been uncertain what he'd seen. His bullet plashed against a rail some distance away and went whining into the night.

'Friend,' I shouted, thickening my Estonian accent. 'Comrades escaped from Strabinsk with stores – food and ammunition. Don't shoot.'

Now I could see him, a boy with a rifle at his shoulder and his head too high to aim it properly: looking at where he wanted the bullet to go rather than looking down the sights. 'I'm going to walk slowly towards you. Please fetch a comrade of the officer type.'

I walked with my hands as high as they'd go. It was just dark enough to have stumbled over a shovel or something and got myself shot. I poked holes in the sky and approached him gently.

Below me, along the wharf area of the riverside, the gunfire was heavy. Nothing seemed to be happening elsewhere, only down at the river. Right now the gold was being unloaded from the barges. The Czechs would have occupied fixed positions in the warehouses alongside the wharves so they could give cover during the operation. When the gold train had left, they'd drop back, abandon the city and follow in their own trains. Meanwhile the Reds'd be trying to worry them out of their positions before they were prepared to leave, that was how I read it.

In front of me there was a flurry of movement. The sentry had got an officer down from one of the lorries parked on the crossing. The two of them were waiting.

I could tell from his accent that the officer was one of those who'd been making no headway in the Tsarist army and had turned their coats. He'd be worse than a Bolshevik if he rumbled me.

But it was all right, he only wanted to get back to sleep.

He rubbed his chin and yawned. 'Suppose I'd better inspect your lot, though God knows we'd take help from the Devil if it included ammunition. Make your driver a signal to come in. I'm not walking all the way down there.'

It'd been Joseph's idea to tie a couple of crossed red flags to the front of the train. The officer liked that. He had the sentry shine his lantern over our propaganda pictures and liked them too. He liked Mrs D.'s madeleines even though they had no coconut on them. Best of all was the tumbler of vodka.

Tornado whinnied eerily within his wagon.

I shouted, 'Kobi, how often have I told you, keep the horses quiet when we halt. You're just telling the enemy there's a train-load of horse reinforcements arriving, that's all you're doing.' I thumped the wagon with my fist. 'Hold still, damn you.'

The officer scratched himself. 'All horses?'

'Yes, Comrade Excellency.'

'Pass. I just want the rest of my sleep. Can I bunk in one of these wagons of yours? No, best not to try it. Might get nabbed by that swine Piatnitsky. He'd have me flogged, wouldn't think twice about it.'

Joseph offered the officer another slug. Shoving his tumbler forward, he said, 'Coal tenders as well, I see. They'll be useful. Go on down the track for a couple of miles and you'll come to Stavka – headquarters. You'll find Comrade Trotsky's train at the junction with the westbound line. He'll tell you what to do.'

'Fine fellow, Comrade Trotsky!'

'Fine, fine man. Dedicated. Wholly without scruple. That's how we want our leaders. No namby-pamby stuff for us, eh!'

'That's right! Men of steel, men like Comrade Prodt!' I said, and when I saw the blank expression on his face – 'or Glebov, whichever name he's using now. Muraviev's men are as afraid of him as they are of Comrade Trotsky.'

'Ah yes, People's Commissar Glebov! The stories one hears about that fellow! Enough to make one's hair curl!'

The violet of the sky seemed to have got into his eyes and made them weird, as if he had rabies. But it was only the sentry playing with the lantern, which was one of those with coloured slides – white, green and orange. 'Look, Comrade whatever your name is, just get on down to Stavka and report there. I'll send this boy with you in case you meet another blockade.'

The lad unshouldered his rifle and climbed into the cab. Shmuleyvich caught my eye and nodded. Then he showed him the wire to sound the whistle and had him give a toot-toot for the lorries to get themselves shifted off the crossing. Nice touch that by Shmuley, giving him one last treat.

We glided down the glinting rails between rectangular wooden houses, vegetable gardens, small horse pastures and sheds for a milking cow. The sky was at a standstill, scarcely breathing. I went in to see how Xenia was. The clock showed half past two. We had four hours in hand.

Forty-nine

BELOW AND in front of us was the Volga, wide enough to take an entire fleet steaming abreast. In that strange light it was gleaming like a huge strip of salmon-coloured tin.

At a sharp angle on our left was the Zilantov Monastery. The way the railway line was curving round, the closest we'd get to it would be at the back, at the foot of its hill. We dawdled along until we came to its private siding. I switched the points to get us in and switched them back afterwards. Then I sent Kobi to reconnoitre the track up to the monastery.

The Bolshevik boy soldier was shitting himself. As soon as Shmuley and I had started to talk he'd have known what was coming. I felt sorry for him, ridiculously sorry. I said to him, 'It's the luck of the draw, as it was for my wife.' Shmuley let him go and as he scrambled down the ladder from the cab I shot him from above, through the top of the head. We took him by the ends and lugged him into the bushes. There was no weight to him, must have had worms.

Anyone who thinks that this civil war of ours had any element of chivalry needs his brain hosed out. It was an affair so purely Russian that when other nations attempted to intervene, they retired, baffled. Being for our purposes and ours alone, it reflected on the one hand our national temperament and on the other our history. The first ensured that it would be disorganised and provincial and the second that it would be marked by instances of unspeakable viciousness, so cruel as to fall into the realm of medical experimentation or even vivisection in some cases. I'm not referring directly to the fate of Elizaveta, though obviously hers is one such example.

What's it like to fight in a war when so terrible a thing can happen to someone's wife? Or where a prisoner risks being fed head first into the firebox of a locomotive, as happened to General Staklo? I'll tell you. It means that when one's skin depends on killing a man promptly, one does it, as I did that boy at the foot of the Zilantov Monastery. He wasn't old enough to have seduced his sister or shot a policeman. Maybe he'd never even got round to stealing apples. Morally, he'd done nothing whatsoever to deserve his death. Yet he had to die, because had he lived he could have compromised my plans – and then I would have died.

God's will is the only answer. One cannot blame history for everything.

But who am I to talk about morals? By others' standards I'm the most despicable creature alive. I've seen the revulsion in the eyes of people who know what I did. But I don't really understand what is meant by the word 'morals' – that is, I don't understand its precise meaning, one that can be applied at any time on any day without having a dictionary in one's hand. I ask myself, What's the point of having a word that only fifty people in the world completely and thoroughly understand without arguing? I didn't need a grounding in morals to see that she was in agony, that her body, her mind, her very life, were all of them ruined. Nor did morals have any relevance to what happened next – to what I did. Any half-decent man would have done the same.

Xenia informs me that my vocabulary is stocked only with imperatives and the selfish words like *must*, *me* and *ought*. I say, What do you expect? The fact is that they come to me like the most faithful of dogs. I don't even have to whistle: they're there all the time and have been since my father died of the plague and left me and my mother with a minus sum in everything that matters for modern living.

Only Elizaveta was capable of tempering my selfishness.

Her death has intensified my feelings of *againstness*. Inevitably so when daily I have to consider the rawest of all our words, which is survival. My grandparents on both sides would have had no concept of it. The closest the Doigs would have got to it was *rubbing along*, which would have been second nature to them. Until my mother's generation, the Rykovs were wealthy enough to be immune.

I now see that survival is too lofty an idea for the bourgeois. It's only when travelling in the bilges that one can perceive with total clarity what the alternative is.

Bread is survival. I'd rather have bread than morals.

That boy – the look on his face moments before I shot him. He knew he was doomed, yet hadn't there been a residue of hope in that quick lick of his lips as he decided to try escaping down the ladder? Some tiny notion of survival?

Or was it my fancy? Was I trying to make out I'd given him a chance?

I said sorry to him again, I said it twice.

Then I went to the compartment to tell Xenia that I was leaving her in the monastery till I'd finished. She was on her knees, praying – had been crying. I said, 'No time for that,' raising her and kissing the tip of her nose.

'What was that shot for?' she said, knowing very well what the answer would be.

'The boy we picked up from those Reds – our safe conduct to Stavka.'

'Did you have to?'

'It was him or us. That means you as well.'

It wasn't the first death she'd been close to. Maybe it was the boy's age that was affecting her.

She said, 'I saw his soul going up to Heaven wrapped in a grey cloth – like a bubble released from the floor of the ocean. I heard the shot – then I saw him, split seconds afterwards.'

She had her case packed. She was good like that. I picked it up. She said, 'Charlinka, do you believe you're going to meet Elizaveta when you die?'

I thought I knew where she was heading, that she'd been dwelling on her position as my future wife and was jealous of Lizochka and my love for her.

I said jocularly, 'Are you afraid you're going to be the wife who didn't make it to Heaven?'

She gave me a confused look. She disapproved of my attitude to religious matters though still acknowledging the advantages of being married to me. That was how I interpreted it.

We went along to the dining car where everyone except for Shmuley was gathered, all in Red Army uniforms. Mrs D. pulled the hem of her skirt up to show me her bathing costume. Strong legs, getting stronger as they rose, well able to sustain Shmuley.

'Black was the only colour my mother allowed me,' she said. 'None of us could have guessed how important red would become.'

I said it looked fine.

'This OK too?' She shook a lilac bathing cap at me.

'Yes, but black your face and arms. Engine grease or soot from the stove, get Shmuley to do the same. Kobi?'

He'd been quiet of late, there being no demand for heroics until now. He was leaning against the door to the galley, his face as cruel as a cat's. I asked him about the track to the monastery. He said, 'There were two men guarding it. I cut their throats. Neither was in uniform. Impossible to say which side they were on.'

'Tornado?'

'Look outside. But the lady'll have to ride him astride, legs apart. There's no woman's saddle for her.'

Beside me Xenia drew in her breath sharply. It hadn't occurred to me that my little shopkeeper might never have been on a horse before. 'Just this once, no distance to speak of,' I said to her. To Kobi, 'Where's the Rykov flag, the one we brought from the palace?'

'In the same place it always was,' he replied, a little nettlesome.

I checked with Jones that the wireless van was running properly.

Stiffy said, Did I have any further duties for him, by which he meant sending out messages but not wanting to say as much in case the women thought about black Fokkers homing in on us and got jumpy. Yes, I said, the most important one of the lot. He blew on his fingers and did a little exercise with them as if preparing to play the piano.

All that remained was the armoured car and even as the thought crossed my mind, I heard a great rumble as Shmuley took it down the wooden ramp to the platform.

I said to my people, 'Got everything? If things go right, we won't be seeing the train again.'

They were silent at this, thinking about the alternatives, about how the hell I was going to get them out of Kazan.

Fifty

THE HILL rose above us, on top of it the monastery within its battlemented walls, the domes of its churches robed not in their usual nocturnal shimmer but in that violet colour that had been with us since Chirilino. Then it had been something of meteorological interest. Now it was sinister, even a portent.

Xenia looked up at the monastery. She looked up at Tornado. She looked at me. 'I refuse.'

I said, 'You'll be riding pillion behind Kobi. All you've got to do is hang on. There's the track. There's the monastery. Half a mile max.'

One would have said there were no bones to Kobi, just old tanned leather, supple as the wind. When on horseback he became part of a horse. They loved him. Even as I was pondering over Xenia's little rebellion, Tornado turned his head to Kobi and snuffled among his clothes – for food, reassurance, or maybe hinting at a need for orders. Kobi spread his fingers round Tornado's muzzle. The horse and the hand made love to each other as Kobi waited for my command and Xenia stared up at the monastery.

She began to say something – pugnacious by the way she set her mouth.

I nodded to Kobi. In an instant he had one hand gripping her coat collar and the other cupping her ankle and had flipped her onto Tornado's back. Squealing and terrified, she clung to the reins, to his neck, his mane, to anything.

'Don't look down,' I said to her cheerfully.

Kobi said, 'She's OK. She's that frightened she won't dare try moving.'

But she did. Gingerly getting herself upright – but not letting go of a thing – she yelled at me, 'Why don't I get to ride in the car like any other woman would?'

I said what was true, that Stiffy and Jones didn't want a woman in the wireless van. No offence but that's the way it always was in the armed services, the presence of women being liable to lead to a loss of concentration. I myself would be going in advance in the armoured car with Boltikov, to force our way into the monastery. 'It could be dangerous,' I said. 'There's no knowing if the Reds aren't already in there. And if they are . . . well, my little peach, I'm just not going to let you do it.'

'So how's Annushka getting to the river? You're going to make her ride horseback as well?' Her dander was up. She was enjoying looking down on me, which was certainly a change. 'And on the way back?'

That last bit was getting too clever. I said, 'Don't blow your knickers off, lady. Everything'll work out fine for Annushka . . . Kobi, if you hear nothing, follow in five minutes. Mrs D., Shmuley, fit yourselves into the armoured car. Boltikov'll sneak you down to the river after we've taken the monastery.'

'Yeah, first let's beat up some monks, get our eye in,' Boltikov said to Kobi.

'Joseph, you stay with Stiffy. When he's finished transmitting I want you to help him start dismantling the wireless. We won't be taking the van with us. Leapforth, you come with them as far as the monastery. You're going to be Xenia's bodyguard while I deal with Glebov.'

He smiled. I'd have needed to be a decrypt expert myself to have made anything of that smile.

I went on, 'Remember, everyone, darkness is our friend. We need to be out by dawn and not a second later. Any questions?'

'Well?' said Stiffy. 'What about it then?'

I realised I'd failed to give him what was crucial – the last message for Glebov. So I did that, stuffed it crumpled into his hand and ran to the armoured car for I was in a hurry now that I'd reminded myself about the dawn deadline.

Boltikov was the driver. With Mrs D. and Shmuley in a turret apiece, I had to squeeze in beside him. Getting in and out of those Austin armoured cars was hell. Only a snake would have found it easy. I was on the point of inserting myself (which had to be done feet first) when Stiffy shouted over, 'Can't read this, sir. Is it Lola? What comes after that? Lola who?'

'Lola shit. Lobachevsky, idiot. Has a statue near the French Hotel, off the main street. Where I'm planning that Glebov and I will meet. You cock that up and I'll strangle every breath in your neck. Repeat the guy's name.'

'Lobachevsky, SIR!'

Boltikov engaged gear as I slipped in beside him. The windscreen was open, up on struts, and I kept it that way. Boltikov had brought one of the machine guns from the train and had Shmuley rig it up so that it could be fired from the driver's seat.

We went rumbling up the stony lane. When we reached the top of the hill it was to find the whole of Kazan revealed to us.

'A gun emplacement up here and you'd soon force an enemy out,' I shouted to Boltikov over the roar of the engine. 'This is where Trotsky should be.'

Which made me wonder why the Reds hadn't made a beeline for it, but it was too late to turn back now as the monastery's iron-studded gate was bang in front of us and if a regiment of Bolshies were only waiting until they could see the whites of our teeth, they'd be opening fire any minute now.

Boltikov was fingering the gun, wanting to give the gate a burst. But I knocked his hand away. We halted facing the gates. Boltikov said, 'They'll open inwards?'

I pointed at the judas gate in the left-hand one and told him to cover me.

Inside was a small wooden lodge house with a window to receive food and alms and all that keeps a monastery functioning and monks plump. Peering in I made out a nightwatchman, asleep in front of the remains of a coal fire. Not an old man, but getting that way. I rapped on the glass. He gave a great start, looked around in alarm and seized his rifle.

He came out full of hostility. I said if I'd been a Bolshevik I'd have shot him as he slept. He quietened down, and a small present of money completed his surrender. He replenished his fire and as he did so began to tell me about his previous job, which had been keeping the birds out of a grove of apricots with a wooden rattle, how his son had been his assistant, how the grove had belonged to an Armenian, how it had been valued at fifty thousand roubles per desyatin, how that was a lot more than the value of the monks' apple orchards—

The door behind me flew open. It was Boltikov, angry as a swarm of bees. 'What are you doing, for God's sake, reciting the Bible? You tell us dawn, and then slow everything down yourself. The horse is here, with Kobi and the woman. Come on, man, come on.'

'How many monks are there?' I asked the nightwatchman.

'Eleven, Excellency, and the Archimandrite. I was coming to that.' He bowed to me, palms conjoined below the tip of his brushwood beard.

Boltikov hustled him out. Lame and muttering, he shuffled over and unbarred the gates. Kobi riding beneath the old vaulted archway with Xenia hanging onto him, the old man took his bow so low that you'd have supposed he'd mistaken my Mongolian killer for Christ the Redemptor.

He wanted to get going with more stories but I grabbed him. Gesturing round the compound, I said that if he wanted to live, he should tell me what the buildings were used for.

On the north side was the refectory, dormitories and offices, a long low building on two floors. On the other side, its towers, turrets, crosses and cupolas lording it over the city, was the main church of Zilantov – All Souls.

There were no lights showing anywhere, not even a glim where some late-night praying could have been going on. In fact, that nightwatchman could have been the greatest humbugger in existence with all that stuff about guarding apricots: there could have been a thousand Bolsheviks lying in wait for us. At any moment we could have heard the snickety-snick of their rifle bolts driving home the bullet. At any moment, Glebov's soupy voice, 'At last, Doig.'

We were grouped in the shadows of the gateway, the four of us and the horse. Behind was the armoured car with Shmuleyvich and Mrs D. The gunfire down at the wharves was brisker than ever.

Boltikov nudged me. 'A racing man would give longs odds against any of us being alive in twenty-four hours. Just a feeling I have.'

I said back to him, 'Yeah, the numbers aren't particularly in our favour. Any time you want to quit – the train's down below. I don't mind.'

Now whispering in case there really were a thousand Reds in front of us, he said, 'You're a bastard, Charlie. Not one of us can leave and you know it.'

'You could get killed if you stay.'

'You're crazy. This whole business with Glebov and Elizaveta has rotted your brains. It's mush, that's what you've got in there now. I should have got out when I could – should have jumped from the train.'

I didn't mind what he said. After a year and a half I'd got within maybe a mile of Glebov – and I wasn't going to give up on him now. On this day, 7 September, I'd been born and since I couldn't have myself a cake with thirty candles I was going to have Glebov's head, and furthermore I was going to help myself to a pinch or two of the Tsar's gold so that in twenty-four hours I was not going to be a corpse thank you very much but at the helm of the future, which'd make a change so help me God it would. I may have been crazy. But I was doing all right so far.

'Go, conqueror!' I shouted at Tornado and whacked him on the butt so that he reared and gave my girl a nasty turn.

The cobbles crackled under his dancing iron-tipped hoofs. The walls behind which the eleven monks were enjoying their last manly pleasures before the avalanche of atheism arrived, threw back the echo. Lights were winking in the maddening sky – the green and red tails from signal rockets. Something was about to happen down at the wharves.

Kobi brought Tornado curvetting back to where I stood. Xenia had recovered. She called down to me, 'Thank you, Charlinka, thank you from every vessel in my body. Such a place has always been my dream.'

'For Christ's sake listen to that,' muttered Boltikov, looking at Xenia in disbelief. Then to the nightwatchman, 'Hey, whatever your name is, toll the big bell, let's get some action round here.'

The sound made me shiver, that big-bellied pot of iron from the time of Peter the Great booming through the violet night.

236

Even the Marxists down at the river must have had second thoughts about God on hearing it.

Heads appeared like magic from the casement windows of the dormitory building, all shaggy-looking as if they'd been taken completely by surprise, as if they'd never heard a single rifle shot and knew nothing about a war going on.

'God will protect them,' said the nightwatchman mildly.

From a window in the central part of the building, which jutted out from the rest and was probably the council chamber, a thin imperious voice called out, 'What is it, Sergei Sergeivich? Have the dogs of Satan come for us?'

I strode over and stood a little way out from him. Eyes close-set above a bent and bony beak and a cleft chin stared down at me. He had to be the Archimandrite. 'Well, have you come to shoot us? Is there enough light to shoot accurately or do you expect us to provide candles?'

'Old man,' I said, 'stop your nonsense. I have a train waiting for you below. It has coal, some food, and the firebox is still hot.'

'Where's it going?'

Kobi, joining me on foot, said, 'So much for staying in Kazan with his God.'

'Strabinsk – Irkutsk – then America if you feel like it. It's yours. Go wherever you want.'

Kobi: 'That way you'll get to keep your guts inside you.'

The abbot fellow shouted down, 'Why are you doing this?'

'Want me to change my mind? Want a taste of martyrdom?'

He looked around, I suppose to gauge the feelings of the monks. But the other heads had all vanished, every one of them. They weren't going to miss the chance to escape. He said, 'I see. This is what the skunks were always after, to save their skins. It's being left to me, God's ambassador, to proselytise among these Communist heathen—'

'Let me shoot the buzzard,' said Kobi. 'That'll make them hurry.'

'But don't hit him,' I said, and as the sound of the shot died away I turned to the nightwatchman: 'Count them out for me. I want the place emptied.'

They assembled in the courtyard. When they were all spoken

237

for, I sent them waddling down the track with their suitcases and homespun grips. One had a carpet flexing fore and aft of his shoulder, another was clutching an ornate samovar – an heirloom never to be abandoned, like my Rykov flag.

'God go with you,' I shouted, in particular to this man with his samovar.

The Archimandrite, going last, was pulling a handcart. 'Our holy books,' he said. He embraced and kissed me. 'God will reward you. May you scatter our enemies.' He faced the monastery and bowed to it.

The nightwatchman said, 'But my wages—'

'Take them in kind. There's plenty of stuff lying around,' said the man and then he fairly scampered off, the cart bouncing behind him.

Boltikov said, 'Why did you do that, Charlie? How are we going to get out if things go badly?'

They were all here now, including Jones and Stiffy with the wireless van. 'Listen up,' I said, 'that's a fine question Alexander Alexandrovich has just asked. The reason I gave them the train is this: so that no easy way out is left to us. We have to succeed. If we don't capture a gold barge, we'll die here.'

What I didn't say was that that train of ours had no chance of getting out of Kazan without being attacked by the Reds. Trotsky would snap it up and then those monks'd be dead soldiers of Christ.

Fifty-one

S HE'D CHAFED, she said, her skin wasn't used to that sort of thing – and sat down on a bench with her thighs parted.

I wanted to leave and get on with the business. But – this was a bad few moments for me. Fact was that I'd removed her from her straightforward life in St Petersburg, had made her follow the flag almost to Siberia, and was now going to dump her in a monastery under the guardianship of Smiler and a nightwatchman whose last job had been scaring birdies off apricots.

Something greater was owed to her. Marriage would square her away when the time came. But Odessa was fifteen hundred miles distant and none of them likely to be peaceful. While now was now and Trotsky and his army of rapists were at our heels. She was risking her life—

'You should have left me,' I said, taking her hand. 'Said, "Goodbye, Charlie," and found your way back to St Petersburg.'

The idiot nightwatchman was hovering around us instead of going to look for valuables. He started up, 'Their bees, that's what they were most concerned about, and the profit from their skeps. The monastery honey! Big money in the city, *barin*! In the summer they'd sit where the lady's sitting—'

'Scram!' I shouted at him.

'Leaving you . . . yes, I've often thought about it,' she said, yawning. Then in a light, dreamy voice, 'The fighting, it seems unreal from up here. In fact, everything has been unreal since I left home . . . Oh, I'm so sleepy.'

'Give in,' I said. 'There'll be a bed somewhere for visitors. Jones'll wake you up when the time comes and then we'll slip down the river – invisibly – with the hand of God pointing the way – and – and God at the tiller also.'

I believe I'll remember it forever how she looked at me, this girl who'd rescued me from the most horrible of my memories and who now sat on the bench with her chafed thighs, those eyes staring up at me – those great balls of eyes, more out than in, fantastically soft in their grey green, which was like the underdown on a finch that's its final and most secret layer of warmth, the eyes which were completely heart-conquering and pleading for love, protection, babies and steadiness in a man. Everything about her was soft at that moment: lips, cheeks, eyes – her whole wonderful and uncommon face – which characteristics were magnified by the great bundle of her hair, on which Moses could have floated for months.

She said, 'But in reality I could never have left you,' and put her other hand over mine. 'Don't be impatient with me. I can see it in your eyes. Open them wider, I'm not a Red about to shoot at you. Look at me, Charlie.'

I said – I've no idea what it was.

Then she said with such sweet simplicity that my breath fell back into my lungs as if it had tumbled down a staircase, leaving my brain gasping for air, exactly the same as when I clinched it with Lizochka – she said: 'God knows but you're a hard man to love. But I love you, I love you a million times over. Perhaps it could only have happened in these circumstances. Living in an apartment would have been fatal to us.'

She paused for my rejoinder or for some movement. I tightened my grip on her hand. The small-arms fire swelled and faded down at the wharves. Boltikov should have got Shmuley and Mrs D. there by now. They'd be picking their way through the abandoned stores and the rubbish and the stunted alder bushes on the river's edge . . .

She went on, 'Yet at the same time I despise myself. There are limits to what a woman who has no money can do. Remember that always. Whenever you think of me, Charlie, say to yourself, But she never had a chance to be the woman she really was. Promise? Say it out loud, then—'

'Why, Colonel Doig, this is a great castello you've got yourself up here. I've been in a few places since I left Grand Rapids but this beats them all. Some money in religion, I'm athinking—'

I said to the brute, 'Thanks for knocking.'

'Hey, did I interrupt something? But you know, Colonel, this is no time for spooning. That's for idle folk, that's what me and the little lady'll be doing while you go out to work. Lean on the battlements and watch the pretty lights, shall us, lady? Quite a spectacle down there. Glad I don't have to be part of it.'

'How's Trotsky to make contact with you, Jones? You going to wave flags at each other?' I said, getting back to the job.

'Don't you go worrying your head about me. These Reds, they're not short of a dollar or two between the ears.'

'What do you mean by that?'

'Figure of speech, old boy.'

Suddenly I had the feeling that something had passed out of my hands. I'd been nudged over and someone else had taken a grip on the lever. Was there another issue of which I knew nothing? Was it the rustle of betrayal I was hearing?

I searched Jones's face for a sign of the dagger – some lack of control round the mouth, an aversion of the eyes, impudence, satisfaction, I wasn't sure what.

Stiffy came lounging up, saying he and Joseph had got the wireless ready for removal from the van and what next. I told him to go and find something else useful to do and to bloody well keep his helmet on in a battle zone – speaking from the corner of my mouth, not leaving off my scrutiny of Jones, not giving him the chance to change his face.

Xenia now said, Where was this nice warm room for her lie-down, and I had difficulty concentrating on that as the thought was ripping through my mind, But is Stiffy also part of the betrayal? Are he and Jones acting in consort, partners for Uncle Sam in some act of political chicanery? It was queer that the two of them should have been sent on a mission to the centre of Russia with only book knowledge of the language.

I looked at him, our ginger-haired Peter Panski . . . I thought, If Stiffy, why not Joseph, why not Boltikov? Could they all be against me?

I thought, Shoot first: shoot before you're shot. What was

the point in thinking of myself as ruthless if I wasn't prepared to be ruthless? I looked round wildly. They had me surrounded: were obviously waiting for a signal. Jones would be their leader – that 'old boy' stuff. I thought: I'll shoot Jones and see where it gets me.

I went for my pistol holster, scrabbling at the metal catch.

'Doig!' protested Joseph, just managing to get a tray with a glass of tea on it out of the way of my elbow. I looked down at him, at his slight, dark, upturned face. The tea was strong and at the bottom, glowing sullenly, was a huge clot of the monks' cherry jam.

'You need it, Doig. You are our leader.'

I looked at him, astonished that I should ever have had the idea of putting a bullet into him. I was out of my skull with nerves, that was all, Glebov being so close. I imagined gripping a colossal lead weight in each hand and letting them pull my shoulders down. I slowly expelled my suspicious breath, taking it up into my nose and then pushing it out all humid over the beginnings of a smile.

Jones said, 'It's scary having a weapon so handy, isn't it? If you lose your temper, if you even have a bad thought about a guy, there's the answer, bumping against your hip. A man is to his gun as a pig is to his slumbers, it all happens quite naturally.'

He grinned at me, showing everything in his mouth, like a man really pleased with himself.

There was that sensation back again. Beneath the soles of my feet I felt the lip of the abyss. The updraught was making my trousers flap. It was no good saying to myself that danger had been my companion since I went birding on the cliffs as a boy. That was silly, that was the way one became careless with risk.

I said to him, 'When this is over, I'm going to make a trip to Grand Rapids and ask a few people if you got born with that smile. You know, came out of the hole saying, "Love me, folks." Maybe no one'll have heard of you.'

'Make sure you get my name right.'

'I'll take a list. Meanwhile you guard my woman with your life. Hear that gunfire? When it starts to roar like a nest of bees being poked out, you'll know I'm in action. An hour after that I'll be back for her.'

'Then?'

'Not your business. Whistle up a cab and go find Trotsky, that's what you can do.'

Fifty-two

STIFFY CALLED to me from the wireless van. He and Joseph were considering how easy it'd be to remove the wireless from its baseplate, whether in fact it'd be possible.

I asked him if he could still transmit. He said, Had I gone crazy, with the Reds just round the corner? I took him by the nape of his neck, squashed him into his chair and turned the switch to Send.

'LOBACHEVSKY MEETING HISTORICALLY INEVITABLE SO NO MONKEY BUSINESS. Send it and don't argue.'

Stiffy said, 'Pardon me, but would a man with Glebov's command of English understand "monkey business"?'

'He knows what a monkey is. Just do it. I'm tired of being thwarted.'

When he'd finished, I had him unscrew the armature and give me the sending key. I said that when I came back for the girl, I'd be in a hurry. He and Joseph were to follow me in the van, to stick tight up my arse or they'd get lost and then what would happen to them – 'Eh, Stiffy, eh? What'll the Reds do to old ginger-knob from Bristol, which name they know only in connection with the grandest hotels in Europe?'

This I said glaring at him from close range. I was fairly certain that somewhere among all his cardboard boxes and tins of odds and ends would be a spare sending key, that, if he wished, he could be up and running again within seconds. But I wanted absolute radio silence from now on. I was going to enforce obedience one way or another.

He agreed, Joseph being my witness and as a Russian understanding everything about intimidation.

Boltikov came roaring up to the monastery having delivered Shmuley and Mrs D. Kobi stuck his head out of his turret, laughing, so I knew there'd been fighting. He shouted, 'Vaska's had it.' I saw that the machine gun in the right-hand turret was somehow lolling. I thought to myself, That's going to be awkward dragging his corpse out, but thank God, he'd fallen on the field of battle – where Boltikov had also been wounded, in the arm. He was steering with one hand, the armoured car bouncing off the topside bank as if he were drunk.

I shouted to Joseph, '*Zhivo*, tea for them both,' and while this was happening learned that Shmuley and Mrs D. had been set down close to the river and that the last few barges were being unloaded in the godown. A derrick was hoisting the cases of bullion out of the hold and swaying them straight into the rail wagons alongside. The barges were being taken out of the godown as they were emptied and anchored in the river. There was a whole row of them, Boltikov said, bristling with weapons in case Trotsky's torpedo boats tried anything.

'Christ,' he said, as Joseph handed him his tea, 'you can do better than that. Bring me the Vladimir. If the monks haven't got a reserve of it somewhere I'll chew my cock off.'

I said to him, 'No sign of that submarine they were talking about in Strabinsk?'

He said, 'Not even a Bolshevik dickhead's going to sink the gold. Think of fishing it up again, brick by brick. However . . . a submarine on the Volga . . . well now . . . we should think about that, Charlie.'

I said, 'How many barges still to be unloaded?'

'Three at most. From where I dropped Mrs D. and Shmuley, I could see through the godown from one end to the other. There are two wharves, each with its own railway line.'

'Only one railway is shown on Jones's map,' I said.

'They become one a few hundred yards from the godown. The reason they have two is so they can load and unload from two wharves at the same time. But they're only using one wharf for the gold.'

'So only one of the lines is being used?'

'Correct.'

'We could capture all three barges?'

'That'd be sixty tons. Enough to die for.'

I said it looked like he almost had, nodding at his arm.

Pinked only, he said, and told me how. They'd met a White patrol – it being no-man's-land down there – and Vaska had forgotten he was in a Red uniform. He'd leaned out of the turret to greet one of the patrol, thinking he recognised his brother. That had been the end of him, just like that. In his death throes he'd jackknifed out of the turret and come slithering down the bonnet. He, Boltikov, had – that selfsame instant, no joking – changed down a gear to get the hell out. Whoosh! had come Vaska's bloody corpse clatter-bang past his head. Instinctively he'd bobbed to one side. It had saved his life. If he hadn't, the shot would have hit him slap in the chest.

'Luck's running along beside me,' he said, and gestured as if patting the head of a dog.

'What are you waiting for, Doig?' shouted Kobi from his turret. 'He can fill himself with drink afterwards.' He traversed his machine gun through its full horizontal range of 240 degrees, going 'bup-bup-bup-bup' like a child.

I wriggled into Vaska's turret. Boltikov waved Joseph away. He was going to keep the Vladimir bottle with him, keep it under close supervision.

As we rattled down the hill, I bowed my head:

'Father in Heaven, Lord of my life this night, look after me. Preserve me from the bombs, bullets, cannon and bayonets of my enemies, from all their shit. Preserve especially my cock. Allow me to come through it in one good working piece. Bring Glebov into my power. Spare my people. Keep the pigs away from my woman. This is the prayer of Charlie Doig with his eyes shut. He knows he has sinned the full roster.'

Coming out of the monastery gates at the bottom of the hill, I beat on the outside until Boltikov stopped. I'd forgotten to check the dynamite. Yes, he shouted back, the box was under his seat, the Bickford cord all over the place as usual, like clothes line.

What about the signal cartridges for Shmuley and Mrs D.?

'Do you take me for a child?' he yelled. 'Yellow, yellow, white, all lying here in the right order. Have a look for yourself.'

Craning my neck I saw them, cartridges as thick as Bologna

sausages. I said, 'See you don't get them wet. That paper'll swell if you do and they won't fit in the breach.'

By way of a reply he farted, a tinny blast within that car.

I said, 'Lay off the Vladimir. Better still, chuck the bottle out.'

He laughed at me, but he drove down to the docks as I'd instructed, warily, not rushing it, so that it would appear to any onlooker as though we'd conquered the place and were on a tour of inspection.

Fifty-three

S TIFFY HAD told me the latest: the Whites held the docks and the surrounding warehouses. The Czechs, their allies, held all the southern railway system up to the point where they'd run out of men. The northern section of the railway, where we'd entered Kazan, had been the centre of the thrust by the 3rd and 4th Red Armies. These men were pushing south all the time, palpating the Whites at every point, probing for weak flesh.

'Good luck, sir, that's what I say. Good luck to us all, come to that,' Stiffy had said nervously.

The key to the gold was the railway. Ownership of one was useless without control of the other. And the key to the railway was the position of the locomotive that was to haul out the laden wagons. It had to be waiting there with steam up or what the Whites were doing was pointless.

Wholly in doubt was the disposition of the forces around this locomotive. It was here, I guessed, that the White and Czech command structure would be at its weakest. The Whites had the docks, the Czechs had the railway. So who'd be responsible for the actual point at which the two met – at the locomotive?

There'd be tension. The Whites would be afraid that they'd load up the railway wagons only for the Czechs to make off with the gold. The Czechs would be blaming the Whites for not unshipping the gold quickly enough. On the one side would be men too watchful to function and on the other side men shouting, 'Hurry, you bastards!'

Were I Trotsky, that would be the point at which I'd drive in a wedge and work it round, harassing and worrying this jealous, tender junction. It was the obvious place to attack.

Perhaps he'd be there himself: have donned his trademark greatcoat and wise-owl spectacles, emerged from his personal train with his hair standing on end as per the photos, and gone to gloat. He'd be in the shadows. A spare, vicious figure. Five foot seven, 150 pounds of bitterness and spite. He'd think himself invisible. But his spectacles would be glinting red from the flames, the explosions and the gouts of blood that'd start flying when I got going. I'd recognise him all right, Mr Shitsky.

'Doig,' I'd say, arriving from behind his shoulder and offering the simplest introduction. 'Your chum Glebov raped my wife, he and his gang.'

'What of it?'

'You dare say that, "What of it?"'

'They were justified on account of their poor allocation by history. Women must learn about the necessity of class warfare as well as men. They must be educated in reality. The days of the Smolny dancing classes are over.'

He'd look me over with contempt, not knowing that in my hand, in my pocket, in my heart's most absolute intention, was Kobi's Mongolian stabbing knife.

He'd say, 'I know you. You were at Smolny on that historic night, you were the mushroom seller. Oi! You men over there! Arrest Charlie Doig, the notorious criminal and descendant of latifundists. The usual bourgeois-liberal tendencies are at work within him like termites. Let us hasten the process of disintegration. Put him in a space vehicle and let science look after him. Up there amid the ice fields and meteorites and the graves of his obsolete gods.'

'You value your ideas too highly,' I'd cry, and whipping out Kobi's knife I'd have his scalp off in one swift and gleaming motion and be tossing it, hairy and dripping, with his smart-ass eyes hanging down like buttons on a thread, to his dog, probably a German shepherd. All men of history have been dog lovers and most of these very same men have also been un-principled liars and self-enrichers, if not psychopaths. Starving, the disloyal carnivore would gulp down its master's scalp in a oner. Then it would start to howl in terror and Trotsky's eyeballs would come pinging out of its anus boiling over with all sorts of clever-dick arguments about the inalienable right of syphilitic Bolshevik soldiers to rape women.

Yes, I'd do for Trotsky as well as Glebov and then I'd go into exile. It'd be heigh-ho for the good life in Chicago, not having to wonder every minute if my woman was still alive, sinking a beer when I felt like it in one of those steep-staired cellars where talk could be had with normal people like the salts from the days of windjammers and harpooners who'd been towed for weeks in their rowboat by a Leviathan –

> It was on the good ship *Lockjaw*,
> Well nigh a fortnight out of port,
> Our engines dead, the sea a-tremble,
> And lifelong water running short,
> That V., our luscious commodore,
> Laid aside her snow-white snort,
> And said, 'So I shall be our SOS,'
> And stripping off her naval dress,
> Her sword, her pants and epaulettes,
> She angled nude across the shrouds,
> Angelic imprint on the clouds . . .

Boltikov shouted up that he'd heard it all before, when I was in my cups, the entire performance. Was I going crazy? Was it all too much for me? Should he pass the Vladimir?

I said it must be the strain of keeping the show on the road, meaning drunks like him. Why didn't he and Kobi sing something to keep me awake?

'From *Don Carlos*?' he shouted back. 'That fantastic aria – it was Chaliapin at his best – you remember, the night that Lenin struck—'

I said No, in case the Reds heard him – which was ludicrous since we were five tons of metal bouncing over cobbles, but it was what I said. Then, 'Do that new one of Lenin's, the Internationale,' I said. 'It'll make a good impression if things go wrong.'

But he and Kobi couldn't bring themselves to do anything so

disgusting, even though they were wearing Bolshevik uniforms. The only tune we all knew was 'God Save the Tsar' so that was what we sang as we rumbled through the ancient Admiralty Quarter.

We were in the eye of the storm. Not much of life was in evidence. A couple of looters, then nothing more until a White cadet officer jumped out at a street corner and levelled his pistol at us. A burst from Kobi's Maxim did for that show of courage, the youth spinning round and his military cap flying off like a discus. Rounding the corner, we came across his patrol running for their lives. Kobi wanted to pepper them even though they posed no threat to us. He'd no idea of right and wrong. Killing was his pleasure. If he could, he would. But here there was nothing to be gained. He'd already shot the officer and by doing so had put our credentials on a proper footing if any Reds were around.

I shouted over to him, 'You'll have your fun later.'

Boltikov teased the cork from the Vladimir bottle with his teeth and started in on *Don Carlos*. I leaned down, grabbed the bottle and chucked it over my shoulder, in among the spare wheels and tyre levers.

'Forget the bloody opera, just get going, lickety-split – you see the fire-watching tower over there?'

My head had suddenly cleared – it was the incompatibility of Verdi and Karl Marx. I was no longer thinking of being dead or alive by dawn but alive only.

Alive, alive O!

And the O was the oxygen that was a light blue streak in front of us, the flare still gleaming from the top of the fire-watching tower to tell everyone, in peace and war, that the building was too useful to be destroyed. Earlier in the night the Reds had captured it. The last Stiffy had heard it was still in their hands. If the Whites had regained it or the Czechs, we were cooked, turning up as we were in full Bolshevik regalia.

'Hang on,' shouted Boltikov, and with his bad arm dangling, one-handedly dropped down a gear, wrenched the wheel over and slewed our armoured car to a halt beside a brazier.

I made out the dull shapes of five men sitting round on wooden warehousing cases. They could have belonged to any of the armies.

Pulling down the peak of my colonel's cap, I leaned on the edge of the turret and regarded them in silence. It was a good feeling to be holding them down by my eye alone. I said in a low voice, 'What the fuck are you doing on your butts? Who's in charge?'

This man idled out of the gloom, smoking. A Czech would never have behaved so casually, would have shot at me on the spot. So now the odds were fifty–fifty, Red or White.

Hands on hips, insolently, he began to walk round the car. 'What name have you given to this heap of yours?' he said, not removing his cigarette. Its paper was stuck to his lower lip. The cigarette's glowing end bobbled as he spoke.

'*Chort*,' I said – the Devil – breathing again, for he was clearly a Red.

'Indeed, *Chort* is it,' he said, coming round to below my turret and looking truculently at my colonel's tabs.

Swifter than a swallow at flies, I plucked the cigarette off his lip. 'Open,' I commanded. And when he did so, as I knew he would on account of Bolshevik discipline, I popped the cigarette into his mouth, and catching and twisting his lips, held him fast. His mouth was vertical, like that of a child who'd suffered from the midwife's forceps.

'Listen, comrade, I am Colonel Sepp of the Estonian Mechanised Regiment. I've fought over one thousand miles to give succour to the proletariat of Kazan. That man up there, who'd shoot you as soon as spit, has come from Mongolia. We are the world, yes, the fucking great future, the unquenchable spirit of the working classes. Who are you? A nasty, mannerless oaf. Unless you're looking for a bullet, you'll one, respect an officer's uniform, and two, tell me when you had the last report from the tower.' I gave his lip another hitch to encourage him.

A second man came out of the shadows. He spoke his name fawningly, but it could have been anything as he had a thick peasant's accent and the engine was still running.

Kobi covered me as I got out of the car. I said, 'Where's your officer? Is that him up the tower?'

When the fellow said it was, I clicked my fingers and held out my hand for the field telephone. There had to be one. These squaddies were just the messengers. The man at the top of the tower'd phone down some shift in the White position and off one of them would trot to Stavka.

It was answered immediately. I expect the observer had got lonely after his initial excitement up there, looking out over the docks and the shooting.

'Sepp, commanding the Estonian Mechanised Regiment. New orders from Stavka, to be delivered in person. Stay at your post. My man will bring them up.'

Kobi had pulled down the lid of his turret. I could see his flat Mongolian face peering at me through the slit. I said, 'Get out. This is your job.'

'Yes, Colonel,' his voice disembodied and metallic, like Boltikov's fart.

Leaning against the hull of my armoured car – *Chort*, the Devil, good name for it – and him standing in front of me rather sloppily, I said, 'Tell Boltikov what's happening. Say he can blow these men to pieces any time he feels like it.'

'Yes, Colonel.'

I called the messengers over, got them standing in front of me, smouldering, eager to pick a fight. I said to the man whose lip I'd had, 'Look, comrade, rank matters. Because I've never feared death and have positive ions between my ears, I'm a colonel. Because I'm a colonel I command an armoured car with two 7.62mm Maxims – water-cooled, six thousand rounds apiece. But you just have popguns and a couple of rounds each. Think about the difference before you try anything.'

Kobi – hell, can those Asian guys be impassive. I took a paper from my inside pocket and handed it to him.

'There's the orders, take them to the top and report back to me.' I pointed him at the metal ladder.

He said, 'He's the only man up there, is he, Colonel?'

His dark eyes flickered. He was trying me. OK, Kobi, but don't overdo it.

'Yes, the only one. Off you go, quickly now, man.'

He made me a deliberately cockeyed salute. I stepped forward and gripped him by the slack of his coat. There was no need to be saucy, no advantage to be gained of any sort. I stuffed my face into his – eyes popping, hissing, spattering him: 'For Christ's sake get up there and bowstring the bastard. Then look round and see what's happening.'

Fifty-four

No sooner had Kobi disappeared up the tower than this lone cloaked figure goolied out of the night, head weaving, hands behind his back, inspecting everything. He walked like someone who knew he was important. I smelt trouble the instant I saw him. And I was certain of it when the messengers stiffened to attention, which they hadn't done for me even when I pulled rank on them.

'Sepp,' I said to him, 'Colonel Sepp commanding the Estonian Mechanised Regiment.'

'Comrade,' he said, no more, voice as flat as a plate. He could have been one of the big names, one of those militant Jewish philosophers trying to get their own back on the world via Bolshevism. He took a torch from the pocket of his cloak and began to walk around the armoured car: a lean, schoolmasterly type who'd miss nothing.

He halted. I knew where his torch was pointing: Muraviev's death-head insignia – a scarlet skull with a thick black line through it. Joseph must have painted it out more than a hundred times, but it still showed.

I got a thoughtful look from him, head to one side.

'Good tyres,' he said. 'Sensible of you not to have put on combat wheels.'

But I wasn't fooled, and when he'd completed his inspection and was walking over to the messengers – when Boltikov's line of fire was clear – I banged on the hull.

It was close range. It made a mess of them, picked that little Yid up and dumped him five yards back. But why take a chance?

That's what survival always comes down to. Only vain people take chances.

One of the messengers had fallen over the box with the field telephone. I dragged him off and got hold of Kobi. He was perfectly composed, took it for granted that the burst from the Maxim had routed all the dangers beneath him. In fact, you might have thought he was up the tower sightseeing.

'Looks good. The Whites have got floodlights rigged up the length of the train. I can make out everything, except in the godown. Can't see under the roof. There are no more barges waiting below so they must be unloading the last of them. Train's got steam up. Maybe we should hurry a bit?'

I asked him, What about the Reds? I was sure they'd have a force close by, waiting to profit from any misunderstanding or jealousy between the Whites and the Czechs.

Kobi said, Nothing doing that he could see.

I said, 'Sure?'

He said, 'Maybe you want to come up and see for yourself?' – a bit of his usual lip creeping in.

But I couldn't leave Boltikov alone, him and his bad arm. What if another lot of Reds turned up and found him surrounded by their dead pals?

I said to Kobi, 'Try making your eyes round. That way you'll see more.'

There was shooting going on all the way through the northern part of the city and along the railway track there. Small-arms stuff, nothing big at this hour of the night with ammunition so scarce. And through the docks and warehouses and all the little alleys and grimy chandlers' offices, it was the same. In short there was a decent racket all round us.

Nevertheless, Kobi's reply reached me with the clarity of birdsong.

'If I heard myself saying to anyone what you've just said to me, I'd say to myself, "Hello, cunt, you're at it again." Where would you be without me, Doig? Answer me that. Then I'll tell you where the Reds are.'

I said, 'You want me to take a hacksaw to the ladder?'

He laughed, knowing it was an empty threat with time running out on us. Kobi's laugh, coming down a field telephone?

Like an oak tree creaking in the wind, a remarkable noise from so whippy a man. Maybe all Mongolians have that sort of deep, gruff, grunting laugh.

Then he said no more. I knew he wouldn't let me down. He'd be imprinting the Bolshevik positions in his mind, visualising the thrust they'd be preparing, the thrust that we'd get in before them, how the ground might look in the places where the shadows were thickest . . .

The telephone tingled in its box. 'Doig, there's a Red signaller down there trying to lamp me a message.'

'Show him your own lamp, then. Just flash it around a bit while you have a final look.'

'Can't. It must have gone over the side with the officer. He went through the roof of the warehouse. Didn't you hear?'

'Then come down damned quickly.'

I ran over to the armoured car. Boltikov stank of Vladimir. He said, 'They'd be very foolish to attack now,' and closed his eyes.

I shoved him out of my way and took a tyre lever to the box of Happy Christmas dynamite – thus stencilled on the lid by the All-Nippon Explosive Corporation – and grabbed an eight-inch stick and a detonator: whipped off a length of Bickford cord.

Kobi touched down lightly, knees flexing. He saw what I was up to and would have helped, only I wanted to hear his report before the tower went up. Afterwards we were going to be too busy to hang around.

'The Whites put a flare up, that's the only reason I could see. The Reds've got a train on the unused line half a mile back from the godown. Looks like they're getting ready for a charge – going to slide up parallel to the gold train and jump it.'

'Coaches?'

'Horse wagons, a string of them.'

'Same idea. The Whites have blocked that line?'

'Yes.'

'How substantial?'

'They're doing it right now. Rubble. Carting it in with barrows.'

I finished laying out the Bickford and cut the fuse: muttered to Kobi, 'I can't think why the Whites didn't blow this place up when they could have.'

'Too stupid,' he said. And then, grinning, 'That Bolshie signaller'll get more of a reply than he bargained for.'

Elation is a good explosion viewed from a safe distance. There was a terrific flash and then these bluish-grey petticoats of smoke, curling and billowing. In the middle of them the tower went up like a rocket stick – not very far, but it got its feet off the ground before toppling away from us like a giant.

'Lucky it fell the right way,' said Boltikov, blearily.

'Stuff it, Jeremiah,' I said and took the wheel. I'd never thought the tower'd go anywhere else, dicky-bird luck being perched on my shoulder with a nice tight sphincter.

I was fairly bubbling as I manoeuvred *Chort* through the back lanes of the dock workers' hovels – ghastly places, low-lying and full of ague. I said to myself, These people are no different to anyone else. They just have to get to the end in as good an order as they can. Maybe revolution is the best thing for them, will improve the quality of getting there. But once they've wiped away the past, there'll be nothing left to hate. They'll have to fabricate new demons. Or try loving each other.

Hate and love, the only constants—

God bless the pair of them! I cried out, and dragging *Chort* round a corner, found I was in a cul-de sac.

But this was ridiculous, to get us lost at such a critical point. They were the same wretched little wooden houses on either side, quite evidently deserted. I stopped and got out, thinking to get my bearings from the direction of the gunfire. And what happened was that in my very first breath I smelt the dawn.

I steadied myself. Don't panic, man. Look to the east and tell me if you see even a glimmer of pale.

I did – and breathed again. The violet glow had left the clouds: there was nothing up there but blackness. It had been my mind at work, the craziness brought back by tension.

I felt my pulse: spoke to myself and got calm. And then it was no longer the smell of the dawn that reached me but the smell of the Volga: cordage, wet tarpaulins, creosote, tobacco, dried fish, motor oil, sails, boats, the effluvium of Kazan's drains. But it was a warning not to dally, and I looked round desperately for a way through to the wharves. There were narrow passages that the dock workers used but I wanted something I could get an armoured car through. I needed a seven-foot clearance.

Kobi said, 'What's that at the end of the street?'

'The back wall of a warehouse, idiot,' I replied.

'I don't think so. There are gaps in it. I saw a lantern moving on the other side.'

I ran to it – and I ran back, having found it was only a wooden paling and that on the other side was the railway track with a train as Kobi had described it from the top of the tower, and that lying around on porters' trolleys were Red soldiers, shagged out and smoking.

But was it the same train that Kobi had seen, the one lined up for action? There was only one way to know.

We were doing thirty when we hit the paling – when we took it out by the roots. It had been built upright but I'd spotted a sliver of space that the dockers' kids had been using to get onto the railway to forage for coal and I went for it. If the baulks fell forward we'd have a hard time getting over them without tipping. But if they went sideways – which they did, splintering, crashing and pulling down an entire section of the paling that had been nailed with a cross-beam.

'Now!' I yelled to Kobi, who let rip with his Maxim over the heads of the soldiers – so that they'd know not to trifle with us.

Empty drums of something went booming over the railway lines like gongs. One of the soldiers who was more alert than his comrades tried to stop us by pushing his trolley under the wheels. We rode over it, crunching it to shreds. Then we were among them.

No one ever got out of an armoured car quicker than I did. I was like a djinn, like a magic puff of smoke, and then I'd caught hold of the Red closest to me and had him fast in my embrace. Christ, he smelt but I was nothing very pretty myself and the point was that I was hugging him like a lover and kissing his furry cheeks and hugging him again, squeezing him against my body at the same time as saying to myself, Until his ribs crack, Charlie, until they bloody well crack.

I held him at arm's length. My eyes were soaked with tears.

He said, 'Why did you fire on us then, comrade?'

'What do you expect, if you skulk around in the dark like adulterers?' – and I fell on him again, a short burly man whom I smothered.

'Talk sensibly, Estonian.'

'Not at you but over you! Yes, over your heads! You were never in danger! We thought you were White traitors up to some knavery and wanted to take you prisoner. Yes! It's true! We were after a share of the money Comrade Trotsky has promised. Can you blame us? Still, all's well that ends well—' and I would have hugged him a third time had he not pushed me away and said, 'Money? What's all this about? How much? Cash?'

'You knew nothing?'

There were about a dozen of them altogether, ragamuffin soldiers. I went round them one by one, shaking hands, drawing each of them into my embrace and asking for forgiveness. They said they were an advance party: that they'd been waiting for orders from an officer stationed on the fire-watching tower that had just been blown up: that now they were headless and unmotivated.

One of them came up to me and peered at my tabs. 'Comrade Colonel!' He saluted me sharply. And now they looked at me very differently, knowing that as a colonel I could save them from being shot for insufficient bravery. Also, in the eyes of each of them and particularly in the eyes of the man I'd hugged, stirring unresolved but hopeful, glinting flashes of silver, was the matter of the cash. They'd all heard the word. Some of them would never have seen even one live rouble in their short lives. Magic was in the air – my magic.

'Gather round me, boys,' I said. 'Now, this is how I plan to get ourselves some benefit from Comrade Trotsky's promises . . .'

Give a man a chance at women, pelf or a good strong horse and world revolution vanishes entirely from his mind.

Fifty-five

THE ENGINE driver was my problem. No Shmuleyvich this one but a man with a wedge-shaped nose and a long swaying neck like a cobra.

I said to him merrily, 'Let's get that money, eh, Ivan Ivanovich!'

'And not wait for the rest of the comrades? Is that brotherly, Comrade Colonel?' Like voice, like man – small, mean and whining.

'Why? They may have given up trying to get to us – been cut off by the enemy, maybe killed. Or they may've found a good billet and gone to bed! That'd be just like them, wouldn't it! So what I say is this, why share Comrade Trotsky's cash if we don't have to? Ten thousand roubles – listen to the sound of that, boys!'

'Ten thousand divided by twelve isn't enough. I must have a thousand for myself. Who's the driver? I am. Who's going to risk a bullet first? I am. You can't deny that, comrades.'

Taking a chance with the squaddies, I said to him, 'You want a thousand? Done,' and kissed the little swine.

'That's all very well but the barricade they've put up: how's that to be dealt with?'

'With the snowplough over there. Push it aside. Easy as picking your nose.'

He was relentless: 'What about my safety? I've no fireman in the cab. I'll be alone. I'll get shot to ribbons.'

I said, 'Oh, but I'll be at your side, comrade, your boot alongside mine, as it should be. Together we'll take our chances, together we'll strip those lice of their illegal spoils. The age of the proletariat is dawning and we shall be its first ray of light. What say you all?'

I glanced to the east. Get on with it, Doig! Then, make haste slowly. Work the crowd properly, take your time, don't get it wrong.

'Thank the Lord for that,' said the driver sarcastically, with a snaky twist of his neck.

But I sensed he had no support among the soldiers. I called Kobi over and said loudly, 'Our comrade friend here has some difficulty with the new style of military discipline. Have him slot onto the snowplough and be ready to go in four minutes. If he argues shoot him and find me another driver.

'Your widow would receive the Order of Lenin as well as the thousand roubles,' I said soothingly to the driver.

He said, 'Fat lot of good that'd do me,' and wanted to argue, but when the soldiers openly laughed at him, I knew he was in the bag.

While he was putting on the snowplough, the Whites shot up a flare to see what was happening. It floated above us like a fizzing star at the end of a tiny white petal of a parachute. We threw ourselves down, in between the rails, in there with the dog shit. Bullets pinged off the rails around us. Raising my head I could see that the loading derrick had given up. In the mouth of the godown there were stevedores bent double, portering the gold across on their backs.

Halfway between the barge and the wagon stood an over-seer. In his hand was a knout. Every man returning unloaded to the barge was getting a flick across his spine. We were all in a hurry.

(A man near me was struck. The thump of a bullet striking flesh has a completely different resonance to one striking wood, for instance, or a sack of wheat. Flesh has a wetness to it.)

My worry was that if we were pinned down for long, the engine driver would get cold feet, decide to forgo his prize money and make a run for it. There were couplings to be attached for the snowplough. Only he knew how to fix them.

Then Boltikov – ah, Alexander Alexandrovich, my saviour! Let me be charitable, let me propose that the required angle of fire was too steep for the Maxim and that the parachute had to drift lower before you could shoot. Let me not say you were sleeping and awoke . . . At any rate he opened up, a terrific and

quite unexpected noise behind us, and demolished the parachute with his first burst. In the silence, as the flare plummeted
into the Volga in a white streak, we heard the tinkle of his spent
shells falling to the floor in the turret, brass upon iron.

The man lying next to me muttered, 'That'll worry them
hearing a Maxim so close. Next thing we'll know is shells
coming our way.'

I leapt to my feet. I flung up an arm. I wanted only a sword
and a scarlet shirt to be Garibaldi. 'Hooray for Alexander
Alexandrovich and his marksman's aim!' I banged on the
armoured car for emphasis. Boltikov pushed up the lid of the
turret and stuck his head out. There was enough light for
everyone to see the sling knotted round his neck. 'Wounded as
well! Yes, comrades, braveness can be learned. He'll be covering
us all the way in. He'll give those Whities a bellyful of lead.
Remember, a bucket of roubles for each of you! Hurrah!
Hurrah!'

Our train appeared with the snowplough, looking like an ice-
breaker. Kobi leaned out of the cab and gave me a good signal.

There was still some muttering so I went among the men
whispering 'Roubles, roubles,' and making the universal recog-
nition signal between thumb and forefinger.

But even then I might not have done it had the gold train not
chosen that moment to whistle. The idea went through them
like an epidemic: it's going and with it my fortune.

Someone shouted, 'Let's get on with it, Comrade Colonel.
You lead and we'll follow!'

'Then let's move it, *zhivo, zhivo*,' and I scrambled up onto
the footplate to join Kobi and the driver.

Kobi wanted to go down the track at full throttle. But I knew
that if we hit the barricade at speed the front wheels would just
ride up the rubble and we'd crash over onto our side.

So we went steadily towards the godown with the plough just
skimming the rails. Of course we were being shot at from all
angles. They were trying to put their fire through the portholes
on either side, to get us in the mouth. But the Reds had thought
of that one and had fitted up mirrors so we could take shelter
and still see what was in front of us – which was the barricade
of rubble.

On the parallel track was the gold train. Behind was the black maw of the godown, figures scurrying, red spittle-spurts of fire.

'Medal time for the hero,' I said to Kobi and out went the engine driver, arms thrashing, like a child learning to swim.

'Send a thousand to the widow, don't forget now,' shouted laughing Kobi.

'Hold on,' I shouted back, there being a bit of wheel spin as we struck the rubble. Then the shattered bricks parted and we were through, covered in dust and sneezing, the godown eighty yards away and the Whites beginning to run like dysentery.

It was Kobi who was on the side of the cab next to the gold train, that was the way it'd worked out. His was the judgement. If he got it wrong we'd be marmalade on the rails.

'Now!' he shouted and was gone, knife in his left hand, to grab hold of the gold train's handrail with his right hand and haul himself along the footplate and into the cab.

I was a second behind him, stumbling as I hit the footplate because Kobi jumping first had the best of the target. Grabbing a stanchion – swinging round – off balance – I glimpsed astonished faces in the train we'd deserted. Then my foot got a hold of something solid and with a heave I was in the gold train's cab, Luger in my fist.

A fantastically red face was staring at me, blue eyes half an inch out of his skull, mouth wide open, dreadful teeth. I shot him, two in the belly, without thinking.

Kobi, on the other side of the man, said drily, 'Thanks, Doig. Lucky for me he's so fat,' and jerking out his knife, gave him a push so that he fell past me, outwards onto the clinker. He grinned across at me. 'Head for home now, shall we?'

I looked at the pressure gauges, expecting to find a good head of steam. However, this was not the case. What had that driver been thinking of?

'Shovel for your life, man,' I shouted, and ripping open the firebox Kobi did so, with swift savage strokes of the long-bladed shovel, not wasting a second of time, not bothering to spread the coal evenly in the corners of the firebox.

I smoothed the throttle forward. Christ, was that engine cold, heaving out these dense lethargic gasps as if on the point of death.

Behind us, in the godown, the driverless Red train smashed through the buffers into the river, a sensational noise of plunging water and steam and cavernous thumping explosions even amid all the gunfire.

Risking a glance out of the cab, I almost had my eyebrows shot off. The White soldiers had recovered from the surprise, were coming up the line from the godown – running fast, dodging in and out of the wagons. The Czechs on the barges out in the river began shooting. I flung myself onto the floor of the cab, dragging Kobi down with me.

Move, bastard wheels! Move faster!

The night was thinning. Dawn couldn't be far away. There was no time left – we were in minus time. Maybe the great bugaboo had caught up with me at last. Maybe it was the end of luck: *konets* – the end.

Lying there I closed my mind to everything except the hiss of steam and the oily suck of the dilatory pistons. You know how this is in a steam train, the small initial tugs as the slack between the wagons is taken up and the reluctance with which the first revolutions are accomplished as the engine assesses the weight behind it.

The bullets arrived like raindrops. The sand buckets were riddled before we'd covered five yards. Both lamps above my head were shattered. Shards of hot glass rained upon me. I covered my head with my hands.

There's not much room down there on the floor of a locomotive cab. Kobi's face was inches from mine. I could see not only every single hair sprouting from the mole on his chin but the flecks of coal dust in among their roots. Did I actually like this man? What would we do when everything was over: say goodbye and walk away as if these extraordinary adventures had never occurred? He'd saved me from death. He'd killed everyone I'd asked him to. Our adventures had been truly colossal.

Might we die together – here, side by side? Was that what Fate had in mind?

I thought, Please, Fate, let me kill Glebov first. Afterwards—

Then, no, by God, not even then would I give in. Fate should take the dog for a walk and get herself amused by something else – by the shape of the clouds or by a fox running off with a live chicken in its mouth. Eventually these bad times would end. Either I'd see them off or they'd peter out of their own accord. When that happened, I wanted Kobi beside me. We'd try our hand at being professional mercenaries. Our knowledge of death would be second to none—

The pressure had to be higher by now. Reaching up I pushed open the throttle lever.

The Czechs had grabbed a couple of launches from some-where and were coming up the river after us at speed. Maybe it wasn't their bow waves out there but those of Trotsky's torpedo boats. It didn't matter which. Everyone was after us, Whites, Reds and Czechs. OK, that had been my plan, so that Shmuley and Mrs D. could swim into the godown at their leisure and cut loose a barge. Who was going to bother about one boat drifting away downstream when wagon after wagon of gold was disappearing in the opposite direction?

However, success was coming at some risk. Before long someone would think of blocking the line or shifting the points to stick us down a siding.

'No bloody Fokker'll shit on us this time,' grinned Kobi from his coal-smudged face. 'They love the gold too much.'

I grinned back. We had pressure on the dial, were fairly rocking along. I had good feelings. Within every successful man a buccaneer is always stretching.

I said, 'What do you say we just go on?'

'Till the coal gives out?'

'Further.'

'Make a run for it, you mean?'

'Yes. Mongolia?'

'With the gold?'

'Yes. Hire ourselves an army. Conquer a territory. Pass suitable laws.'

'You're teasing me, Doig.'

The long slow bend I'd picked out on the map was coming up. There was no question of halting the train with that sort of pursuit behind us. They'd smell a rat. The Whites I wasn't afraid of, but the Reds and the Czechs – they'd send their hard men after us into the city. We wouldn't have a chance. Nor would my girl. And then Glebov would go unpunished.

Some buildings were coming up on the river side of the line. They'd screen us for a bit. That'd be our chance to jump, when we slowed to make the corner. I stuck my head out, hand on the air-brake lever.

The bullet went past my head with a quick dry whistle.

Fifty-six

I TOOK BACK everything I'd been thinking about home and dry. Kobi said, 'Where did that—?'

I slammed on the air brakes, the handbrake, Emergency Only. The wheels locked and screamed. Sparks bloomed, I could see them in the mirrors, whole necklaces rippling away. The wagons cannoned against each other violently, slamming shit out of the buffers. That sniper had to have been a mountaineer or a gymnast to have hung on through all that. But was he alone?

A lump of coal hit the floor right at my feet. I looked up. A hand shot out to stop the whole lot sliding down. Filthy, but a hand and not mine or Kobi's.

'Christ,' I shouted, 'they're everywhere, like fucking serpents.'

Kobi had his knife out. I cupped my hands and up he went like a bird and grabbed that man's hand and began to sever it at the wrist. Next, they were rolling around at my feet and the coal was falling in a black landslide and the train was rocking because of the bend and some bad joints in the rail and I couldn't make out which body to shoot as they were both like survivors up from the Underworld with the coal dust all over them – but then a knife appeared that I recognised and I knew what was what immediately.

The two of us alone in the cab again, Kobi laughed his great deep laugh and said, 'If you hadn't braked he'd have had us both. Leaned over the coal stack – one pop, two pops, both of us dead.'

I said, 'Time to leave,' and racked the throttle up to give someone a hard time when they tried to stop the train. Then we grabbed our rifles and jumped, I hard on Kobi's ass.

A terrific pang, darkness as complete as death, then Kobi was standing over me throwing foul-smelling ditchwater onto my face from his cupped hands. I flexed my arms, legs, back. He said, 'You caught my boot as we landed.'

I felt my face, felt the texture of the blood on my fingertips. I arched my head back, trying my neck. I saw a steep bank. We'd hit the ground exactly where a culvert came out that led the topside water underneath the railway. I stood up, felt everything again, flexed my legs, ran for a few paces on the spot.

'Kobi, I don't feel so good.' I didn't collapse but I was close to it I was that dizzy. I got myself sitting down and then lying down, flat on my back.

Kobi shouted – so it seemed – 'You've got a date with Glebov, remember? Will I have to look after you for the rest of my life?'

I said, 'Why are you shouting?'

Then I heard it. No one else could have. Only I, with my heightened sensitivity after the bang on my head, could have heard the change in the pitch of the water coming through that culvert. It couldn't have been a big flow to begin with. We were still in summer conditions – 7 September. But it had been dammed up and released. Swish, I heard it go and presently a freshet of water came out, not two yards from where I lay.

I put my finger to my lips and pointed at the mouth of the culvert – tried to convey to Kobi the motion of someone crawling through it. We'd gone down one side of the track and the White I'd shaken loose had gone down the other. That's how it had to be. Then he'd hit off the culvert, put his head to its mouth, heard us talking, had a brainwave. Bold fellow.

Was he on his belly? Unquestionably. He'd have wanted to come out in a position to shoot.

So he'd dragged himself along by knees and elbows, shoulder blades pinched together, getting as wet as a herring. He'd have paused, maybe to put his rifle off safe, have felt that pulse of water surge away as he started to move again. He'd have heard our voices cease. He'd have thought, I'm a dead man, I'll be drilled either by a bullet from in front or by a bullet from behind. He was doing what he'd signed up to do – being a soldier. And now he was bottled up in a culvert, unable to stand or run or do any single thing that would physically dissipate his sense of fear.

Maybe he had no fear. But I did not see how this could be for someone on his belly in a death trap.

There was a slab of concrete, railway detritus, balanced at an angle against the mouth of the culvert. Kobi pointed to it and told me in sign language what he wanted to do. His face was alive with merriment, his teeth as white as daisies.

I saw his idea immediately. If the man didn't want to be drowned, he'd have to crawl out backwards – he'd never get himself turned in that pipe. And I saw the reason for Kobi's laughter, for who would undertake to crawl backwards out of a dark hole in a civil war, when men are especially unparticular? Ankle tendons, hamstrings, testicles, asshole. One by one these targets would present themselves to the interested party.

I nodded.

Taking care he didn't get shot at, Kobi lowered the slab over the mouth of the culvert.

What could that fellow be thinking now he was in total darkness? His pay was fifty kopeks a month, enough for forty cheap cigarettes. Was he considering the relationship between money, risk and life? Was he thinking that a stipend of forty cigarettes was putting his life at too great a discount? Was he furious? The only life he was ever going to have and he'd been bamboozled into surrendering it for forty gaspers?

Kobi was fishing around in the spoil from the culvert for lumps of clay to block off those gaps – to make it watertight and drown the man.

I said to him, 'Leave a hole for him.' There was no reason why the man should die so long as he didn't get in my way. After all, we were both fighting the Reds.

Lying head downwards on that steep bank, I put my mouth to the lip of the culvert and shouted, 'You're lucky I'm Charlie Doig. Find your own way out.'

He must have been able to pick out the edge of my skull against the lighter shade of the night. The bullet struck the concrete slab at my side, almost making me deaf from the crack of its impact. I threw my head back, feeling a tiny sliver of concrete hit my forehead. The bullet must have ricocheted back up the culvert and struck the man, for there was a muffled roar. But that could just have been his anger at missing me.

I stood up. What spirit that man had! I said to Kobi, 'I could do with a hundred men like that.'

Kobi said to hell with that, we should move out pretty damned fast. The Whites wouldn't be far behind. Besides, I had that appointment with Glebov. We climbed up the bank onto the railway, crossed the track and set off at a trot.

Fifty-seven

BOLTIKOV WAS in a bad way. His arms were clasping the steering wheel, his forehead resting on them. Had he thrown down his cards – given up – prepared himself for death? A year ago he'd been the fat fellow who'd had a chocolate named after him. Now he was half the weight. I had the sudden feeling that maybe all that vanished flesh had contained the essence of Boltikov. The warehouse in Constantinople that was going to be choked with bales of furs and Bokharas and tapestry rolls – lidded chamber pots clanking with incredible chunks of Siberian gemstones – the awesome calculations of profit – had his capitalist ebullience been lost without trace?

I hauled him up, looking for clues in his shrivelled eyes. Maybe it was just the loss of blood, even a lack of sleep.

I said, 'Next stop Odessa. From there it's an easy boat ride to Constantinople.'

In a pale voice he said, 'It'll take more than Annushka Davidova to get me right . . . Looks like you need her too.'

'A gash when I left the train, then a chip of flying concrete.'

'That whole business looked terrific from where I was. The way you jumped from one train to the other and left those Reds to go into the river. It was worth a St Andrew's. The blue sash – you'd look good in it. I'll send you a citation – from Heaven. That's where I'm off to. Not long now.' He groaned terrifically – turned his shoulder to show me his blood-drenched sleeve and the pool of blood on the floor.

But I thought this was all far too positive for a dying man. And I was right. For when I'd re-dressed his arm and let him have a couple of Mrs D.'s madeleines, he began to perk up. It was then that I discovered the reason for his poor sentiment.

He said, 'You see, Charlie, something turned inside me when you gave the train to the monks. I couldn't say anything: it just wasn't the moment. But all my stock was in that wagon. The entire picture collection of the Benckendorffs plus some carpets you know nothing of plus other similar items. Are you aware that you gave the monks a Rembrandt? The self-portrait of him and his dog Betsy? It was Benckendorff's, filthy but unmistakable. Now God has it. I can't bear the thought of God owning my Rembrandt. He'll never spot it, He hasn't got half the eye that I have.'

'It's not God but the Reds who'll have your Rembrandt.'

'You're making it worse.'

'What's the answer then, Alexander Alexandrovich?'

'Get Glebov. Make a start on the bastards.'

'*Poshli* – let's go.'

Somewhere just off the dockyard a church clock struck six. It was the time I'd given Glebov.

I had Boltikov drive me and Kobi over the causeway to Kazan proper. About a couple of hundred yards from the Lobachevsky square he let us off. I told him to wait and keep off the bottle.

I never doubted that Glebov'd turn up. Historical inevitability would be impossible to resist. Also, he'd come out of inquisitiveness. He'd come because the Bolsheviks were winning. And he'd come to renew an old enmity.

He wouldn't want to walk up the hill as I was doing. He was too fat, too short in the leg. And he was a vain man, wouldn't dream of arriving panting at a rendezvous.

No, he'd walk out alone from the Uspensky Cathedral. His men would keep to the shadows, pretending not to exist – the threat of the firing squad having been stated for anyone who emitted the smallest human sound apart from breathing. He'd go to any lengths not to scare me away. He'd want me to believe so sincerely in this piece of theatre, which would be that of two adversaries staging a philosophical tourney beneath the statue of the man who achieved fame from his discourses on Euclid's Fifth Postulate, that I'd come trotting out *doux comme un petit agneau* and so deliver myself up to death.

He might bring a photographer along. The tripod on its silent rubber ferrules – the black drape – then the bulb snatched at instead of being squeezed, someone being too excited by this moment, which was unrepeatable, which was of the very highest drama available to mankind: my execution.

Fifty-eight

THE DARKNESS had changed to a broken grey. A long pink strip of tomorrow was stretched across the horizon like a measuring tape.

'Remember, he has a moustache now,' muttered Kobi.

We'd taken over a tea house on the square. Once it must have belonged to a wealthy merchant for there were cornices in the rooms, plaster cartouches of flowers, trumpets and Cupids above the windows, and outside balconies with iron-work as intricate as lace. Now it lay deserted, its windows blown out, shit on the floor, the walls pitted with bullet holes. Only the cake stands and the chandeliers had proved sacred.

We were on the first floor. Kobi was going to put up a flare for me: I didn't want to be blinded by it so I'd taken up a position on the opposite side of the room. We were half in and half out, the muzzles of our rifles resting on the lowest curlicues of the balcony.

The stock of the Mannlicher .256 was cool against my cheek. I looked through the telescope. Soon it'd be light enough to do without a flare.

One shot. Then run like hell. One shot – my best.

The bust of Lobachevsky, head and shoulders, was directly in front of me on a tall black drum of granite. To its left one of the cobbles stood out through having been painted white. A mark for the bandmaster at parades?

I caught it in the cross hairs. So what type of moustache would I see down the scope? Would I actually notice? I'd be going for a body shot. With one of the new expanding bullets I'd wreck him, would utterly destroy the rapist.

Below the statue a circular metal table had been placed. A chair was tipped against it to keep the seat dry. Was it for him or me?

Dawn was at my elbow now. I could make out the difference between the groups of bushes, could see that the beggars slumped sleeping on the lawns were actually piles of autumn leaves. I saw too that the chair had a metal frame and that its slats were wooden. In the centre of the table was a socket to hold a sunshade.

A faint gleam rose from the gold lettering of the inscription:

MATHEMATICIAN
NIKOLAI IVANOVICH LOBACHEVSKY
2 November 1793 to 12 November

The date of his death was unknowable in that especially dark corner.

I remembered the last time I'd waited for Glebov. I'd killed a perfectly innocent man believing it to be him. So now I started by disbelieving.

Which was correct, for the man with wild white hair who appeared out of nowhere and came weaving across the square was clearly a drunkard, a small narrow-haunched squeaky-farting man in slippers or galoshes, I couldn't say which, being able to make out only his bare ankles, which flashed like ivory beneath the bottoms of his trousers. Grasping a black umbrella halfway down the shaft and waving it as if at a tram that hadn't stopped, he wobbled dribbling and babbling towards Lobachevsky.

'Dog! Apostate! May you always feel empty, may crayfish trample you flat, may . . . may . . .'

He rounded the statue and spotted the table and chair. 'Oh, *borzhe moy*, how noble of that waiter to remember the needs of an old man . . .'

'Get out, dottled old fool. Go! *Provalivai* – scram!' said Kobi, not shouting but not quietly either.

The man's head went up. He looked towards us, trying to get a fix. I couldn't let him near. He'd come wheedling in, clasp us in his arms, would swamp us with his embraces. I might as well

276

go into the square with a loudhailer and say, 'Here's where we are, Prokhor Federovich.'

By the same token nor could I shoot him.

The fellow stared and stared at our tea house. I said to myself, It's chance, he didn't really hear Kobi, how could he in that condition. It's just that he's eaten cakes here once or done something here that's triggered this spasm of memory.

He took half a dozen tottering steps towards us: 'Why should I be afraid of anybody? Am I not pure? I was baptised and lo, the holy water still endures, in my soul, like a lagoon . . .'

He turned half round, with a sweep of his open palm as if on the stage, 'Can anyone doubt what I say?'

Putting his head right back so that his white beard was cocked up like a hen's tail feathers, he shouted at the sky, 'Jealousy!' He glared ferociously round the square. 'Liars! Murderers! Fornicators!' Then he shuffled over to the table and sat down – sat perfectly silent and still, contemplating the cobblestones between his parted knees.

'What now?' said Kobi.

'Wait.' It was all that was possible, even though it was growing lighter with every minute that passed.

Suddenly the man gathered himself up, hammered on the table with the handle of his umbrella and shouted at the statue, 'I hate all Bolsheviks!' He hung the umbrella on the back of the chair – climbed onto the seat – climbed from there onto the table, which lurched beneath him.

Bony knees bent, arms flung out, hands steadying the air, cautiously turning to face us: 'Ha ha! Whoever you are over there, observe the power of the God-fearing . . .'

Jabbering to himself, he began to feverishly polish his spectacles.

His mouth was moving. I could see every detail through the scope. He was thirty yards away, that was all. I could have put a bullet through his forehead by moving only my finger.

Eighteen fifty something, that was when Lobachevsky had died. Only the last digit remained in shadow now.

I said to Kobi, 'When I can see if it's eighteen fifty fucking four or nine or whatever it fucking is, if the bastard's still up there you go and pull him in here and slit his fucking throat for him.'

He said back, 'It's not the same for Glebov. He's winning. He can wait for us all day.'

Eighteen fifty-six. That was when the chump had turned his toes up. I said to Kobi, 'Go and do it.'

He said – frowning, not like him at all: 'Maybe you are sentencing me to death. If Glebov's watching—'

'So what the hell else are we to do? It's halfway light and we're about to have three armies searching for us.'

'We could come back another day. Dead men can't do that.'

The sun was racing down Lobachevsky's plinth now. His nose had got to the stage of leaving a shadow beneath its ridge. I could make out the dust on his eyelids, that on his left breast was the Order of Stanislav. Christ, he looked smug up there.

Kobi said unexpectedly, 'What's that noise?'

I said I didn't know.

He said, 'It must be Boltikov. He wants to get out of town. People'll be around him, getting curious, maybe hostile.'

But it wasn't an Austin engine that I was now starting to hear. It was deeper and throatier than any armoured car.

I started up. My eyes locked with Kobi's. 'That bastard—'

The Fokker came up the hill, following the street. Came low, almost brushing the houses, its black wings waggling. Its exhaust was a pale blue streak dotted with red sparks. The pilot banked opposite the cathedral – had a look at the square. He was alone in the cockpit, his leather-capped head sticking up like a toffee apple on the end of its stick. Impossible to tell whether he had a moustache.

He took the plane out in a loop in order to make his approach with the rising sun at his back.

The voice of the old man rose and hung wavering in the little bushy square, 'Hail, great spirit of Our Lord Jesus Christ . . .' He took a pinch of his trouser legs and hoisted them, showing a glimpse of his alabaster shanks – then knocked out a foot-tapping routine on that perilous table: swaying, undulating like a houri, the sun faintly kissing his long bouncing white locks.

The air whined through the Fokker's rigging as it came in behind us. Then it was directly overhead, the beat of the engine reverberating down the broken flue of the tea-house stove.

It came into view, its wings smeared with golden bars of sun like a tropical butterfly.

The pilot – hunched, solitary, goggled. Going away from me at about 120 mph, dipping as he dropped the nose to attack, showing me his shoulder blades.

Was it the same man as before? And was that man Glebov?

The plane lurched as it met the slack air in the square. I had him in the scope, had him, lost him – saying to myself, between the scapulae, get him plumb, be calm, squeeze don't pull. But my finger was never really at the point of decision. My heart, my grip, my sighting eye, something was always jiggling too much.

The old fellow looked up from his dance. Ceased – threw his arms wide open. 'Alleluia!' – it must have been something like that. I just saw his gaping mouth.

The Fokker closed on him, diving so sharply that the pilot took the risk of clipping the statue as he pulled out. He must have known it wasn't me. Yet he did it, had that man's joyful face fat in his sights as he rammed his thumbs against the trigger levers.

Maybe the old man's last thought was devoted to flamenco. Maybe it was spent addressing the soul of Russia. But it was quickly over. The bullets lifted him off his feet and off the table and slammed him against the plinth – arms outspread, Christlike, head hanging to one side. He remained there, as if impaled on the lettering of Lobachevsky's epitaph. Then he slithered down, the table partially breaking his fall.

Kobi said, 'That was not what we expected,' which was undeniable.

The Fokker rose and without once circling the square set off due west – to the monastery. Not wavering, not looking for other targets, heading straight for Zilantov. Half a mile: a minute for that plane.

What took him there? To fetch Jones for that meeting of his with Trotsky or to screw my woman? Had to be one of them.

We ran down the hill to the armoured car. Boltikov had fallen asleep again. We hauled him out of the way. Kobi got into a turret. Then I smoked that car back across the causeway and up the winding hill to the monastery. A couple of families with handcarts were heading out of the city. 'Should have done it a week ago,' I shouted as they took to the ditch. A thump – must have been their dog. They'd have to eat it sooner than they'd planned.

O woman, woman – moaning softly I barrelled that great hulk of a thing round the bends. Had he abducted her? Could two people fit in the plane? He'd squash her in somehow. Then what would I do?

The huge wooden gates were open, just as I'd left them. But I didn't drive through; it was too obvious a snare. I skidded the armoured car round ready for the getaway and killed the engine, even though it would need the crank to start it again.

The drive had shaken Boltikov back into the world of the living. Kobi and I poked him into a turret and swivelled him round so that his Maxim was aiming through the gates. We'd be in a hurry on the way out. We'd need covering fire. Glebov was in that monastery somewhere. I could smell him.

Fifty-nine

THE NIGHTWATCHMAN was back in his chair in front of the fire – dead, a bullet through his temple.

Keeping to the shadows, Kobi and I flitted round the courtyard wall to the dormitory building. In the gable end was the servants' entrance. I could just make out the fore-edge of the door: it was off the latch. It hadn't been like that when I left Jones and Xenia there.

Kobi said, 'Is it a trap?'

But there was no alternative. I led the way in.

The stone threshold was bowed from the passage of millions of feet over the last three centuries. The stairs were a left-handed corkscrew: steep, tight and dark. A rope had been strung up the wall to act as a handrail. The stone had that coldness that comes from never seeing the sun. I went slowly, always turning, enough to make me distrust my bearings.

Silence wasn't possible. Our boot soles scuffed every step. One of mine had a bit of flint embedded in it which scraped across the stone.

Even our breathing was a giveaway. One holds it back when danger is anticipated. But eventually it has to leave.

If Glebov was waiting for us at the head of those steps, he'd be giggling to hear us approach. That was an idea that crossed my mind. *Giggling*. Spluttering his fat little face in half.

I knew something solid was in front of me when the current of air in the stairwell ceased. I was climbing each step as if death was five seconds away – both hands stretched out, Luger at the ready. Its butt was slippery with sweat.

I expected a door but it was a curtain of heavy felt. I poked it:

there was nothing the other side. Next I explored how it was hung – a rod and rings beneath an overlap of felt. Flattening myself against the wall I squeezed past, giving Kobi my hand so he knew to do the same. Not a ring moved.

The room felt large. I could sense the space in front of me by a hollowness in the air, which was clean and new after the clammy atmosphere of the stairwell. Was it the council chamber we were in? I thought it had to be, with its windows looking out over the courtyard – where the abbot had stuck his head out to ask if we were Bolsheviks.

But if there were windows facing the courtyard, why was there no daylight showing? Where an abbot had leaned out, the sun's rays could come in.

Answer: because Glebov had had someone go round securing all the shutters. To confound me as if by a blindfold. To overpower me with his mystique. Clever comrade, bigsy Mr Glebov.

But it seemed to me, standing there getting my eyes accustomed to the light, that Glebov's was poor reasoning. A battle, maybe the crucial one of the civil war, was going on in the suburbs of Kazan. Trotsky, whom nobody dared defy, couldn't be more than a mile away. Six hundred and seventy tons of gold were disappearing in a driverless train. Another twenty were in the barge. So why should Glebov take time off to make these elaborate preparations for me?

Could it be that I was more important to him than Trotsky – than the gold – than the outcome of the battle?

Do you need me, Prokhor Federovich? In a fix, are you, comrade?

I slid my feet across the planked floor, not wanting to trip on rugs or furniture. Slats of light started to appear in the louvres of the shutters. Gradually I realised that the room was empty of everything except a wooden reading stand in the centre.

In the left-hand corner was the door leading out.

A corridor, gloomily lit by skylights high up the wall. Cubicles on our left, squats, the smell unmistakable. Here the floor was linoleum. We had to be close to the monks' sleeping quarters.

But he wouldn't be receiving me in the dormitory: his sense of cruelty was too refined for that. I strode down its length, through an incredible odour of used bedwear, men's unwashed clothes, candle stubs and cats. Breviaries lay on the floor, abandoned in the flight to get aboard my train.

I whispered to Kobi, 'Where is he then?'

He pointed at the door leading out – raised his eyebrows.

'Glebov's mine. Some things just can't be shared.'

He looked blankly at me, maybe not understanding fully how it was between me and Glebov. Then he padded out of the room, back down the way we'd entered.

My skin was tingling like an anthill. Revenge would be mine for the remainder of my life. It would be like a meat loaf, knobbly and nourishing. Would never melt or go mouldy. Would attract no rodents. I'd carve a slice from it whenever the memory of Elizaveta got too bitter, and when it was finished, I'd be cured.

A physician might have known where my energy was coming from. It was thirty-six hours since I'd slept. And I was hungry, God damn Hercules but I was hungry. Hungry and choking with anger.

Everything desperate that had ever happened to me was in my expression as I kicked that door down and went flying in, neck stretched out, fanning the Luger to left and right. My eyes, the tip of my nose, my snarling lips, all were charged with a determination of brutelike proportions to get rid of the past by a single murderous deed. My father's debts, the plague that slew him, falling in love, the whole bag of tricks that life had played on me was stacked in that look. Every blood cell in my body was red and boiling. I could have torn someone limb from limb such was my physical strength.

Nor should I forget nor shall I what was most important of all.

'Elizaveta!' I bellowed as I hurtled into that softly lit room. Elizaveta, my life, my love, my eternity.

The oak door caroomed against the wall and flew back onto my shoulder. I flicked it away. Glebov, Lenin and Marx lined up in front of me, that was my vision. They'd have been smirking in their intellectually condescending manner. 'Charlie Doig, loser,' I'd have read on their faces. Then I'd have shot them to pieces, shattered them with the hard facts of my Kriegsmarine parabellum bullets. 'And fuck you the most, Karl Marx,' I'd have cried, 'for being the daddy of these lice.' Then I'd have shot him again and again for what his theories did to my Elizaveta, pincushioned him as he lay there in a welter of his petty jealous blood.

Of course not one of them obliged me. But that didn't worry me as there was someone just as good.

Sixty

WINDOWS SHUTTERED: floor littered with bearskins: a coal fire, just lit: in the very corner of my eye a medieval brass-hooped chest against the wall. That was at first glance. Then, at an angle from me, a desk. On it was a black upright telephone, its cable severed about nine inches from its base; a vase of white long-stemmed roses in full bloom, and a lamp with a bare soft pink bulb.

Why was the fire lit and the bulb pink, Doig?

Don't expect me to answer smart-alec questions. I was dispatching the past to oblivion, was as tight as a spring. And what was important to me at that moment was in the chair behind the desk. Lolling, half in and half out of those firelight-flickering shadows, eyes unfathomable but with that same damned sardonic smile pulling one corner of his mouth down – Captain Leapforth Jones. The man from Grand Rapids, the decrypt wallah, the President's undercover negotiator.

'Whichever it is, I don't believe it,' I snarled and in the same breath I shot him, giving him no chance to reply. I didn't know how he'd been turned by Glebov and I wasn't going to ask. I fired an inch to the left of the pink bulb. The bullet entered his skull exactly where I aimed and flipped his head back. When the smoke cleared I gave him another one in the same place, to make sure.

His head fell forward. But he was still smiling at me.

I reloaded, strode round the desk. The chair was drenched in blood. I pulled back his coat. The bullet hole in it was plain – in the chest. I'd shot a dead man.

A door opened in the wall on my left. A sharp bright light

shone out. Figures moved silently across it, filing into the room. The door was closed behind them; the light vanished.

There were six of them. They lined across the end of the room in the semi-darkness, legs astraddle, arms folded across their chests. Latvians, with bulky black leather jackets that whispered when they moved. Chunky Browning pistols on their hips, no nuances there.

The situation required no discussion. They didn't bother to draw their weapons or search me. They were the victors and I was not. I laid my pistol on the desk. Jones's glassy stare caught me. I winked at him. *Contra mundum*, old boy, nothing unusual about that for Charlie Doig.

I walked up to the guards. Loneliness and fatigue, in equal proportions, that's what I was feeling. Only pride kept me from admitting that I was done for.

They looked straight past me. I was shit to them.

Quit that miserable way of thinking, I said to myself. Don't let them get you down. They daren't look you in the eye because they know it's you who's the hero.

I halted in the centre of the line. In my pocket was a whole lot of Kerensky metal currency. Jiggling and jangling it, I said, '*Vot?*' meaning 'Well?'

They said nothing. Russians can be like that. No one can wear a face like a wall better than they. It comes from fear of the knout. I walked up and down the line of thugs, examining each black-pelted face in turn to embarrass them. My shoulders, which had been at half mast, began to rise. The theatre had been set: I had nothing to do except amuse myself. If at the end I was executed, so be it.

'Well, where is he? Don't keep me hanging around.'

The door behind them was opened from the inside – and this time left open. The same bright light poured out. I found I was looking directly into the abbot's private chantry, at the altar wall and thus at a portrait gallery of their saints, one next to another, a row of halos and garish costumes. To the left, a rood screen plastered with gold leaf. All the trappings of divinity were on display, in which I must include the person I saw at my very first take.

Who was meant to be seen first.

Who was seated on the abbot's throne wearing an evening dress of pink satin and long white gloves.

Who was idly swinging the leg crossed at her knee, who was tapping the ash off her cigarette onto the silver communion plate – who was the woman I loved.

She'd been eating caviar off the knife, which she was licking slowly, like a cat. The pot was on the altar table with a silver ladle sticking out of it.

The guards parted, making a frame for her.

My heart, what can I say about that poor pained lump? What can I say about the sudden weight in my eyelids, my shoulders, my knees, about the anguish that came flooding up from my lower stomach, about the death of self-esteem, about the sheer pointlessness of living if this was all that was going to happen to me every time I got going?

'So it was you all along. From when you touched me up in the tram. And there I was, thinking what a lucky chap I was. Bitch.'

I moved forward. Part of me wished to strangle her. I got my hands ready. I can see them now, out there in front of me, like claws. But another part insisted that too much had passed between us. I knew immediately which was right. My hands fell away, I shook my head.

I didn't want to be fair to her. Who had been fair to me? However, we had lived together as man and woman should. She had brought my soul contentment and my body relief. In return I had borne her to safety and made her a promise of freedom. Love had passed between us. It was the right word. Neither of us had been faking it.

But somehow Glebov had a grip over her. Either he'd seen me at Smolny or his spies had heard I was living in St Petersburg. So he'd sent her into action. She'd snared me because she had to.

I squinched up my eyes and examined her face.

There was no triumph there, no glitter in those green eyes, no malice. What I saw was sadness. She was being forced to act out a role. The bright colour of her dress, the fancy shoes, the cigarette, the pose – none of those belonged to the Xenia I knew. And to have made her sit in the abbot's throne and use the communion plate as an ashtray – it must have wrung her heart dry to do it.

I stepped towards her. The guards closed ranks against me. But I'd been up against far worse that night. Imposing on them my height and sheer force of character, I prised the scum apart. They grunted to each other in their wretched dialect but quietened down when they saw I wanted only to speak to her.

Leaning against the door frame I watched her smoke. We'd been together a year and I'd never seen her even touch one before. She'd rouged her cheeks and used a light tone of lipstick, again things I'd never thought part of her. She was wearing sheer white stockings too – showing them off to me as she waved her dainty foot around. Where there were stockings'd be a garter belt, with pouches for money and hooks for scalps.

How sorry for her should I feel? How sorry for myself?

Be realistic, Charlie. Don't over-consider the lady. Think about getting out of here and think quickly.

That was what the less exhausted part of my brain said. But the rest of it was sluggish and coarse and saying to me, How come you got cunted again, Charlie?

I said, 'Got a different name now?'

Of course she didn't reply, just drew on her cigarette and pouted. She was waiting for Glebov. He'd do the talking for both of them.

'Frightened, were you? He's not nice with his women, you know.'

In a low voice she said, 'Thank you for showing me what love is. Thank you for your heart, your honesty, your strength. I would rather have chosen death than this.'

'Why, that's good to hear,' I said, wishing to show her the extent of my hurt.

'God is the only real man in my life. You know that. What I did with my lovers was for my personal pleasure. Except you, Charlinka.'

So God was in there as well as Glebov. It didn't surprise me. She'd said her prayers twice daily, undertaken the correct periods of fasting and stood in freezing churches for hours at a time, chanting and bleating with the breath coming out of her mouth as white as manna. Who in their right mind would volunteer for such discomfort?

Everything in this era was so mixed up when you thought about it, so stood on its head.

And so unfavourable to me, what with the six animals behind me and some other disadvantages to my situation.

I said to her, not having moved from the doorpost, 'Life's a spittoon, no question about it.'

Her eyes shifted. The black jackets rustled. A voice behind me said, 'And you, Comrade Doig, are going to have to drink from it.' It came from below my shoulder level because he was such a dwarfish runt.

Sixty-one

FIVE FOOT five or a little more. Dark slicked-back hair, going bald on the crown. Pale blue eyes. Tufty, truculent moustache, something of the badger about it.

The moustache was an obvious difference. Also there was something new in his eyes. Where before they'd been shifty they were now firm, and where there'd been jealousy I saw confidence. Otherwise I'd got in front of me the same Glebov as the man Kobi and I had tossed screaming into the back of a White hospital wagon.

Or maybe not quite the same. There was his broken leg to be considered.

'You running again yet?' I said.

'I even dance,' he said back.

'No amount of dancing'll help you get away from me.'

'But I have my Fokker.' If he hadn't been some ways shorter than me, he'd have been able to smile down on me. That's what he was trying to do.

'You flying it yourself then?'

'Sometimes. But in general I just give the orders. You must remember who I am.'

He had a bearskin cloak lined with dark blue cotton draped round his shoulders. Beneath it he was naked except for a red towel round his waist and a pair of loose leather slippers. He'd got here, shot Jones, fixed up his welcome for me, had his men stoke the furnace in the bathhouse – and had been enjoying Xenia, both of them slippery with steam, while I'd been groping up that dank staircase.

I said, 'You've been busy.'

The fat was hanging from him in corrugated rolls of creeping black hair. His bosoms quivered as he chuckled. 'Life is always busy for those at the top.'

We were so close our bodies were almost touching. I thought, This was what lay on my Elizaveta?

He said jauntily, 'You look clapped out, Comrade Charlie. You should model yourself on me. Half an hour in the baths works wonders for a man's energy. I'm going to need all mine again in a few moments, for my chick. She's ravenous for my body. All women appreciate a good lover. Seems you were too eager, comrade . . . Doesn't she look sophisticated smoking through that amber holder! It belonged to royalty, of course. I had quite a few knick-knacks from their rooms.'

'Including Anastasia?'

'For three days only. Then she died – the bayonet had gone in too deep. You know, she was fatter than I am – and only seventeen. She'd have been a royal mountain if she'd had the chance. And the other thing I was going to say about the woman you know as Xenia but who is actually Nadya is that she told me you always smell. Isn't that right, darlingka? And I agree with her. You smell like a loser, Doig.'

He padded off into the chantry, yanked Xenia out of the abbot's throne and took it himself. He flapped his hand disparagingly at the portraits of the saints. 'So many baubles, such unnecessary riches. No wonder the people detest their priests . . . Comrade, close the door, will you? No point in bewildering these baboons with conversation that's over their heads . . .' He shouted to them, 'Play a game of Riga poker. Recite Lenin's April Theses. I don't care. But stay handy – do you hear me?'

I pulled the door to.

'Latvians, good for only one thing – killing people.'

'You've gone up in the world. Was rapist, now People's Commissar.'

'You never thought it would come to this, did you? You thought the bourgeois principles of your class were certain to prevail, as they always have done in the past. That's why you came after me with such obstinacy, saying to yourself, Reason must out. But ours is the reason you should have listened to. What you lacked was the intelligence to see that destiny was against you. I myself spotted her coming a long way off and let her give me a ride. A certain breed of man has this gift. Oh yes, I've licked and licked and licked. That's the way to get on, knowing where to lick. I don't mind talking to you like this. Things are going my way. The fact is that you're of no importance, a minor figure, like a junior captain in the old army. Luck doesn't want to know you any more. If I don't have you killed, someone else soon will.

'I may call you comrade but I don't mean it. You're not one of us. You don't even have the excuse of being a Jew . . . Pass me that cigarette, Nadya . . . This day's been so good to me . . . The reason I call you comrade is purely out of habit. We all call each other comrade – like brother. It's a healthy custom.'

It was obvious he wanted to talk about himself – and I had nowhere to sit. I stuck my nose out of the door. The Latvians were lounging on the desk playing cards. I told one of them to tip Jones onto the floor and fetch me his chair.

Anyone stealing my pistol would be shot, I added.

'Through the stomach,' Glebov yelled. 'I'll have no thieving in my units.'

The Latvian carrying the chair looked from Glebov to me. I told him to place it opposite Glebov's throne.

'Wipe the blood off it before he sits down, animal,' Glebov said to the man. 'There's a rag on the hook over there,' pointing to a stole embroidered in cream and gold.

Xenia lit another cigarette and lay on her back on the altar. Her shoes stuck up vertically. They were lime green. The colour went better with her pink dress when she was standing.

Glebov said, 'Vladimir Ilyich has decreed that God no longer exists. Therefore all religion ceases to have a meaning except in the context of historical error. Unless an American will pay a good price for these tapestries and so forth, they'll be cut up and used for blankets in our hospitals. Something like that. It's not my business.'

Xenia said dreamily, looking up at the chambered turquoise roof, 'Am I your business?'

'You wouldn't be here if you weren't.'

'There was a rumour in Strabinsk that the new government intends to nationalise women,' she said. 'That's pure spite.

They may be the wives and daughters of the *boorjoi* but that sort of woman deserves as much respect as the rest of us. It's we who bring children into the world. We are the future, not you, Prokhor Federovich.'

'Enough of the lecturing. Leave a man's work to men.' To me he said, 'She's angry because when she was young she knew nothing about the vinegar douche. A girl called Lili was the result. I made Lili my captive – my pawn, comrade. She was the lever I used to get her mother to enslave you.'

I looked up sharply, surprised. I said to Xenia, 'I did you an injustice.'

Grinning, Glebov said, 'And she trapped you with her body, didn't she? She's got an aptitude for that line of work. Haven't you, woman?'

She said, 'He's a bastard. They all are. One chink and they rip you open like a can of beetroot. I'll give you a tip though, Charlie – he's afraid of spiders. Would you believe it? Tiny little insects, a fraction of his size . . . So you thought I did it for the money?'

'Yes.'

'I did it for my daughter. I do everything for her. I went to the baths with him for her. I'm wearing this dress for her. Soon I'll be sucking his stinking cock for her. But the worst thing of all I've done for her is to lie on this altar and mock God. May He open His merciful heart and forgive me.' She crossed herself twice. 'He's the vilest man in Russia.'

'Comrade Trotsky is far worse,' Glebov said. 'The most common words in his orders are "Shoot them". Not March or Halt but "Shoot them". In comparison, I – I am a saint.'

I laughed at him. I didn't mind if he shot me for it. Russia was strewn with corpses, its rivers and weirs blocked with them. If death was so commonplace, it had to be easily suffered. I laughed with all the bitterness I could summon, leaning forward in my chair, right into the face of the man who'd ruined my life and now pronounced himself a saint.

He held up his hand like some Roman emperor. 'I and my comrades, Vladimir Ilyich and Lev, we are in the process of changing the world. We are doing this for the benefit of all its peoples. The class system has to be destroyed for that benefit to be released. Therefore this war is taking place. War means necessity. There can be no exceptions, not even for young brides.'

Was I going mad? Glebov lounging in his bearskin, Xenia rigid on the altar – and these stupid, barbaric assertions—

I rose, kicking back the chair. Automatically I patted my pistol holster.

He said, 'On the desk out there. Minus its bullets or heads will fall.'

God, how I detested that knowing grin of his. I eyed his neck. Would the guards hear anything? Would Xenia start howling?

He said, 'That Mongolian youth of yours does all the murdering, not you. You don't have the experience, so don't look at me like that. See, I know everything about you. She kept me well informed. No detail was omitted. Because of her daughter . . . You mustn't blame her, Doig. You know how it is between women and their children.'

'I should have killed you.'

'But you're weak. When the moment offers itself, you fluff it. They never come again, those moments. But yes, you should have.'

I'd had him, trussed, in the forest. I could have killed him in one of ten different ways, at my leisure. Then I'd backed down. And this was the consequence: defeat, humiliation, maybe death.

I said, 'Next time there'll be no mistake.'

That was what I meant, but in another part of my brain I was thinking, Hang on, Charlie, that's for the future. The short-term problem is how to improve your situation. I said with a sigh, 'You're right, I am weak. It's from my mother's side, her female reserve.'

'You've inherited the aristocrat's typical ignorance of the rules for survival. Because he's read a stirring tale in a novel, he thinks he can easily battle through. Of course he does! There he is turning the pages before a good coal fire while upstairs his fattest housemaid is rolling in his bed to get it warm. Such a man believes sincerely that in a contest for existence he can perform as efficiently as a plate-layer on the Siberian railway. That's rubbish. First, his hands let him down. They're too soft to chop enough wood to keep the fire going for even one night. Here! Look at mine! Look at the pad on that thumb, how hard it is . . . Then there's his lungs – servants have done all the running for him. Pouring out his coffee, that's all he can manage. Maybe a walk in his garden. Thereafter he's exhausted. The weakness of his body spreads to the mind. It takes hold. He can't form his words properly. He's finished. He dies.'

'So what am I to do?'

He wagged a finger at me. 'That's a better tone. You've stopped speaking through your nose. When I was in Berlin, "on leave" as we exiles called it, I heard people speaking like that everywhere. The effeteness of wealthy European industrialists disgusts me. However, now that you're prepared to accept that you're inferior – there, you don't even bristle when I say that . . . Bring your chair close to me. Nice and close. There's something I want to say.'

I obeyed. I found his knee between mine. He'd just shoved it there.

'There are only three of us who matter in Russia today. I count Vladimir Ilyich and the Jew as my absolute comrades – comrades in the most spiritual sense, you understand. We have taken vows, have mingled our blood before witnesses. We have one goal. Nothing can come between us.

'That said . . . Well, Vladimir Ilyich is in the capital and the Jew is completely engrossed by his desire to film the capture of this city. No one loves him more than I do but there are times when he goes too far. Stavka is like a caravanserai. All the specialists in Russia are there. Eight men at the wireless sets, two in his private cinema, one in his darkroom waiting for film, another four grinding out tracts on the duplicators – and so on. It's not right. Action first, *then* the propaganda. It's a beaten foe that makes the best believer. Another thing . . . You know that I have my men everywhere—'

'And women,' said Xenia in a voice husky from the cigarettes.

'Trotsky owes his life to me. That man you knew as Jones – he was an American assassin. He was sent to kill Lev because the Americans thought him the most dangerous of us. A complete amateur, of course. It was going to be poison. We found it on him. Lev was going to be poisoned like some sort of vermin.'

Sixty-two

HE CONTINUED: 'I know the minds of the counter-revolutionary swine as well as a mouse knows its wainscoting. Nothing can be concealed from me. Nothing, nothing, nothing. Wireless telegraphy and the Russian brain are like that – twins!'

I said, 'You're a big man. I bet you had Jones's messages unscrambled in – what was the longest one took?'

'They were all easy. My men watched his train like they watched yours. Watched till you put up your aerial. Then they listened.'

'And now?'

I said it encouragingly. Something was on his mind, something prickly, something like a plot. I wanted him to get there soon and to include among the details a safe conduct out of Kazan. I didn't fancy playing a leading role in Trotsky's film.

Glebov said, 'Thanks for leaving Jones and the woman so available. I suspected a booby trap. Nothing so interesting. Jones tried to run away. Mr One-Step Jones the baboons call him. They're quick off the mark. I had them stick him in the chair to make your nerves rattle. I said, "And get the American smile back on his face so he looks 100 per cent realistic." It was difficult. They had to put wooden wedges between his jaws. And you fell for it!'

He got up and tried a quick cowboy draw, only the bearskin cloak snagged his arm. 'Pow! Pow! A good bit of fun so early in the morning, eh, Charlie?'

That was new, the Charlie bit.

'Comrade?' I said.

He rewrapped the towel round his waist, ran his fingers

through his hair, became businesslike. 'We'll be quick about it. You must understand that Bolshevism is no different from politics anywhere. Theory is one thing. Reality belongs to another continent. And what's real is this: there are 5,391 railway miles between Moscow and Vladivostok and our population is 155 millions. What do those two facts tell you? That we're not some stupid little country like Britain, that's what they say. We're big. In fact we're the biggest in the world. And what does that mean? It means power. Big always means power.'

'What are the views of Vladimir Ilyich and Comrade Trotsky?'

He seized the point of my chin, thumb just below my lip, and shook my face. 'Who's conducting this conversation?'

'You, comrade.'

'Good. Horses that believe it's they who are in the saddle get shot. There's another lesson in power for you.'

'Yes, comrade.'

'Sufficient power for the three of us is either in existence now or can be created. Our appetites are as normal as those of any other victor. The three of us will share our power and exercise it benevolently. We are no monsters, Charlie – good Comrade Charlie. Our achievement in Russia is without precedent. We have called into being a marvellous new world. Truly. Come back in a century and tears will spring to your eyes to see the way a just, contented society works.'

I groaned, making him smile pouchily. 'You know what? I agree with you! In a century! When we're dead! What use is that? It's now that counts. You're the same as me. Now or never, that's what men like us say every morning upon awakening. So you see . . . you and I . . . well, I'm not the man to turn away the chance of a lifetime. But you don't have my knack. You're not going to get any power unless it's handed to you. This is where you and I can benefit from each other . . . you and I, Charlie . . . don't you also get the feeling that we have a shared destiny?'

He rose, went to the altar and fondled Xenia's breasts, without intention, idly playing with them.

She closed her eyes.

He said, 'To have supreme power over other people can be a terrible thing. One's every dream is attended to. Want a woman:

snap fingers. A boy: snap fingers. When a man no longer needs to try, his life becomes pointless, that's what a philosopher will tell you. But should I therefore turn my back on power?' He laughed, a little bark of a thing. 'Of course not! I want to have my way. I want to be on top.'

'Yes,' I murmured.

'The power exists. Am I to turn myself into a charity and hand it over to someone else? Well, I'm not mad, that answers that one. But to stay powerful I must keep in sight the man who most wants to kill me. There! That's why I want you to work for me. No reason can be as good as that one.'

I stood up. Things were coming to a head.

'Those monks and that nice train you gave them – they did their best with the driving levers but God had no suitable advice for them. The mess they made of it, Charlie! Then they tried to run away – all in their robes – you can imagine how that excited Trotsky's men. Immediately after that the gold train, which because of you had no driver, ran up its backside. Yes, a big smash and just at the wrong time. Unfortunately, the Czechs had more men in the area than we did. And so . . .'

He sighed, his voice going soft. 'You can guess what I want. Only you have the braveness and stupidity to lead such a mission. You can have as many of my men as you want. But you have to act quickly while there's still liquidity in the situation.'

'You'll never get it out of the country. Even if you do, what'd you do with it?'

He bent over Xenia, squeezed her lips into a bunch and kissed them. Smoothing back her hair and looking into her eyes, he said softly, 'The young man wants to know what I can do with money. Darlingka, what an extraordinary question. He just hasn't been listening to me.'

'Well?'

'Who said anything about getting it out of the country? You get the gold for me and I'll give you ten tons of it right now.'

'Nothing doing.'

'Fifteen. It has the highest purity in the world, you know.'

'Nope.'

He narrowed his eyes. 'Let's start again. Sixteen tons plus the rank of General plus a job as my Chief of Staff.'

I frowned to disguise my elation.

'Plus the girl,' he added quickly.

I was sure now that he'd heard nothing about Shmuleyvich and Mrs D. having cut loose the barge. He'd have made some reference to it. It'd have come into the bargaining somewhere, along with their lives.

'The girl?'

'Lili. Nadya's daughter. My captive.'

'What's wrong with her? Blind? Lame? Harelip?'

'Guards! Bring the girl in . . . Now, General Doig, you'll learn the advantage of working for Commissar Glebov. Do as I say and promotion comes fast. General! It suits you, Charlie.'

The door opened.

Sixty-three

WHAT CAN I say? What is believable from a man racked by
sleeplessness, hunger and revenge? But it was no vision.

I lightly pinched the flesh of her bare arm – above her elbow,
avoiding a gentle blue nerve – and released it. The white print
made by my fingers filled out and turned pink. It was real – it
was Lili.

She smiled at me without any coyness. The thugs who'd formed
her escort, the abbot's chantry, her gussied-up mother, Glebov
in his bearskin cloak, it must have been an extraordinary scene
for her. Maybe she was used to such circuses wherever she'd
grown up.

Maybe also there'd been no mirror in that house and she was
unconscious of her beauty. She held herself so well – demure,
friendly, unspoiled.

I'll call her fifteen, though I know Russian girls develop young.
I glanced over at Xenia to take a cross-bearing on their respec-
tive ages. She'd swung her legs off the altar leaving the cloth
all runkled. She was clutching at it convulsively, watching Lili
and me intently. When her daughter came in, she'd gasped and
her eyes had become radiant – then she'd clapped a hand over
her mouth, as if to subdue or even eradicate her joy.

So if Lili was fifteen, Xenia had to be – but what did it
matter? She'd been spying on me, working for my enemy for a
whole year. She was out of my life.

She wanted to say something. I cut her off. 'Keep 'em
bouncing. You'll always find a man.'

Tears formed in her eyes, for God, for the girl, out of shame
for what she'd done to me – I didn't care. I waved at the pot

of caviar. 'Don't get it on your dress. Caviar stains – irreversibly, like you've stained me.'

Then Glebov was pushing Lili at me and saying, 'But the daughter is an improvement, General. Don't take my word for it. Listen to what her teachers have told Nadya. Go on, woman, tell the General.'

When she refused to speak, he said, 'I'll tell you what they say – that Lili's quite exceptionally intelligent as well as obedient and dutiful. Good mixture in a woman, eh!' He gave Lili another little shove. 'Don't be afraid of him. He's only Charlie Doig.'

Her face – broad, very Russian, with the same creamy skin of her mother. Hair – light brown, a little darker than tea-and-milk, sweeping back from her forehead in thick waves. Strong hair too, well rooted in her scalp and getting good nourishment from it so that the fibres were thick and glossy.

Hands – unworked. The nails cut very short, like her mother's.

White blouse buttoned on the side, like a military tunic, with a narrow pleat masking the buttons. Full high breasts, lovely for cupping. Taut waist – a neat figure in her long dark broad-cloth skirt: about normal when she'd finished growing, perhaps even on the tall side.

We stood facing each other. Her palm lingered in mine. I remember that very well.

Such eyes! The blueness of wild flowers, horizon blue! All the gaudy colours of sainthood around us were in an instant obliterated. Gone! Just Lili's huge young eyes left. They were bigger even than Xenia's, had slopes on which the light glistened. And that blue – no sharpness anywhere, only the soft strokes of our northern latitudes.

I was mesmerised.

From a distance Glebov said, 'A very great improvement on the mother, wouldn't you say?'

I wanted to ask Lili how much of Alexander Pushkin's poetry she had by heart. Of course she was intelligent, one didn't need a teacher's report to realise that. One could see it in her whole attitude, in the way she was standing, in the firmness of her handshake.

I became conscious that Xenia was making warlike noises in her throat, like a wild animal that sees its offspring threatened.

I found she was glaring at me. I thought: mother and daughter, is there a law against it?

Lili took her hand from mine. 'Good morning, General,' she said. Her voice was as light and strong as her hair. When it deepened, it would resonate through a man's life, maybe even through history. It was a voice that'd be able to halt runaway horses or kill flies.

Without a tremor – I didn't attempt to reason with myself: the necessity of acting as I did overwhelmed me – I said to Glebov. 'Comrade Commissar, I decline all your offers of employment and I decline the rank of General.'

He looked me over. 'Twenty tons, then.'

'Save your breath.'

'A fixed annual sum? You must give me an idea. I want you. I want to hug you close to me. To the bosom – right in there, next to the skin.' He threw back his cloak and showed me his chest and lardy breasts.

'Nope.'

This revolting man spread out his arms. 'Charlie, Charlie, be sensible. Does destiny mean nothing to you?'

'Nope.'

'Two women then? A different woman each week? A Negress?'

'Nope.'

'Listen: last time we met you spared my life. Had you carried out your threat I would have killed myself, right there, in the forest. Without eyelids – no surgeon could have given me new ones. Without them – *nichevo*! I'd have preferred to stare at nothing – in fact, I'd have preferred death. I was trying to repay you by making you up to General. And a job on my staff, just when I'm at the peak of my career. Had you accepted, you'd have been assured of a long and fruitful life—'

'As your servant, let's get that clear.'

'But now . . . Well, I'll show you the sort of master you're turning down. I'll show you what generosity is – I'll still do you a favour. Today your life is spared, and tomorrow and every day until I'm established in power. Then I shall come after you and I shall kill you. Why? Because I cannot afford to leave you alive forever. There, let that be the treaty between us.'

He reached up and grasped my lapels. 'You're too bold to be

dead. You *impose* yourself so well on situations . . . Just you and I and the gold – we could pick up dead men's papers anywhere. Then disappear as Jones pretended he was going to do. We'll – how would he have put it? – we'll vamoose! We'll be the richest vamooseniks in the world. Your king – *nichevo*. That fat French crocodile – *nichevo*. Mr Banker Morgan – *nichevo*. But me and you – *millioners*.'

'No.'

'For the last time?'

'No.'

'Then I shall kill you. When I feel like it. In a week, in a year, how should I know, I'm Russian. You have a chance to run away. I've said you can. I'm a man of my word. But you're a thousand miles from safety in every direction. I shall find you however well you hide. Then our acquaintance will end.'

There were four of us in that chapel – Xenia and Lili were standing arm in arm, watching. But suddenly, as we deliberated on those words, 'Then our acquaintance will end,' it seemed as if a fifth person had entered the room and was occupying its very centre. I turned my head towards it, as did Glebov, as did both the women. No one spoke.

At length Glebov said with a sigh, in a soft, unlikely voice: '*Es wird vollbracht* – it will end.'

We still didn't move. That figure, that presence, remained in the centre of the chantry – in the shape of a pillar, that was how I conceived of it.

Was it Elizaveta signing off, was that the fifth person in the room?

I smiled. She'd helped me down the steps at Smolny when Lenin, Trotsky and Glebov were only yards away. Now she'd come to my help again. I bowed to her, bowed properly.

Glebov said harshly, 'No need to do that. Just get out before I change my mind. Take the daughter. Enjoy her. Enjoy what time you have left.'

Sixty-four

LILI TOOK a pace towards me, looked back at her mother. Huge tears were starting in Xenia's eyes. They were the saddest eyes I've ever seen. Her cheeks began to pucker. Of a sudden she seemed to be six inches shorter. Weights were dragging her down, the weight of her past.

She said to Lili, 'Go with him. Bear his children. The future needs rescuing. All of Russia's women must start preparing for that day.'

They embraced. Forlornly, they clung sobbing to each other.

Xenia broke away, her face aflood. 'Charlinka, it was to preserve Lili that I sinned. I have lied to you. I have sold you so that my daughter may live. Forgive me. Now I give you Lili. It is my atonement. A daughter – no mother could give more.'

I said, 'Go in peace with yourself.' It was goodbye.

I grabbed Lili by the hand and made for the door. I hoped Glebov had primed his thugs. I didn't want for us to be riddled by those big Browning bullets.

Behind us there was a scuffle. Turning I saw Xenia break loose from Glebov. Her face was on fire, her pink satin dress stained black with her tears. She was desperate, mad with grief. She ran past me like a wild animal, went straight through the room, past the guards and out of the far door.

Lili ran after her but I caught her halfway across the anteroom. She tried to pull away from me, a big strong wriggling girl. I said to her, 'You'll meet her again. Just let her be by herself right now. She's seen God.'

'Ten minutes' prayer'll cure all that, not a serious condition,' said Glebov coming up behind us. 'Here, animals from Latvia, leave us alone for five minutes. I want to have some private talk with General Doig. Go find yourself a bottle . . . Lili, block your ears. What I have to say is not for a maiden.'

We were standing besides Jones's body, where he'd been flung to the floor. I leaned back against the desk, hands behind me groping for my Luger.

Glebov said, 'Take it, Charlie. That shows how straightforward I am. Anyway, I've got the bullets,' he chuckled, tossing one up and catching it. 'But a nice weapon. Lovely balance. Handsome, too. The Germans are good engineers.'

Lili had paused with her hand on the doorknob. Glebov said to her, 'Make up your mind then. In or out, which is it?'

She said calmly, 'I'll wait for General Doig.'

He said to me, 'You'll be far better off with a woman you can train from the very start. Speaking of which, or rather speaking of Nadya, or Xenia as you call her, do you realise that she's the second woman we've shared? Our destinies lie together and there's the proof for you. You should think again about my offer, General. I'm not going to repeat it.'

'You bastard murdering dwarf,' I said and as quick as a falling axe I grabbed the roses from the vase. I didn't feel a thing. Those stems could have been blades of grass for all I knew.

I wrenched his towel off. I caught him by his slick hair, pulled his head right back. His pale blue eyes staring up at me began to register a complaint – 'Remember Elizaveta,' I snarled, then I snapped his head forward and with my right hand I harrowed him, yes, that's right, I dragged those lacerating roses and every single one of their bayonet thorns through his crutch and round his testicles and his vile rapist's cock. I *scrunched* them into his flesh, I *wiped* them up his cleft and round his jingle-bag, ripping and gouging until he screamed like a boar having its throat cut. I must have come close to circumcising him.

Lili cried out. Looking up I saw her cover her face with her hands. 'Run, Lili, run like hell,' I shouted at her – and shoved Glebov's head down again.

I was panting. Between my breaths I was conscious of hearing my own voice, not shouting but hissing at him, 'Elizaveta, Elizaveta,' as I raggled those roses again through his balls. Looking down I saw his blood pouring, streaming down the inside of his thighs. Jamming his head even further down, I scraped the roses up his belly and round his face and stuffed them into his screaming mouth.

I could hear the Latvians pounding up the stairs. 'For Elizaveta. On account.' Then I grabbed my Luger off the desk, wrenched open the door and ran after the girl.

But she was still there, bent over, doing something with her underwear. 'For Christ's sake, get going,' I screamed at her.

She stumbled – then her drawers came free, were tossed away, and she had her hampering broadcloth skirt pulled right up, like a tyre round her waist, and was running in front of me. God, did she have movement in those buttocks. She could run all right, no girly nonsense about tripping along.

Down the stone staircase we went, bouncing off the walls, maybe not the only way out but the only way I knew, over the bowed threshold and across the courtyard to the gatehouse. Once guns have started firing all you can do is to run and hope. When they haven't, you run far faster, trying to outpace the bullets that you know'll be coming soon, or even to outdistance them. Did we run, oh how we ran through the early light of that September day, and she barefoot.

A little drizzle had fallen while we were with Glebov, so that the cobbles were greasy. I prayed neither of us would slip. Twist an ankle and what next? Would Lili stop and come back to lug me to safety?

She might have. She ran like a champion, stride for stride beside me, skirts hoisted and those strong pink legs pounding away in the corner of my eye. Head and shoulders back, breasts bouncing like coconuts.

Would Glebov keep his word and let me go after what I'd done to him?

My lungs were going like bellows. Every second I expected to be shot. I had the same fear as before, at Smolny: that Glebov would wait until I was a few yards from safety – until I thought I'd got there. Then wallop, and the sky would go black.

Kobi was shouting at us. He was lying on the cobbles by the gatehouse. He had a machine gun set up on a tripod. I thought – he put half a dozen rounds over our head – I thought, the bodyguard have come out and we're bang in his sight line. Lili had the same idea. We swerved left and right simultaneously and Kobi put in a long burst between us, the bullets fanning the air as they passed.

That must have sent them back inside. Then we were through the gateway and standing, gasping, in the shelter of the armoured car.

Boltikov was revving the engine. 'Go go go,' I shouted and began to cram Lili into one of the gun turrets, made awkward by the Maxim's firing handles and the spare wheels stacked at the bottom. Humiliating Glebov had given me a buck. He'd be the laughing stock of the whole 5th Army when the story got around. Dead was best but what I'd done wasn't bad.

'Who needs sleep?' I said grinning.

'Not this one,' she laughed, showing me her fine young teeth, strong as a hippo's.

Then Kobi had me by the shoulder with a grip of iron. Annoyed, I tried to throw him off but he had me fast. He was pointing to the church and its bell tower and saying something I couldn't grasp.

'Don't piss on me,' I shouted above the noise of the engine. 'I know she's in the church. She's saying bye-bye to her sins. What do you want, that I ask her along for a river trip?'

'Use your eyes! Up there on the bell platform, what do you see sticking out? Yes, Doig, the Reds have put two field guns up there.'

I couldn't believe it. Between my leaving for the docks to free the gold and my return to the monastery for Xenia, the Reds had had two three-inch field guns swayed onto the bell-tower platform. Over a ton apiece and then the ammo. Christ, those guys knew how to get things done.

'Where's the box of Happy Christmas?' I shouted at Kobi. 'Charge, fuse – Christ, they'll shell the whole fucking city to bits unless we get them.'

'I already laid it,' he shouted back. 'Charge set and ready to fire.'

'So what's stopping you?'

'The church'll go with it.'

'What's a church?'

'Your woman's in there.'

He'd stopped shouting. Was looking at me with those not-understandable oriental eyes. I stared back at him, my head angled forward, like a vulture.

He said casually, 'Your woman, your decision, Doig.'

I couldn't believe it. Within an inch of success and now bitched by the woman who'd betrayed me. I looked to see where Lili was. Not to be seen, fishing around somewhere in the bottom of her turret to make herself comfy.

Should I run across the courtyard and fetch Xenia out? The guard could shoot me on the way there, could shoot both of us on the way back. Would probably aim for my legs, to bring me down so that Glebov could play around with me.

I said to Kobi, 'What lengths of fuse have you got?'

'Five minutes and half an hour.'

'Cut me a five.'

Sort of patting me for my decision, he said, 'She'll get to Heaven quicker.' Then he was kneeling on the ground, matches ready.

But I could *drive* over there in the armoured car to get her and be in no danger at all. They'd be lucky to hit the tyres firing only with rifles.

Kobi called up, 'Quick, boss, they're coming out – they're going to rush the tower. Yes? Do it now?'

Boltikov opened up on them from the driver's seat, which made them retreat again. But it wouldn't be for long. They'd use the other doors, scatter as they burst out, get to the bell tower, cut the Bickford cord and turn the guns on us.

'Is she your mother, for God's sake? Why are you waiting?' He'd struck another match, was holding it within his cupped hand.

But still I hesitated. How would it be in years to come with two dead women on my card? Oh yes, I could say in conversation, I was caught up in the Bolshevik Revolution, I know what hard decisions are like. But what would I say to myself at night, when I was alone?

'Yes or no. *Wake up, Doig.*'

They'd got hold of a machine gun: put a burst through the gateway, making us go to ground. Could I actually get to her now, even in an armoured car?

My head sank. I said in a low voice, 'Blow the church then,' not wishing to mention her – to be explicit.

'Thank God!' Leaning swiftly forward, he lit the fuse. I watched the tiny smouldering glow set out. In five minutes, so long as the fuse hadn't got damp—

'Wait!' I couldn't help myself.

He looked up at me angrily. 'Is one woman worth more than the lives of all of us here?'

My foot was poised to grind the spark into the cobbles. He flicked the fuse away, jumped up and grabbed me. Before I could say a word, he had one arm bent up behind my back and locked there, almost pulling the ball out of my shoulder. I heard the hiss of steel and felt his knifepoint below my ear. 'We'll watch the fuse together, boss.'

The decision was out of my hands. Suddenly I was tired, tired as a dog, tired beyond the point of argument.

You want to know how slow time can go? Try watching a five-minute fuse.

Kobi was right. Of course he was right. Either the guns were blown up or they were turned on us. A pea-brain could have worked it out. So why had it taken me so long? Because the very first thing I thought of was her head flying through the air and once you have that in mind for your lover, you have memories and regrets and images of joy that are so conflicting that everything must be delayed while they're sorted out.

I stood stock-still, Kobi's knife touching the big vein.

Watching the fuse smoulder was like watching a worm having its tail eaten away by old age. Kobi kept the knife there the whole time.

Not moving, just watching the fuse, I said to him, 'Lili still down at the bottom of the turret?'

'Yes.'

Pray God she didn't surface and start bellowing for Mama. She was in the best place in view of Mama's circumstances.

I thought, What if I saw Xenia come to the door of the church – right there, not a hundred yards away, in her pink satin dress and white hose and elbow gloves and lime-green shoes? What if she was scared by all the firing – saw the armoured car –

waved for me to come and rescue her? Would I be able to forgive her enough?

And thus I got myself into the position of *begging* the fuse to hurry. Even that's too soft a word. What I wanted most was to go down on hands and knees and fan the little snivelling trail of smoke until the spark fairly crackled. I'd have done anything to shorten those five interminable minutes simply because I was too tired to deal with any more of that type of question. A man should be able to kill his wife if that was the best thing for her. He should be able to agree to the death of a treacherous lover if the alternative is mass slaughter. Whoever has to make such decisions should not be penalised. But no man should be given both an Elizaveta and a Xenia to deal with.

I had no prayers suitable for the occasion – no God prayers, I mean. I could do nothing but watch the fuse, watch Boltikov's bullets pocking the wall of the dormitory building and hope that Xenia was up to her smutch in a conversation with her Maker. Sin, I whispered, have her list her sins starting with the man who came into Zilberstein's shop, that'll take a fair bit of time—

Then miraculously the fuse was up to the little nick I'd taken as a marker. I said to Kobi, 'Let's move!' and broke away from him. I hammered on the hull for Boltikov to get going and jumped onto the running board. The thugs must have been watching the car. As the wheels started to turn, they came pouring into the courtyard, firing at us as they ran. But we were away, went crashing down the hill into Archangelskiy Street, rounded the bend at its foot on two wheels and didn't stop until we were in cover, down by the little Kazanka river.

I had to say something to her – to defend myself. By her death, maybe a hundred or a thousand lives would be saved. But it was I who'd passed sentence, I who'd taken on the mantle of executioner. No matter that she'd done the dirty on me.

'Xenia, only about fifteen seconds of your life remain . . .' that was how I started, and so it came to pass that while I was speaking to her and she was speaking to God up she went, my erstwhile peacheroo, and of the manner of her death I say only that better cannot exist if that's the way your mind turns. God and bed were her main delights. To have died hand in hand with God was the more fitting of the two.

There the bell tower went, not ding-dong ding-dong but a vast crashing roar, and there Xenia went, shoes separately, and there the two field guns went. Up, up and away, all of them to better times.

First had been the tremor, the church and tower shivering. Then the explosion itself, huge but dull, from somewhere in its bowels. Then the core of the church had risen, it seemed in one piece, into the unsuspecting sky. The golden onions, cross erect, had climbed to God. They'd halted – wavered – toppled inwards upon themselves, and then the whole brute force of the explosion had taken over and a black column of smoke had shot out and debris and saintly relics and God knows who else beside Xenia had blossomed out in looping arches – exactly like a cherry tree in April. And *then* the noise smote us, making us duck. We looked goofily at each other, our ears ringing.

Lili appeared with eyes as big as cartwheels.

There was no time to take her for a sedating walk or anything like that. I said to her straight out, 'Lili, your mother was in that building, praying. She'll be dead. I'm sorry. I couldn't get her out.'

Up there in the turret, looking down at me: 'Did you try?'

'There were two field guns in the bell tower. We had to destroy them. The bodyguard knew that – had a similar idea, to get to the dynamite before we detonated it and then to turn the guns on us. On you and me, Lilenka.'

'So you tried?'

'No one could have crossed the courtyard.'

'But you tried? You tried to help my mother?'

'Yes, I tried to help her.' It was what she wanted to hear.

She gave me a fraction of a smile, tears somewhere in the background. 'Maybe she wouldn't have left with you anyway.'

'Why not?'

'Not if she was praying hard for your soul.'

'Why'd she do that?' I knew we were wasting time but this was a conversation I wanted out of the way.

'After all the wrong she did you? You know what she was like better than I do. She sent me away to grow up.'

'You did it fast. Oh Lilenka, you hold the record for growing up.'

She started to cry, shaking her head, the tears flying off her cheeks onto the machine gun. It was good. We respected her for it.

Our pale hero, Boltikov, the only one of us who was a parent, climbed up and clasped her tightly with his good arm, drying her face off with a rag and both of them starting to laugh at the streaks of oil on her cheeks.

Kobi was beside me. He said, 'Before I saw the guns in the tower, I heard Tornado trying to smash his stall down, to get out. I let him go. I drove him across the courtyard and out under the gatehouse arch. He knew me and wanted to stay. But I wouldn't let him. Outside he has a chance. So handsome a horse always does.'

'You are soft, Kobi,' I said, laughing and crying because suddenly I'd been touched with a needle to the heart that Xenia was dead because of me and yet an hour earlier this hard-hearted man, my accomplice in her death, had thought so well of the animal kingdom that he'd driven a horse to its freedom. It was perverse but so was everything else around me.

What I suddenly yearned for was to find the war ended, to hear Tornado trumpet and looking up to see him galloping towards us with Xenia clamped to his neck, his hoofs plocking through the dampened dust and his one good eye shining like a coal from his black-and-white clown's face.

I embraced Kobi, drawing him into me and holding him there as I would have a woman, by his bony ribs.

He pulled back, examined my face with his hands on my shoulders. I had no idea what was going on behind his oriental eyes. My race – my whiteness – barred me from knowledge of all the pulses that had brought him from orphanhood in Mongolia to my side at this spot, below the smoking monastery of Zilantov. They were fixed on me, those sombre, diamond-shaped eyes, asking the least-known question of all, the one by which men's hearts speak to each other.

'*Ty moi brat* – welcome, brother,' I said, and we embraced again.

The shooting had stopped throughout Kazan as all parties pondered the significance of the explosion. Rooks were circling above the monastery's grove of cottonwoods in a frenzy, folding their wings and diving into the smoke. They would have suffered too. Their nests, maybe even their ancestral nests, the views they'd been brought up with as fledglings, their family members . . . It was always the weakest that suffered.

Sweet Lord, what a business it was! Just staying alive—

'You're knackered, Doig. I'll get us there.'

That sounded so good, like silence to a dying man. I thanked Kobi and described the contingency plan if Shmuley and Mrs D. weren't at the agreed meeting place. He and Boltikov got together to plan the safest route to the Volga.

I sat down.

A heron creaked past, legs trailing. On the hill the rooks babbled. I thought, Did Glebov go up in smoke too? But the effort of thinking was too great and I found that the idea of his death by other than my own hand gave me no pleasure.

Sixty-five

NOTHING HAD changed, that was my first thought on awakening. There was still a babbling noise close by, and the sky above me was still so vast. That feeling of space, of endless cornfields, of vistas, of skies, trees and lakes – of eternity itself, is what we call *prostor*. No Russian has ever believed that *prostor* can be experienced when one is dead. So I had to be alive.

Moreover, there was a lilting motion beneath me, and when I sat up to investigate, I found I could move easily.

I was facing the stern of the barge, on its deck. A mattress was beneath me, a pillow under my head, a light quilt over me. A mile away down the deck, Shmuleyvich was doing something at the stern. We were stationary, lazing beneath the sweep of a huge willow tree.

Shmuley looked up and saw me sitting there. He waved and shouted.

'Good morning, General!' It was Lili, from the window in the back of the wheelhouse. I was beneath it, where somebody could keep an eye on me.

Mrs D. was in there with her. Something had fouled the steering. They'd put into the bank. Shmuley had stripped and gone over the side to free it.

He and the women began a shouted conversation down the length of the barge about my health. I wasn't yet in command of my complete senses. I could think only that Xenia was dead and that beneath these eighty feet of planking were thirty tons of the Tsar's gold. How could it be otherwise if we had possession of both the barge and our lives and Kazan was no longer in sight?

I called up to the ladies, 'Is it there? Have you checked – seen, touched it?'

They smiled on me as if I were a baby. I loved Mrs D. Everything went well when she was around. She was so solid, so enduring. Look how she'd nurtured that worthless husband for so long, there was steadfastness for you. She was grinning down at me, had her arm round Lilenka's shoulders. Two warm faces in the window, in the sun. I loved them both.

'Everyone present and correct?' Again they smiled on me. It was stunning – that we'd come through such an ordeal losing only three of us. Marvelling, I fell back with a shout. That all this should have happened to me by the age of thirty!

Then Mrs D. was kneeling at my side with her medical bag, asking if I was all right. She took up my wrist. Moaning softly, I feasted my eyes on her bosom.

'Stop pretending,' she said commandingly, at which Lilenka, watching us from above, giggled.

She tapped my chest, got out her stethoscope. In an ominous voice, 'Did your father have heart problems?'

'He died of the plague,' I said, looking up into her masterful eyes.

'Be serious.'

'I am.' (By rolling back my eyeballs, I could see Lili still leaning out of the wheelhouse.) 'What have you found wrong?'

'It should be lub-dup, lub-dup, the four valves snapping shut in pairs. But with you . . . Your heart is scored. In normal times I'd send you to a hospital for examination.'

I sat up sharply, knocking her stethoscope away. 'Scored? My heart *scored*? It's more than scored, Annushka, it's stencilled. Your people in the hospital, they'd find Elizaveta to begin with and then Xenia – and God knows who's yet to come. Let's work out how much space there is. How big's my heart, the area that'll take a chisel?'

She gave me the steely eye. 'Don't be frivolous. For a long time I've wanted to speak to you about your attitude. It's morally pernicious. You'll end up lonely and cynical if you continue down that road. I've seen it a dozen times in my professional life. You'll take to drink. A temperate existence is what everyone should aim for. I'm keeping Lili away from you—'

'Waste of time. She's a goner.'

'—under lock and key if necessary. And you, Charlie—' She broke off in a sudden bunch of smiles and started patting her hair. Looking up, I knew why: padding down the deck towards us was Yuri Shmuleyvich. Thick mud-streaked legs, everything mud-streaked, big furry stomach, swinging arms – it was how he approached, swatting aside the sprays of brown and jaded willow leaves. Love was written in capitals across his black and bristling face as he advanced upon her.

'Be temperate now, Annushka,' I murmured.

She rose twittering, the stethoscope dangling from her neck.

He coiled a massive hand around her waist – bent her backwards – planted his mouth on hers. Her jaws parted. Her hands were up his back in a flash, nails digging into his muddy flesh.

He broke away, gazed adoringly on her, whacked her on the bottom and said to me solemnly, 'Every morning I thank God for big women.'

She went up on tiptoe and kissed him. 'Men are such brutes.'

'Some are,' he said agreeably, pulling on his pants. Whistling he went into the wheelhouse, turfed Lili out and started the engine.

The barge edged out into the river. And there was another welcome sight – on the far bank, Kobi astride Tornado, motionless, like a Red Indian, their two images fused into one in the water's reflection.

I raised both fists and shook them in triumph. He waved back, slipped his rifle sling and fired a couple of shots into the air.

I said to Lili, 'How did the horse get here?'

'He was grazing beside the road. Kobi hopped out and hitched him on at the back of the armoured car. He rode him onto the barge. Tornado just stood in the middle of the deck, looking around as if he owned the boat. When we got into the middle of the river, he was so big he acted like a sail. So Kobi's riding him along the towpath. Isn't he beautiful?'

'And Boltikov?'

'Improving. I'm just going to wash his bandages.'

'Stiffy and Joseph?'

It was Shmuleyvich who replied. 'Getting the wireless to work. Got a knock on the way here.'

316

'The aerial?'

'Safe and sound. Hey, boss, give me the course for Odessa, will you?'

We all laughed. Nothing to come could be more difficult than what we'd just pulled off. 'Oh, south and west in a general manner of speaking,' I said cheerily. 'Anything for a man who's feeling peckish? Do we have a cook on board?'

'Be patient,' said Mrs D.

There was no other traffic on the river. The war had made it too dangerous unless a crew could defend themselves. Thinking of which – but Shmuley interrupted me, saying, 'We should find ourselves a pilot. This river'll have bad places as well as good, sure to.'

Now I noticed someone had positioned a machine gun on the roof of the wheelhouse, which allayed my worries in that direction.

The right bank had the usual steep bluff with the towpath hacked out at its foot. On the left the countryside was flat for a bit, letting the river spread out and wander among marshes, stew ponds, duck decoys and a few houses on stilts. Then the forest took over again.

I lay back. The sun was at its sweetest. It was a beautiful early-autumn day: yellowing birches, maples just starting to colour, poplars spearing to the sky, which was itself perfectly blue – *perfectly*, from horizon to horizon, as if the day had decided to set an example to all the other days that God intended to follow it.

Russia, O Russia! World without end, world of every emotion known to mankind at twice normal proof. Could I ever leave it?

Lili was draping the washed bandages over the rail to dry. I called to her. She finished her job and sat beside me, touching. I took her hands between my paws and said, 'What's the best memory you have of your mother?'

Those eyes, just like Xenia's but bigger. I thought, I'll eat my hat if she's fifteen. Seventeen, more like.

She cleared her throat: the truth was coming. 'The best, the very very best? All right – when she said goodbye to me. In the chapel. Then she ran out – remember? She freed me. I loved her for that.'

317

'She gave you good advice – having my children. They'll be terrific. My father had his faults but I make up for them.'

'My mother never loved me. I was a nuisance, I interrupted her life. She paid for me to be away, with her sister. Every month she sent Anna Marevna rouble notes folded in carbon paper so the post office clerks couldn't see it was money. Once in a blue moon she came down to visit me. I just wasn't part of her life.'

'Sounds like an honest arrangement.'

'I think Anna Marevna took all the guilt upon herself . . . I'm not old enough to understand about guilt. All I know is you have to have done something really horrible. You've done something, haven't you? Tetka Anna used to mutter about it when she got to know whom Mamasha had gone off with. You shot someone? She wouldn't tell me more.'

She prattled on. I wasn't taken in by her innocence, no matter that her eyes were fantastic and made me tremble. She was leafing through my history, maybe fantasising about the children we were to have. A light gusting wind had sprung up. Poplar cotton was blowing across the river in drifts, like snowflakes. On it came the smell of my country – the fields of rye and oats, the rivers, the woods, the small black cattle, the bathhouses on a Friday evening. I lay back on the quilt, gazing at the sky.

I'd done it! Got the gold, turned the corner, recaptured luck – grabbed it by its horny ankles as it passed, as one would a chicken.

It was then that he came, while I was thinking about luck and the gold and Lili's breasts and the way her buttocks had shifted against each other as we ran from the monastery; while I was thinking that everything comes right in the end so long as one has a calm attitude towards life.

Sixty-six

W E STOOD, we listened, heads cocked. Below, Stiffy and Joseph were having an argument in Anglo-Russian. The noise was so faint that we couldn't hear it when they suddenly started shouting at each other.

Lili said, 'Are you sure you're not imagining it?'

Shmuley said, 'If it's one of those destroyers from the Romanov Bridge we're as good as sliced and dried.'

'Not worth the effort for one small barge,' said Mrs D. 'They've got bigger fish to fry. Anyway, it's gone now.'

But I knew what had been making that insistent humming noise, having heard it the previous dawn at close quarters. Glebov would have been too cowardly to dabble iodine down below, but he'd swabbed himself clean, had a few hours' sleep – and come after me. No need to search upstream, towards the bridge. One way only that a gold barge would go. And it would be Glebov himself. No hired assassin this time. He'd want to get me in his sights and pump bullets into me until I was mince.

I said to Shmuley, 'It's him. He may have got bandaged bollocks but he has hatred in his heart.'

'Women on board, doesn't matter to him?'

'Not a bit. He's without mercy.'

He said nothing, spun the wheel to take us back under the willows on the flat side of the river.

Kobi had heard the plane too. He'd urged the piebald to the top of the bluff. Warriorlike he sat on the horse, hand shading his eyes, gazing upstream.

I said to Shmuley, 'What did Kobi take with him?'

'Two rifles and half the ammunition.'

319

I tried to send the women below, down there with Stiffy and Joseph. Lili would have gone but Mrs D. refused point-blank. She was going to stay with her man in case he was wounded. Moreover, if the barge were holed, it'd sink like a stone from that weight of gold and if she were below decks, she'd never get out.

She didn't care for that idea, 'Strong swimmer though I am, as you know very well and should be more grateful for than you are.'

That put me in my place.

'Yuri can't swim well. He told you he could in order to stay with me and protect me – you know, when we swam into the godown. Now it's my turn to look after him . . . Lili, do what you want, girl.'

Lili glanced mischievously at Shmuley and Mrs D. – plucked at my sleeve. 'This morning Yuri asked her to marry him.'

I said to Mrs D., 'Is that so? Hope you said yes. Then you can use him as a shield. He's beefy enough to soak up a whole belt of ammo.'

'Don't say that,' Mrs D. said, ready to have another go at me.

I told her I'd say what I wanted and the barge was mine and she could swim for it if she wanted but since Glebov hadn't been blown up in the monastery, here he was again and was she going to help me or wasn't she.

But still she wouldn't go below, nor would Lili. I had to resign myself to that. Next I collared Joseph and Stiffy, one in each hand, and kicked them onto deck, sparing no part of the boot. I wasn't going to be beaten at this point. I didn't know how. But it wasn't going to happen and they were going to be part of it not happening.

We set about collecting mattresses, planks, loose partition boards and any old stuff we could lay our hands on to make the wheelhouse safe.

Joseph began bleating, 'Excellency, Excellency, how can we put the mattresses up there if a *machinka* is already there?'

'So get it down,' I roared.

The old squaddie surfaced in Stiffy. He shoved Joseph out of the way. Shirt off, he walked the machine gun on its tripod to the edge of the wheelhouse roof. I took it from him, some weight in it. Twenty yards forward was a winch bolted to the deck, a big old iron thing with double handles. I dragged the gun into its shelter and set it up. Stiffy ran over dragging a belt of ammo in each hand.

Hearing the sound of the Fokker getting louder, I glanced up and there it was, only quarter of a mile away, wheels almost touching the water, dancing in the sunny shimmer like a giant fucking hairy black spider.

Shmuley cut the engines. We were eighty yards from the willows and a good thick patch of osiers. But it'd be a neat piece of helmsmanship to get the barge under cover without grounding her.

Even neater would be to get there before Glebov got us.

His distance, four hundred yards. His speed, one hundred miles per hour. We had eight seconds to live the rest of our lives.

Looking at it another way: four hundred rounds per machine gun – therefore eight hundred separate chances of death.

Had I been any use to the world? Did my beetle really count for anything? Was there anything else I could be proud of?

The noise of the Fokker suddenly shrank. We looked up together, Stiffy flicking the sweat off his eyebrows with one finger. Glebov had swung away. He'd calculated that he'd time to get round in front of us and take us head-on. He was going to rake us all the way down, from bow to stern, about twenty yards before we got to the trees.

'Tickle her up, man,' I shouted to Shmuleyvich. Our impetus had slowed drastically. We were almost down to drifting speed. But we could still get there if Shmuley gave the barge some boot.

I had another thought, stemming from something Shmuley had said earlier: maybe I could induce Glebov to give us the breathing space we needed by exhibiting our women. Maybe when he saw them out there on deck, all soft and innocent, he'd become polite, compassionate, gentlemanski Glebov. I've said it before, when a revolution comes along, people try out new personalities. They have to, to survive. One should be surprised by nothing in a revolution. Novelty is their purpose.

The women had gone into the wheelhouse for shelter. 'Kick

'em out of there,' I shouted to Shmuley. 'Get 'em where he can see them. Have 'em take their blouses off and shake their tits out.'

Kobi started firing. His rifle shots punctuated the rumble of our engine and the howl of the Fokker. I could make out Tornado safe among the trees. That'd have been Kobi's first priority. If we were killed, he'd have a means of escape.

A series of crashes from the wheelhouse: Shmuley was bashing the glass out of the windows with a wrench, to stop it flying about when the bullets struck.

He thrust a broom into Lili's hand. 'Here, girl, into the river with that glass, it'll take your mind off things. Don't listen to him about showing yourself. You're not a tart.'

Stiffy and I were beside the machine gun, watching to see what she'd do – which was to saunter over to us as if there wasn't an enemy within a hundred miles. She pointed to a minuscule piece of glass at my feet. Vast shards of the stuff were lying in heaps round the wheelhouse. But that wasn't the point. That partic-ular fragment of glass was where she was going to start.

It had been hot work barricading the wheelhouse. She'd taken off her tunic top. What was left was a vesty sort of thing tucked into her skirt band. She smiled up at me. Not coyly, not flirta-tiously, more like experimentally. Then she bent to her work, harassing that piece of glass towards the scuppers with the smallest and least effectual dabs of her broom that any human could have devised.

White white shimmering skin, smooth as milk. No blemishes of any kind. Ribs just visible. And nodding beneath her shift, like lazy young animals, her glamorous, sweating breasts.

Stiffy drew in his breath sharply.

I said to him, 'Changing your mind about women?'

'Never seen anything like them,' Stiffy said.

Then tossing a burst of gay laughter at us over her shoulder, Lili threw herself into the sweeping, sending great heaps of glass cascading over the side.

'Blimey, the things I can tell Mum,' exclaimed Stiffy.

Then we huddled as close to the winch as we could. But it was a pretence, and we knew it. When Glebov started to strafe the deck, only luck could save us.

Looking round, I saw Lili was still out there, checking that she'd got the last of the glass. 'Get into the wheelhouse,' I bellowed. 'Don't be such an asshole.'

Her huge blue eyes stared at me, then went flickering towards the Fokker. She propped the broom against the wheelhouse—

'Holy God, woman, stop fooling around. Get inside, go below, get out of it.'

She paid attention that time. It was the last I spoke for a while.

One hundred miles per hour – I gave him a good lead. The barrel swung easily: Kobi had kept it well oiled. In the same sight line I saw Glebov's bullets tripping up the deck towards me. Tufts of wood were springing up at great speed, in two distinct furrows. They were pointing straight at us. Only the winch could save me. As for Stiffy – God what a din there was, and smoke and the rattle of empty shells, and soon I'd be firing vertically overhead and my throat'd be full in his sights, would be white as a lily, would be waiting for the carotid to be split by a small dull cone of lead dug by man from the earth.

Dug by whom? What was his name? Put his foot on the spade and up it comes and he says to himself, That'll do for Doig – was that how it was, that I was to be killed by some ignorant horny-handed peasant?

Then without warning, the barge stopped dead – not brick-wall dead but near enough. I was flung against the winch – turned and flung, shoulder first, my head striking one of the handles. Stiffy – he was sent skidding down the deck, ended up yards away.

The pain was like having an arrow through my shoulder. I worked my arm a bit – got to my knees. Everything had slid off the wheelhouse roof. There was no sign of Shmuley. Mrs D. was at the wheel.

'Mudbank,' she shouted. 'Got to be.'

The Fokker – God knows what had happened to its bullets. Must have skewed everything for him, us stopping like that.

Lili staggered out holding her head. She'd got her tunic back on – looked unmarked, thank God. A splinter of wood in that young flesh'd have been the worst sort of crime.

'Watch out!' shouted Mrs D. 'He's coming in again.'

This time we were dead mutton. He wouldn't overshoot us a second time. He could take all day, make every one of his bullets count.

I went to haul the gun round to face the stern; it was where he was bound to come from next. Stiffy was out of it – alive but not doing anything very quickly. My shoulder was hell – then Lili was there to help me. One – two – three: we grunted together as we dragged the gun round.

I had my back to the winch now. We had no protection of any sort when he attacked.

She lay flat on the deck – gripped both sides of the ammunition belt, said, 'Like this?'

'Get out, woman! Get back under cover!'

There was no time for more. A sort of silence fell upon us. Angels were hovering, death was approaching.

Shmuley had reappeared, had the engine racing, trying to back us off the mud. But we remained stationary, all eighty feet of us. We were up at the bow – well and truly grounded. The nearest tide to lift us off was at Gibraltar. We'd have to wait for a winter flood. Could be Christmas.

I thought of Christmas and the black Fokker attacking through a snowstorm.

Glebov completed his turn and levelled out for the kill.

Stiffy had slithered back to his post, was trying to push Lili aside.

'Get ready, General.' Not budging, brave as a lion, her little fists clenched with battle-fever.

'Wait till you see the whites of his bandages,' said Stiffy.

We were going to die in good humour. And I was going to die in love, which Alexander Pushkin had always wanted to do.

Think ranges and trajectories, I said to myself. Concentrate. *Kill the swine.* One bullet through his black leather helmet, that's all that it needed. Jaw, skull, earhole, I wasn't particular.

He was coming in even lower than before, wheels only inches from the river. He'd have to climb sharply to clear the willows. His belly would look the size of a Zeppelin – if I was still alive to see it. So I'd aim for his head and keep my thumb on the button. *Hope* for his head, that was nearer the truth.

'Now!' said Lili and Stiffy together.

I started firing.

I can tell you nothing about the next twenty seconds, which were a yammering delirium of sound and smoke. I'd had the idea that Glebov'd be so full of choler that he'd shoot too soon, would maybe lose control of himself and run out of ammunition. If he kept a straight head on him I'd see the bullets running up the water towards the rudder: see them entering my barge over the stern counter, ripping the wood as they had the last time. I'd fling myself on top of Lili, to be killed or not. I'd keep my eyes open and watch the bullets approaching up the deck. That way I'd know the future before it arrived.

The vibration coming up my arms from the machine gun was like having my shoulder struck with a jackhammer. But I set my jaw and let rip, firing straight at his goggles. Lili's forearms were constantly jabbing into my sight as she fed the belt through. Flecks of cordite and hot oil were flying out of the gun's action, spattering us left and right.

The Fokker was about level with our stern. It began to lift to get over the willows. Then Glebov flumped the plane back down – steadying it, wings rocking like anything, but maybe coming in at too flat an angle. I thought, It's like the attack on the train, he hasn't got the nerve at come in at the best angle, a steep one – then there he was above us, engine screaming, flying wires howling like a tortured animal, so low that Lili could have reached up and had his wheels for earrings.

He'd hit the trees, had to, would never pull out in time – the notion was no sooner in my head than an updraught off the river, maybe from a pack of air gathered under the willows, swept him up and over. Was this a new manoeuvre? Was it proof of what everyone was saying about the Fokker triplane, that it could dance on a kopek?

I watched it rise – saw it waver – cursed sun and sweat for making everything blurry.

Stiffy said in an inquisitive voice, 'Is that an aileron hanging loose, sir?'

Baby hope drummed its heels in my breast. I grabbed Lili by the hair and shook her head, it being just handy.

The Fokker rose, engine pitch unchanged – no, maybe it was plucking at the air a bit. Its angle grew steeper, like a rearing horse.

Was he wrestling with the controls in there? Was it actually possible that something had been hit?

I jumped to my feet. 'Shoot, keep on shooting at him,' I shouted to Kobi even though he was hundreds of yards away. Now the plane was getting to the vertical and not moving at much speed at all. Maybe there was an emergency lever he could pull, maybe he'd have everything ironed out in a couple of seconds and with a chuckle would swoop down and kill us and our stupid hopes.

The Fokker was stationary, hanging in the sky. Anyone could have hit it. And Kobi had my rifle, which had a scope.

'Get him, Kobi,' I yelled, quite out of control, 'get the bastard.'

The Fokker was reaching the limit of what was possible for an aircraft standing on its tail. Its engine began to pink; a tinny echo nearly above us. I thought, May the bastard's heart be pinking too, and I thumped my fist into my palm.

Stiffy whispered, 'He's had it. God bless that bullet.'

It was the signal. The Fokker accepted the impossibility of what it was trying to do and toppled onto its back.

For seconds it hung there. I thought, Christ, he hasn't been hit, he's just showing off, playing with us. Then the engine cut out. He went into a spin, the triple wings setting up a swishing fluttering sound as the plane spiralled down. Faster and faster it fell – but not plummeting, it was impossible with wings like that unless they came off. The propeller was dragging him down, that great heavy wooden propeller. If he was alive, he wouldn't know what day of the week it was, the rate at which the Fokker was spinning.

The willows hid him from our view. We waited. Seconds later there was a long slow ripping noise – then silence.

'God bless and sanctify that bullet forever,' said Stiffy. He turned, snapped to attention and saluted me.

Shmuley and Mrs D. walked towards us, hand in hand, little Joseph tucked in behind them with Boltikov. We looked upon each other – with smiles, love and wonderment.

Shmuley said, 'Now for Odessa.'

I said at large, 'Where's Lili, then?'

Mrs D. thought she'd nipped into the wheelhouse and went to see, saying, 'Poor mite, what a baptism of fire.'

Wreckage from the Fokker began to drift down the river. A bit of its fuselage with the Red Star on it bumped along our side and I fished it out with a boathook. We agreed to nail it to the wall of the wheelhouse. Thinking about souvenirs made me ask Joseph if the Rykov flag had got onto the barge. When he said, Yes, of course it had, I took upon myself an air of triumph and looked gaily round the group to include them all in my suggestion, that we improvise a flagpole and hoist the Rykov wolf. Here and now, while the going was good.

Joseph and Shmuleyvich, happy grins from each of them, thinking about the gold. Boltikov was smoking the celebration cigar he'd been keeping. And here was Mrs D. – God, what a tremendous day!

'Annushka,' I started, going to embrace her – but she held me off. She pushed me away to join the others. Raising herself up, making herself bigger and more important – the signals were unmistakable: 'Glebov was Lili's father. She's just told me.'

I spoke my first thought: 'Had to be someone.'

Then it struck home. 'But she helped me! She helped me kill him!'

Implacably Mrs D. went on: 'What else could she have done? Ask yourself that. Anyway, you know what it means: she's lost both her parents in one day.'

She looked at me as if I'd personally slit their throats. Boltikov, harrumphing, stroked his jaw. Shmuley, he didn't dare go against her. Perhaps none of them did. They regarded me as men will in these circumstances.

So she had it in for me, for whatever reason. She wasn't saying anything about Elizaveta, about how it was Glebov's due. Or how I'd saved her from the Reds and got her a new husband and a share in a shipload of gold. Oh no. With some people it's only emotion that counts.

Shrugging, hands in pockets, I strolled up to the bow to see how deep in the mud we were.

I sat down on the towing bollard. I took my shirt off and felt all round my shoulder: bruising only, nothing serious. A few more scraps from the Fokker floated past – wood, canvas, what looked like a pencil.

When would life change so that everything went well at the

same time? Was every effort I made destined to fail or were my efforts simply insufficient? How the hell was I to have known that Glebov was Lili's father? And how was I to handle this knowledge? I didn't think I could look at her body in the same way.

However, it only reinforced the lesson: be surprised by nothing. And there would be other lessons too, I was certain, that would rise up and strike me when their time came.

The shadows of the past were in there murmuring with the river. There was one good thing, that Glebov was dead. The memory of Elizaveta would start to fade. She'd release me, become an occasional visitor only, become someone I could take by the hand in the dappled sunlight and talk of things past.

I wouldn't be bitter, wouldn't rail against life. I'd say to it, Thank you for everything, everything: for war, revolution, love, the struggle. There's no lot sweeter than trying, no fate more joyful than to be a pilgrim. I'd say, Thank you for not having taken my life. Thank you also for Xenia. Too bad she and Glebov got tucked up together and produced Lili. It would have been a delight to breed with her. She'd have got the Rykovs on their feet again. Whatever errors there've been, put them on my slate.

To Elizaveta I'd say, No love could have equalled ours. We were closer to Heaven than God Himself. And for the last time I'd draw down the lids of her empty eyes, my fingers not lingering.